A STONE DENIED

MÓRDHA STONE CHRONICLES - BOOK 7

KIM ALLRED

STORM COAST PUBLISHING LLC

A STONE DENIED
Mórdha Stone Chronicles, Book 7
KIM ALLRED

Published by Storm Coast Publishing, LLC

Copyright © 2022 by Kim Allred
Cover Design by Amanda Kelsey of Razzle Dazzle Design
Print Edition June 2022
ISBN 978-1-953832-16-0
Large Print Edition June 2022
ISBN 978-1-953832-17-7

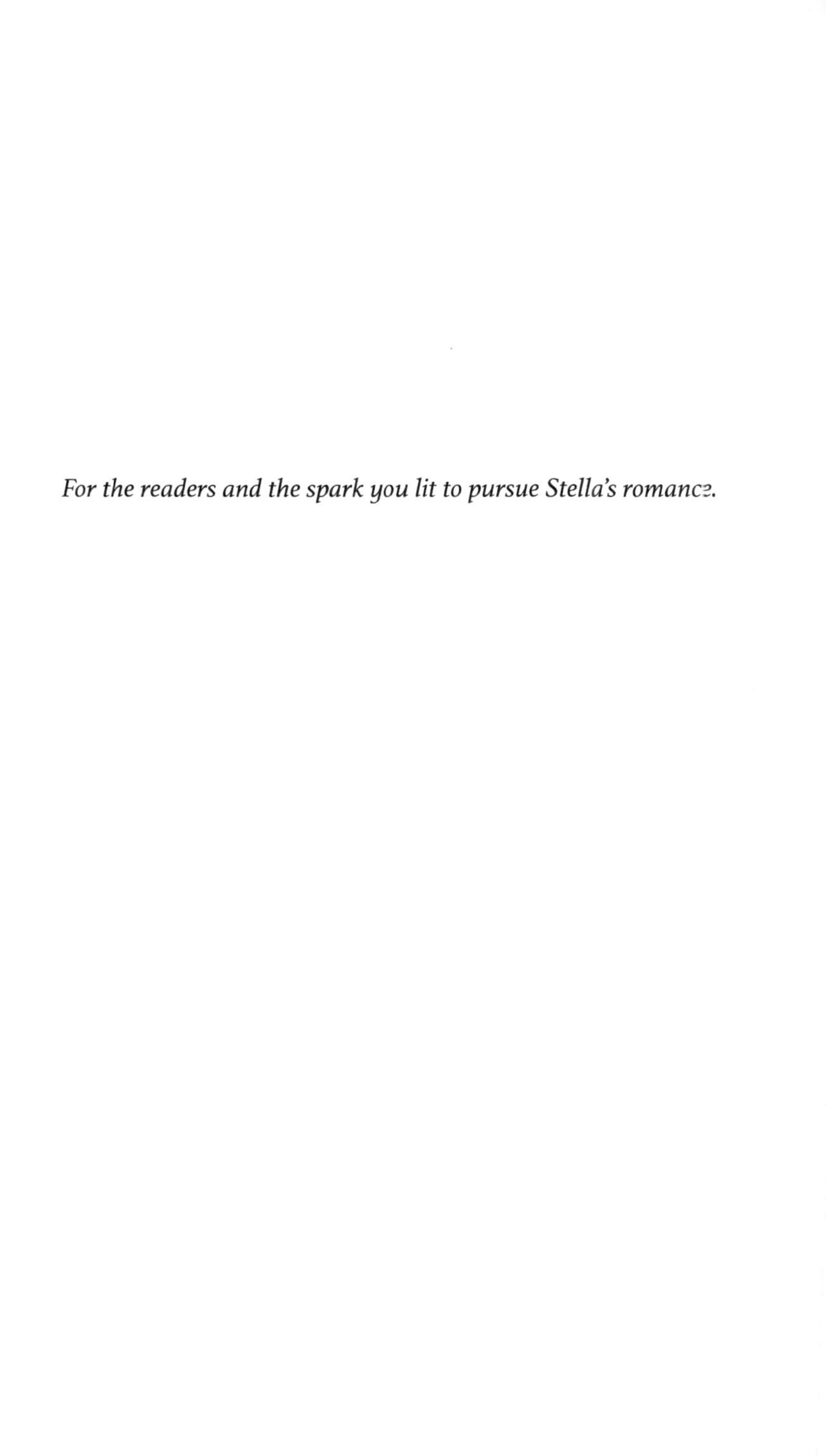

For the readers and the spark you lit to pursue Stella's romance.

"I am not the same, having seen the moon shine on the other
side of the world."
Mary Anne Radmacher

1

Baywood, Oregon – Present Day

Stella Caldway grumbled as she stuffed the oversized mug of coffee into the cup holder. The lid slipped off, and splashes of cream-colored liquid sprayed the console, passenger seat, and her long, cherry-red rain duster.

"Damn." She opened the middle console and pulled out a wad of napkins, quickly soaking up the mess.

This was the second time during an already long morning she'd spilled coffee. The first time, right after she'd finished dressing, the coffee had run down her linen pants. After exchanging them for another pair, this time something a few shades darker, she tried wiping the stain out but gave up and tossed the slacks into the dry clean pile.

The coffee also managed to spread to a client folder and seeped into the top pages of the final contract, where earlier, she'd fought with a recalcitrant printer. Sighing, she'd spent another thirty minutes reprinting the contract and creating a new folder.

Once the car's interior was clean and back to normal, Stella pushed her auburn hair back and checked her makeup in the visor mirror. Grateful there was nothing to fix, she glanced at her watch, then swore to herself. She gave a last look at the house, reconsidered her plans, then drove out of her small circular driveway.

She hated being late, priding herself on being the consummate professional. One thing she'd learned early on, very little in real estate ran on time. Inspectors ran late, customers wanted to see just one more house, sellers changed times when a house could be shown. It never bothered her. She found she could adapt to any situation, always diverting disgruntled homeowners or buyers with other distractions. The one thing she could control was herself.

However, this morning, she'd definitely woken on the wrong side of the bed. If she knew what was good for her, she'd cancel her meetings and go back to bed, but there were only two appointments, both for contracts with new customers. Her first meeting went without a hitch. One contract was signed with a commitment to have a list of houses for their review in two days. Their wish list was pretty simple for new homeowners, and based on the decor of their rental house, she'd already made a mental list of a couple homes they'd adore.

She stopped at a local coffeehouse for a refill, and with plenty of time before her next meeting, decided to head to the inn. Ever since the large group of family and friends had returned from their holidays in France three months ago, Finn had split his time between assisting Jackson with the remodeling of the inn and preparing his sailboat for a week-long trip down the coast of California.

AJ was excited for a little time away, but if Stella had to guess, her friend was more thrilled to see Finn's eagerness to set sail. She figured this was just the start of long sailing trips, and she'd be jealous if the thought of being on the waves didn't make her stomach do flips. Standing on a dock was enough to get her seasick.

Although AJ and Finn were probably hoping for time alone, everyone sighed with relief when Maire had suggested she and Ethan tag along. She'd locked herself away after France, eager to study the pages of Sebastian's journals they'd discovered hidden in the monastery. After two months, Maire hadn't fully completed the translation. It turned out, of the two journals they'd found while on holiday at the monastery, Sebastian had used the second one to copy what he'd felt were the more prominent parts of The Book of Stones before he'd sent the separate sections away to be protected. Maire determined there were missing pieces Sebastian hadn't copied but hoped that with more time, she might be able to make an educated guess on those gaps. That decision seemed to be enough for her to return to a normal routine, and everyone settled into their lives.

Since Stella wouldn't be sailing with them, she agreed to watch the inn, stopping by every day to refill bird feeders and water the indoor plants. Jackson had taken the week off, and the sun had decided to show itself on what was turning out to be a lovely early-spring day.

She was turning into the inn's driveway when her phone rang. Checking the screen, she smiled and activated the speaker in the car. "Hi, Isaiah. What are you up to?"

Isaiah was Jackson's grandson, who had returned the previous summer to help with the inn's remodel. He was supposed to go back to California for the fall semester but decided to finish his degree at the university in Eugene. Professor Emory, having once been a tenured professor at the institution before retiring to buy an old bookstore, had helped him transfer his transcripts and credits.

"I'm on my way back to Baywood. I'm still an hour out but just got a ping from the inn's alarm."

"Really?" Stella slowed as she drove down the driveway. "I'm just now pulling in and don't see any other cars except the ones that belong here." She laughed. "It's probably that crazy seagull that AJ keeps feeding. I'm running late this morning, so I haven't put his snack out yet."

Isaiah chuckled, and he raised his voice to compete with the wind gusting in the background. "It's possible. It was definitely him two days ago."

"Yeah, the poop in front of the French doors was a dead give-away," Stella spoke louder and shivered, not understanding how he could drive over a mountain pass on a cool morning with the windows down.

"Ari seems to know how to make an entrance."

Ari, or Aristotle as AJ named him, was a one-eyed seagull that looked as if he had been in one too many bar fights. He'd somehow discovered AJ's soft spot for gulls and found his way to her back deck. Once she fed him, he became the inn's very own seagull, showing up every day at the same time, waiting for his snack. Turned out he was quite patient, and though he'd fluff his feathers in a disgruntled way, he always waited no matter how long it took for someone to come home. Ethan was the one who started calling him Ari. He thought it was funny since Ari was a bird, and his nickname was pronounced as if it was spelled airy. No matter how much AJ had tried to stop it, everyone called him Ari except for her.

Stella parked her car and rolled down a window before shutting off the engine. She waited a beat. "I don't hear anything."

"Not even squawking?"

She shook her head then remembered to vocalize it. "No. But that's not unusual. He likes to surprise people."

Isaiah snorted. "And I just thought it was Grandpops who did that."

Stella grinned. "Well then, I guess Ari is in good company." She got out of the car. "I think everything is okay."

"Maybe you should wait until I get there. Do you have time to come back later? Ari will wait, and so will the plants."

"I have a meeting in an hour, then I just want to go home, soak in a hot bath, and forget this day happened."

"That bad?"

"You don't know the half of it."

"I'd still like you to wait. Or better yet, I'll feed Ari and cover your other tasks. I'd feel better."

"Tell you what. Since I'm already here, why don't I just slip in, see what mess Ari made this time, then call you back? Five minutes tops."

There was a long pause. "I'm not going to change your mind, am I?"

Stella mounted the stairs, pinched the phone between her ear and shoulder, then dug in her purse. "It's all quiet. If anyone was here, they would have heard me pull up then scrambled to get out. And with no car, how much could they steal? Probably early spring breakers, and worst case, Finn's stash of homebrew will be gone."

"Now that would be disastrous."

Stella laughed. "Five minutes, and I'll call you back." She hung up after she heard his grunt and tossed the phone in her purse while holding on to the set of keys she'd recovered. She opened the front door and breathed in the deep scent of cedar and lavender that always permeated the house. When she saw the mail on the side table, she cursed under her breath. She'd forgotten to grab it today, considered walking up to retrieve it, then decided there was always tomorrow. Her purse dropped next to the stack of catalogs, bills, and other junk advertisements.

It was such a beautiful day, and her chores wouldn't take long. She would have time for a cup of coffee on the back deck. Might as well squeeze whatever enjoyment she could out of the day. AJ kept a variety of single-serve coffees, and she strode to the kitchen to start a cup brewing while she inventoried Ari's mess.

When she walked into the kitchen, she felt the chill and immediately found the broken window in the French doors. She raced over, hoping Ari hadn't flown through it and died. What would she tell AJ? It wasn't like running down to the local pet shop to buy a replacement goldfish.

She pulled to a stop and stared at the floor. Nothing but broken glass.

"Ah, there you are."

She spun around, her hand sliding to her throat when her gaze fell on the tall stranger. Before she could turn to run, the man leaped toward her, and in two strides, grabbed her upper arm. Having taken some self-defense classes offered by one of the larger Realtor offices in town, she knew a thing or two. She turned into him and stomped on his foot with the stiletto heel of her boots.

The man screamed and released her, pulling his foot up like an injured paw. Stella shoved him and ran. He caught the edge of her rain duster, but she didn't stop, and the sound of the material ripping at its seams made her growl.

The only question was where to run. Finn still hadn't completed the panic room. AJ had drummed it into Stella that the library and the master bathroom were the safest places in the house. She headed for the library but switched mid-stride as she reached the staircase. The safety of the library was actually within the armory. They'd activated the alarm before leaving, and for some reason, her perfect memory was failing to come up with the code for the door. She didn't think she'd have time to figure it out. The scuff of boots scrambling on the slick hardwood floor ramped up her frenzy.

She took the stairs two at a time and had just reached the top when a hand grabbed her shoulder. Then she was tackled, falling hard on the landing with the man on top of her. She rolled, kicking and punching, a couple of her strikes connecting, but all the man did was grunt.

Then a piercing pain slammed into her head just before her vision winked out.

The tingling sensation became painful enough to wake Stella. When she moved her leg, she released a whimper. Not sure what had happened, she pried her eyes open, but the light was too bright. Her head pounded, and when she reached for it, discovered she couldn't move her hands. That forced her to peek through squinting eyes. She was back in the kitchen, tied so tight to a dining room chair, she was losing feeling in her hands and toes. That explained the pins and needles making her eyes water.

The pounding in her head made it difficult to keep her eyes open, but she pulled herself together when the man entered the kitchen. She studied him more closely now that she wasn't running from him. He was dressed strangely, the tailoring all wrong. His worn jacket hung halfway to his thigh, and the collar of his shirt rose too high on his neck. His vest...she gulped... wasn't a vest but a waistcoat. Her chest tightened, threatening to close off her breath when a nagging truth slammed into her. This wasn't a thief. Well, he might be, but he'd come a long way to rob someone. Like maybe two-hundred-years long.

No. No. No.

Why hadn't she waited for Isaiah? Because she had been in a hurry. Because she didn't think anything truly bad could happen in Baywood. She stifled a self-deprecating laugh. Because she thought, as AJ and Finn had, that the nightmare with the stones was over. And she would bet every last cent of her very fat savings that this man was here because of the stones.

He leaned his hip against the counter, arms crossed over his chest, and his expression a bit wild-eyed, which didn't lend a comforting feeling.

"Where's the stone, Miss Moore?"

Stella blinked then shook her head, which only made the headache worse. "What?"

"The Heart Stone. It must be here for the smaller stone to have found you."

Yep. He was a thief. And if the clothing hadn't told her enough, his English accent confirmed it. She hated when she was right. And, of course, he had a stone, or he wouldn't be standing in AJ's kitchen. How long had she been unconscious? She glanced at the microwave. If she was reading the numbers correctly, only five minutes had passed. It seemed longer.

He gave the outward opinion of being calm—for the most part. He continued to lean back, his posture relaxed, but his gaze bounced about the room as if taking everything in and was uneasy by what he saw. Her best guess was this was only his first or second jump. A mixture of an extremely dangerous man and a scared rabbit. She was fairly certain that wasn't a safe combination.

"Who are you?" Her voice cracked, and she glanced longingly toward the jug of water she used for the plants.

"My name doesn't matter. What matters is what I came for. The Heart Stone. If you just give it to me, I can be on my way, and you can get back to..." He scowled as he waved at the kitchen in general. "...however you live with all this."

"I don't know what you're talking about." Her head began to clear, and she bent her neck slowly from side to side, hearing a slight snap as pressure released and the ache receded, though it hadn't left entirely. Now that she could think, she retraced her steps since arriving. Then his earlier words came to her. He thought she was AJ. That made sense since she'd bounced through the door and into the kitchen like she owned the place.

He stared at the ceiling, seeming to contemplate his next move. After a prolonged moment, he prowled around the dining room and kitchen, which were designed to be one spacious open area. Every time he stalked past her, she went rigid, not sure what to expect.

After the third pass, he grabbed her hair, pulling back so hard and fast that one moment she'd been staring at the horrifyingly slow movement of the clock on the microwave, and the next, she gazed at the ceiling. His grip was so tight, she was positive he'd rip her hair from her head as tears streaked down her face. The pounding in her head returned, but she refused to scream. Instead, she slammed her lids shut so she wouldn't have to look at his menacing face as he leaned over her.

His body odor and wickedly sour breath made her want to choke. "From everything I've heard about you, I figured you'd choose the hard way. So be it." While still clutching her hair, he raised a fist.

Before he could release the punch, she yelled, "Finn has it. All he told me was that he put it in a safe place. That I didn't have to worry about it anymore." The words raced out of her as she spun her tale. While she hated lying, she was pretty good at it. The fact she was terrified for her life added a huge dose of reality to her story.

The man paused, then slowly released her hair. Stella rolled her neck, and though she didn't feel the satisfying snap, the intense thrumming lessened. She blinked back tears and noticed the clock change. Isaiah was still forty minutes away.

When her view was blocked by a hulking form, she stared up to eyes full of doubt—or maybe confusion. He stood within striking distance though his arms were crossed again. "I don't believe you."

Without missing a beat and needing to stall for time, she went with a partial truth from something AJ had shared with her. "When we returned from the monastery, I wasn't myself." She glanced down, nibbled her lips, and lowered her voice. "I began seeing things—people who should have been long dead. I couldn't sleep, worried that a day like this might come." She sniffled for effect, then choked out a half-laugh. "Guess someone owes me a big apology."

After a silent moment, she lifted her chin and stared him in the eye, releasing part of her rage. "He decided it was best if I didn't know where he put the Heart Stone." She smirked. "He bought into that whole out of sight, out of mind theory."

He pulled away from the counter and stalked toward her.

She couldn't stop from daring to go a little farther. "It appears I was right all along. I'm hoping I'll live long enough to tell Finn I told you so." Did she want to know whether he was planning on killing her?

He smiled, though it wasn't very pleasant. "Now we have some honesty." He strode to the bay window and stared out to the shimmering ocean. Good fortune turned her way when he stood there for ten minutes before sighing. "I didn't want to do it this way, but we knew we might not have another option."

Stella wanted to scream. No one would hear her, but it might release the terror worming its way through her and picking up speed like an express train as he turned. She released an audible sigh when he walked past her.

He reached into an inside jacket pocket and pulled out two pages of parchment. He selected one, stuffed the other back in the pocket, then placed the first one in the center of the kitchen island, using the empty flower vase as a paperweight. The vase AJ always kept filled with fresh flowers from either her garden or Stella's. Now it sat empty—and AJ was two days away from being of any help to her.

When he turned toward her, he pulled a knife from his boot. Her stomach dropped as if she'd been tossed from a penthouse window and was hurling toward the asphalt. She shook uncontrollably and couldn't stop, even when all he did was cut the bindings to her arms and legs.

She immediately moved her hands and feet around, rubbing each wrist and grimacing as the blood rushed into her extremities. He turned his back on her for a moment as he pulled out another smaller piece of parchment. Stella didn't wait to see what it was.

She was up, flying through the kitchen and rounding the corner, making one more attempt at the stairs and the master bathroom. She didn't even make the stairs before a fist grabbed her hair and pulled her to a stop.

"You are a foolish woman," he hissed and spun her around.

She kicked him in the shin and swore. She'd been aiming a lot higher. Before she could regroup, he slapped her so hard, she understood the phrase "seeing stars." At the same time, he kicked her legs out from under her, then grabbed an arm along with her hair and dragged her back through the kitchen toward the French doors. He stopped long enough to open the door. Thankful her raincoat protected her from the broken glass, she continued to protest as he lifted her by the waist and pulled her through the door.

Once they were on the back deck, he fished in his pocket and retrieved a small piece of paper. She squirmed as he grabbed the chain from around his neck and pulled up a medallion with a familiar tricolored stone. With one glance at the necklace, she doubled her efforts to throw him off balance, but his arm was like steel. He squeezed her to him until she got a second dose of his stench. He managed to keep one hand on both the medallion and the slip of paper.

When she heard the Celtic words, she squeezed her eyes and shouted, "No. Let me go. We can wait for Finn."

The wind picked up as if in response to his words, and she twisted in his grip to monitor the ocean and the sky.

The fog was coming. So fast. Too fast.

In the distance, she heard the slamming of a car door. Isaiah? He must have broken speed limits the whole way. She stared at the fog, felt the pounding of the man's heart against her back as he pulled her closer.

Isaiah wouldn't reach her in time.

The world went silent as the fog enveloped her in bright, white light.

2

———————

London – Spring 1805

Viscount Theodore Beckworth dismounted and handed his horse to the footman before turning to stare up at the gentlemen's club. This particular establishment wasn't one he was familiar with, which was the point for this evening's meeting. He had to admit to being a creature of habit, and didn't usually frequent this part of town. He shook his head, still hardly believing that he and his one-time nemesis, Finn Murphy, were members of the same club near Hyde Park. Small circles, they say.

He checked his silver pocket watch, incredibly in one piece after his trip to the future and all the hell that had broken loose after that. Five minutes. He didn't want to spend more time here than necessary, not when there could be eyes everywhere. He'd requested a private room, but that didn't mean they'd comply.

This group was a fidgety lot, and it had taken him half the London season to get this close. Instead of attending balls and smoking cigars with the upper crust, he'd been sneaking about the aristocracy, dressed like the old street urchin he'd once been, simply to track the movements of his two targets.

It scared him how easily he'd fallen back to working the streets. Since becoming the Viscount of Waverly, he'd remained close to two London gangs, or what he referred to as his crews, meeting with a few men whenever he was in town. This year, he'd spent the season with one particular crew, staying in their humble homes instead of sleeping on a plush feather bed at the club or one of the fine manors.

This type of work wasn't what he'd expected when he'd agreed to help Hensley, England's favorite spymaster, but the old man assured him this was an extreme exception. He'd assured Beckworth his true value was rubbing elbows in higher circles —-or so the man had claimed. Yet, in the last six months he'd worked for the man, this was the second job he'd been assigned as nothing more than a common thief. What if this was only the beginning? That wouldn't do at all.

His one previous job for Hensley had been to meet with a tailor who had information that one of the members of Parliament had a bastard child with a French woman he kept hidden in the West End. Under normal circumstances, no one would care. But during a war with Napoleon? That could put the minister in a compromising position. And though on that occasion, Beckworth might have been dressed with more respectability, he was still spying on a man to catch him with his mistress. He shivered. This would be the last assignment that would force him to work in the trade where he'd begun. Hensley could find another man to roam the back streets of London. Beckworth could think of a few names right now.

When he walked through the front door of the club, he paused. The layout wasn't much different than other clubs he'd been in, including his own, but he'd been blessed with a fine eye for fashion and décor. It wasn't difficult to see the age behind the furnishings. The carpets, once a rich burgundy, had dulled to muddy brown and showed a well-worn path. The edges of peeling wallpaper leaked out from beneath the boring landscapes adorning the walls. His ability to notice such details was most likely something he'd inherited from his father. The Duke of Dunsmore had been of noble birth, and had he not gone mad, might have one day publicly recognized Beckworth as his son, bastard or not. He shook it off, grateful he'd been lucky enough to get out of the man's clutches with a title and an estate.

"Can I help you, sir?"

Beckworth turned to find an older gentleman giving him a once over, and by the frown on the old man's face, he was coming up short. He almost snorted. Had someone dressed like him shown up at the door to his club, Beckworth would have probably given the man a similar look. No matter. He had no intention of entering this club again.

"Yes. I'm here to meet with Mr. Sinclair."

When the man raised a brow, Beckworth sighed. "He's expecting me."

The old man gave him a more thorough study, his sour expression never wavering. "Very well, if you follow me."

Beckworth was led to a lounge that must have filled a quarter of the first floor. This room was in far better condition than the foyer, probably because this was where the members would spend most of their time. A long, polished wood bar filled out most of the back wall, and overstuffed leather chairs were arranged individually and in groupings. A dozen gaming tables were currently quiet. They would see more action in another couple of hours, and if he had to guess, there would be a second gaming room farther in the club.

"I'll advise Mr. Sinclair of your arrival." The man left the room by way of the main hallway but made a left rather than a right toward the front lobby.

The library, dining room, and various other rooms would lead that way. The guest rooms would be on the second floor. It was always good to know the layout of a place before meeting with unknown contacts. One never knew when a hasty retreat was required.

He waited at the bar and ordered an Irish whiskey, keeping an eye on the main door and the two others the footmen had been using. His second drink was being poured when a man stepped next to him.

"Are you Beckworth?"

Beckworth turned toward the grisly voice and studied the man. His clothes fit the establishment, but the man could use a bath and a shave. Was this the best contact they could send? Maybe they weren't taking him as seriously as they should.

"Mr. Sinclair?"

"Yeah. You said you had something for us."

Beckworth glanced around. "I asked for a private room. I can't be seen talking with you."

"Well, this is the best you're going to get. Now, what is it you think you have we'd be interested in?"

"And do you have something of interest in exchange?"

The man scratched his scruffy beard and glanced behind Beckworth.

It required every ounce of willpower not to turn around. One of the three doors was behind him, and his back itched not knowing if he should be concerned. But nothing would happen inside the club, so he relaxed and sipped the whiskey.

"It will depend on the value of the information you supposedly have."

"Oh, I have it..." Beckworth trailed off, and his eyes widened for a split-second when he noted two men enter the room. He turned his back to the main door and lowered his head. His hand trembled, and he tucked it out of sight. "But I'd prefer talking where we have more privacy."

The man turned to see what made Beckworth nervous. The man's interest in the new arrivals suggested he might know the burly man that walked in. Not everyone knew the spymaster, but Beckworth took it as a sign he was on the right track if this man knew who Hensley was.

Hensley was with two other gentlemen and didn't glance their way. Beckworth kept his back to him and growled under his breath, "Unless you find us a more private place to talk, I'm out of here. I'll find someone else interested in what I have to share."

When Sinclair gave Hensley a second glance, he shook his head. "This is private enough."

Damn. Beckworth wanted this to be his last night in London. But this idiot was going to drag it out. Maybe it would be best to leave and spend a few days at Waverly. This illusive gang might become more amenable if they had to wait for his return.

Beckworth drained his second glass, tossed a few coins on the bar, and walked out without saying another word, making sure to keep his head down until he was out the door.

After collecting his horse, Beckworth considered his options. He should have known this meeting could be a bust. They were a suspicious lot, based on what he'd learned from the one or two contacts he'd made, and trying to discover the leader of the group had been like catching the wind.

He was hungry and tired. If he had any sense, he'd go to his own club and get a good night's sleep before traveling to Waverly in the morning. But he'd only ridden a couple of blocks when he spied a pub and stopped on a hunch.

He selected a back corner, paying well for roasted pork and a mug of ale. After an hour of watching men come and go, he began to question his instincts. Not a single person of interest had wandered in or out of the place, and another fifteen minutes passed before he stumbled out the door. He must have been tired because he questioned whether he'd turned down the right alley when he didn't see the street kid with his horse.

His senses finally triggered the danger he'd walked into. His horse was there, but the street kid was gone, replaced by four hulking men.

He sighed. His hunches were working just fine, it was his ability to sense trouble that was faulty. He continued to stumble as he made his way to his horse, only glancing up when he was ten feet away and giving the men his best confused stare. He recognized one of the men as Sinclair. "What's this about?"

"You said you wanted privacy. We're here to give you that."

Beckworth only had seconds before he heard the men behind him. He turned and reached for his blunderbuss pistol, but something hard slammed into the back of his head. His legs collapsed before he took another step.

***

Beckworth woke to darkness, and he squelched the panic when he couldn't move his arms. He could barely breathe through the scratchy fabric of a hood. He calmed his breathing so he could hear over his drumming heartbeat.

No voices. No footsteps. But the heavy, nasal breathing of someone, maybe more than one someone, was unmistakable. They were close.

He waited. If they'd wanted to kill him, they would have done it already. Whoever hit him wanted something, and since he had nowhere to go, he could wait with the best of them. He wasn't sure how long he sat there, maybe fifteen or twenty minutes, when footsteps approached. It sounded like two or three approaching from his right. Scuffling of boots, the scrape of chair legs on a wooden floor, someone clearing their throat.

The hood was tugged off and lantern light temporarily blinded him. The lamp wasn't more than two feet away, sitting on a makeshift desk made out of scrap wood. Without the hood, he could smell the tang of the Thames. They were somewhere near the docks. The faint scratch of boats rubbing against the pier floated through the broken windows that ran along the tall walls. He guessed the building to be an old warehouse.

The back of his head ached and his arms and legs were tightly tied to the chair. It wouldn't take them long to grow numb. Two men stood next to the door, and two others stood behind a man, who sat across the desk from him and wore a mask that covered a good portion of his face.

"Who are you?" Beckworth's voice was rough, and he coughed to clear his throat of tiny fibers from the burlap bag they'd used for a hood.

"Give him some water." The masked man pushed a skin across the table, and one of the men at the door picked it up, grabbed Beckworth's chin, and forced his mouth open to squeeze water in.

Beckworth struggled as the other men laughed, and half-choking, spit out the water.

"Enough." The man tossed his head to the right, and the man returned to the door. "Sorry. The men get restless."

"Why did you kidnap me?"

The man held out his hands in an apologetic gesture. "This isn't a kidnapping. We just wanted to speak with you."

The man's voice was muffled behind the mask, leaving his voice indistinct, yet it seemed familiar. Beckworth shook his head, trying to clear the cobwebs. He'd been tired and shouldn't have had that second ale. His head ached from where they'd hit him. "You could have just asked."

"We've been watching you." The man sat back and folded his hands across his stomach. He appeared relaxed, but his dark eyes narrowed as he considered his prisoner, his gaze shifting to the men at the door and then to the pounding emanating from the floor above.

All statements aside, Beckworth was tied to a chair. He'd be foolish to consider their action anything less than a personal attack.

The masked man held his gaze, a slight smile forming. "You've caught our interest since your work with the Duke of Dunsmore."

Beckworth kept his expression calm, almost bored. "You and every other scoundrel."

The man laughed, but it didn't hold any humor. "I'd say that makes us fitting partners."

Nerves tingled across Beckworth's skin. Was this the contact he was hoping to meet? The ropes tying him to the chair stretched when he straightened his position, and he almost laughed when the men at the door stepped forward as if he were making a run for it.

"On the surface, you seem to have returned to the steadfast Viscount of Waverly, rubbing elbows with the aristocracy and even those in Parliament. Yet, behind the scenes, you've been seen associating with some rather..." The man tilted his head as if considering the correct word. "I'll just call them somewhat unscrupulous people."

Beckworth sneered. "Present company excluded, I assume."

The man studied him, his hands folded across his stomach.

"I never really liked you, but you do amuse." In a flash, he leaned across the table in what Beckworth assumed to be an intimidation tactic. "But, I can assure you, I'm as unscrupulous as they come."

Beckworth's heart rate increased and his knee bounced. Rather than reining in his physical responses, he let them go unchecked. He didn't like where this was going, but it couldn't hurt to show a bit of fear.

"We weren't sure about you." The man leaned back and rested his mud-encrusted boots on the table. He pulled out a knife and dragged it along his leg, the tip scraping against the cloth. "You were seen with the spymaster on several occasions, and you got rather chummy with that Murphy fellow."

Beckworth sneered. "If you were watching that closely, then you would have noted that my half-brother stole my manor while I was away. I'd work with anyone to get it back."

The man stared at Beckworth for a long minute. "That is a possibility and something we considered."

The man kept using the word "we". Did that mean he wasn't the boss? Was this the illusive Gemini, or had Beckworth gotten himself caught up in some other madness? The fact they knew about Hensley didn't bode well. If that was the case, he would have to limit all contact with the spymaster, which meant he'd be on his own.

"Then we watched you meet with one of our contacts earlier this evening. It didn't go unnoticed when the spymaster showed up. Yet, you went out of your way not to be seen. That gave us hope you weren't the countrified gentleman you present to everyone."

"You're boring me with this trip down memory lane. Can you get to the point? These ropes chafe."

The man dropped his feet to the floor with a loud thump, then stabbed his knife down on the table, letting it stick. His eyes appeared like coal-black orbs in the dark mask. "We're offering you a job. We're picking up where the duke failed."

A cold sweat ran down Beckworth's spine. How did they know the duke had been up to something? Did this have something to do with the stones? Those damn things were going to get him killed.

"It's really rather simple. More consultative work than anything. Let's just say your experience will be of value."

"If you're getting involved with what I think you are, you're all as mad as the duke."

He shrugged. "Maybe. But the reward is worth the risk of a bit of madness." He stood. "You'll be well paid for no more than a fortnight's worth of work. You'll be given a few days to consider our offer, but our plan is already in motion."

"What have you done?" Beckworth let a touch of panic creep out. It would be impossible to hide it.

"All in good time, but the package will soon be en route." The man strode toward Beckworth, stopping a mere foot away. "You'll be watched until you give us your answer." He bent down to whisper his final threat. "A wise man would give strong consideration to joining our cause. And if you think you can get a message out to anyone while you're making your life-changing decision, think again. Not everyone at Waverly is in your pockets."

The blood left Beckworth's face before the hood was thrust back on and everything went black.

3

———

Baywood, Oregon - Present Day

AJ tossed the last duffel onto the dock and took Finn's hand as he assisted her off the sailboat. She stretched, lifted her arms into the air, leaned back to suck in a breath of clean ocean air, and almost purred. A week on the ocean, but nothing smelled better than sailing into their own port.

"Can you grab those last two bags? We can bring the cart down later to remove the perishables and get her stowed away." Finn carried a duffel over each shoulder and one in each hand. He looked like a Sherpa prepared for tackling a mountain climb.

Ethan was equally loaded down and had already started his schlep up the hill. Maire waited with her own duffel. AJ chuckled at the number of bags. It had only been a week-long excursion. They'd need a bigger boat if they planned a longer trip.

She shook her head and grabbed her gear. "All I want is a

real bath in our large tub. I didn't think sailing could be so exhausting."

"Next time, Finn should hire sailors to do all the work. My shoulders are twice the size they were before we left." Maire's quip was met with an appalled glance from Finn, and AJ laughed.

"I offered that suggestion before we left. It garnered the same expression." AJ nudged Finn, and he followed Ethan's trail.

When they reached the top of the path, the men headed for the front of the inn while AJ turned to cross the lawn. "I want to check on the feeders."

"You know Stella has been filling them." Maire followed her toward the stairs that led to the back deck.

"Yes, but I want to see if she's already been here today. She prefers to come later, but it depends on her schedule."

AJ stopped at the base of the stairs and surveyed the landscape. Her mother's garden club had been the inspiration for most of it, along with a few ideas from Stella. The makeover had required a small village to create pathways, till the soil, haul compost, and plant a variety of flowers. All the old plants had been removed with the exception of the roses on the north side of the inn, and she could hardly wait to see what buds had emerged to fill her kitchen vase.

They climbed the steps, and AJ steered for the back deck to check the hummingbird feeders, but stopped abruptly when she spotted someone sprawled on one of the loungers. She stumbled forward when Maire ran into her.

The French doors flew open, and Finn stepped out. "AJ?" His call sounded urgent, then shocked when he added, "Isaiah?"

The body on the lounger unwrapped itself, and Isaiah emerged from under what AJ noted was a sleeping bag. What the hell?

"Did someone forget to give you a key?" She laughed, but it

came out as more of a choke when Finn stormed toward the man.

"What happened here? Where's Stella?"

At Finn's words, she dropped her bags. His tone wasn't one of a simple question, like maybe Stella had gone to the store. It was clipped and harsh and her stomach did a flip. Dread as thick as sap wormed its way through her veins. With the French doors open, she noted one of the panes was gone, replaced by a piece of plywood. She counted to ten, her old and usually reliable aid in calming her nerves. It wasn't working.

Maire's hand touched her arm, but she ignored it, her focus on Isaiah as he rubbed his eyes, coming fully awake.

"Thank god you're home. I left messages, but I wasn't sure if you could get them at sea." He untangled himself from the sleeping bag.

"I'm not going to ask a second time. Where's Stella?" Finn's expression was a mixture of anger and fear.

AJ grabbed hold of the railing.

"She's been gone for two days."

"Let's go through it once more from the beginning." Ethan handed Isaiah a glass of water.

Isaiah drank most of it in three swallows before wiping his mouth with the long sleeve of his Henley. He'd been settled into one of the living room chairs. It was obvious from the fine beads of sweat along his brow, his dazed expression, and determined set to his jaw that he was still getting his emotions in check.

AJ attempted to get her own anger and fear under control by pacing between the living room and dining area. Her fists clenched and unclenched with each step, aching for the solid grip of her dagger. When Isaiah blurted out that Stella had been gone for two days, a coldness had seeped in. Every inch of her had turned to ice when she'd spotted the kitchen chair with the pieces of cut rope strewn across the floor. A potted plant had been overturned in the hallway, and Stella's purse was on the entry side table. She'd overheard Ethan tell Maire that Stella's car was still parked out front. Isaiah had left everything as he'd found it, with the exception of starting repairs on the French door.

It wasn't until Finn pulled up the security feed that the whole story came together. Mostly. The letter the kidnapper had left behind confirmed their worst nightmare. That was when the ice turned to fire in the pit of her stomach. And the flames raged when she heard Isaiah's tale.

Finn stepped in front of her, and she adjusted her course to walk around him, but he grabbed her shoulders and led her to the couch, pulling her to him so she couldn't get up.

Maire dropped to her other side, just as shell-shocked as the rest of them, her focus someplace else.

"The first indication of a problem was the security alarm I received from the inn. I was already on my way back from Eugene. We'd been getting alerts all week." He lowered his head but gave AJ a quick glance. "It was Ari. He flaps around and pecks at the door, just enough to trigger the alarm. And he leaves plenty of evidence he'd been there." He gave them a slight smile, but it slipped away.

"I left a message for Adam, but Joyce said he'd be in court most of the day. I called Stella next. She'd just turned into your driveway, and she said right away it was probably Ari. There weren't any unexpected cars in the lot. I asked her to wait, or that I would stop by as soon as I got to town, but you know how she is." He glanced around and everyone nodded. "She was already opening the door, said everything sounded quiet, and she'd call back in five minutes. I tried her twice, and when she didn't call back I broke speed records all the way here."

He rubbed a hand over his closely shaved head, and when he looked up his eyes glistened. "The fog moved in fast. It was on me before I got out of the car. I barely found the stairs to work my way around the deck. By then, the fog was already lifting and no one was there. I came in through the French doors, saw the broken glass and figured that's what triggered the alarm. After seeing the rope and the letter, I watched the security video. Then I knew." He finished the glass of water, his hand trembling as Ethan took it from him.

"I was going to call Adam, but I knew you'd be back in a couple of days and, honestly, what could either of us do? We couldn't call the police, and it wasn't like we could follow them." His voice faltered.

AJ had a hunch he wanted to add "back in time" but couldn't quite seem to spit it out.

"Can I see the letter again?" Maire reached out and waited for Ethan to hand it to her.

They'd decided Ethan, with his security background, would be the best one to lead Isaiah through what happened. No one wanted Isaiah to think this was his fault. He'd done everything he was supposed to do. At this point, AJ blamed herself for pampering Aristotle. What a calamity of misfortunes.

Maire sat back and perused the note. AJ glanced over her shoulder. Between the frilly handwriting and the early modern English, it took a moment to decipher the words.

"The note references *The Book of Stones*, and this incantation, though quite similar to the original ones, has been enhanced. It's comparable to how I've modified the incantations, but more, I don't know, rough around the edges I suppose." She stared at the page, her finger running along the incantation, and she nodded. "The author of the letter believes this incantation will send us to a specific location and, more importantly, a specific date. I can't be sure, but it's possible they found something Sebastian and I didn't have access to."

"That seems incredulous. Have they even tested it?" Ethan appeared as perplexed as the rest of them and didn't seem to expect an answer.

"We know from Sebastian's journal he left for Maire, he'd found new incantations that came from one of the sections of the Book." Finn glanced around the room before his jaw tightened. He shook his head. "I was going to ask for coffee and just looked for Stella." No one spoke, but gazes dropped. It had been an automatic response. Stella was always the one popping up to play hostess. AJ squeezed his arm as she got up to start a pot. "It appears this person has a piece of the Book."

"Or had at one time," Maire added. "Based on that same journal, Sebastian mentioned sending all four sections to trusted sources. Unfortunately, since Sebastian didn't date his journal, we don't know if he wrote it before or after the date on this letter."

"For all we know, we're the ones who end up retrieving the section of book from whoever sent us the letter." AJ hadn't left the room yet, interested in where the conversation was headed. When brows rose, her exasperation grew. "Well, we're not leaving Stella to fend for herself. This isn't like when Finn took me back. Even when I was mad at him, I somehow knew he'd be there for me." She lowered her voice. "Even during the worst of it."

Finn stood and put an arm around her. "Of course, we're going after her. But we need to know what game is being played." He gestured to Isaiah. "Come on, let's go grab some lunch while AJ and Ethan clean up. Then we'll make plans." He turned to Maire. "They already have a head start on us in addition to the incantation they believe will take us to an exact location and point of time. We have to assume the man who took Stella used a similar incantation. They probably wouldn't want much time to lapse before our arrival. It's a risk keeping a hostage. What do you think?" His question was directed at Ethan.

"I agree. At this point, all the advantage is theirs."

Finn refocused on Maire, his face softening. "I have no intention of following their rules. I know I'm asking a great deal, but I need you to find a way to manipulate that incantation, both in time and place. I want to arrive days earlier and close to one of our allies."

"Oh, well, as long as you're not asking for much. I'll just go get my decoder ring." She flipped her hair back as if she were an angry teen, and AJ wondered how she knew about decoder rings. But for all her sass, AJ noted Maire's unfocused gaze. She was already working on the problem.

AJ held out her hand to Maire. "Let's get you set up in the library. It's nice and peaceful."

"How about if I go with you?" Ethan asked Finn. "I'd like to go by the house and pick up some new clothes and our weapons. It would be easier if you could put us up until we leave."

AJ noticed Maire hadn't asked for her notes or the journal. She hadn't seen her with them on the boat, but Maire was possessive so it didn't surprise AJ that she'd kept the documents close. "Go ahead, there isn't much to clean up. I'll take care of it after I get Maire situated."

"Isaiah, call Adam and Emory. They'll be helpful with the planning. We leave in four days." Finn glanced at AJ, his gaze hard and filled with worry. "I don't think our nerves will last any longer than that."

AJ turned the lock and stepped inside. The silence, mixed with the scent of roses, slammed into her like a logging truck. Emptiness overtook her, and she clutched the door before the sensation dropped her to her knees. She sucked in a sob and pulled herself together, closing the door quietly behind her.

As much time as Stella spent at her real estate office, AJ hadn't felt the loss there as much as she did standing in her friend's foyer. The office had been her first stop to check mail and Stella's calendar. She contacted Alexis, Stella's backup, and told her Stella had a family emergency and would be out of contact for at least ten days. Had she been overly optimistic?

Now that she was at Stella's place, worry and fear for her friend flooded her. She'd been able to tamp it down while she was with others, but once she'd cleaned up the mess, she'd had nothing to do. At some point, her brain had shut down, and she wasn't reliable to make correct decisions. An eerie paralysis had settled over her. A visit to take care of Stella's business and home might help get her head back on straight.

AJ checked the windows, watered the plants on the porch, cleaned out perishables from the kitchen, and emptied vases. Once she'd finished caring for everything in the house, she stared at the back patio. A couple of lights in a far corner had already turned on though it wasn't yet four o'clock. Everything was so peaceful.

This was where Stella truly lived. She always found something to pick at: a brown leaf here, a wilted flower there, but from AJ's perspective, the garden was lush, wild, and complex—just like her friend.

She stepped outside and picked up the comforter Stella always left on the patio lounger. It smelled of Stella's favorite perfume—an exotic floral scent. AJ wrapped it around her, fell onto the lounge chair and curled into a ball. Unable to hold back any longer, she let the tears fall. Now she understood how Stella felt when she'd disappeared with Finn.

Stella hadn't known where AJ had gone, and though she'd suspected Finn or Ethan would have been with her, the thought hadn't appeased Stella. This was worse. Stella didn't have anyone with her she could trust. She had to know they'd come for her. But she was in the hands of an unknown enemy, who thought she was AJ. What if her captives discovered who she really was?

She nestled into the warm comforter. Fifteen minutes for a pity party, then she'd get back in the game and lock away her worries for another time.

Something nudged her. Then another, and she swatted at the air, thinking it was a fly.

"AJ, wake up."

She pried open a lid. The lashes stuck together, and she wiped away drool from the side of her mouth. Her forehead scrunched. "Finn?"

He messed her hair like she was a good dog, and she scowled while batting his arm aside.

She sat up and glanced around. "I fell asleep."

"Aye."

"I was only going to take fifteen minutes." She squinted up. The sun was still up, but the shadows had grown longer.

"It probably hasn't been much longer than that. Maire called when you didn't return when expected."

"Good grief."

"We're all worried about Stella, but we also know it's more difficult for you. Don't blame us for our concern."

He pulled her up and walked her to the wicker patio chair. He sat, the chair swallowing him as it did everyone, and pulled her onto his lap.

"Isn't Ethan and Isaiah waiting for us?"

"No. Since your car was here, I had them drop me off. Though I can't guarantee how much food will be left if we dawdle long." When AJ tried to get up, he pulled her back. "We have a few minutes. I wanted to talk to you alone."

He pushed an errant strand of hair away, tucking it behind her ear. "I know we've discussed this when we've found ourselves in precarious situations. We have to tuck our emotions away and stay focused on the mission." He chuckled, but there wasn't any humor in it. "I can't believe I used the word mission, but that's the simple truth. Based on the letter, we know they want the Heart Stone. So this business is once again unsettled." He squeezed her. "I don't know how long before we can call it done, but it appears with all Sebastian's careful planning, someone found something."

AJ considered his assessment, and found it a likely call, but it wasn't the only possibility. "What if someone else knew about them? Maybe we didn't catch everyone like we thought we did."

Finn nodded. "At this point, there are too many possibilities, leaving us with nothing but guess work."

After a couple moments of silence, AJ murmured, "I'm so worried about her. She hated the idea of going back in time."

"I know. But consider this. Stella is a fighter and extremely intelligent. The kidnappers believe she's you. And they won't do anything to harm her until I show up with the Heart Stone."

AJ perked up. "And Stella would know that, so she'll do anything to prevent them from knowing who she really is."

"Does that help?" His gaze was tender, but his brow creased.

She ran a hand across his forehead and pushed his own lock of hair back. "I say we go home and put our plan together. Then we start training in the morning."

4

Waverly Manor, England – 1805

Beckworth handed two envelopes to Barrington. When his butler reached for them, Beckworth held onto them for a tentative moment. He'd never questioned Barrington's loyalty. Never thought he'd have to. That was the problem with trust. It was intangible. Something one had to feel, to know with bone-deep certainty. Even then, sometimes a person had a blind spot. He'd had little cause to trust most people through his life.

One could pay for loyalty, but there was always someone with more money. Worse, there were men despicable enough to threaten the weak in order to gain an advantage. He'd been that perpetrator on several occasions, directed by those above him. Yet, nothing threatened loyalty like the seeds of doubt. Gemini might know nothing of Waverly, let alone anyone that worked at the manor. But that was the rub. How did he know for sure?

Two nights ago, he'd woke to find he'd been tossed like a

bum into a London back alley. He'd ridden nonstop until reaching Waverly late last night, and when he'd walked through the door something had felt different. He couldn't put his finger on it. That tingle told him there was either a spy hidden at Waverly or his nagging uncertainty was growing. The stones and the trouble they brought were a large portion of his unease and clouded his judgment.

Barrington waited, refusing to pull on the envelopes until he released them. After Beckworth let go, he mumbled an apology. "I don't seem to have my thoughts together this morning."

Barrington nodded. "I'll have these posted immediately." He took a step but hesitated. "Is everything all right, sir?"

Oh, absolutely. I'm sitting here trying to determine if someone I've known for half my life is betraying me. No worries.

"It will pass." He couldn't look Barrington in the eye.

"May I sit, sir?"

Beckworth sighed. This was where they'd put all the cards on the table. He wasn't sure he wanted to know the truth. But a long time ago, they made a promise to each other. If Barrington ever had reason to discuss something on a personal level, it would be on equal footing, sitting across the table from each other.

"Yes, of course."

When Barrington sat, Beckworth stood and pulled a bottle of scotch and two glasses from a nearby serving table. He poured generous amounts then returned to his seat. He took a long, slow sip, his eyes closing with pleasure. One of his best bottles. He opened his eyes to find Barrington smiling at him.

"What?" He almost wiped a sleeve across his chin in case he was drooling.

His butler shook his head. "If either of us thought we'd be here all those years ago, we'd think each other mad."

He settled back in his chair and lifted his boots to the desk. "I don't think I mentioned I saw Toby on one of my last visits to London."

Barrington sneered and sipped the scotch. "Is he still the bumbling idiot?"

He grinned. "He's managed to stay alive after all this time. Works in his sister's herb shop and finds part-time odd jobs. But he still stays connected to the old gang."

"For all his faults, he was a loyal one." He lifted his gaze to meet Beckworth's. When he didn't get a response, he continued, "You know Henry meant everything to me."

Beckworth fidgeted and shifted his focus to the bookshelf. "You don't..."

"Stop." Barrington took a long swallow and winced as the liquor burned a trail down his throat. "I wouldn't bring up my nephew if it wasn't to make a strong point."

He lifted a brow. It must be one helluva point for him to drudge up one of the worst days in both their lives. A thought occurred to him.

"Why do you insist on working here?" When Barrington's eyes widened, he amended his question. "You've had dozens of other opportunities. If you insist on being a butler, you could have your choice of dukes and earls."

"I was meant to work in service. Butler suits me. And I dare say, I've had more excitement in my years at Waverly than I could find in a nobler home."

"Yet you stay. If it's for Henry, there was never a debt to repay."

Barrington drained his glass and slipped it toward Beckworth, who added two more fingers. "It wasn't what you did for Henry. No one could have predicted the calamity of that day. You have protected our family time and again, always with great risk to your person. And not once did you ever ask for anything in return." He shook his head and ran a hand over his balding head. "We didn't know each other very well back then, yet you took action when no one else would." He caught Beckworth's gaze and held it. "I knew right then what kind of man you were. One that I could trust with my life."

Beckworth couldn't speak. Didn't have the words. But the tension that squeezed his chest slipped from him in waves. If he'd been standing, he'd be nothing but a limp rag on the floor. There was at least one person he could trust.

"I was thinking." Barrington scratched his neck, and another smile, this one more wicked, lit his face. "If say, for some reason you're not at liberty to disclose, you were concerned about the staff, perhaps the Deveraux plan might be the best approach."

The Deveraux plan. Where had he heard that name before? He leaned back and stared at the ceiling. After a moment, he laughed. "Max Deveraux. I haven't heard that name in ages. Now he was a squirrelly one."

Barrington chuckled. "Right to the end."

"Oh?"

"He had quit the game and went to work at the docks. Got drunk one night and fell into the Thames. Drowned."

"Well, that's a shame. He was a good man."

"I think his wife left him, and he used the bottle to ease the pain."

They sat in silent memory until Beckworth slapped the desk. "So, we scatter false messages through the household and see what we turn up."

"If there is a mole, we need to root them out one way or another. In the meantime, everything you deem private will be handled through a secondary flow. No one associated with anyone in the manor."

"Is that doable?"

"I believe so."

"Let's start with Libby and Donald."

Barrington nodded. "If we can clear them, that will give us a great deal to work with."

"Excellent." He finished his scotch and rolled the glass between his hands. "You know we should do more of this."

Barrington stood. "As soon as we get you out of whatever the spymaster has gotten you into." He gave a slight bow with a matching smile, then his expression became blank as he left the room. The consummate professional.

If Libby or Donald could be cleared, that would mean he hadn't been a fool after all. He didn't want anyone in the manor to take the bait, but he had to look at it realistically. His staff was well paid, and he never asked more of them then he considered fair. He'd come from a similar background, so he understood what it took to make people happy. As it turned out, it usually wasn't much—a good job and a secure home. Living in the country, working at a fine house, and earning a fair wage was a dream for many of them. But the war had impacted everyone. He couldn't blame someone for trying to earn a few extra schillings to feed the family. He knew little of Gemini but doubted the man cared about the damage he left behind.

Beckworth stretched, tugged at his lacy cuffs, and stood to scan the gardens. His study in the east wing, used for his private business, didn't have a window, but he was surrounded by books, and that was almost as good. The west study was used for manor business. It was twice the size of his private study, was more comfortable for accepting visitors, and it had the best view of the estate. The only thing marring it today was the poor weather.

Now that he was confident his letters would get out, his focus turned to his next step. How to respond to Gemini's offer. He didn't have a choice in which answer he'd give the man, just how to deliver it. As much as he'd prefer to walk away from all this business, Gemini was already a thorn for Hensley. If the stones were involved—when would it all end?

The last few days had done nothing but sour his mood.

Barrington knocked on the door, startling him out of his thoughts.

He smiled as he turned. "Yes?" His smile faded. "What is it?"

"You have a visitor. Lady Prescott."

L ady Prescott? What the devil was she doing here? Beckworth had seen her once after his holiday party, about a month ago at Lord Melville's birthday gala. It had been an overnight affair, and while they'd both teased and bantered during the weekend, she'd flirted with several men. After hearing Fitz tell stories of their indiscretion, Beckworth wouldn't be surprised if she'd added another conquest that evening. But what was she up to now? She might appear to be scouting for a husband, but he suspected there was more to it.

"Did anyone accompany her?"

Barrington pulled himself up as if he wasn't already straight as a board, his nose almost wrinkling with his response. "She travels alone."

"She does seem to play her own game."

"She asked if she might wait for you in the solarium. Something about wanting to see the gardens."

Beckworth smiled. "She did seem to enjoy them the last time she was here." He sat at his desk, pulled a page of stationary from a drawer, and uncapped an inkpot. "Show her to the solarium and ask Libby to bring her tea."

Libby was the best spy in his employ, and her role as a lady's maid put her in an excellent position for snooping. He disliked having to test her, but he'd been given little choice.

"Very good, sir."

He completed the letter, took time to review it, and satisfied, signed it. On the way to the solarium, he diverted through the kitchen. He searched three rooms before finding a young lad polishing shoes.

"Jax," Beckworth whispered.

The boy gave him a quick glance, then sprang up, a shoe dropping from his hand. "Yes, sir."

"Come here. Quick now."

The boy ran over, wiping stained hands on his black work pants, his forehead scrunched in thought. "Can I help you, sir?"

"Is Mr. Huntsmith going to town today?"

The boy nodded. "He's already pulled the cart around."

"I want you to go with him. I promised someone would help him with the barrels. I would also like you to take this letter and post it for me. There will be something extra for you."

Jax scratched his cheek. The creases in his forehead disappeared and his dimples emerged. "You know I'll do it. I love going to town. You don't have to give me anything."

Beckworth grinned. "I insist you allow me to do something for you anyway. But not until after the deed is done."

"Agreed." The boy snatched the letter, stuffed it in the pocket of his pants, grabbed a biscuit that had been sitting next to the shoe box, and scampered out the door.

He was taking a chance with the boy, but he'd known Jax since before he could walk. His parents had worked on the estate for the previous viscount. His father was a smithy, and his mother was one of the house maids. Both hard workers. Jax had originally been put to work in the stables, but he'd been useless except for talking up the horses. What he did demonstrate was a fascination for everything around him, and Beckworth understood—the young lad was bored. He began leaving books in the stable where Jax ate lunch. It took three days before Jax picked up the first one.

Beckworth had then requested Jax be assigned a tutor for one hour every day. He thought the parents would prove difficult, but they surprised him. Some people could be stubborn, but this couple saw opportunity for their boy and heartily agreed. Now, Jax worked in several areas but usually went wherever he was needed. Beckworth was positive the parents could be trusted, but it would break his heart if Jax had been unwittingly lured. He'd know soon enough.

When he strode into the solarium, Lady Prescott was seated on the sofa that faced the garden. A tea service had already arrived, and she was adding milk to a cup.

"I'm sorry to keep you waiting. Your visit is a splendid surprise." Beckworth gave her a quick bow before taking a seat across from her.

"It's me who should apologize for arriving without announcement. I've been in Bristol and was on my way back to London when I remembered you're almost on the way." She tilted her head a bare inch and frowned. "You can't see the garden from there. Come sit next to me." She smiled and sunshine seemed to break through the dull, gray day. "I promise I won't bite."

He inwardly sighed. If only he didn't distrust her. He'd throw caution to the wind and let her drag him upstairs. Or to the linen room. Either would do. But while his lower half was all-in, his instincts held him back, cautioning him to step carefully. He knew better than to question a gut reaction.

He moved to sit next to her—a little closer than what would be considered socially acceptable—and wasn't surprised when she leaned toward him. Her perfume wafted over him, something soft and dreamy.

"Would you like some tea?" she asked. When he nodded, she poured a cup.

"You said you were in Bristol?"

If the direct question troubled her, she didn't show it. "I've been visiting with an old friend of my mother's. Well, they knew each other a long time ago. She lives outside Bristol, and I'll be staying with her after the season."

"Not with Lady Singleton?"

She hesitated, then gave him a regretful sigh. "I'm afraid that didn't work out."

"I see." He didn't see at all but was beginning to. Whatever game she was playing, she had a strategy worked out. Or perhaps one that wasn't going quite as planned. Suspicions weren't facts, but they were strong enough for him to remain wary. "I take milk, no sugar."

"What? Oh, yes, the tea." A light blush rose to her cheeks. "I'm afraid I was musing over your lovely gardens. Even with the gray skies, I see several bits of color."

Her blush was impossible to fake, but had he caught her fabricating more lies, or had she truly been pensive? Damn, but he hated these ruses. They used to be fun. What had changed?

"We'll have to take a short stroll after tea."

She nodded enthusiastically. "Also, I hate to ask, but you're the only one I seem to know well enough in the area."

His brow rose, but he didn't respond. He did nothing more than glance at Barrington when he replaced the teapot with a fresh one, but he caught the butler's slight nod. They had a spy at a door. Most likely Libby. If so, their plan was coming together.

"Lady Hawthorne doesn't go to many parties. It seems she's

not invited to many, either. Your parties are the talk of Bristol, and I thought…"

"That an invitation or two from me might lead to more parties." He'd been tempted to let her struggle with the request, but a gentleman wouldn't do that.

Her smile was coy, and she ran the tip of her tongue over her lips. If she was attempting seduction, that wasn't the way to go about it. Not with him.

"I think that can be arranged. Though I honestly can't tell you when the next one might be."

"Oh, well of course, not during the season. In fact, that's why I'm heading back to London. Did you have plans to spend time in the city?"

He sipped his tea then shook his head. "I've not made any plans for the spring."

"That doesn't sound like the viscount I've heard so much about."

He chuckled. "I'm really rather dull except for my parties, and most of those are for hunting. I'm a man of leisure and never know when I might grab a horse or carriage and visit neighbors."

She wrinkled her nose. "It does seem rather boring." She tapped a delicate finger on her chin. "Why don't you follow me to London? I know of a small but quite elegant home in Hyde Park that has recently become available for the season." She turned up the charm, her deep sapphire eyes melting into deep pools.

He sighed. "I can't tell you how wonderful that sounds."

Her alluring smile turned into a pout. "I know when someone's going to make an excuse."

"No excuse. Just the truth. While I might have estate managers to care for everything, I do have tasks to perform, and I'm afraid I've yet to make arrangements for any departure."

She perked up. "But you are making plans to be away?" She lowered her head. "That seemed too forward. I'm sorry."

This time he waited her out, wanting to see where she'd steer the conversation.

"You could follow a fortnight behind. That would allow time to have the house prepared and see what invitations we can garner. As long as I know you'll be able to come."

He'd intended to clear his calendar for the next few months to return to London. He had a job to do for Hensley, and he had no idea if or when Gemini would reach out. He'd found the man in London before; he could do it again. What better cover than to have his own apartment with his own beautiful house guest. It would be easier to uncover her game if she were close. Could he juggle time with her and Gemini? He did enjoy a challenge.

He gave her his most charming smile. "Your offer definitely bares consideration."

After the promised stroll through the garden, Lady Prescott seemed eager to get back on the road. Once her carriage rolled down the drive, Barrington stepped next to him on the front landing.

"Are you sure you want to get that close?"

"You're not afraid I'll let a beautiful woman distract me, are you?"

Barrington didn't respond. His gaze monitored the carriage as it followed the curve in the road until it turned out of sight. "Gemini is dangerous. He's spent years in hiding, or more likely, hiding in plain sight. Either way, he didn't survive this long by playing nice. Having another puzzle to work out, beautiful woman aside, could be a distraction."

While Beckworth might have been thinking along those same lines, hearing them spoken out loud by someone other than himself unnerved him. "Let's stick with the plan and hope we don't get any surprises."

"I'm afraid you have one waiting for you in your west study."

Beckworth entered his study to find Libby sitting in one of the guest chairs, her knees bouncing. He'd never seen her anxious.

"Libby, is there a problem?"

When she began to wring her hands, he couldn't decide what to make of her behavior. She was a streetwise young woman who'd grown up in one of his old crews. She'd been on his staff at Waverly for a couple of years now and made a marvelous spy, capable of working in various roles in the house. Was she truly Gemini's inside man?

"If I were you, sir, I'd watch that one."

That was unexpected. He poured a liberal amount of whiskey for both of them. At this rate, he'd be drunk before lunch. "Lady Prescott?"

He handed her the glass and sat in the opposite chair rather than putting a desk between them.

She gulped the first two sips of whiskey. The tension in her shoulders eased, and she settled back with a gentle foot tap the only sign of her earlier agitation. "Sorry, sir, but that woman worries me. I asked around Corsham about her and no one's heard of her. That's to be expected if she's not from around here, but a couple of weeks ago one of the lady's maids that work for Lady Agatha mentioned a Lord and Lady Prescott that live near Lancaster. But the Lord is dead now."

"Lancaster? That's rather far north of here, isn't it?"

Libby nodded. "It's possible this Lady Prescott is from another line or not related at all. But after all her nosing around at the Christmas party..." She shrugged and stared into her glass. "I just thought I'd put a word out and see what came back."

"I appreciate that, Libby."

"Oh, and that story about Lady Hawthorne in Bristol? That's hogwash."

Beckworth downed the rest of his drink. He wasn't sure he wanted to hear any more. "Go on."

"I suppose Lady Prescott could be staying with her, but the woman's two sons live with her, including both wives and five children between them. The estate is meager in comparison to Waverly."

"And how did you come by this so quickly?"

She winked at him. "You must not have met Rosalind yet."

Beckworth squinted. The name was familiar. "Ah, the buxom new scullery maid."

Libby snorted. "That's the one. She came from Lady Hawthorne's kitchen staff. And she's not a shy one. She wanted out of that house so badly, she took a lower position to work here. That one never stops talking."

He studied her. "And you can have this information confirmed?"

Libby smiled. "Of course, sir. A couple of the girls have the day off tomorrow. We were going to Corsham for lunch at the inn. If Rosalind could have the day off, too, well, she still writes to one of the footmen."

Beckworth laughed. Libby joined in, though she would have no idea that most of his mirth came from his sheer relief that she couldn't be a spy for Gemini. Unless she was going to pass along information about Lady Prescott, but he couldn't see how Gemini would care one whit about her. But Libby was a smart one, she could still be duping him.

He set his glass on the desk and decided on one more question. "One thing doesn't add up. It would be easy for me to confirm Lady Prescott's story if I had a mind. Why would she take such a risk?"

Libby polished off her whiskey and placed the glass next to his on the desk. "I could be wrong, and we'll know by tomorrow night. But my best guess? Whatever she's up to, it's the end of the game, and she knows you won't have time to investigate."

5

England – 1805

The blinding light of the fog was nothing compared to the intense cramping that seized Stella in what appeared to be an attempt to turn her insides to the outside. The man's grip on her arm pinched, and though she hadn't eaten since breakfast, she was pretty sure puking was next on the list. Her only pleasure would be finding a way to turn around so the asshole who got her into this predicament caught the brunt of her returning breakfast.

When she didn't think she could take anymore and darkness edged her vision, her feet hit solid ground and, not anticipating it, she crumpled like a wet teabag. The bright light receded and the rushing in her ears disappeared, but her stomach spasmed. She managed to crawl a few inches before rolling into a ball.

She heard a grunt behind her, and assuming her abductor was in the same hampered condition, she pushed aside the effects of her roller-coaster ride and scrambled on her hands and knees. Not sure where she was or where to go, the urgency to flee from the crazy madman drove her toward the trees. She made it to her feet and stumbled several yards before her heel caught on something, and she went down.

An instant later, she was hauled up by an arm. The man didn't chide her. Instead, he turned in a slow circle, taking in their surroundings while Stella oriented herself. They were in a clearing in the middle of a forest. The air smelled different—cleaner, with tinges of earthy and woodsy scents. It had recently rained. The ground wasn't muddy, but the dirt was soft. And here she was in her favorite four-inch boots. At least her feet were dry, but the heels would prevent any hope of escape. As if she knew where to run.

She wiped the dirt from her face, picked leaves out of her hair, then stared at the man who'd kidnapped her. He didn't seem to notice her as he continued his study of their surroundings. She closed her eyes and forced the panic to take a back seat. It wouldn't help now, and she assumed there would be plenty of time for an anxiety attack later. Right now, she needed to keep her wits about her. That was what AJ would do.

AJ. They were still two days out. Of course, that would be two hundred years from now. But once they were home?

The man had left a note. Isaiah had been seconds from reaching her. Surely, he would have seen the fog and knew what that meant. They would come for her. She glanced at the man next to her. The fear returned regardless of her attempt to ignore it. Her previous decision to pull on her big-girl panties lasted all of five seconds. She didn't know their true intent or how long they planned on keeping her alive.

She decided to test him on his communication skills. "Where are we?"

Without a response, he pulled her toward the woods. She resisted, but he was stronger and simply yanked her down the road, hauling her up each time she tripped.

"You have to slow down unless you plan to drag me the whole way. My shoes don't work well in mud. And where exactly are we going?"

The man spun unexpectedly, and Stella raised an arm in self-defense. "The main road isn't far. I suggest you keep up. I have no problem dragging you. My orders were to simply keep you alive. And a few bruises or broken bones won't kill you."

She began to say something, then thought better of it. At least the plan didn't include any killing, though the boots might break her neck. If they were truly two hundred years in the past, the last thing she wanted was a broken anything. She focused on where she stepped and tried to keep up, but when they got to a wider road, she collapsed.

"Get up, woman." Spittle fell on his chin. He was mad as hell, but what did he expect after abducting her, forcing her through a stomach-wrenching journey in light as bright as a thousand suns, then dragging her about like some unwanted baggage?

When she refused, he let go of her and performed another slow turn. He appeared lost. Maybe that was why he was as growly as a bear. He gave her long look.

"If you run, I won't be so nice. You'll still be able to walk with a broken arm."

He kept staring at her. Assuming that was a signal she could walk on her own, she nodded. He turned and stormed down the road.

She scrambled up, but instead of following, she considered her options. Her gut instinct said to take flight. No surprise there. She had no misgivings that she would run from a burning building rather than race into one. And this situation was no joke. Her only weapons were her instinct to survive and her smarts. If she did run and managed to get away, she could die in the woods without food or water. Someone worse could come along, though it was hard to imagine how that would be possible. But the real clincher was his brutally honest truth—he would snap her arm like a tree branch and not give her screams a second thought.

She straightened, pulled down her sweater, and followed after him. If he wanted to outpace her, that was his problem. They might have to walk for miles, and these boots were made for city streets not hiking. The road was smoother than the first trail, but it was still strewn with rocks and divots. The last thing she needed was a sprained ankle.

An hour later, she sat on a boulder while the crazy man paced. She pulled a pebble out of her boot and rubbed her feet. Blisters had already formed. Another five miles, and she would let him drag her the rest of the way by her hair. She was starving, thirsty, and exhausted. Moisture filled her eyes when she remembered waking up that morning. She'd been so close to going back to bed. Why hadn't she listened to Isaiah? *Oh god, AJ. How did you survive this?*

"Are you sure you know where you're going?" She shouldn't aggravate him, but honestly, he could have made a wrong turn on any one of the roads they'd traversed.

"You need to walk faster."

He stalked off. At least he didn't hit her. Based on her experience with Finn and Ethan, men from this era didn't like to be questioned in areas they felt knowledgeable. Good to know some things never changed.

She took her time putting her boots back on, squeaking at the pain before pushing it aside. After straightening her sweater and rain duster, she wiped debris from her backside, pushed her tangled locks back, and took a tentative step. The blisters weren't too bad, but she didn't fool herself. Things were bound to get worse long before her luck changed. Right now, all she wanted was food and a bed. The ground would suffice, but when she glanced at the sky, the clouds worried her. The last thing she needed was to be soaked on top of everything else.

They stopped twice more before Big and Tall—the name she'd given her kidnapper—got tired of waiting for her, and, disregarding her indignant yelp, tossed her over his shoulders. His body was hard bones and even harder muscle, and the blood rushing to her head made it ache. She closed her eyes. At least her feet were grateful. But after twenty minutes, she couldn't take it anymore. Before she could bargain with him, he dumped her into a pile of leaves. She hit hard, the jolt knocking her teeth together.

"Give a warning next time." She rubbed her backside.

He'd already walked on, and when she turned to see where he was going, her eyes widened. A rickety cabin, its roof questionable, the porch floorboards peeling away, and the shutters hanging lopsided, appeared as hospitable as a wolverine's den. But smoke drifted out of a crumbling chimney, and she pictured a roaring fire with her curled up in front of it. The fragrant smell of something roasting caught her attention, but it wasn't coming from the cabin. A campfire was ablaze several yards from the porch, and three men sat on crates circling it.

A snap from behind her made her turn. Two more men walked out of the darkening woods, rifles resting on their shoulders. No one spoke. Big and Tall stopped several yards from the cabin. He didn't speak to the other men, didn't even acknowledge their presence. He just stared at the cabin.

Several quiet minutes passed until a woman walked through the door and stopped at the top of the porch steps. She was dressed in snug black pants, a white shirt, and a black vest. Her boots stopped just below her knees. Her blonde hair was tied back in either a ponytail or braid, it was difficult to tell which from this angle. And though she was too far away for Stella to see the color of her eyes, it wasn't hard to tell from her expression that she was mad as a hatter.

"You're late. You should have been here three days ago." With each graceful step down the stairs, the woman seemed better suited for an elaborate ball gown.

Big and Tall stalked toward her, uncaring of the men who stood and stepped closer. "I wouldn't be if the incantation you gave me was correct. We came through five miles from here."

The woman's demeanor instantly changed, and she took the final steps to meet him, placing a hand on his cheek. "I don't know what went wrong. It worked the last time."

"We should have run more tests."

"We didn't have the time." She took another step when he backed up and turned away from her. "Gaines!"

So that was his name. Stella preferred the one she'd given him.

He stopped long enough to give her a tight-lipped smile. "Don't worry. I'll make up a story why I'm late. But we have a larger problem."

She nodded. "If the incantation isn't predictable, our guest might also be late." She shrugged. "Easy enough to plan for. We might have to wait, but we'll be better prepared. I didn't want to have to deal with a hostage for that long, but it's better than missing the window."

He nodded. "I'll be back tomorrow night."

"Be safe." Her voice had softened, and the tension around his eyes lessened.

Stella's eyebrow rose. Was this an area Stella could exploit? She'd have to give it some thought. It didn't require a rocket scientist to guess that Finn was the guest this woman was expecting. Was the woman in charge?

Gaines walked to a group of horses, saddled one as everyone watched, then rode off without another word.

The woman stared at the empty road where Gaines had disappeared for several long moments before swinging around to Stella. She stomped toward her, her earlier grace gone, and stopped a foot away, staring down with a curious expression.

Stella refused to be daunted and took her time to stand, wincing as she stood on sore feet. She tugged her sweater down, swiped the leaves from her backside, and brushed her hair back from her face before giving the woman a haughty glare.

"You're AJ Moore?" The woman's head cocked to one side. She was either sizing Stella up to whatever expectations she had regarding AJ or suspected she was a fake and was deciding the best way for Big and Tall to off her when he returned. Or rather than wait, she might ask one of her other questionable associates to handle it.

"Yeah, well, you haven't caught me on my best day."

The woman's eyes widened, and then she laughed. "My word, I think you're someone I could truly get along with. It's unfortunate we're on different sides." She winked at me. "That could change."

Stella brightened. "Oh, good. Does that mean you'll just whisper a little incantation and send me home?"

The woman's gaze sparkled with delight, but it could have been madness. "It would have been easier if you'd just given up the stone. Now we have to deal with all these secret meetings and additional planning." She glanced off to the distance, and Stella assumed she was mentally rearranging her party calendar. "No matter. It's just another inconvenience." She gave Stella another perusal then noticed the boots. "My word, how did you walk in those shoes?"

Stella grimaced. "Not easily."

"I imagine you're hungry."

"And thirsty."

"Fine. Jessup, take Miss Moore to the cabin. Find something

for her to eat and drink. She'll be your responsibility until we get back to the house."

Stella stepped back when Jessup grabbed her arm, and like Big and Tall, preferred to drag her to the cabin rather than let her walk on her own. Where were all the gallant men this century supposedly produced? This group must have focused on the caveman approach to handling hostages they'd read from some outdated kidnapper's handbook.

She continued to struggle against him until she heard the woman call out, "And don't damage her too much. She needs to be presentable when Murphy arrives."

<hr>

The interior of the cabin was as bad as Stella imagined. Sections of the floor resembled Swiss cheese, the edges of boards rotted through. A light breeze whistled through gaps in the walls. A matching set of a chipped pitcher and basin sat on a hewn counter that stretched along one wall. Hard to believe, not the worst kitchen she'd seen. A table with four chairs sat on one side of the room and a hearth on the other. A piece of fabric hung over a doorway that led to a storage room or maybe a bedroom. She was fairly certain it wasn't a bathroom.

The only bright spot was the heat blazing from a roaring fire and the smell of something cooking. Her stomach growled.

Jessup pointed toward the table. "Sit."

She gave the room a more thorough scan while she waited for the food, but she hadn't missed much, except for a couple more chairs and a side table. They must be desperate if they'd spent three days here waiting for Big and Tall to show up with his hostage. A bowl was dropped in front of her, and brown juice splashed on the table and the front of her raincoat.

She stared into the bowl and questioned her decision to pick up the spoon, but she was starving. If she was going to be of any use to Finn and AJ when they arrived, she had to keep up her strength. The thick gruel didn't look appetizing. When she stirred it, large chunks of meat surfaced. A piece of bread was tossed on the table before a mug slammed down next to it.

Her stomach overruled her concerns of food poisoning, and she took a small bite of the thick stew. The taste surprised her. It wasn't anything she'd pay for, but for a starving person, it was good enough. She used the bread to sop up the dregs of the stew, not knowing when she'd get another meal. She also drained the cup of water.

After clearing the table, Jessup grabbed a dark bottle and another mug. He poured a fair amount of a tawny liquid into both mugs, and she caught the telltale scent of alcohol. Then he dragged a chair over until it touched hers and plopped down. Her eyes watered from his foul odor. Three days of sitting around, they had more than enough time to find someplace to bathe.

He turned toward her and placed an arm on the back of her chair before chugging down a couple swallows. "Go ahead and drink. You'll want to keep up with me tonight."

The stew made a rumbling sound in her stomach, and she rubbed it, damning her sensitive stomach as she considered her options. If someone had come on to her like this at home, she would have threatened him with the pepper spray she kept in her purse. But her purse was still in Baywood, and she didn't even have a stick of gum in her pockets.

She stared at the bottle of alcohol. How much would she have to drink to forget where she was? Would it be enough to drown out her anxiety, stress, and fear? She had to keep her wits, so she pushed the mug away.

"I could use more water."

Jessup stared at her, but his gaze didn't meet her eyes. His focal point was well below her chin, and she pulled her raincoat tighter.

"You won't need that fancy coat. I'll keep you warm enough."

She had originally been impressed by the blonde woman, who appeared to be in charge of this motley team, but she would need to lower that five-star rating if these men were given free rein to do what they wanted. Maybe this was how the men blew off steam. Would a woman let another be abused on her watch?

Without a weapon, she'd have to try a different tactic. "Do you know who Captain Finn Murphy is?"

Jessup leaned back, barely outside her comfort zone. He scratched his cheek, then his chest. The man probably had lice. "I've heard of him."

"What do you think he'd do to someone who abused his wife?"

"We have enough men to deal with him." He puffed his chest like a preening peacock, but his words didn't carry any heat.

She laughed. "You think Finn will be coming on his own?"

He blinked. "That's what Gemini said."

Gemini? That wasn't Big and Tall. The woman had called him Gaines. Was that her name?

She shrugged. "If that's what you want to believe, but I think I know my husband better than whoever this Gemini is."

He considered her statement, but the gleam in his gaze suggested he wasn't scared of too many things. When he reached out, she twisted to evade his grasp. He caught her left breast and gave it a squeeze, which evoked an immediate, instinctual response.

She slapped him.

Next thing she knew, she was on her back, still sitting in the chair. He grabbed her arm to pull her away. Her raincoat had fallen open, freeing her legs, and she kicked out. It was a horrible angle, and she didn't think she'd connected, but a leg went out from under him. If he hadn't been trying to step over her while grabbing her arm, he would have easily missed the kick. She took advantage of the odd timing.

She scrambled up. Her first thought was the door, but she'd have to get past him. She turned for the makeshift kitchen, found a clay teapot and threw it at him. Her aim had always been true, and this time was no exception. He tried to duck, but his timing was off again, and the teapot hit him in the side of the head, shattering when it hit the floor. Somehow, that wasn't enough to take him down, but he paused a moment to rub his face. His expression unsettled her. A hard, burning anger had burned away the lust.

She scanned the room, searching for anything to defend herself. She spotted a butcher knife near the basin but wasn't sure if she'd be fast enough. He followed the direction of her gaze and reached for his belt. No. Not the belt, but the dagger she somehow hadn't noticed.

She switched direction and ran toward the hearth, knocking over the three-legged table piled with a tall stack of books and a mug. He leaped over it without pause, but she kept moving. She reached the door, hoping to at least get the blonde woman's attention.

The door stuck, and before she could pull it free, he grabbed her arm, turned her around, and swung his fist. She half-expected it and ducked, but not fast enough. His fist clipped her jaw, and she fell backwards. He was on her before she'd reached the floor. She squirmed, but he was stronger and pinned her arms above her head before straddling one of her legs.

She waited for his next move, and he didn't disappoint. He reached for his belt again, and she knew it wasn't to grab the dagger. She took the opportunity to bring her knee up while he was off-kilter and couldn't help grinning when she connected.

His eyes went blank, and he made a funny shape with his mouth as he tipped over, holding his manhood with both hands.

Stella crawled away, using the tipped over chair to push herself up. He rolled around on the floor while she stumbled toward the kitchen for the knife. When she passed the table, another thought came to her. She grabbed the bottle of alcohol, and when he twisted away from her, she broke it over his head. He stopped moving.

She nudged him with her boot, but he remained motionless. She found one of the heavier books that had fallen on the ground and hit him over the head again. Just for good measure. She glanced around the room. For as little furniture the rundown shack had, they managed to knock most of it around. The whiskey had disappeared into the cracked floorboards, but not before leaving a splatter mark a good foot or two beyond where Jessup lay. The alcohol had splashed over her pants, raincoat, and part of her sweater. She swore under her breath. It wasn't like her clothes were going to survive this trip, but now she smelled like a distillery.

On her way back to the counter, she rubbed her jaw. She winced at the pain and pulled her hand away when she felt sticky wetness. Blood. She touched her lips. He'd split her lip. This day kept getting better.

When she reached the counter, she studied the knife. It was too big to stuff in her pockets, and it was doubtful they'd let her walk around with it. She rummaged through two cabinets and a few drawers before she found a paring knife. Not the best defense, but it was better than nothing. Next, she searched the mess from the side table that had been knocked over and grabbed a piece of paper that had fallen out of one of the books. She wrapped the knife so it wouldn't poke her and stuffed it in her pocket just as the door opened.

The blonde woman stormed in with two men behind her.

Her gaze flew to Jessup, then to Stella, and finally to the rest of the room. Stella could only imagine what she looked like with her wild, unkempt hair, her hand protecting her pounding jaw, and blood still dripping from her lip.

The woman stood over Jessup and kicked him. He didn't move. She glanced at the men behind her. "Get him out of here." She strode over to Stella, who backed up a step. The woman grabbed her chin, and Stella winced.

"I told him not to touch your face."

The remark rekindled Stella's anger that had been flowing just beneath the surface since Big and Tall had ambushed her in Baywood. "So, rape would have been okay as long as he didn't leave bruises."

The woman wouldn't hold Stella's gaze. "He was only meant to scare you enough that you wouldn't try to run."

"After everything you've heard about..." Stella stopped. She'd almost said AJ. No one talks about themselves in third person unless they were crazy. She wasn't there yet, but it was something to consider.

The blonde finished her sentence for her. "I've heard more than enough about Murphy. Which was why Jessup was only supposed to intimidate you."

Stella wasn't expecting Finn's name to crop up. AJ was proficient with daggers and a bow and could handle herself in a variety of situations. That would explain the scare tactics. Stella doubted this woman would run from a fight, but maybe she'd pegged her wrong and that was why she surrounded herself with so many men.

When one of the men returned after removing Jessup, the blonde pointed at Stella, "It's your turn to watch her. Hands off unless she tries to run." She picked up one of the books then turned back to Stella. "Clean this place up. There's a mat on the far side of the hearth. Stay there if you don't want any more trouble. We leave at dawn."

After the blonde stormed out of the cabin, the new man positioned himself in front of the door. Stella glanced around. She couldn't trust this man any more than the last, but now she had an excuse to hold a broom or some other tool in her hand. But would it be sufficient until AJ and Finn came for her?

6

———

Stella groaned when something nudged her shoulder. She pulled herself into a tighter ball, protecting what little warmth she'd conserved. The second prod was harder, and she pried open an eye to see two boot-adorned legs. One boot came forward again with a shove forceful enough to push her onto her back.

She stared up at the blonde woman.

"It's time to get up, princess. We leave in thirty minutes. If you want to eat, now would be the time. We'll be riding for several hours before another meal."

Stella considered that. She was more tired than hungry, but she'd be miserable if she didn't eat something. Correction. She was already miserable, and though she wasn't sure how, it could definitely get worse.

"Coffee?"

The woman laughed. "There might be some dregs left. Next time, be up with everyone else. I gave you a pass this morning, but that's the last one. You've been in this time period before. You know how it works."

Stella groaned again when she tried to move stiff limbs. The muscles had tightened overnight in the chill air. She'd woken several times to see the fire burn to nothing but embers, had been tempted to add wood but had been too tired to rise. Now, the fire was restored, and she forced herself into a half-crawl as she inched her way to it, closing her eyes to revel in the heat.

"Gemini, there's someone coming."

The blonde woman's head snapped up. "Gaines?"

Stella didn't glance up until she heard the blonde woman respond. So, she was Gemini. It could be a first name, she supposed—if her parents had grown up in the sixties with a commune of hippies. The thought made her giggle, and when she noticed one of the men giving her a strange look, she laughed more. Perhaps if they thought she was going loony they'd leave her alone.

Gemini had moved to the door. Two men stood beside her with muskets. She hadn't known the difference between a musket or rifle until Ethan had explained Maire's weapons; the rifle having more accuracy and longer range. AJ didn't like using firearms because she wasn't comfortable with priming flintlocks. Stella, on the other hand, was well versed with modern weapons. Her father had taught her to shoot when she was a kid, and she kept that skill honed at a local shooting range. Being a single woman in a one-person office, she knew how to protect herself. But other than clubbing someone over the head with it, she didn't have a clue how to load a firearm from this era.

Another thought occurred to her. Maybe AJ and Finn had already arrived. If it was them, she had to help. She glanced around the room, but it was as barren of weapons as it had been the previous night. She stood so she could search the counters, her muscles screeching for her to cease and desist. Bowls and mugs cluttered the space, and as she suspected, the butcher knife was no longer there. But the warmth of the fire heated her backside, her body soaking it in, and she refused to move.

While everyone waited to see who was approaching, Stella performed an internal survey. Though nothing was broken, her feet hurt, and there were definitely blisters. Her body ached all over, but she assumed that was from the tussle with Jessup. Her mental state was the most questionable. If she didn't have to play the role of AJ, she would still be rolled into a ball, not caring if they just left her in a cabin in the middle of the woods.

AJ's words from their holiday in France kept repeating in her head. "There were days that only thinking of you, what you would do in a particular situation, got me to the next day." If she had been AJ's touchstone when she traveled back in time, then AJ could be hers. No pity parties. She squared her shoulders and focused on the men standing on either side of Gemini.

Their rifles were pointed toward the floor, but one kept rolling his shoulders and the other tapped the musket against his leg. Without warning, their weapons rose.

Gemini stiffened, but then her shoulders eased. A single name rushed out with relief. "Gaines."

Stella couldn't discern if Gemini was thankful the rider was one of her own or if there was something deeper between the two.

Everyone went down to meet Big and Tall while Stella focused on her own situation. A kettle hung from a hook on the fireplace. Stepping closer, she smelled caffeine. There was either coffee inside or she was hallucinating. She tapped the handle and found it warm but not too hot to handle. There weren't any clean mugs, so she filled the basin from a nearby pail of water and washed one. The liquid in the pot was lukewarm and bitter, but it was coffee.

She placed the mug as close to the fire as possible to warm it up, then returned to the basin to wash her face. The water quickly turned the color of mud with a splash of red from the dried blood on her lips. The cut was sensitive, but most of the tenderness had been from the punch. Another lesson—duck faster.

Gemini said there was food, but the woman must have a wicked sense of humor. Stella frowned at the hard piece of bread and cheese and picked up what appeared to be jerky. Her stomach growled, and she wasn't sure if the slight nauseated feeling was from a lack of food or preemptive disgust at the meager offering. She bit off a piece of jerky and continued to chew as she retrieved the mug. The coffee wasn't hot, but it was warmer than before, and she slurped it down before shuffling back to the counter to eat the rest of the meal. She managed another half cup of the sludge while the cobwebs in her brain receded. Almost back to her old self.

Big and Tall entered the room, filling the door frame. "Let's go."

Stella stared at him as she finished the last drops from her mug, which she placed on the counter before picking up the last piece of cheese. She grabbed her raincoat and strolled out the door, hoping Big and Tall didn't see her fear.

Everyone was mounted, their horses spread haphazardly in the clearing. Gemini's mount faced the cabin next to a riderless horse.

Stella gulped. She didn't know how to ride a horse and couldn't remember being on one since her parents had taken her to a county fair with pony rides. She'd been six at the time. AJ hadn't ridden one until her first jump to the past but, if Finn could be believed, was a much better rider now.

There was no way she was going to be able to pull that off. The scuff of boots startled her out of her panic. There was only one horse without a rider. Of course, she'd be riding with Big and Tall. They wouldn't want AJ to have her own horse. It would be easier for her to escape. Little did they know she wouldn't get more than twenty yards before tumbling off.

Big and Tall stormed past, grabbing her arm and forcing her to race to keep up. At least her feet would get a reprieve and stop screaming in agony. When she reached the horse and stared up at the saddle, her misgivings returned. The horse turned to stare at her with one coal-black eye, and she took a step back.

"Nice horsey. If you even think of biting me, I'll bite back."

The horse lifted its head, snorted, then turned away.

"That's better." She grabbed the saddle, preparing to lift her leg into the stirrup, when she was suddenly in the air. Big and Tall had thrown her onto the horse. She landed on her stomach and scrambled to get a leg over the beast. Big and Tall shoved her forward so he could mount.

There were several snickers as she struggled to find a safe position. She flipped her hair back, smacking Bit and Tall in the head. The guffaws increased, and Gemini worked hard to hide her laugh.

"Sorry." She wasn't, but she hadn't meant to hit him, he'd just been in her way.

Without waiting for Gemini's command, Big and Tall kicked the horse, and they were off. Stella grabbed for the saddle while leaning forward so she wouldn't have to touch the angry man. After thirty minutes of the group riding fast down a narrow trail, she couldn't hold the uncomfortable position any longer and leaned back just as Big and Tall steered the horse into a tight turn. She wasn't sure exactly what happened, but one minute she was on the horse, and the next, the horse reared and both riders tumbled off the back.

Stella landed on Big and Tall and heard his grunt, but her focus was on the horse that appeared to be backing up instead of going forward. The only thing she cared about were where the hooves were, and she skittered away, her spiked boot hitting something too soft to be the road, forcing another grunt from the man beneath her. She ushered out another apology, but kept moving until she slammed into Gemini, who'd probably come to help.

Gemini grabbed her shoulders and shook her. "From everything I've heard, you're supposed to be a decent rider, but you act like you've never been around a horse before."

"Just goes to show you shouldn't believe everything you hear." Stella's tone was waspish, but she was still assessing her physical condition. When she glanced up to see Gemini's frown, she sighed. "Sorry. It's been a while."

Gemini gave her an assessing look that made the spot between her shoulder blades itch. Stella straightened her coat, ignoring the woman. Big and Tall had managed to get hold of his horse and limped back to the group, holding an arm across his chest. She should probably apologize again, but she didn't like him and, as a captive, didn't think it was required.

"Maybe you should have her sit behind you. That way the next time you fall, she can soften your landing."

Big and Tall swung around, scanning the men to see who'd spoken, but they were all laughing. He glared at Gemini, who'd thinned her lips and had to turn away to hide a grin.

"And maybe we should let her ride with Jessup so she can occupy her time with wandering hands." Big and Tall gave Stella a sneer.

"She rides with Gaines. But I agree, she rides behind. I doubt she'll want to fall again and will hold on tighter." Gemini mounted her horse. "We're behind schedule. There are too many hours ahead of us to deal with any more antics." Not waiting for Gaines, she turned her horse and raced off.

The rest of the men followed. Several were still laughing, and one gave Big and Tall a leering grin and wink.

Stella didn't want to get back on the horse with Gaines, but Jessup would have been worse. The excited gleam in his eye when the idea had been suggested made her sick. No doubt about it, he had revenge on his mind.

Focused on the safest path to survival, she shuffled to the horse. Big and Tall flexed his right hand with some difficulty, and guilt crept in.

"There must be an easier way for me to mount." She kept her eyes on the saddle, not daring to look at him.

"I'll mount first." His tone was even, and he was surprisingly gentle when he pushed her aside. He swung himself up then gazed down at her. His stern expression didn't ease her tension, but he held out his hand. "Put your left foot in the stirrup, grab my hand, and when I pull you up, throw your right leg over the horse."

She ran over the instructions a couple of times, visualizing the act. Of course, she'd seen it done dozens of times in Westerns. Who had she been dating that made her watch so many of them? Eric? Stuart? No, it was Matthew. That made sense. He always wore cowboy boots, which she'd assumed was just his questionable fashion sense until he'd invited her to his parents' farm. She'd been forced to end it when he started talking children and cattle.

She was still smiling at the memory when Big and Tall waved his hand at her. Not wanting to test his impatience, she managed to get her foot in the stirrup and, stuck in that position, grabbed his hand. She almost flew up, her momentum faster than she anticipated, and was almost hurled over the other side. The only thing that stopped her was grabbing Big and Tall's shirt.

Once she settled, she beamed. "Well, that wasn't so bad."

He kicked the horse, and Stella immediately grabbed a

chunk of flesh through his shirt, her nails digging in. Big and Tall howled at the unexpected grip.

"Sorry," she yelled but smiled. It seemed Gemini's plans had gone awry since dragging her into their time. She might not have weapons, but she'd been known to create chaos.

7
———

Stella slid from the horse and fell into a heap, no longer caring whether it would trample her. Eight hours in the saddle with only two short breaks along the way, and she was ready to tell them they had the wrong person. She wasn't meant for this time period. Her legs were numb, her backside ached, and her fingers were permanently frozen into tight grips where she'd held onto Big and Tall for most of the ride.

She rolled over and stared at the gray sky after the horse was led away. At least her feet didn't hurt anymore. All she required was a blanket, and they could check on her in the morning to see if she was still breathing.

"Get up. You'll have plenty of time to rest while we wait." Gemini stood over her, blocking her view of the sky.

"I don't think I can stand. Or walk. Probably can't crawl, either."

"Jessup, put her in the back room." Gemini nudged her with her boot. "You can either walk, or Jessup will carry you."

With a grunt, Stella rolled over and managed to get on her hands and knees. It took a couple of tries to get her feet under her, and she cringed at the pins-and-needles sensation running through her legs.

"What a disappointment." Gemini's muttered comment as she walked away didn't discourage Stella.

The words gave her some relief. They still believed her to be AJ and assumed they'd received false information regarding her abilities rather than considering her to be an imposter. Jessup grabbed her arm, and she braced herself to be dragged up the steps of a farm house that was, thankfully, more appealing than the rustic cabin.

She barely had time to note a hearth, a larger kitchen, and more furniture before she was led down a short hall. He opened a door and shoved her inside. She took a few steps and tripped over a rug but gripped a dresser to remain standing.

"Don't touch anything."

The door slammed, and a bolt slid into place. The only window in the room had been boarded over with multiple nails. A single bed and a second dresser were the only pieces of furniture. The rest of the space was filled with bags and trunks. It reminded her of any guest room that doubled as storage.

She ignored everything and tumbled onto the bed, falling into a long overdue sleep.

A loud knock on the door woke Stella seconds before the door burst open. She managed a croaked, "What?" Her brain was fuzzy, and her first thought was of Jessup coming in to try something, but he wouldn't have announced his entry.

Gemini, looking freshly bathed in clean pants and shirt, strolled in and dropped a tray on the dresser.

"You have thirty minutes to eat, then someone will come to take you to the privy and allow you a short walk. You'll spend the remaining time in this room where you can stay out of trouble."

"How long will that be?"

Gemini considered her, possibly weighing the pros and cons of what to divulge. It was more likely she wasn't sure when Finn might show up, considering Big and Tall had been late in delivering her from the future.

"A couple of days. You'll be on a schedule for your personal needs and some fresh air. Food will be brought to you." She slammed the door on her way out, followed by the bolt sliding home.

She collapsed back on the bed and stared at the ceiling, worried about going stir crazy. AJ and Maire's ordeal in the cells at Waverly reminded her how much worse her incarceration could be. Finn's stay as a guest of Reginald had almost killed him. She had no room to complain, not that she would stop the whining.

The aroma from the tray made her stomach grumble. She'd had little to eat since breakfast.

Before rising, she did a physical check. Her muscles were sore, she'd have bruises from her fall from the horse, and her backside ached. She'd be happy if she never saw another horse. Her legs wobbled but cooperated when she shuffled toward the dresser.

The tray held a bowl of stew, a piece of bread, a mug of ale, and a lantern. She tasted the stew, shrugged, then ate every drop, using the fresh bread to mop up the bowl. Her only complaint was the single mug of ale. She could have used two. While she waited for Jessup to retrieve her, she considered the bags and trunks filling the tiny room, but before she could give any consideration to snooping, the rattle of the bolt gave her a couple seconds to prepare for her visitor.

Jessup stood in the hall. "Let's go."

He didn't move, forcing Stella to pass within inches of him. She blasted him with a singe-worthy glare, but he held his leering smile, following one step behind her. When she reached the front door, he pushed her aside to exit first. Dusk had settled, and a handful of men roamed the yard, giving her a quick glance. There were more here than at the other cabin, and they milled about caring for the horses, building a fire in front of the farmhouse, or on guard patrol as they walked the perimeter with their weapons in plain sight.

Off to the right, barely visible in the dimming light, was an old barn with doors hanging askew and a patchwork roof that hadn't seen livestock for some time. To the left, an overgrown field lay fallow. A rusted plow could barely be seen through the tall grass. Large oak and elm trees were scattered near the house, but just beyond the fields and barn, a dense stand of trees surrounded the farm, and Stella remembered from the ride that she hadn't seen the house until they'd passed through the trees. Visitors would be seen before they made it across the field. The perfect security. It reminded her of the inn back home, and it surprised her that she'd been thinking like Ethan and Adam.

Somehow, that made her feel better, and she turned her meager pace into a steady march all the way to the outhouse then past the edge of the field until Jessup forced her back to the cabin. If she was AJ, she needed to immerse herself in the role. AJ had escaped from her captors twice, and though she'd been caught both times, it had all worked out eventually. Stella's predicament was different, but if she could get a horse... She snorted, picturing herself hanging from the saddle as the horse careened out of control down the drive. It was nothing more than fantasy, but she took pleasure in Jessup's suspicious frown.

After being led back to her cell, which she considered an apt label, she fell into her standard position and flopped on the bed to stare at the ceiling. That lasted five minutes. She sprang up and studied her surroundings.

Jessup told her not to touch anything, which was nothing more than baiting a cat with a fish. You don't lock a woman up for days in a room filled with luggage and not expect some snooping. She'd only checked two bags, which held clothing, before Gemini returned.

"I have to leave. Gaines will remain to ensure you stay out of trouble. You better hope Murphy makes the appointment on time."

Gemini left without waiting for a response, but what was there to say? Stella had the most to gain by Finn arriving quickly. After waiting fifteen minutes and no one returning, she assumed she was on her own until morning.

It wouldn't take her long to go through each of the dozen or more bags and trunks. If she gave each one a quick assessment, she could note which ones required a more thorough perusal. She began her search in the farthest corner and worked methodically. The trunks would probably hold the more valuable items, but not everything of worth came in velvet boxes.

After going through four bags of clothing, she opened a trunk filled with fine evening gowns, day dresses, and undergarments. She sighed when she closed the lid. They were probably all filled with clothes. The next trunk didn't disappoint. More dresses, but after pushing through all the silk and lace, her hand touched on something at the bottom, and it wasn't the trunk. She ran her hand around the edges of what felt like a soft covered book or ledger.

She glanced at the door. Her sense of time was better than most, and she guessed an hour had passed since Gemini had left, but who knew if Big and Tall or Jessup would check on her before morning. She could wait until after breakfast, but after her nap, she wasn't tired and decided to risk it.

She peeled the fabric away layer by layer until the journal appeared. It was tied together by a red ribbon. Her heart raced like a jackhammer as she lifted it out and laid it on her lap. It was more a folder than a journal. She untied the ribbon and sifted through the collection of pages—newspaper clippings, a will, letters that appeared to be discussions between family members, though the handwriting was difficult to read.

The last documents were contracts for the purchase of several land parcels in Lancashire. Real estate—finally, something she could understand. The older form of English and the script-style handwriting made the reading difficult, but she caught the important sections. The document was for purchase of land by a Lord Selby Prescott some forty years ago, assuming Stella was in the first decade of the nineteenth century. There was another single page dated June of 1804, requesting a change in ownership due to death of Lord Prescott. The petitioner was Penelope Prescott, and the request was denied.

What did this have to do with the stones? Prescott wasn't a name AJ or Finn ever mentioned. Was Gemini related to these Prescotts? This couldn't have anything to do with her kidnapping. This group of outlaws were too obsessed with the accuracy of incantations and the Heart Stone. Maybe it was nothing.

She stuffed the papers back where she found them, making sure they were tucked in the bottom of the trunk. After going through several more bags with various styles of men's clothing, she opened a smaller trunk filled with jewelry and silverware. Were these important to Gemini, handed down from mother to daughter, or something to trade? The jewels looked real to her, and if the silver was pure, it could be melted down.

Disgruntled, she returned to the bed having found nothing to help her current situation. Not one item connected to the stones, and of the handful of books she'd found, none were written in Celtic or any other foreign language.

She pulled off her boots. Three blisters had opened, and she had nothing to protect them. There had been more than enough thin fabric in the trunks. Perhaps she could fashion a bandage. She stood to open one of the trunks and tripped over a boot.

She bent to move her boots and noticed the edge of another trunk under the bed. Where was her head? Everyone checked under the bed. She dropped to hands and knees and tugged out a small overnight-sized trunk. Whatever was in it was heavy. A lock kept it secure.

Damn.

She had nothing to pick a lock. Concerned someone might come in while she mulled over options, she shoved the trunk under the bed then laid down. There were several items she might use at home but crossed most off her list immediately. She needed something thin yet strong enough to not snap in two.

A groan slipped out as she beat a fist against her forehead. This whole experience had played havoc with her critical thinking. She sprang off the bed, wincing as her sore muscles reacted, and put her ear to the door. The farmhouse was quiet. Time to find out what was in that trunk. She reviewed the luggage she'd scoured through earlier, recalling what each one held.

She set the lantern down and knelt in front of the second trunk, pushing the duffel off the lid. One box of hair accessories and another two with jewelry lay underneath two layers of gowns. She pulled out anything that might work—a hairpin, a broach, and a jeweled stickpin.

Her first two attempts with the lock were failures. On her third, she closed her eyes and guided the hairpin by touch alone. A few seconds grew to thirty, and she brushed her hair back, sweat dampening her forehead. A soft click made her smile, and she slipped the lock from the clasp.

When she opened the lid, she fell back, mouth opened in surprise. The chest was filled with coins—silver, copper, and gold. A pirate's treasure. She picked one up and held it under the light of the lantern, finding nothing she'd be able to decipher.

She considered her options. The money was unorganized, as

if someone opened the box just long enough to throw money in. Unless they counted it each morning, no one would notice a few missing coins. Guilt for stealing lasted until she took her next breath. She was on her own with no money, which meant if she did find a way to escape, she had no transportation or food. Money made all the difference.

She ran her fingers through the coins and pulled out several, and having no idea how the monetary system worked, made an assumption—the larger, the more valuable. But where to keep them? She couldn't just stuff them in her coat pocket.

After replacing the lock and shoving the trunk under the bed, she placed the hairpins and jewelry back in the trunk, but not before removing two handkerchiefs. She wrapped up her stolen loot and stuffed it under the lumpy bed. She was closing the lid when she noticed the tiny, beaded handbags large enough to hold her stash. She grinned. Who went on a trip without bringing back a souvenir?

8

———

Baywood, Oregon - Present Day

AJ stared out the bay window where Maire and Finn sat on the deck in deep conversation. Maire had been agitated since breakfast. She'd spent the last four days hidden away in the guest bedroom or locked in the library where she could concentrate without interruption. Ethan forced her to come out for meals, but she spoke little, ate quickly, then excused herself to go back to work.

"She feels like she's failed everyone." Ethan stepped next to AJ and handed her a mug of coffee.

"We can't expect her to decipher miracles when she has no access to the required material. And there's nothing we can say or do that will make her feel better." AJ squeezed Ethan's arm and returned to the kitchen, adding finishing touches to a large salad. She placed plastic wrap over it and shoved items aside in the fridge to make room for the large bowl.

A knock on the door was followed by, "It's just us." The

sound of her mother's voice brought some comfort to AJ's strained nerves.

Her mother rushed into the kitchen, followed by Professor Emory, Adam, and Madelyn. They all held bags brimming with heavenly aromas. She hadn't eaten well since Stella had been taken, but her stomach growled in anticipation for what was supposed to be their last meal before the jump. But Maire hadn't come up with a new incantation.

"Where are the kids?" AJ pasted on a smile and gave her mom a hug.

Madelyn pulled food containers from the bag, placing them on the counter. Emory transferred the content to dishes. "With the babysitter. Charlotte has been asking about Stella every day. We didn't think it would be good for her to be here without..." Madelyn wiped her nose. "Well, it just wouldn't be good for her."

AJ put an arm around her. A year ago, the two of them could barely stand to be in the same room together. Now, they had a closer relationship, initiated by Stella and Adam working together when AJ had disappeared the first time with Finn. Somehow, Stella had become a part of their family, especially with Charlotte, who carried a deep fascination with Stella's origami figures.

How crazy to think one ancient stone necklace had been the fulcrum in establishing such a large network of endearing friends and family, some separated by two hundred years.

"I have the paperwork if you want to get that started." Adam lifted his briefcase and pointed toward the hall. "It would be nice to have it done before dinner."

"Sure, let me get Finn. The library is yours." She turned for the deck where Finn and Maire still chatted.

An hour later, the group gathered around the dinner table. They passed bowls and plates of food around, a combination of homemade and takeout. The conversation wasn't stilted, but it was quieter than normal. Stella was good at keeping the conversation going, and AJ sensed her absence weighed on everyone.

She frowned as she placed two barbecue ribs on her plate. It wasn't just her missing friend. Maire's defeatist mood sucked all the optimism out of the room like a Dementor extracting all the happiness out of a person.

After dinner, Finn brought out the Jameson and wine while Adam made coffee. Once glasses were filled, he sat and stared out to sea, his hand reaching for AJ's. "We all agreed it wouldn't be wise to use the incantation the kidnapper left us. Though it's meant to bring us to the right time and place, it will also be a trap. They would expect me to use the Heart Stone, and while we were disoriented from the jump, they could easily grab it and that would be that."

"But they wouldn't know you wouldn't come alone." Ethan spoke to the group, but he watched Maire, who also appeared transfixed by the ocean.

"Aye, but how many will be waiting for us?" Finn turned to Maire, his expression soft and without disappointment. "Maire has worked diligently to find another solution, but we need alternatives."

AJ tapped her fingers on the edge of her wineglass, staring into the dark, red liquid. "We could use Heart Stone and the original incantation, which would take us to the monastery."

"Or you could use the updated incantation with Ethan's stone." Adam leaned over his pad of paper, different colored pens within reach. He'd taken the role as planner and had already sketched out three columns, filling in the heading of the last column as he spoke. "We believe," he paused to glance at Maire, who hadn't moved, "you should land at Ethan's last point of origin, which would be the woods at Waverly when you traveled back for Finn."

"But neither incantation will land us at the correct time." Ethan kept his gaze on Maire, but if she noticed it didn't show.

"I know I'm new to these planning sessions." Madelyn scooted closer to the table. The fact she was here and not at home with the kids spoke volumes about her commitment to Stella. And while AJ had only recently gotten to know her better, the one thing that was never in question was the woman's tenacity. She'd proven it when Charlotte had gotten sick, and again by the way she'd dealt with Adam when he'd hidden his gambling debt from her. "The letter implies this new incantation will take you to a specific place, on the right day, at an exact time. I thought the ability to manipulate time specifically required the torc."

"A torc?" Helen asked.

"It was a neck adornment worn primarily by Celtic nobility and warriors." Emory answered from the kitchen where he was doing the dishes. He wiped his hands and turned toward the table. "In this instance, the silver torc had been created by the druids to hold the Heart Stone and the five smaller stones. It was believed that together, the stones would provide the power along with the correct incantation to take the wearer to a specific place and time."

AJ glanced at Maire to see if the discussion would get a rise out of her, but she continued her vigil like a person in a trance. The revelation of this new incantation had rocked the group when they'd first discussed Stella's kidnapping, which was bad enough and had everyone on edge. But Maire had been affected the most, and while AJ couldn't be positive, she expected most of Maire's time locked away had been in the same posture—staring into nothingness, wondering what she'd missed. Maire and Sebastian had been through the druid's book, also known as the *Mórdha Stone Grimoire*, and a good portion of *The Book of Stones* several times, and there was no evidence a single stone could do what the kidnapper suggested.

When they'd first gone over the druid's book, Maire thought there was a missing piece the druid had deliberately left out. Sebastian had disagreed and considered the druid's incantation faulty. But they'd only had two days to review the book before Maire had been forced to jump to the present with AJ and Finn to protect her from being kidnapped for a third time.

"I wonder if the druid's book would have helped." AJ snorted at her own statement. The druid's book was in the past, and no one had found it at the monastery when they'd been there for Christmas. From what Maire had shared, Sebastian had provided a location for it, but his journal was in code, and Maire hadn't translated that section yet.

Without warning, Maire jumped up, knocking her chair over, and ran from the room like she'd been prodded by an electric charge. Her feet pounded up the stairs as everyone turned to Ethan.

He shrugged and picked up her chair, looking as perplexed as the others. "She hasn't said much of anything all day."

Several minutes later, feet tromped down the stairs, but as Maire entered the kitchen, her pace slowed, faltering a step before lifting her head to finish her march to the table. She dropped a six-inch-thick folder on the table and cleared her throat.

"I know you're going to be mad, and if you want to yell at me, you can do it after we've saved Stella." Her glare traveled over the group, but everyone still appeared stunned from her earlier, swift departure to interrupt her flow. Satisfied, she opened the folder and dragged out a variety of pages—old parchment paper with words written by quill, modern-day paper, colored stationary from both time periods, and pink and yellow sticky-notes.

AJ stared at her. "Is that the druid's book?"

Maire glanced at Ethan first then returned AJ's gaze. "No." She took a deep breath. "It's a copy of it."

Ethan choked on the whiskey he'd been sipping. Adam reached out as if wanting to pull it over to read.

Finn groaned a disappointed sigh, "Maire, didn't we tell you not to bring any of that with you."

Maire squared her shoulders and gave him what AJ imagined was their mother's disapproving stare. "Well, it appears, dear brother, that it's a good thing that I did. This—" she jabbed at the stack of pages, "—will be our advantage.

"Part of this was my own fault. I was stubborn, not believing someone could come up with a more precise incantation. And quite simply, I wasn't able to see the wood for the trees. My focus had been on using Ethan's stone for our jump. The kidnapper would have had a similar stone to get here and back. So, I assumed the kidnapper must have found one of the sections of *The Book of Stone* and the incantation was meant for a smaller stone. I'd like to know who they found to translate the Book. I can't believe Sebastian would have assisted them."

"And that's something we'll ask when we meet them." Finn watched Adam as he wrote bullet points in his pro and con columns.

"Right. Sorry. I've spent the last four days focusing on the information from *The Book of Stones* and Sebastian's journals. Sebastian had suggested a couple of new translations that were supposed to provide more accurate timing, but we also need the correct location. I considered the Heart Stone might be a better option for using the incantation, but I needed to understand how the incantation differed from the others we have. All the while—" she poked at the pages from the druid's book again, "—this was sitting not ten feet from me most days." She shook her head with a curled lip. "I don't know where my head was at."

AJ squeezed her hand. "Maybe you were worried about your friend."

Maire laughed. "It's always the rest of you coming to my aid. All I had to do was sit and wait. I didn't have to worry what might be happening to you. At least not like this." Her smile faded. "So, while you were talking about what dismal options we were left with, and AJ mentioned the druid's book, I was almost too embarrassed to tell you anything."

Ethan's low grumble made Maire smile, and she laid a hand on his shoulder. "I never translated the entire book, nor was I able to copy all of my translations, especially when Reginald returned earlier than usual. But I think the most important pages are here.

"The druid's original time tests were with the Heart Stone, trying to determine how much it could do on its own. He had a few successes but wanted to run the same trials on the smaller stones. I need to take his earlier incantation work and compare it to the one the kidnapper left and the two Sebastian developed. Hopefully, I can determine a key that can be used to manipulate one of the incantations. Maybe one or two more should we not end up where we want the first time." She glanced down and ran a loving hand over the parchment. "I'm going to need some time."

Ethan rubbed her back. "All the time you need."

Finn nodded. "Aye. This is the closest we've been to a successful option." He tapped Adam's notepad. "Let's plan from the assumption Maire will be successful. We'll need to provide the place, date, and time. Let's work through our options."

Two days later, AJ reached for the mailbox, her body slumping over it as her breath heaved. Sweat dripped from her brow, plopping into a puddle from the overnight rain. When her breathing evened out, she lifted her head to find Finn and Ethan, hands on hips, waiting for her twenty feet away. She hadn't even noticed them.

She waved at them. "Go on without me." She paused for her lungs to refill. "I'm just appreciating the beauty of the morning." Neither of them held back their grins, and she couldn't stop thinking evil thoughts. She spent her training days climbing, honing her dagger and bow skills, and running three miles every other day. When what she thought was a five-mile run turned into ten, she knew she was in trouble. It was by sheer will she was even standing.

The men waved in response and continued their run down the driveway to the inn. The minute they were out of sight, she rubbed her side where a cramp brought tears to her eyes. She focused on long, slow breaths and took a few steps, thankful her shaky legs kept her upright. Before she turned down the driveway, a familiar sedan rolled down the street, and she thanked the heavens as she waited.

The car pulled into the driveway, and Adam rolled down his window, already chuckling. "Finn made you run."

"Ten miles."

Her brother was a runner, but she didn't think he stuck to a routine. He cringed. "I thought you were doing five."

"So did I. Mind if I ride with you?"

"Get in."

When AJ fell into the soft leather seats, she moaned with relief. "You have to promise you made me get in."

Adam laughed as he drove to the inn. "Mom's been cooking all morning. I think she has a feast prepared."

This time she moaned with annoyance. "Promise to help keep the afternoon lighthearted."

"That's two promises in less than two minutes. I'll have to charge you extra."

"I don't think I've ever thanked you properly for all the help you've given us. Me."

"You're not going to get all touchy-feely, are you? I have a reputation as a partner in a law firm to uphold."

"Your reputation is safe." She glanced out the window. This was harder than she expected. "We don't know what's waiting for us."

"You never do."

"I just wanted to make sure everything is right between us."

"This isn't one of those 'you don't think you'll be coming back' talks, is it?"

AJ didn't respond. Everyone was coming for lunch—Mom, Emory, Jackson, and Isaiah. Maire had found the key to the incantation, and rather than wait until morning, they would have a late lunch and then leave. It was impossible to not think of it as a possible farewell. She rubbed her face, pushing the dark thoughts away.

Once Adam turned off the car, he turned toward her. "Based on your interpretation of events, I'll have to disagree and declare that everything isn't settled between us. If memory serves, you were supposed to find a particular broach for me."

AJ slapped her forehead. "I forgot." She had made a couple of calls to antique stores specializing in roaring twenties jewelry, a passion of Madelyn's, then forgot everything when Stella was taken.

Adam grabbed her hand and squeezed it. "Then it looks like you'll have to come back and complete your promise to me. You still owe me."

She gave him her best smile, but deep down, she wasn't sure

their luck would hold for another trip back in time. "You'll keep Mom busy while we're gone?"

"Madelyn has the next two weeks planned. Mom won't have a moment alone."

"Thank you."

"Just don't make me have to come get you."

<hr>

"Another perfect meal." Emory kissed Helen on her cheek as he passed by with a stack of dishes in his hands.

Helen glanced at Adam then AJ before she blushed and waved a hand as if dismissing him before setting a coffee pot on a trivet. "I'll leave this here and get the cream and sugar."

Adam winked at AJ, who turned in time to see her mother nudge Emory with her hip. The two had gotten closer after the trip to France, and though she'd been concerned about the two-hour commute that separated them, she decided fate would find a way. It had worked for her and Finn, and they'd overcome a two-hundred-year gap.

When she returned her focus to the table, she noticed Finn's heated gaze on her. Her cheeks warmed. Damn, but he could still make her blush, and she gave a quick glance to her mother, who was on her way back with the cream and sugar. Her mother pretended not to notice, but her lips twitched.

"Have you made a decision on where you want to go?" Adam poured coffee in the waiting mugs.

"We'll try for Hereford one week before our scheduled meeting." Finn spread a map on the table. "This was the simplest map of England I could find." Four locations, spread across the southwestern part of the country, had been circled in different colors.

Ethan pointed to the northern most circle. "Our first stop is Hereford. We don't know exactly where we'll end up, but most likely close to the village. That was one reason we chose to go at night. Less chance of being seen. We have gold and silver with us, so we can buy horses if needed.

"Why Hereford? Isn't the meeting spot down by that red circle?" Madelyn leaned over the table and ran her hands along the lines connecting the dots.

"We'll need men, and the earl is in a position to provide them. Thomas, his Sergeant of Arms, has been with us almost from the start. He'll want to be involved." Ethan sipped his coffee. He'd been drinking the brew all day and should have been bouncing off the walls. AJ couldn't blame him. She'd drank more than her fair share. They wouldn't see another decent cup until they returned.

"From there," Finn directed Madelyn to the farthest west circle. "Hensley's estate. He needs to be made aware of the situation. And with any luck, he'll know where Jamie and the *Daphne Marie* are."

"Will you need a ship?" Adam took the plate of apple pie his mother handed him. He pushed the ice cream on top of the pie, took a large bite, and closed his eyes in blissful appreciation.

"We need to be ready for anything." AJ's plate barely landed in front of her before her fork was digging into the flaky crust minus the ala mode. "The monastery is the center of everything that happens with the stones and books. And, as Finn and Ethan reminded me several times today, we always seem to end up there."

"The yellow circle is Waverly?" Madelyn asked. This was the first time she'd been included in a strategy session. AJ couldn't remember a time she'd seen Madelyn without makeup, except for when Charlotte had been hospitalized several years ago.

There were dark shadows under her eyes, and Adam didn't look much better.

The truth was, they were all in bad shape. Finn and she might be getting sleep, but it was from sheer exhaustion. Between training, strategy sessions, and preparations for closing two houses, they fell into bed like zombies each evening. The worst part was their worry over who'd taken Stella. What conditions was she being kept in? She would know they'd come for her, but time ticked away waiting for Maire to work magic. AJ's only consolation was them arriving in England before Stella was brought back. And how weird was that?

"Shouldn't you have this Thomas guy stop at Waverly?" Madelyn's question shook AJ out of her woolgathering.

Finn tapped the map, probably remembering their heated discussion on the topic. "AJ wanted to stop there after Hereford, but Beckworth won't have any men to organize for the cause. However, we could still use him, which is why we'll stop there on our way to the meeting in Basingstoke."

"If we get the earl's blessing, we'll have Thomas head for the meeting spot straightaway." Ethan pointed to a spot neighboring their destination. "They'll stay in a neighboring village while they survey the area. They'll be discreet, but we have to know what we're walking into."

"Wasn't it the earl's men who were with Maire when she was kidnapped the last time?" Adam wiped ice cream from his chin as he pushed his spotless plate aside.

"That wasn't their fault." Maire responded before Ethan could. "It appears you weren't told the entire story. I slipped away without the guards knowing and went to Peterstow. There was a young woman that worked at the apothecary who was rumored to know something of the druid's book. I was taken on my way back."

"Yes. I missed that piece." Adam pulled the map closer and

traced his finger over each circle and their connecting lines as Madelyn had. "The plan is sound, but is a week enough time? Everything seems rather spread out."

"We can't be sure we'll have a week." Maire placed a sheet of paper on the table. "I've created three incantations. All three will work but with different possible outcomes. The more I've reviewed the current incantations we have available, I'm not sure the one we've been given will be as accurate as they expect. One would think they'd tested it, but perhaps not."

"So, we need to be ready for any possibility." Finn was thoughtful rather than dismayed. AJ supposed that should make her feel better.

"What I have determined," Maire continued, "is the reason the kidnappers want the Heart Stone. It's what we've always known. The only way to truly predict where and to what time you might travel is either with the torc or the Heart Stone itself. The smaller stones just don't have enough..." she seemed to search for the right word, "juice I think you would say. Not enough power to provide dependable accuracy."

"But how else would they have gotten here?" Madelyn's perplexity was understandable depending on how much Adam had shared about the stones.

Maire nodded. "Remember, the small stones seek the Heart Stone. The kidnapper would use that incantation because he wouldn't know what date or location to jump to. One thing I've never determined is why the smaller stone doesn't connect to the Heart Stone in its own time period. Maybe it's a flaw in the incantation, or maybe it ignores the Heart Stone in its own time, or a dozen other possibilities. It's all quite frustrating. But I've strayed from our current concern. They would have had to use a similar incantation to the one they gave us in order to return from where they left since they didn't retrieve the Heart Stone."

"So which of the three incantations will you use?" Adam asked.

When no one answered, Finn gave Maire his signature grin. "Dealer's choice. Maire will make the final decision once we're on the dock. Though I think she already has one in mind."

Maire lifted her shoulder in a half-shrug, which appeared to signal the conversation was over.

Several minutes ticked by before Helen stood. "Let's clean up while our travelers prepare."

Two hours later, after hugs and promises were given, AJ followed Finn, Ethan, and Maire, each with their own stuffed backpacks and duffels, to the end of dock. Those remaining behind stopped halfway down the path.

The travelers had changed into time-period clothing and all except Maire carried a pistol, sword, or dagger on their person. Finn ran through a final checklist while the others checked their packs and duffels to confirm each item he rambled off. He finished with the last items that only AJ and Ethan carried.

"Medical kits."

AJ nodded. "Both kits have bandages, antiseptic, tweezers, scissors, antibiotics, and healing salve. Maire added herbs to each of the kits, but they should be last resort if we don't find something fresher wherever we'll be."

Finn nodded. "The stones?"

"I have mine sewn into a pocket." Ethan patted a pocket of his pants.

AJ lifted hers from around her neck and drew it over her head. She handed it to Maire, who would be reading the incantation.

"That's it then." Finn stepped close, and the rest followed.

They all waved to those on the path before linking their arms together, their duffels making the position awkward. Maire glanced at the sheet of paper she gripped in both hands.

This was the moment.

AJ wasn't sure where or when they would show up, but she trusted Maire, who'd gotten them this far. She had positioned herself so she could see her mother and Adam. Emory, Madelyn, Jackson, and Isaiah circled around the two like sentinels. She stood straighter, wanting them to see her confidence that they would return, and Stella would be with them.

Maire's lips moved, the words buffeted away by the soft coastal breeze. Her voice must have been loud enough because she heard Madelyn's cry of surprise. AJ didn't have to turn around to know the fog was coming.

The four inched closer, their grips tightening. The world went quiet, and she closed her eyes as the fog enveloped them.

9

England – 1805

The next afternoon, Gemini and five of her men returned while Stella was out on her after-lunch stroll. The woman grinned like she'd won the lotto and ran to Gaines. For a hot second, Stella thought she'd throw herself into his arms.

"He's on his way and should arrive by tomorrow evening I would think."

"How do you know?" A short, bearded man with a scar on his left cheek and a red scarf tied low around his neck growled out the question.

"Because…" Gemini's tone took on an air of trying to explain why the sky was blue to a child, "Roberts followed him when he arrived at the gentlemen's club. He was given the note, which he immediately read, then stayed at the bar for another hour. Three whiskeys later, he burned the letter in an alley, got on his horse, and headed west out of town. Exactly as we asked."

Red Scarf, Stella's name for the scowl-faced man, didn't

appear appeased. What guest could Gemini be talking about? She hadn't been expecting Finn for another day or so. Maybe something changed. Even so, the mention of a gentlemen's club was odd.

"Miss Moore!"

Stella turned, half-expecting to see AJ, but found Gemini staring at her.

"Are you with us, Miss Moore? Or do continuous time jumps leave one addled?"

Oh, yeah. She was Miss Moore. Two days in, and she still couldn't remember her role. It must be the lack of caffeine. The smell of coffee wafted into her room every morning and evening, but all they gave her was a tin of water. The abrupt withdrawal would explain the drumming headache.

She brushed off her pants and gave Gemini a shrug. "Sorry, I wasn't paying attention. Did you ask a question?"

Gemini held a riding whip that she tapped against her thigh. "You'll need to be more presentable for our guest. Jessup will bring hot water and soap to wipe the grime off you. And try to do something with that hair."

Beckworth ducked into a nearby alley, stopping to wait for his shadow. The man had followed him, rather poorly, all afternoon. It was a wonder Gemini hadn't been discovered before now with the group of bumbling fools working for him. He pulled out the message he'd been given while sipping whiskey at the gentlemen's club, wondering what game Gemini was up to. The directions seemed simple enough.

The package has arrived. We require your answer. Meet us at the old Stratmore farmhouse four miles southwest of Basingstoke by six tomorrow evening. The man that runs the pub can give you directions. Destroy this letter after you've read it.

What was this package? If it had involved the duke, then it had to be related to the stones. Did they uncover the stones or one of the books? And if they did, had something happened to Sebastian?

The old monk had irritated Beckworth the first time he'd visited the monastery in northern France. He was always sneaking around, disappearing and reappearing out of nowhere. That was before Beckworth learned of the secret tunnels under the monastery. The monk proved quite resourceful in helping to rout Reginald and Dugan. He would hate to see anything bad come to the man.

He pulled out his silver pocket watch and rubbed the surface before opening it—almost four o'clock. If he started now and found an inn on the way, it would still take him most of tomorrow to reach Basingstoke, assuming he didn't want his shadow to lose him. He'd prefer to be alone to investigate the area first, but Gemini hadn't given him enough time.

Beckworth shook his head at the shuffle of boots entering the alley. He bent over as if to pick something up and noted someone ducking behind a stack of crates. He'd have a good laugh with his old gang over this shoddy tail, assuming he lived through the evening.

He made a demonstrative show of using his flint and steel to burn the letter. The paper turned brown, then black, as it curled in on itself. He kept hold of it until ashes fell and nothing but a corner remained. Certain Gemini's man had seen him perform the requested task, Beckworth returned to the club to have the footman bring his horse.

When he was on the road heading west out of London, he stopped under a tree to check his weapons. His sword hung from his saddle, his Queen Ann blunderbuss pistol rested in his belt holster, and a dagger was hidden in his boot. If Gemini had wanted him dead, he'd had plenty of opportunity, but going in unarmed would be one of the more foolish things he'd done. If they want to take the weapons, so be it. He should have listened to Hensley and stayed clear of Gemini, but somehow, he would have been dragged into this business with the stones one way or another.

———

Beckworth stopped his horse just shy of the trio of men waiting next to a campfire, an empty spit visible in the dancing flames. A couple of tin cups sat on a nearby rock.

"It's about time." A grizzly old man, short and stocky, spit at the ground, then wiped his chin with the back of his hand. He glanced at his companion. "Get Gemini."

Finally, the day of reckoning. Would he meet the real Gemini or another imposter?

Beckworth leaned an arm against the saddle and studied the bushes and trees that skirted the clearing in front of the farmhouse. He counted five other men in the nearby trees, but there would be others staying out of sight.

"You need to hand Randall the reins." The man gestured with his chin to a man who walked out of another stand of trees opposite the farmhouse where several horses had been tied. "He'll take good care of your mount."

Beckworth gave the clearing another scan before obeying the request, handing the horse off to the man with a weather-beaten face, a hand with two missing fingers, and a slow smile. Randall laid a gentle hand on the horse's neck and patted it several times before leading it away toward the other horses. At least his horse would be treated well.

He turned back to the trio who'd first greeted him then squinted toward the farmhouse. The twilight hour cast the porch in darkness, and the light from the farmhouse obscured the shadowed figure standing in the doorway. This wasn't the large man he'd met in London. The person was slight of build and, while he couldn't make out the face, the curve of hips was unmistakable. A woman.

She strolled down the steps and across the small clearing with purposeful strides. When she drew closer, he sucked in his breath. It couldn't be. But then it all made sense. She was dressed in pants and shirt that fit her shapely form as if tailor-made, and her blonde hair, tied back in a long braid, swung gently behind her as she strode toward him. Her eyes glittered with satisfaction. "Viscount. How nice of you to join us. You're late." Her pleasant tone turned stern on the last sentence.

"Gemini, I presume." Beckworth fought back the rising bile as he considered their previous conversations. Nothing, other than her odd mannerisms and rakish behavior, had given him any clue that she could be Gemini. He grimaced at the jokes Jamie and Fitz had made that Gemini could be a woman. Her desire to get close to him made sense now. "Does Lady Prescott actually exist, or did you make her up?"

She stopped a foot away from him and batted her eyes as she gazed up at him, a smile on her sensuous lips. "Oh, she does, but she's quite young and rather clueless. She's been a recluse since her elderly husband had a torrid and quite public affair before he dropped dead one day." She held up her hands, and her smile widened. "I didn't have anything to do with it, I assure you."

"And the real Lady Prescott?"

"Tucked away in a quiet seaside port."

He shook his head. "And she's your backing?"

"She's quite naïve, and her estate manager a gullible man, but both very trusting in their charity to support the war effort."

"She keeps you well supplied in men and arms."

Gemini shrugged. "She's not the only one." She turned and snapped a finger. Two wooden chairs were rushed over and placed near the fire. "We'll need some refreshment as well."

"And who was the masked man in London?"

She laughed. "I do love a good game. Gaines does personal meetings for me. He doesn't always impersonate Gemini, but since you'd seen him at your holiday hunting party, it was our best option."

"And your recent visit to Waverly was to gauge my plans."

"You think I'm an enigma, but you're a puzzle I'm still working out."

Beckworth watched two men race to do her bidding, carrying over a short table, a bottle of whiskey, and two tins. One of the men poured the alcohol before backing away.

Gemini sat and picked up a cup, swirling it around before upending it. She grimaced as the alcohol went down then poured herself another one. "Sit. We have much to discuss."

Beckworth followed her moves, swallowing the drink as soon as he sat, but when she offered him more of the swill, he shook his head. "Let's get to it."

She smiled at him. "If you're here, I assume you wish to join us?"

"I have to admit, I don't know why you're interested in me."

"That's simple." Her tone turned teasing. "Because you have a stone and know how they work."

He wasn't expecting her response and found it difficult to hold his blank expression. "And what stone might that be?"

She tittered. "We really don't have time to play games, Beckworth." Her face softened. "I wish you'd let me call you Teddy."

He couldn't help but sneer at her tinkling laugh, which at

one time had made his cock stir. Now, he couldn't imagine a more detestable sound.

She waved her hand and laughed more. "You'll come around once you know our entire plan." She leaned forward, her big blues lit with excitement. Was there a bit of madness behind them as well? "I know you worked for the duke. And I know he had the torc, stones, and a section of *The Book of Stones* in his hands before he was killed."

His mind raced, but try as he might, he couldn't remember anyone knowing about those items except the duke, Dugan, and Reginald. Perhaps a servant or two, but Dugan wasn't the sort to leave witnesses.

"Fascinating." When Beckworth gave her a startled glance, she took a long sip of whiskey before returning his stare. "It's not often you show your hand, but I see the wheels turning as you wonder how I would know such things." Her smile disappeared and a more feral expression replaced it. "You were there. At the monastery. Tell me it wasn't you that killed Dugan."

"Dugan?"

"He wasn't one to show his feelings, but he kept a very warm bed."

The thought that he had seriously considered bedding her himself made his gut wrench. "If you mean to take up where the duke and Reginald failed, you're going to get us all killed."

She finished her drink and gently placed the cup on the table. "Maybe. But think of the reward." Her gaze turned to the men around the camp and her voice lowered, her eyes still bright with passion—or mania. "Can you imagine? Traveling to the future. Gathering information to sell to the highest bidder. I am, after all, a purveyor of information. And while that mad king and fool Napoleon rage war, I'll have time to auction off the keys to the kingdom. Can you imagine the fruits waiting for the eager explorer daring enough to wear the Torc of Stone?"

"It's not as pleasant as you'd think," he muttered under his breath. He poured a second glass, draining it in a single swallow, needing the heat to burn away the growing numbness. "What do you know of *The Book of Stones*?"

"More than you, I imagine, and not nearly enough." She sat back. "I know there are missing pieces of the Book, and I have some ideas where they might be. But I can't do anything without the Heart Stone. And I mean to get it by any means necessary."

Now, Beckworth laughed. "I think you'll find that impossible to do."

She winked. "I would have to disagree. Within a day or two, I'll know exactly where the Heart Stone will be."

A troubling awareness squeezed his chest. She knew something he didn't. And while everything she'd shared was dangerous enough, something told him he was going to have his world, and his loyalties, tested. She nodded to one of her men, and he turned toward the farmhouse and whistled.

Time stopped as Beckworth waited for whatever surprise she had in store. He glanced behind him and noted the three men standing between him and his horse. They had all moved in from the trees as if mesmerized by what would happen next. He returned his gaze to the farmhouse, where a man appeared to be dragging someone behind him.

His heart raced. This century's Heart Stone was safely buried within Buckingham Palace under the watchful eye of Lord Langdon. The other one was with AJ and Murphy two hundred years in the future. He squinted as the two drew near the door, the shorter one fighting every step. The taller one had the advantage, and when he finally made it through the door, he pushed his captive in front of him.

Beckworth blinked. It couldn't be. He whipped his disbelieving gaze to Gemini. "What is this?"

She downed another shot then stood as she laughed. "I tried

to get the Heart Stone, but Miss Moore was rather stubborn, so I had to move to my next plan. In a matter of days, Murphy will bring me the Heart Stone in exchange for his wife, and hopefully lure his sister out of hiding."

He could only stare, his mind racing, unable to keep up. How had Gemini accomplished this? Then her words cut through his confusion, and he took a closer look at the bedraggled woman standing with her head held high, fury raging in her gaze. Her frosty posture contradicted, or perhaps emphasized, her physical appearance. Her clothes were stained with filth and what might be dried blood. Her mud-caked boots, based on his short time in her era, were probably expensive, though it appeared the heels had been broken off. Her auburn hair, wild and untamed, framed a surprisingly clean face. A burning anger was clear and present in her stony gaze.

Gemini thought this woman was AJ? How the devil did that come about? But Gemini said it herself. If she'd been close to Dugan, it made sense she would have access to one of the smaller stones and incantation. Yet, everything she'd told him so far made it sound as if she'd never traveled. Which means someone else went to the future. The only remaining question was how they mistook this woman for AJ.

"I want no part in this." Beckworth backed up a step. He hadn't signed up for this. When AJ and Murphy arrived, and they most assuredly would, he'd be right in the middle of it all.

"We made a deal."

"You didn't give me much of a choice. Beyond that, I didn't think there would be any harm in divulging what little I know."

"Then what's the problem?"

"You didn't say anything about kidnapping anyone." He glanced at Stella. He'd seen her with AJ a couple of times while he'd been in Baywood, but one moment stood out from the rest. She'd been on the street looking through a store window and had taken his breath away. He remembered how she'd backed up and managed to step on two men's feet. They'd been so quick to apologize.

When she stared at him now, there were only two emotions reflected on her thinned lips and narrowed gaze—fear and resolve. That could be a very dangerous combination. If she pushed the wrong buttons and something happened to her, there would be no measure to AJ's rage—or vengeance.

His hands closed into fists as he controlled his breathing. It was all he could do to hold in his own furor. He turned on Gemini, ignoring her coquettish smile.

"I think it bears repeating. You're going to get us all killed."

Ten minutes earlier, banging on the door had woken Stella, and she required a moment to remember where she was. Dread filled her when the door flew open and Jessup hovered there. Resignation forced an audible sigh when she noted his evil grin. Hadn't he learned anything the last time he tried something?

She jumped up, wincing at her continued aches. He didn't need to get any ideas with her sprawled on the bed. "I thought I got food first, then a walk." She straightened her shoulders and pushed her hair back.

He gave her a suggestive perusal, his gaze firmly on her breasts. "This isn't a walk. Just a showing."

Did that mean Finn was here, and this was some form of proof of life? No. Her brain, still foggy from being roused from the first good sleep since arriving in this time period, finally caught up. They had been waiting for someone to arrive before Finn. Someone they had followed to ensure they were on their way, which made it sound like they didn't trust this person.

She turned her back on Jessup to put on her boots, disgusted when she noted the heels were coming off. Two quick tugs tore them the rest of the way off, new irritation flaring at the waste of exquisite boots. She stood and tested them with a few steps. It was a strange feeling, but walking would be easier.

"We don't have all day."

Stella straightened her sweater and brushed at her pants for no reason other than to settle her nerves before marching to the door, bracing for any sudden moves on his part. He allowed her to pass but refused to give her an inch, forcing her to brush against him as she passed. She only managed three steps before he grabbed her arm.

Tired of being dragged around, her instincts kicked in, and she pulled away, bringing her other arm up to slap him, but he blocked her with a forearm. She tried a kick, which connected but probably hurt her as much as it did him. He didn't let go but backed far enough away to stay out of her reach.

"Settle down. I don't care if the boss won't like it, I'll teach you a thing or two." His menacing leer added depth to his threat.

She was past caring and was planning her next attack when Red Scarf poked his head in the door.

"Stop messing around and get her out here. You know what happens when the boss has to ask twice."

Jessup sobered, suddenly taking his job more seriously as he strode to the door, uncaring of Stella's attempts to break free. When they reached the doorway, he pushed her out, and she almost tripped but somehow kept her feet under her.

She couldn't have slept long. Twilight provided enough light to see the men at the edges of the clearing and a table near the fire where a man and woman stood. Gemini grinned like the proverbial cat that swallowed a tasty meal. Then Stella focused on the man. A cold shiver ran through her, and her mouth turned as dry as the Oregon sand dunes.

Beckworth.

She rubbed her head, remembering the last time she'd seen him. He'd slammed her into the kitchen cabinets at the inn before grabbing AJ and jumping into the past with her. If Gemini was after the Heart Stone, Stella should have anticipated this man showing up. After all he'd done, AJ trusted him. And now, here he was conspiring against her, putting them all in harm's way.

She glowered at him and noted the recognition in his gaze. The charade would be over as soon as he told Gemini she had the wrong woman. That she wasn't AJ. Then their ongoing conversation registered, and her confusion grew.

The two of them had some type of deal, yet he'd been surprised by Gemini's bold kidnapping. Now, he wanted nothing to do with it. He must know he was a dead man once Finn arrived. Yet, he still didn't reveal her true identity. Why not?

Beckworth had backed away and seemed genuinely upset, but Finn had called him a manipulator. She racked her brain for what else she knew of him. A London street kid, a henchman for the duke, but then appeared to switch sides.

Each time he glanced at her, she couldn't tell if he was confused or irritated. By the fists he held clenched at his sides, there was definitely anger boiling underneath his thinly held control. Before Jessup dragged her back through the door, two men made a grab for Beckworth as he advanced on Gemini, who couldn't stop her uncontrollable laughter.

She stumbled into the farmhouse with Beckworth's crazed screams following her.

"You're going to get us all killed."

10

———————

AJ landed hard, as if someone had tossed her out a second-story window. Her duffel slammed into her head, and she cried out when a body landed on top of her before rolling away. She crawled a few feet, her brain still adjusting to the jump. At least the bright light and horrible stomach cramps were gone. Then she vomited.

Note to self, next time crackers and ginger soda before a jump.

She rolled over and stared at a sky filled with stars and a crescent-shaped moon. Wherever she was, it was better than landing in a rainstorm like she had when she'd jumped with Beckworth. She turned her head and breathed a sigh of relief when she found Finn attempting to stand. Off to the side, Ethan crawled toward Maire, who was doubled over with her own stomach ailments.

They'd landed together and it was night. Now, they just had to confirm the last two pieces—location and date.

She considered the environment around her. The stars were bright, the air carried the bite of an early spring, but it was the smells that told her they weren't in their time anymore. Sweet and pure with the scent of wet grass and wildflowers. The ground beneath her was damp from either an overnight fog or a recent rain. With a sigh, she rolled over and got to her feet.

By the time Finn joined her and dropped his duffel next to hers, Ethan and Maire were making their way over.

"Does the landing get harder each time, or am I just getting old," Ethan grumbled as he dropped two duffels with the others.

"You are getting old, but aye, this one seems the hardest." Finn scanned the landscape.

AJ followed his gaze. Nothing but trees and darkness. The moon was stingy with its light. "It doesn't look like we landed in Hereford."

"Unless we landed before the town existed." Ethan's comment gave AJ chills. She couldn't even imagine how long ago that would have been.

"The location wasn't meant to be exact, just within the vicinity." Maire held her stomach, and even in the scarce light, she looked paler than usual.

"Are you all right?" AJ's queasiness hadn't settled yet. "I brought something for digestion."

"You did?"

She shrugged. "I was thinking of Stella."

Maire laughed. "I have no doubt the food won't be to her liking."

AJ grinned in return. It didn't make much sense, but being in the same time period made Stella seem within arm's reach.

"It won't only be the food that won't agree with her. The coffee won't be up to her standards." Finn had a point, and they all quieted. Stella wasn't the only one in the group who would miss espresso. "Do you know where we are?"

Ethan scanned the area then looked up to the sky. "I can't give you a location, but it should be late winter or early spring based on the constellations."

"Agreed." Finn picked up his duffel. "If we're anywhere near

Hereford or the earl's estate, you'll be the best one to select a direction."

"Let's find a road." He pointed to his left. "I thought I saw a glimmer of light that way."

They grabbed their bags and followed him through the ankle-high grass. Fifteen minutes passed before they stumbled upon a wide and well-traveled road. By then, the trees had cleared, and Ethan guided them to a high point on the road. A valley lay in darkness dotted with an occasional small glow. To the right, the glow intensified to form a deeper concentration of lights coming from homes.

"That should be Hereford." Ethan grinned. "I know where we are now."

"Thank the stars. Where's the estate from here? I don't recognize any of this." Maire looked haggard, and Ethan picked up her duffel. AJ should have dragged her away from the journals and transcribing to train an hour or two a day.

Ethan turned away from the town. "This way. We have a bit of a walk, but we're on the right road to the earl."

<hr>

Two hours later, four weary travelers trudged through the gates of Brun Manor. They made it another hundred yards before two armed men in matching uniforms stopped them. One held a lantern and lifted it high above his head.

"What business do you have with the earl at this late an hour?" The one without the lantern did the talking.

"It's me, Filmore. Ethan Hughes, and I apologize for our tardy arrival."

Ethan stepped forward so the guard could get a better look, but the guard was already approaching.

Recognition danced in the man's gaze, and his face broke into a hearty smile. "By all that's holy, it is you. We thought you were dead."

Ethan laughed and shook the man's hand. "Not yet, and God willing, not any time soon."

Filmore turned to the second guard, who Ethan didn't know, though his features were familiar. "Wake Thomas and let the manor know we have guests."

The younger man handed Filmore the lantern and ran toward the manor. Filmore eyed the rest of the group, and when he spotted Maire, his smile widened, and he ran a hand over his hair.

"Lady Moore."

"Hello, Filmore. I'm glad you remember me."

"How could we forget the first lady to grace these halls in many decades? Let me carry that bag for you." Filmore pulled the backpack from Maire's hands. The bag held her books and notes, and though she wouldn't want them out of her sight, she seemed relieved to be free of the extra weight.

By the time they reached the steps leading into the manor, Thomas bounded through the door and raced down to greet them. He nodded to Finn but grabbed Ethan by his shoulders.

"By God, it's good to see you, old man."

"Likewise."

The two men hugged, and Ethan waited as Thomas shook Finn's hand then kissed Maire and AJ on their cheeks, bringing a blush to both women.

"I suppose if you're here at this time of night, your news can't be good." Thomas led them up the steps. "We told the earl why you had to disappear, but with no letter since then, we feared the worst."

"We were deciding if it was safe to return when we received

word, of a sort, that the business with the stones might not be over."

"I was afraid of that. We'd—"

Before Thomas could finish, another voice, soft but arresting, interrupted the discussion. "Is that my boy? Ethan?"

The earl, older and leaner than the last time Ethan had seen him, shuffled toward him. When he bowed, the earl slapped his arm, bringing him in for a hug. He noted the fragility of the old man, and fear pricked at his eyes. He glanced at Thomas, who lowered his gaze but not before Ethan caught the sorrow in his friend's eyes.

"My boy, so good to see you." The earl released Ethan but held onto to his forearms. "You look healthy and happy. And more importantly—safe."

The earl turned. "Maire, my sweet girl, thank heavens they found you. Thomas told me you were well and back with Ethan, but to see it with my own eyes does my heart good."

Maire fell into his arms, her own wrapped around him. They hugged for some time before the earl stepped back and studied the other two visitors as Ethan introduced Finn and AJ.

"I've heard tales of your adventures." The earl's eyes were filled with mischief, but they grew solemn when he took Finn's hand. "I know your journey was as long and lonely as Ethan's. But..." he glanced at the two women and winked at AJ, "it appears your journey ended as well as his."

"Lydia!" the earl called out. "We have guests. We'll need two rooms in the tower." He turned and grinned. "Don't worry, our finest rooms are in the tower."

Ethan leaned toward Finn and AJ. "It's an old joke."

"I understand you walked here. You must be exhausted, and I need my rest. We'll talk more at breakfast." The earl nodded at Ethan and Thomas then wobbled down the hall.

Lydia, a woman of middle age in a hastily thrown on robe,

bustled out of the dining room, having come from the kitchen where the stairs to the servant's quarters were located.

"Master Ethan, a pleasure to have you home." The woman's warm smile was a happy sight. She'd been the youngest of the countess's lady's maids when he'd first arrived at the manor as a young boy. The earl made her his governess until he'd come of age, then she became the housekeeper.

"If you follow me, I'll take you to your rooms." She wrapped the robe tighter about her and headed for the stairs. Ethan nodded at Thomas when the man jutted his chin toward the hall that led to the earl's study.

He followed his friends up the stairs to their rooms, which were on the second floor of the tower. The guest rooms in both wings were as stylish as any aristocrat's, but the tower rooms were larger and more impressive. Each of the first five floors held two guest rooms. The sixth and top floor held the earl's master suites. It had large windows that allowed him to watch over his entire estate. It was a wonder he could still get up and down the stairs.

Once he and Maire were shown their rooms, he shooed the maid away and started the fire. Maire pulled out her journals and notes, spreading them out on a corner writing desk. He kissed her cheek, which he doubted she noticed, her focus on her notes as she retrieved a quill and inkpot from her bag. He left her to her musings and had reached the bottom of the stairs, turning for a side hall, when he met Thomas coming from a hallway that led to the back of the manor.

"I'll explain inside." Thomas held out an arm and waited for Ethan to enter the study.

Ethan stopped once he entered, his gaze taking in everything at once, and he took a deep breath, his muscles relaxing at the familiar scent of pipe smoke. Nothing had changed in all these years. The old man's desk was piled high with books, ledgers, journals, and if he knew the earl as well as he thought he did, there would be correspondence from his renters and friends from town. Bookcases lined two walls and were as overstuffed as the stacks in the manor's massive library. A framed portrait of the earl and his deceased bride, Eleanor, reigned over the room, but, modesty aside, he'd always cherished the one the earl had commissioned of him when he'd returned from one of his military campaigns. Although a fair likeness at one time, he knew he'd grown leaner and harder since he'd sat for the painting. On the wall farthest from the door, a fire blazed in the massive hearth.

He closed his eyes and sucked in another deep breath as the memories flooded him. Him as a young eight-year-old when the earl first picked him off the back streets of London. He'd been scared and hopeful. The first two years had been difficult, but they'd eventually found common ground. From then on, he'd come to this room every evening after dinner to work on his studies at a small desk the earl had procured for him. Before bedtime, the earl would have hot cocoa served, and they would sit and watch the fire. That scene had played out every night when they were both in residence until the day the earl asked him to take that fateful step into the fog in search of a magical stone.

There had been years of riding lessons, fencing, literature, boxing, weapons, art, and hand-to-hand combat. The earl made every effort to make Ethan a respectful gentleman without a title. As the earl's Sergeant of Arms, doors were always opened to him. Now, that honor fell to Thomas. And while his heart tightened at the thought, his time here at Hereford was done.

"Nothing has changed." Ethan took the proffered chair in front of the fire.

"Did you expect it to?" Thomas poured two glasses of scotch, the earl's favorite, and handed one to Ethan before setting the bottle between them and taking the chair next to him.

"I would have been more surprised if it had."

"This was the only room Maire didn't have time to update."

Ethan sipped the fine alcohol then nodded. "She had no plans for the study, the earl's suites, or his library. She said she knew better than to touch a man's personal spaces."

Minutes ticked by while they stared at the flames, giving the scotch time to work its magic as Ethan built up enough courage to ask the question he wasn't sure he wanted answered. "Truth now. Tell me about the earl."

Thomas topped off their glasses before settling back in his seat and placing his boots on a woven footstool. "He gets frailer by the day. He came down with winter fever after a fall he took. It was a couple of weeks after we heard you and Maire had jumped to the future after the last battle at the monastery. He never fully recovered.

"As you must have guessed, or seen, the stairs are too taxing for him. But you know how stubborn he can be. I posted someone with him at all times so he wouldn't topple down them. It didn't take long before the earl gave in and suggested the solarium might be a better spot."

"Not much privacy with all those windows."

Thomas chuckled. "Lydia was the only one he would listen to. We spent three months enlarging the two rooms on the other side of the solarium to create a respectable suite with its own privy. We moved a desk and reading chair into the solarium where he spends most of his time. He's actually improved some, and Lydia swears it's the sun. But we know it will be a miracle if he survives to see next Christmas."

A notch tightened around his heart. He hated to ask, but the earl's legacy mattered to him. "What of the estate? Will it be left in good hands?"

Thomas shrugged. "The earl has been in talks with a nephew, the second son of a half-brother who lives just north of Nottingham. He's a young man and seems to have a good head on his shoulders. I wager this manor is larger than the one his older brother will inherit. He sounds eager enough and a gentle sort, but that might have been for appearances."

Ethan grunted. It wouldn't be the first time either of them had seen that play out in other noble families.

"What about you?" Thomas asked. "Do you have a good life now?"

He considered the question, not sure where his life was—in this time period or the one he was building in the future. He grinned when he glanced at Thomas. "I have a good woman, there's not much else I need."

"Truer words."

They touched their glasses together and drank. Ethan refilled them and settled back to watch the fire. "So, tell me, Thomas, what is the exact date and year?"

11

———

Beckworth restrained his outrage, sorry he'd lost control as he scanned the men, all of whom had moved closer, most fondling their muskets or pistols. It had been foolish to stalk toward Gemini, but her antics had been a shock. He would never have considered anyone jumping to the future to kidnap someone. He didn't know who this woman was or what other connections she had, but it seemed she was as mad and dangerous as the duke.

Gemini eyed him, probably assessing if he was the one who'd lost his mind, but there was a hint of a smile. It wasn't too late to salvage his shaky position. She motioned Gaines to sit, then snapped her fingers, and one of the men brought another mug. She splashed whiskey in the mugs then gave him her most alluring smile. The same smile she'd used with the suitors who'd followed her around like lost puppies at Waverly.

Gaines frowned. Had she taken up with the man after Dugan was killed? He appeared the jealous type, but his glare toward Beckworth could stem from multiple reasons. There had been animosity in the man the first time they'd met.

"So why all the subterfuge?" Beckworth sat and picked up

the mug, swirling it around before holding it up in a mock salute, then gulping it in one swallow, pleased with the burn that flowed to his churning gut. "Is this scheme something new, or was the plan to pick up where the duke failed?"

He hadn't been lying when he'd agreed to tell her what he knew of the stones and time travel. From what he'd gathered to this point, they knew as much as he did. Anything else he could twist to whatever story she wanted to hear. The one thing she couldn't discover was who'd killed Dugan. She'd been testing him earlier when she'd asked if he'd been the one who'd performed the deed, but he suspected she'd already pinned it on Finn. If she discovered it had been AJ, he doubted anyone, not even Gaines, could protect their captive.

Gemini studied him, and for a fleeting moment, he thought she could read his mind. He mustered his best neutral expression, but he wouldn't trust his ability to remain calm if Gemini had any more surprises in store.

She lifted her mug in response to his toast before finishing the drink. "I've always been good at uncovering information. Most men give women little thought in conversation. A few words here and there, it's not too difficult to learn secrets. It didn't take me long to discover some whispered words were more valuable than others. But when I heard about the stones?" Her eyes glittered with mischief and perhaps dreams of something else. Unimaginable riches, no doubt.

"How did you get involved with Dugan and the duke?"

"You know how much I like parties."

"Ah, so you crashed one of the duke's." When that would have been, Beckworth couldn't guess. One thing he knew for sure, he'd never seen her before she came to Waverly.

She gave him a saucy wink while resting a hand on Gaines, probably to calm the man. He'd already poured more whiskey and was fidgeting in his seat. Was he worried Gemini would reveal too much, or was he jealous of her flirtations?

"Tell me," Beckworth leaned back and placed a leg across his knee. "What's the plan now that you have AJ?" He could dig for more information on how she became Gemini, but his survival instincts had moved to the top of the list along with how to keep Stella safe until Murphy arrived.

"He doesn't need to know anymore than what's necessary." Gaines's growl brought a scowl to Gemini's exquisite lips, but she ignored him.

"Gaines left a new incantation for Murphy. If he uses it correctly, Murphy should arrive at the assigned meeting place with the Heart Stone in the next few days.

Beckworth's heartbeat thumped an increasing staccato. "An incantation that can predict the jump's date and location?"

"Isn't it marvelous? Can you imagine the possibilities?"

"How did you discover it? The duke knew nothing of how the stones worked."

"Gemini." Gaines's tone was a low warning.

She gave him a disparaging glance. "Why don't you check the perimeter? The men have been slacking."

The stare between them lasted long enough for the nearby men to take note before Gaines stood, knocking his chair over as he stalked off.

"I apologize for Gaines. He doesn't always see the big picture."

Beckworth chuckled and responded loud enough for Gaines to hear. "Not the free thinker Dugan was?"

Her gaze clouded over, and Beckworth worried he might have stepped over a line. She recovered, but her tone was frosty. "You don't need to know how the incantation was discovered, only that we have it."

"Then why the need for the Heart Stone?" If she wanted it so badly, had she already tried to retrieve the one from this time period? Now that it was with Lord Langdon, it would be as daring a feat as jumping through time. Any attempts of sneaking into Buckingham Palace where Langdon claimed he hid it would be suicidal.

"The Heart Stone is more powerful. Once we have the torc, the Heart Stone will add more precision to our timing."

He considered the impact in divulging more of his knowledge, but it didn't seem to matter with what Gemini already knew. His brow crinkled. "I thought you needed all the stones to use the torc."

"That's our ultimate goal, but we'll be able to do amazing things with just the Heart Stone."

The more she used the term "we", the more he believed she wasn't talking about Gaines and her men. He didn't have any reason to believe there was someone else lurking in the shadows, but it made sense. He couldn't fathom how Gemini would have discovered all of this on her own. Dugan and Reginald had been clueless to the workings of the stones. Beckworth was positive about that.

"So now you have a hostage, but why the wait for Murphy? Does that play into the incantation somehow?"

Gemini turned and scanned the clearing, but if she was searching for Gaines, he couldn't tell. When she settled back, she studied Beckworth, and he worried she might take Gaines's word of caution to heart, but like so many in her position, she couldn't stop from gloating.

"I had no intention of keeping a hostage for more than a day or two, but a single small stone makes the new incantation less precise. Gaines's last jump was only his second, and we weren't sure how consistent the incantation would be. It turns out, we don't have the accuracy we hoped for in using a smaller stone. But no matter—we'll be ready. The extra time works to our advantage in preparing the location for Murphy's arrival. Once the men have set a wide parameter, we'll have our guest in a tight spot."

"And where is this meeting place?"

She paused, and he could tell by the set of her jaw he'd reached the limit of his questions. "You'll find out when the rest of the men do."

"So, what part do I play in all this?"

"At first, a simple exchange of information to see if you knew something I didn't."

He snickered. Perhaps like knowing she had the wrong woman locked away in her farmhouse. "And you'll reciprocate?"

"Darling, I already have. But, if you prove more useful, I might share something in return."

"And can I expect something more than my continued health as payment?"

She laughed, and for an instant they were back at Waverly as she entertained his guests with some exotic story—probably invented. How could she be so sure of her plan? He hadn't seen anyone in her gang who might know Murphy or how devious the man could be.

"There will be more money than any of us could spend in a lifetime. Treasures wait for us on the other side of time."

She was as mad as the duke, but he had to admit she was more prepared. That could spell trouble.

He spread his arms in a resigned gesture. "So, payment will be from some future venture."

"I can't believe you need money. That's not why you work for Hensley."

Now we're getting to it. "And why is it I work for Hensley?"

She leaned over, her gaze blazing in the firelight. "Information. You're no different than me, you're just playing closer to the rules. We've seen the men you've been meeting in out-of-the-way places, and all under the spymaster's nose."

She must have had someone watching him since the holiday party. He hadn't suspected a thing. She'd been planning this for a long time, and he would bet his most-prized stallion there was a great deal more to her plan. It was possible Gaines wasn't even aware of its depths.

"But even so," she continued, giving him that seductive grin, "before we can truly trust you—and I do mean until Gaines trusts you—you'll have limited access to information." When he frowned, she raised a hand. "There is a way for you to show your loyalty this evening."

"Oh?" His muscles tensed. These types of opportunities never worked in his favor.

"I need Miss Moore to answer a couple of questions for me."

He sat up and poured a nip into his mug. This was an unexpected opportunity he'd be happy to accept. "You think she'll respond to me any better? I'm aiding your kidnapping. She won't be happy to see me."

"I have it on good authority the two of you became fast friends after that nasty episode with the duke. But I understand, unlike Gaines, how critical it is to stay neutral. I'm sure you'll think of a way to get her to talk to you."

He simply bowed his head. Her assumptions were only helping him, but he turned to stare at the fire. He should appear to have some hesitation with the request, so he ground out his question. "What do you want to know?"

She rubbed her hands together, her smile never wavering. "Wonderful. First, I need confirmation that Murphy will bring the Heart Stone. That was part of the deal, but he might use one of the smaller stones for the travel."

"Murphy has the other stones?"

She shook her head, then swiveled to the right at the snap of a twig, but it had been one of the horses fidgeting on the line. When she settled back in her chair, she studied him before giving him another answer. "We haven't accounted for all the smaller stones but suspect he has one."

"Do you have the rest of them?" His worry shifted to Sebastian.

"We know where they are."

What did that mean? Sebastian would never voluntarily hand them over. Were they planning on raiding the monastery?

"Did you have another question for AJ?"

"I want to know where Maire Murphy might be, and her watchdog Hughes as well."

"Maire? She could be anywhere."

"Maybe. Or she might be hidden away with a section from *The Book of Stones*, continuing her translation work. I need to know where she is." She stood. "Jessup will take you to the Moore woman. You have thirty minutes." She turned her head again toward the horses, tilting it to one side, but whatever she was listening for, he couldn't hear it. Before she walked away, her smile turned serious. "This is your first test. Don't screw it up."

Beckworth waited while Jessup opened the door then stepped back to let him enter. He stopped just inside the door when Stella jumped from the bed, probably startled from the unexpected visit. She took one look at him and raced to the corner of the room to stand behind a wooden chair. He remained still. Now that he had time with her, he wasn't sure where to start.

Her gaze flicked around the room before her passive expression landed on him for a heartbeat. Vivid green eyes flashed. She tugged at her filthy sweater before her hand inched down to pick at a piece of string hanging from a rip in her pants. She must be freezing in the clothes with no hearth for a fire.

He scanned the room stuffed with trunks and bags. At least she had a bed, and though it didn't look comfortable, it had to be better than the floor. He noted the long, tattered overcoat hanging from a hook, and based on the buttons and styling, it had to be hers. At one point, it might have been red but was so mud spattered it was difficult to tell in the soft glow from the lantern. One thin blanket had been bunched on the bed where she'd kicked it off. The trunks were no doubt filled with clothing. Hadn't Gemini offered her more appropriate attire?

He took two steps, and when Jessup followed, he pushed the man back into the hall with a sneer before slamming the door in his face. Unsure where to start, he considered his options. It was obvious she wasn't going to be the first to speak. She still wouldn't look at him.

Beckworth pushed two bags off a stool before dragging it toward her but left six feet separating them. Close enough for a quiet talk, but not too close to spook her. He sat, keeping his hands in his lap and showing no signs of aggression. Now that he was closer, with more light from the lantern, he noticed the color on her left jaw. It was still a dark blue, and from what Gemini told him, Stella had only arrived a couple of days before. Had she put up a fight to earn that bruise?

"I think introductions first." He kept his tone low so anyone standing by the door wouldn't hear. And maybe she'd relax long enough for a conversation.

Her gaze darted to his, then away, but after another moment accompanied by a long, exaggerated sigh, she pushed her thick auburn hair back and gave him her full attention. His first thought was that her curiosity wouldn't keep her quiet. He had no idea why he thought that and couldn't help but wonder what she'd been thinking when he'd first entered the room.

"My name is Beckworth, but I think you already knew that."
She nodded.

He glanced toward the door then leaned forward and whispered, "And you're not who everyone thinks you are."

She snorted but kept her voice low. "You're quick. AJ didn't tell me what a scholar you were."

He stared at her. A sharp tongue on this one, and he wasn't sure if he should be offended or intrigued. "Are you going to be as troublesome as it appears?"

"Probably."

This would require a different approach. He tugged at his sleeves, and though he ignored her smirk, he folded his hands in his lap. "Can you please sit?"

When she didn't comply, he sighed. "It's obvious you're not pleased by my visit, but we must agree on a plan until AJ and Finn arrive. Gemini sent me to garner answers from you. We need to decide what those answers should be."

That got her attention. She squinted, probably searching for traps in his statement. With another deep sigh, she stepped in front of the chair and sat, her hands resting on her knees. Quite prim and proper. Her gaze was clear, and that expression that appeared more curious than concerned returned.

"Let's start with an easy one." Beckworth relaxed on the stool, lifting a leg over a knee. "Gemini wants to know if Murphy will bring the Heart Stone." Before she could launch into another scathing retort, he continued, "I have no doubt Murphy will bring it; that's the only way they can time travel. For some reason, Gemini believes him to have one of the smaller stones. Two are uncounted for, so she's obviously guessing. Although I'm not sure how she came into possession of one." The last statement was mumbled more to himself, but Stella straightened at the comment. "Regardless, Murphy would bring the Heart Stone in case there was no other way of retrieving you. Of the two questions Gemini wants answers to, this one seemed the safest to answer, but I wanted your opinion."

Stella stared at him with wide eyes that quickly narrowed. She didn't appear to trust him. What had AJ told her about him? He considered restating the request in case she hadn't followed along.

"What's the second question?"

Now it was his turn to raise a brow. He hadn't expected her to question him. "Why is that important?"

She rolled her eyes, and he almost chuckled. Did she learn that from AJ or the other way around? Come to think of it, a lot of women did that in their timeline.

"You said Gemini wanted answers to two questions. You thought the first one was the best one to answer. But how do I know that if you don't tell me what the second question is?"

He almost barked out a laugh. The little minx was paying attention. He couldn't hold back an engaging grin and noticed the sudden blush in her cheeks. He considered a witty comeback to add a touch more pink, but this wasn't the time to tease.

"I'm supposed to ask about Maire's location."

Her expression went blank, and she turned so she wasn't directly facing him. She knew something after all.

"That won't do." When Stella glared at him, he shrugged. "It's your expression. It's obvious you know where she is. If Gemini brings up Maire, you need to look surprised, like you thought everyone knew where she might be. The way you've positioned your body, you're almost daring me to pull off a fingernail or two to find out what you're hiding." He grunted. "And to think I had high hopes on your intelligence."

"You're not big on winning friends, are you?"

"I have many friends. I must be doing something right."

She snickered but answered his question. "Finn will most

definitely bring the Heart Stone." Then she leaned over, her voice barely above a whisper. "Do you know they're married?"

"Of course." He paused. "Ah. I see where you're going, but Gemini knows this already, which explains why she's positive Murphy will come." He tapped a finger on his chin as he studied her. She should know everything he did, including what he suspected. "I don't believe Gemini is working alone. There has to be someone with more money and influence, but she's only sharing small tidbits of information. She doesn't fully trust me."

She nodded. "The first question was probably a test, either for me or you, maybe both. They must know you've worked with them in the past."

Her statement didn't surprise him. She had to be smart. When he'd been in her time period, he'd seen her face on dozens of signs all over Baywood, advertising herself as an Estate Agent. A successful one from what AJ had once shared with him.

"Maire is with AJ."

The statement startled him. The fact she divulged the information so easily suggested she might trust him, if only a little. "I thought so."

"Wouldn't it be better if everyone thought Maire was in this time period?"

"Quite right. It would give Murphy an advantage if Gemini doesn't suspect Maire and Hughes would be with him. And when AJ reveals herself..." He shook his head.

"What?"

He gave her a halfhearted shrug. "The four of them are deadly together, but they'll be vastly outnumbered." Her frosty glare returned, and she was probably judging his value. "They have me, of course, but I'm not sure what I can do before the meeting. No one will tell me the location. At least they haven't yet."

"As long as whatever we share doesn't lead them to the monastery."

"Sorry, but that's not a secret. Gemini was quite close to Dugan and knows everything he did about the duke, and by extension, the monastery as well. If we have to divulge Maire's possible location, I think we should point them toward the Earl of Hereford. Hughes used to be the Sergeant at Arms for the earl and is still quite close to the man. If Gemini sends someone to check, hopefully there won't be enough time to return before the meeting to validate your answer. Oh, and that reminds me."

He stood, picked up the stool, and smashed it against one of the dressers. Splinters flew and pounding started on the door before the bolt slid back. Stella jumped and rushed behind her chair, arms crossed tightly in front of her as the door swung open.

Beckworth turned to find Jessup staring at the remaining bits of stool scattered across the floor. "Get out!" He took a step toward the man.

Jessup held up his hands. "Gemini doesn't want her hurt."

Beckworth sneered and nodded toward Stella. "Well, thank you so much for letting her know that. Besides, there are ways to not leave bruises. Now get out. I won't ask again."

The door slammed shut, and he tugged at his sleeves. "Well, I couldn't have asked for a better showing."

"Was that supposed to impress me? Give me assurances you're on my side?"

She wasn't going to give an inch. Barely a half hour with her, and he had no doubt she'd be more difficult than AJ ever was. At this point, there was nothing he could say that would make her trust him. His actions would speak louder than any words. For now, keeping her true identity secret would have to be enough.

"I'll tell Gemini that you confirmed Murphy will arrive with the Heart Stone. I'll make it sound as if you were close to giving me Maire's location before Jessup broke in. That will give us another opportunity to talk without prying eyes."

Without waiting for her response, he left before he said something he'd regret. Or she did.

<hr>

When Beckworth stepped outside of the farmhouse, Gemini was pacing back and forth in front of the fire. Her arms hung stiff at her sides, her hands balled into tiny fists. She appeared to be mumbling to herself. A movement to the left caught his eye. Gaines stepped closer, his focus on Gemini as if ready to grab her if she did something crazy.

Something had changed in the short time he'd been away, and it was best if he stayed out of it. He had to think about his own safety if he was going to help Stella survive. He skirted the fire, keeping it between him and Gemini. A prickling along the back of his neck was his first inkling that she'd just heard news that wouldn't bode well for their hostage. And he hated when his sixth sense proved true.

"I'll kill her myself." Gemini's voice, now easily heard around the clearing, only added to Beckworth's concern.

"We need her." Gaines stepped in and grabbed her shoulders, forcing her to glare up at him. "For now. A few more days. We'll keep her isolated and restrict her movements. You won't have to even look at her. Once Murphy arrives and we have him, you kill the woman, and I'll kill Murphy."

"I don't know if I can wait that long. If we know he's bringing the Heart Stone, why keep her at all? She's been nothing but trouble."

This wasn't good.

"Pardon me. Is everything all right?" Beckworth took a step back when Gemini whirled around.

She stared at him like she was trying to remember why he was there. Her focus shifted, and her face scrunched in renewed anger. "Did you know?"

"Know what?" Though it was difficult, he held his ground. Whatever it was, it was going to be bad. Of all the different emotions he'd seen her go through, boiling rage had never been one of them and it worried him.

Her chest rose and fell with each breath, as if she couldn't get enough air. She pointed her finger at the farmhouse. "That woman killed Dugan."

God's blood. How did they find out? He'd only been gone for a few minutes. He glanced at Gaines, whose smile seemed out of place for this situation.

"One of Dugan's men who escaped from the monastery finally made it back to England. He'd been conscripted to a pirate ship to earn his way home from France." Gaines nodded to a man standing next to a horse. "It took him a while to find his way to us, and what a tale he shared when he found out who our guest was."

He advanced on Beckworth, who stepped back to keep distance between them but found himself backed up to the fire. Gaines waved at the farmhouse with almost the same ferocity as Gemini, as if Dugan's death meant something to him. He almost laughed at Gaines's misplaced hostility for the loss of the man. He doubted the two would have gotten along.

"That woman put an arrow through his heart." Gaines flashed a glance at Gemini before turning back to him.

"AJ did that?" Beckworth widened his eyes, trying to show disbelief at the idea. "She could barely ride a horse."

"I'm sure." The man with the horse shifted from foot to foot, but he wasn't backing down.

This was a problem. Beckworth stared at the ground, hiding his emotions as he considered his options. He shook his head. "It was dark. Men were running and fighting in both courtyards as well as the monastery. It was utter chaos. Worse than when the duke was killed. To be honest, I'd missed most of it, I'd been upstairs with Reginald."

"Who you killed." Gaines's statement didn't bother Beckworth.

"The man raided Waverly. He had no rights to it. It never belonged to the duke. I was the better man, and the duke knew it." He glanced at Gemini, who seemed to be listening. "Reginald had been a thorn in my side for years, and he was jealous of me being in favor with the duke."

"Then why didn't you work with him instead of against him?" Gemini asked. Her expression had calmed, but he wasn't fooled. She was deciding if he needed to be killed now or later.

"Let me state it again. He took Waverly from me. That's all I have in this world." He waved his arms about as he spewed his own rage. "I worked years to earn that title, bossed around by the duke and your beloved Dugan, but I did what I was told without question. Then Reginald comes along with the same mad dreams as the duke. He thought he could just stroll in and take my home without me doing something about it?" He stormed past her, setting up his own path to pace in front of the fire. He spun around so fast, his face hot with growing fury, that Gemini took a step back. "You think I wouldn't do anything, work with anyone, who could remove that stain from Waverly?"

"But he had the druid's book. He had everything he needed except the translation." Gemini seemed honestly confused.

He stared at her. How thick was the woman? And to have gotten as far she had? "Aren't you listening? I don't care about the stones. I want to be as far away from them as possible. If he had gone directly to the monastery or taken someone else's manor, everything would have turned out differently. But he didn't. He thought he could take mine, and I wasn't going to just sulk off. There was nothing else I could do but put him down like the mad dog he was."

He wiped his mouth, as surprised as everyone else at the amount of rage that had been bottled up inside. If she wanted truth, she had it now.

Gemini and Gaines stared at him as if he'd gone mad himself, but their glances with each other were communicating more than he could guess. He turned away from the fire and caught Stella's gaze. She had been walking back from the privy with Jessup but had stopped to listen to his tirade. He glanced toward Gemini, who fortunately hadn't seen her. The darkness hid Stella's expression, but her stiff posture told him she'd heard plenty.

He'd worry about that later. Right now, he needed Gemini to focus on him until Stella returned to the farmhouse. If she noticed her now, she might kill her and worry about consequences later. He'd learned over the years, the best way to lie was to stick close to the truth.

He kept his voice low, worn out after his outburst, but also so Stella couldn't hear. "After I killed Reginald, all the fight went out of me. I sat on the bed and stared at him for what seemed like hours. Had I made a mistake?" He caught Gemini's gaze and held it. "I don't know. But I did feel relief that I had my home back. By the time I made it back downstairs, it was all over. Dugan was dead, and his men disarmed. No one mentioned who had killed Dugan. Murphy had been after him, and I assumed he'd done the deed." He glanced away for a moment, then sat in one of the chairs by the table.

He poured a drink, swallowed it down, then poured a second one. "To Dugan. Although I hated the bastard, I'm sorry for your loss." He drank it down and waited, sneaking a glance toward the farmhouse. Stella was gone.

Gemini stared into the trees for some time, then released a large sigh. She strode to the table, poured whiskey in a second mug, and held it up. She turned in a circle, her steady gaze resting on each man. "To Dugan." She finished the drink and slammed the mug on the table. "Break out the bottles, gentlemen. We drink to Dugan tonight."

Cheers erupted, and Beckworth released his breath. Crisis averted for now.

Instead of walking away, Gemini sat down. "So, tell me, Beckworth. What did our little murderer have to say for herself?"

Gaines stood behind her, his eyes hooded, arms crossed, but Beckworth ignored him. "You are correct. Murphy will arrive with the Heart Stone. That was easy enough to get from her."

She nodded with a light smile. When Gaines laid a hand on her shoulder, she reached up and stroked it. "It will be within our grasp." Her gaze flickered back to him. "And Murphy's sister?"

Beckworth tugged at his sleeves. "I was minutes from having the information when Jessup broke in. I don't know what's going on between him and your captive, but she stopped talking."

"You should have replaced him." Gaines's words were unexpected, and Beckworth sat back. Was he talking about him?

"You're right. Move Jessup to the perimeter. From now on, that woman is your responsibility until I can take care of her." Her gaze moved to the farmhouse. "We'll try something different with her tomorrow."

"I can do this. If I hadn't been interrupted—"

She drove a knife into the table, the move so quick and unexpected, Beckworth almost fell backwards off his chair. "I'll be asking the questions now." Her tone was hard, and the fire in her eyes proved her thirst for revenge still simmered.

"Don't worry." Her smile didn't quite reach her eyes. "You passed the first test. Let's see how tomorrow goes. Until then..." She stood and grabbed the bottle. Gaines put an arm around her as they moved toward the trees. He grabbed a blanket from someone's pack as he led her away. With any luck, he'd keep her busy for a few hours.

Beckworth watched the fire, sparks flying when a burned log dropped into the embers. It was times like this he missed Murphy, who made the difficult decisions. But there was only one way out of this, and it would most likely get him killed.

He ran a hand through his hair, stood, and tugged at his sleeves. A crate of whiskey sat next to other supplies. Several bottles remained after the men had taken their share. He picked one up, uncorked it, and poured a portion on the ground before he swaggered to the first group of men.

12

───────

Beckworth leaned against the side of the farmhouse and stared into the trees where Gemini and Gaines had crept hours earlier. He'd spent most of the night chatting the men up with tall tales, making sure they continued to drink. He moved from group to group until they stumbled off to their sleeping area or tipped over where they sat.

Gaines had wandered back to camp at some point, striding directly into the farmhouse. He'd considered following him to be sure Stella was safe, but the man returned before he'd made a decision. Gaines had carried a small bag with bread sticking out of the top and a skin probably filled with wine.

Now, Beckworth glanced at the horizon and the position of the crescent moon. It would be light in a couple of hours. After one more check of the tree line, he crept toward the back of the house, stopping to listen for anyone still awake. He waited a couple of minutes before pulling the door open, prepared for a squeak of hinges. Everything remained quiet, and he stepped inside, stopping once again while his eyes adjusted to the dark hall. Dim moonlight filtered through the windows in the front of the house, and other than light snoring, no one stirred from what he could see from the hallway.

He inched to the door on the right. This would be the first hurdle—getting into the room with as little sound as possible without Stella screaming or throwing something at him. He slid the bolt back with care, wincing at the slight creak as the door opened, and he paused to watch shadows from the front room. When he confirmed no movement, he quickly stepped in and pushed the door closed but not completely shut.

The low glow of lantern light surprised him at this hour, and he waited for his eyes to adjust again.

Stella was sitting up, her back resting against the wall with her arms hugging her legs to her chest. Her eyes were huge.

He pressed a finger to his lips and nodded toward the door.

Her gaze followed his movements, and he took a few steps toward the bed. "I need you to follow me."

She shook her head.

Didn't she understand why he was here and that he was on her side? Then he remembered her outside during his argument with Gemini. He doubted she'd heard everything but probably enough to question whose side he was on.

He stepped closer until he stood next to the bed. She didn't move, which didn't fit his image of her, and he became wary. Then he noticed one of her arms had slipped to her side, her hand hidden beneath the blanket.

"You don't want to do that." He held his palms up. "We can't afford to wake anyone."

She didn't move her arm, but she slumped a fraction, and he released his breath.

"I'm trying to rescue you."

"Why do I need rescuing?"

Without thinking, and in a move too fast for her to deflect, he lifted her chin, turning her head so he could see her lips in the light. Soft kissable lips. "You have a bruise forming in addition to the split lip. It will be sore for a couple of days." He couldn't seem to take his eyes off those lips. While he stared at them, he considered his options—tell her Gemini found out AJ killed Dugan and had decided she doesn't need a hostage anymore, or lie to counter any possibility the woman might do something unfortunate.

He dropped his hand. "Would you prefer staying and taking a chance with another one of Gemini's men? They're getting antsy waiting for Murphy to arrive."

"Why didn't you tell Gemini who I really am?"

"Good question. There was a time I might have been tempted, but I'm not that man any longer."

She snorted. "Or maybe you're worried what Finn would do once he caught up with you."

He wasn't going to let this woman compare him to Murphy. "I leave in five minutes. If you wish to come along, go out the back. I have a horse waiting on the far side of the privy. There's a foot trail that leaves the privy and goes into the woods. Follow it for twenty or thirty yards. Find your way there—quietly. Otherwise—" he tipped his head in a slight bow, "—I wish you all the best. It was a pleasure finally being introduced."

He shut the door, hoping he'd said the right thing. The last thing he wanted was to come back and forcibly remove her. Instead of going out the back, he skirted around sleeping men as he made his way to the front door. He would be the distraction she'd need when she made her move, assuming she was as smart as she appeared to be.

The snoring increased, coming from both corners of the main room, almost loud enough to cover any noise either of them made. Halfway to the front door, he turned back in time to catch a glimpse of Stella in the hallway, who was nothing more than a shadow in a long coat. He couldn't make out her face, yet he was positive she'd looked straight at him before turning and stepping swiftly toward the back door. With her awkward steps, she must know where the squeaky floorboards were. If she'd been planning an escape of her own, where would she have gone?

Did she know about AJ's friends in this time period? She'd known about him, but that would have been from when he'd been trapped in her time. AJ might not have told her everything about this century, but she must know a few names. From his experience with women, she'd have cooked something up—probably getting herself killed in the process.

Once he'd given her enough time to get out, he continued to the front door. Before he reached it, someone stirred. A man rolled over and propped himself up on an elbow, rubbing at his eyes. Beckworth remembered the face. The man had started drinking before the others, and it was a wonder he woke at all.

"It's me," Beckworth whispered. "I'm just off to the privy."

The man stared at him as he swayed back and forth, and Beckworth waited to see which way he'd tumble, betting on him falling backwards. He would have lost that bet as the man weaved one more time before falling face first into the floor.

Beckworth slipped out the door, closing it with a silent push. He tiptoed down the stairs, sticking to the edges of the boards. Once in the clearing, he increased his pace toward the privy.

When he reached the designated spot, he'd expected Stella to be standing next to the horse. He turned in a circle and sighed. She must have taken the opportunity to run on her own. He should have known better. She was proving every bit as troublesome as AJ. He strode to his horse, untied the reins, and turned him so he could mount.

"Psst. Beckworth."

He twirled around. Had he imagined the voice?

"Over here."

He glanced to his left and caught the movement of a hand waving from the bush. He walked over, his steed trailing behind. In the loudest whisper he could muster he chastised her. "This is not the time to be playing games. Come out of there."

She stepped out, her coat catching on a twig before she yanked it free, and within the dim glow of the moon a button flew out of sight. Her hair was disheveled, and she picked at the leaves strewn through it. What a fright, and yet, still a beauty.

"I don't think this is a good idea." She stared at the ground.

"Why not?"

She refused to meet his eyes.

"Quickly, woman. This isn't the time for soul-wrenching admissions."

That got a rise out of her, and she gave him an irritated glance as she straightened her shoulders and pushed back her overcoat to rest hands on hips. "Horses don't like me."

He choked back a laugh. "Really? And how do you know that?"

"It's a bit of a long story. Let's just say the trip over from the first cabin was a bit adventurous, even for Gemini. There were some injuries."

He gave her a head-to-toe perusal, but she shook her head. "Not me."

His brow rose. "Did the horse survive?"

"Funny."

"Well, we can't stay here, and it would be foolish to go on foot. So I'm willing to risk it."

She stepped closer, but when she glanced up at the horse, she shifted from foot to foot before taking a step back.

He shook his head. "You're scared of a horse?"

She bit her bottom lip. "No. Well, they are large, and it's a long fall."

"Christ, woman, you're thinking too much. Come over here, and I'll help you up. I'll have control of the reins."

She didn't move.

He glanced around, positive their lengthy discourse would wake someone. They were lucky there had only been two guards for him to take care of, but it wouldn't be long before Gaines would eventually rouse and check the watch.

He stepped closer until the horse stood in front of her. "He's a nice horse, but they have their own minds, so..."

"That's not helping," she interrupted.

"Let me finish. All I'm saying is that they'll stand still while you're mounting but tend to shift their feet once you've mounted. It can give the appearance the rider might not be in control, but believe me, I am in control. I don't know what you did to spook the other horse..."

"What makes you think it was my fault?"

He huffed and led the horse down the narrow trail. After several yards, he glanced back to ensure she followed. She stayed several yards behind, glancing over her shoulder every few minutes. They walked a quarter mile before his nerves couldn't take it, and he stopped.

When she reached the horse and stood next to the saddle, he didn't say a word other than to hold the horse quiet. She grabbed the top of the saddle and swept her coat back to place her foot in the stirrup. When she pushed off to mount, he made sure her backside landed where it should. He was still holding her left leg as he helped shift her farther up the saddle, only pulling away when it was time for him to mount. He waited for the horse to settle under their combined weight, then clucked the horse into a trot.

Stella tensed when he put an arm around her waist. When she fidgeted, he lowered his head and whispered, "Relax. The horse can sense your discomfort. Lean back. I won't bite. We have a long way to ride." It took another quarter mile before her muscles relaxed, her back pressing against him, he increased their pace.

They rode that way for several miles until Stella's head fell against his shoulder. He tightened his grip in case she woke and spooked, not remembering where she was. Poor thing. She'd probably been sleeping with one eye open since she'd arrived.

He considered his plan. His preference had been to ride for Hensley's but suspected Gemini would expect that. Once she discovered them gone, she'd know she'd been betrayed, and her first thought would be the spymaster.

The second logical choice would be London. It was a large city and easy to get lost, as long as you hid where no one expected. Otherwise, it was irritatingly simple to run into acquaintances if one remained in their section of the city. With his youth and early adult years spent in London, he knew every inch of it. But even so, it would be risky, and AJ and Murphy wouldn't think to look for them there.

Then there was the Earl of Hereford. He'd never met the man and had no idea whether Hughes or that Thomas fellow mentioned his new role as one of Hensley's men. The earl probably had no idea. Stella would be safe, but he might end up in the dungeon. Every proper castle had one.

He glanced down at the sleeping woman in his arms. She was partially correct in his reasoning behind rescuing her. The last thing he wanted was to face AJ's wrath should something happen to Stella, especially if he'd had the opportunity to do something. There was only one place he could be sure she'd be safe, and him as well. The problem was getting there and whether AJ would think to look there. Though, with the stones involved, it was where everyone ended up.

Travel would be tricky with the war. He'd been lucky enough in his last two crossings, both during the war, but he'd had

Murphy and Jamie to thank for that. He had no clue as to the current whereabouts of the *Daphne Marie*. He would have to put their lives in the hands of another captain.

He pushed the horse to a faster pace, positive that Gemini had already scattered her men in search of them. Would she consider his move? She might. As raindrops began to fall, he urged his horse faster and held tight to Stella as he leaned them into the horse. He was banking everything on Sebastian still being among the living.

T he soft whoosh of scattering leaves brought Stella out of her morning dreams. Darkness. The ground racing beneath her. A cold wind in her face as strong arms pulled her close. Branches slapped at her arms. Then she was falling, but instead of hitting the ground she floated, a gentle warmth enfolding her. Or were those arms holding her, carrying her?

She groaned and opened her eyes, groggy from sleep and still bone tired—tired of being filthy, tired of being terrified, tired of no one ever finding her. The floor was hard beneath her, and she winced when her muscles refused to cooperate. She pulled herself up to lean against the wall, her whole body ached, and her stomach grumbled, begging for food.

The memory of the prior evening crashed around her. The horse ride. Beckworth.

She was in England, and this wasn't the room she'd been locked in. This was a different cabin, if one could call it that. A cool wind blew in from a ragged hole under one of the front windows and stone debris circled the crumbling hearth. An old wooden table and a three-legged chair were the only remaining furniture. Dust and cobwebs completed the rustic decor.

Lovely.

She used the wall to help her stand and wrapped her coat around her before stumbling to the window. Nothing outside but a small clearing and what looked like an overgrown cart path leading into the woods.

No horse. No Beckworth.

She was alone.

At first, relief flooded through her, but when her stomach grumbled, worry set in. It was morning if she read the light and cloudy sky correctly. Rain threatened in the distance.

Had he just dropped her off and ridden away?

Some rescue.

She paced the width of the cabin, warming up her muscles and working out the stiffness. Once she felt more like herself, she returned to the rickety door that hung on by a prayer. She glanced back to where she'd been dumped—that wording didn't seem strong enough—where she'd been left to starve to death. That was more appropriate. Then something shiny under the scattered leaves caught her eye.

The object rested a few feet from where she'd been laying. She groaned when she bent to pick it up. It was a silver pocket watch. She turned it over, marveling at the delicately engraved scrollwork etched around the front and back, leaving no room for an inscription. A button on the side released the front casing, revealing the clock with a thin second hand that ticked away the time.

Had Beckworth left this behind, and if so, where would he have gone?

Gemini.

She raced to the window, scanning the yard and the woods beyond. Maybe he was providing a diversion. When her stomach grumbled again, she pictured him returning with a steaming cup of coffee and a bagel with cream cheese. She snorted. Without knowing how long she'd be on her own, water was more important. If there was a cabin, there must be a water source nearby, unless it went dry, which might explain why it had been abandoned.

The front porch squeaked when she stepped on it, and several boards were missing or had rotted away. Maybe being outside wasn't the best idea, but if Gemini's men were around, they wouldn't hesitate to check the cabin. Unsure of the best thing to do, she stepped around the rotting wood and made it down the front steps.

She found the thickest bush she could find, climbed into the middle of it, then hunkered down. After making herself as comfortable as she could while remaining hidden, she listened. Birds twittered as they flitted about, unaware or uncaring of her presence. There might be a small creek behind her, if she interpreted the sound correctly. She checked the timepiece, willing to wait for an hour. But then what? She checked her pants pocket and sighed with relief when she squeezed the bulky object. The beaded purse with her stolen coins were still there. She might not have a clue where she was, and had no food, but she had money. It gave her little comfort.

She dozed off, but her head snapped up when she heard twigs breaking. Leaves rustled on nearby trees, then the thud of hooves. It sounded like a single rider, but she wasn't an expert. A horse's head broke out of the woods on the far side of the clearing. The man appeared to be alone. She didn't recognize the clothing, but his movements were familiar.

Beckworth?

She wasn't positive and couldn't see his face as he dismounted and hurried up the steps, avoiding all the pitfalls of broken stairs. He disappeared inside but was back on the front porch in seconds, scanning the area. It was Beckworth, and he managed to find different clothes.

"Stella!" His voice was nothing more than a whisper, yet she had no problem hearing it. He appeared concerned if his wrinkled forehead was any indication.

He raced down the steps and stood in the yard, turning a slow circle. "Stella." His tone was still hushed, and that could only mean one thing. He didn't want to be heard from too far away. At least he'd come back.

"Over here." She pushed branches away, scratching her cheek in the process.

"What are you doing over there?" Beckworth strode over and stopped just short of where she crawled out.

She brushed leaves from her shoulders and the sides of her coat, then lifted her chin. Her idiocy made her cheeks warm.

His lips twitched, and she was positive her cheeks were turning a deeper shade of stupid.

"I wasn't sure if it was you or one of Gemini's men and thought I should hide." It sounded silly, but she held his gaze, daring him to laugh at what she deemed common sense.

"That was very smart on your part. But now we need to go."

She'd brightened at his first comment but whined like a petulant child at having to leave. "Can't we take some time to eat and get more sleep?"

"We haven't put enough distance between us. Now hurry."

She trudged behind him, then stopped. "Where were you?"

He'd reached the horse and was checking the saddle. "What?" He glanced around and frowned when he noticed she'd stopped ten yards away. His gaze lifted to the sky, and he muttered something she couldn't hear before giving her a hard stare. "I have no idea how long it was before they discovered us gone. My guess is thirty minutes at the most, especially if Randall checked the horses. He's the type of man who'd notice a missing horse. Gemini will scatter her men far and wide to find you. We need to move before they start spreading out."

"Where did you go when you left me alone?"

He huffed and walked the horse toward her until she took an involuntary step back. "Can we talk about it on the way?"

"How am I supposed to trust you when you don't include me in your plans? You're the one who was working with Gemini in the first place."

"I'm trying to keep you safe. AJ would trust me."

Stella rolled her eyes and gave him her best sneer.

He took a step closer and surprised her when he reached out and lifted her chin so she'd meet his gaze. "She does trust me, doesn't she?"

"You kidnapped Maire and then her. You put them in danger."

"I explained that all to her. She said she trusted me."

"Right." Stella brushed his hand away and turned to the horse, not wanting him to see the truth. AJ did trust him. Trusted him with her life. He appeared to be trying to save her, but several months had passed in this timeline since AJ had last seen him. With the war, many things could have changed. Maybe he liked playing both sides.

"I see." Beckworth ran a hand over his head, leaving his blond locks in disarray. He tugged at his sleeves. "Well, no matter. I'll make this easy on you, Miss Caldway. If you wish to go your own way, this would be the time. I suppose I can scrape together enough coin to pay someone to get you as far as Bristol. I don't think Hensley has left for London yet and can keep you until Murphy comes. Hopefully, Gemini or her men won't spot you, but it would be foolish to think she doesn't have men watching Hensley."

He studied the trees while she nibbled her lip. He'd seemed genuinely upset at being told AJ didn't trust him, and her gut wrenched. If she didn't have men chasing her, she could figure out where she needed to go if he would point her in the right direction. Having money in her pocket made a difference. But she did have men chasing her. AJ and Maire hadn't been able to outrun their captors. Beckworth was her only hope. The only one who knew who she was, hadn't told anyone, and seemed confident AJ and Finn would come for her.

"What if we both went to Hensley?"

He seemed to consider it, then shook his head. "It's fine for you to go, but if Gemini's men catch me heading that direction, they won't hesitate to kill me." His smile was unpleasant. "And regardless of what you think of me, I'm not ready to die for anyone."

The words stung, as they were meant to, and she didn't have anyone but herself to blame. Then she snapped her fingers. "I have something of yours."

If he was surprised by the change of subject, he didn't show it. Nor did he say anything.

She fished into her coat pocket and handed him the pocket watch.

He stared at it for a moment. "With all this running around, I'd forgotten. Thank you. It would have upset me to lose it."

A lump formed in her throat. He'd left something important to him, something to tell her he hadn't left her, and she'd tossed the risk he took back in his face with her lie about AJ. She'd never actually said AJ didn't trust him, but her inference was clear enough. "I'd prefer to stay with you until AJ and Finn arrive."

He nodded, but his expression remained unreadable. "We're just south of Corsham, which is the closest city to Waverly."

"I know where Corsham is."

He blinked. "You do?"

She nodded. "When we were making plans for AJ, Ethan, and Maire to go back for Finn, we discussed Corsham and its location to Waverly."

"Hmm." He considered her for a moment, then waved her closer. "Come on. We have to move on. I hadn't planned to be gone so long."

Sorry she'd delayed them, and sensing his concern, she stepped up to the horse.

"I have a dear friend, Eleanor, who lives not far from here. We needed supplies, and I wanted to send a message." He stood back and nodded toward the horse.

"Oh. Right." She grabbed the saddle, and with Beckworth's help, settled quicker than before, but not without complaint from her backside.

Beckworth swung up behind her and immediately moved the horse into a faster pace.

"Why don't we go to Waverly?" She sat forward, trying to keep space between them, though he kept his arm around her waist.

"That will be the first place they look, and I don't have enough security in place. Most of Gemini's men are mercenaries, and I'm not convinced they'd be gentle with the staff if they thought I was hiding there. If they do investigate, I trust Barrington, my butler, to give them leave to search the estate. Although there will be changes made if we make it out of this."

He mumbled the last words and might not have known he'd spoken them out loud. But Stella grimaced at how many people were being put in danger because of her. Her stomach rumbled, only adding to her growing discomfort.

"That reminds me." He released the arm he had around her waist and leaned back as he checked his coat pockets.

"I noticed you got new clothing."

He handed her a chunk of bread and a thick slice of cheese. "That will need to tide you over for another hour or so. And don't worry, I have a change of clothes for you as well."

"If not Waverly or Hensley, what about the earl?" She had to release her grip on the saddle to accept the food offering, but when both his arms braced her, she managed to relax enough to nibble.

He turned the horse to the right when the trail split, and it was another minute before he answered. "Did you know about the earl before I mentioned him the other night? Has AJ been keeping you well informed? You seem to know everyone."

She shrugged and let her body sink back against him. He placed an arm around her waist again, and this time she noted the hard muscle beneath his jacket sleeve. "I have an excellent memory. Once I hear something, it sticks. But, yes, AJ tells me everything." She took a bite of the bread. It was good, though it would have tasted better toasted.

"I'm not sure how much Gemini knows about the earl and his involvement with the stones, but she knew Dugan. So, it would only make sense she's aware of him. The earl's estate would be secure, but it would be a farther ride."

"Gemini knew Dugan?"

"Apparently, they were lovers."

She snorted. "That's hard to believe. I mean she seemed, I don't know, higher class I suppose. But, considering Gaines, maybe not. Is he the replacement or something?"

"He is something. Gemini met me before she dragged me into this mess. I first knew her as Lady Penelope Prescott."

"Penelope?"

"Turns out, that's not her real name. The actual Lady Prescott is presently enjoying a small vacation on the coast."

They rode for another ten minutes before she pieced together his words. "If Gemini had a thing for Dugan, does that mean she knows who killed him?"

She closed her eyes when his body tensed. "How long has she known?"

He only hesitated for a second. "I'd say about a day."

She slumped. That's why he'd insisted on getting her out of the farmhouse. Not to protect her from the men, but from Gemini. Had she given her men orders to capture or to kill? Probably capture her and kill Beckworth. Gemini would want the privilege of dealing with the one who'd killed Dugan. Would she bother to wait for Finn's arrival? Not the best time to be mistaken for AJ, and thoughts of her friend brought on a deeper despair.

At first, it seemed simple. AJ and Finn would come, they'd bring the team together, and rescue her at the meeting place. She should have known better. AJ and Finn always lamented about nothing with the stones ever going right. A large chasm seemed to separate her from her friends, and without quick communication in this time period, how would anyone find her?

Stop it.

In the last few days, she'd fallen in and out of her pity parties. That was enough. AJ spent months searching for a way home, then spent weeks searching for Finn. No one could guess how long she might end up in this timeline, but with Beckworth's reassurances providing more comfort than she would have believed, there was no doubt her friends wouldn't stop searching for her. If Beckworth had a place where she would be safe, and he felt certain AJ and Finn would find her, then everything would turn out. If she could stay alive long enough.

13

The Earl of Hereford pounded his mug on the table, and the voices in the room silenced. Ethan straightened in his chair along with Thomas and the footmen, who were already in strict postures. AJ inwardly chuckled at Ethan's reflexive response to the earl's commands—whether by word or the thump of a mug.

The earl waved at the footmen. "We need the room to ourselves. Leave the coffee."

When the footmen filed out, AJ reached for Finn's hand under the table, and he gave hers a quick squeeze. Maire, having lived with the earl for several months, went back to her notes. Breakfast was finished an hour ago, but they'd remained in the dining room to discuss their next steps.

"Now, let me review the situation one more time." The earl waved his cup at Thomas, who jumped up to refill it. "Your friend was kidnapped and brought back to our time. The kidnapper wants to trade your friend for the Heart Stone. Therefore, we must surmise they either don't know who has the stone in this time period, or they know who has it and decided traveling to the future was the easier option. Does that sound like a fair assessment?"

Everyone nodded.

"In addition, we know nothing of the kidnapper. How well armed is he? Does he have the money to support this endeavor, or is someone else behind this? Do we have anything that might give us a clue?

The group fidgeted, and their quick glances around the table before giving another nod made AJ uncomfortable. They understood all of this, but having the earl verbalize it illuminated how difficult it might be to retrieve Stella.

The earl sipped his coffee then sat back and stroked his chin as he studied the ceiling. "I do find it interesting that the incantation they left behind worked. This tells us someone has intimate knowledge of *The Book of Stones* or *The Mórdha Stone Grimoire.*"

"Certainly someone with more insight than me. My fiddling around didn't work as intended." Maire's voice sounded small, taking all the responsibility for the group not arriving as planned.

The earl pinned her with a steady gaze, proving to AJ that his frailty hadn't impacted his mind. "You arrived in the correct location, a mere two days later than you planned." He raised a hand when Maire started to object. "You're too hard on yourself, always striving for perfection. It might not have been the exact day you wanted, but considering the traveler had no control over time or location on previous jumps, I'd say your incantation was near perfect."

Maire slumped back, refusing to contradict him, even if his words of praise didn't seem to appease her. In the time AJ had known her, Maire had always held herself to a higher standard —sometimes too high. If she only saw in herself what everyone else did. AJ didn't care how much knowledge the kidnapper had, it couldn't be as solid as Maire's insights and adaptive capabilities.

"To be honest," the earl continued, "I think most of your plan is still salvageable."

"We can make it to Basingstoke in time to scout the location, but not if we go to Bristol first." Ethan's concern had been the cause of earlier sidebars until the earl used his mug as a gavel to get the group back on track.

"We don't know the numbers of the other side, so you might be outmatched, but those you'll have at your disposal are well-trained." The earl turned to the sideboard where Thomas had laid a group of rolled-up maps.

"Let me." Thomas picked through the maps before selecting one to place on the table, using mugs to keep it flat.

The earl ran a finger over various spots before sitting back. "I believe one of your earlier concerns was what might be happening at the monastery. The last letter I received from Sebastian, which was a month ago, and penned a month before that, stated all was fine. His smuggling operation hadn't been discovered and no attention was being paid to the monastery. That being said, many things can change in two months, especially with war."

"So, you agree a visit to Bristol is warranted?" Finn asked.

"Oh, absolutely. Hensley has resources at his disposal that I don't. They might not be fighting men, but Hensley's network of informants has grown steadily since last year. And if the monastery has been compromised, you'll need a trustworthy ship to get past the blockades. I have one docked on the Thames, but even with the best captain it wouldn't outrun a patrol."

"Then we're back to the same problem with not enough time." Ethan's posture began to match Maire's.

"My boy, have you grown soft in that new century?"

Ethan straightened, and though his return stare didn't hold a challenge, fire lit his gaze.

The earl chuckled. "I didn't mean anything other than to say you seem to have forgotten your history, and that I was the one who put you on the trail of the stones in the first place."

Ethan bowed his head. "No, sir. I haven't forgotten and agree I could be overlooking something."

AJ looked to Finn at what sounded to her like a dress down, but he watched the earl and gave no indication of his thoughts. Maire, on the other hand, hid a smile, and the knots in her muscles loosened. This was apparently typical banter between the two.

"Good. Then you should know I'm willing to give you as many men as I can. With the war extending longer than many had thought, and with Hensley's encouragement, Thomas has been teaching a handful of men the finer art of infiltration and surveillance."

"And they've become restless to put their training to the test." Thomas had seemed eager for action since their arrival, and AJ questioned if that was for his men or himself.

She hadn't spent much time with Thomas during their earlier missions. In fact, he hadn't thought much of her from the beginning when he'd helped Ethan rescue her from Dugan during the coach ride to Southampton. His derision had been obvious when she'd begged Ethan to return for Maire. While everything worked out in the end, Ethan could have been killed in that glade rather than being left for dead. Over time, Thomas stopped glaring at her and listened to her suggestions, but they never developed the friendly banter she had with Lando or Jamie. Perhaps that was her fault for not trying harder. While they might not have anything more than mutual respect, she never doubted his loyalties, and that in itself was enough for the team.

The earl tapped the map, snapping AJ out of her musings. "While I had hoped to spend more time with all of you, we need to move with all haste. I will send Thomas and his five-man surveillance team to Overton. It's larger than Basingstoke, and as the main road from London to the West Country, it has several inns. If they leave tomorrow, there will be enough time to scout the area. In addition, I'll send another group of fighting men to East Stratton. That village is on the road from London to Southampton, so having a dozen men traveling together during a time of war won't seem unusual. Thomas will coordinate the two groups based on what they find."

Finn and Ethan exchanged glances, and their relieved expressions eased AJ's earlier fear of never finding Stella.

"That will give us time to reach Bristol, advise Hensley, get a message to Jamie, and then ride hard for Basingstoke in time for the meet." Finn scratched his chin. "While we're headed there, I'll need Hensley to send someone to meet Jamie in Southampton. If the monastery is in play, and the kidnappers plan to escape to France, that would be the closest port."

"Beckworth, if he's in residence, would be the likely candidate." Ethan tapped the map where Waverly would be. "He's on our way, gets along with Jamie, and knows his tactics should the *Daphne* be moved. This kidnapper might have enough foresight to keep men watching the docks."

"Sounds like you have a plan." The earl rose. "Thomas, see to the men and have fresh horses provided to our travelers. I'll have footmen up to your rooms to collect your bags. When you're ready, meet me in the sitting room."

He shuffled out the door, and while his movements were slow and awkward, he hadn't lost the bearing of an earl. She might not have met him before, but having been around men of similar titles, and observing Ethan and Thomas around him, she could envision a younger version of the man with the same commanding presence of the older one.

An hour later, after heartfelt goodbyes, the group left the

manor. Thomas and his elite team rode with them until they crossed the river Severn, and Finn promised to meet them in Overton within four days' time.

Once Thomas was gone, this was their first opportunity to discuss the plan between them. But no one spoke until Finn turned to Ethan. "What do you think?"

"I didn't think the earl would be able to commit that many." Ethan stared down the road where Thomas's men had long disappeared. "But it won't be enough if Hensley and Beckworth are in London for the season."

Finn nodded and turned them southwest. Soon, the horses flew down the road and the landscape flashed by. The tension that had dissipated earlier eased back into AJ's shoulders and neck, her thoughts frenzied with renewed worry over Stella. She shook it off. Rather than agonize over something beyond her control, she leaned into the horse and focused on the road.

***

Before leaving Hereford, AJ had changed into pants for the ride to Bristol. She was grateful Finn insisted she keep up her riding skills back home. Not that she minded the extra alone time with him. And though she'd grumbled when he'd forced her on two day-long rides prior to the jump, without that added experience, she would have been an impediment to the group. Time in the saddle aside, she wasn't looking forward to the miles they had to cover in the next two days. She snorted. Where was a coach when you needed one?

They would overnight when it was time to give the horses a good rest. Wherever that was, it would be an evening with a campfire and a hard ground. Fortunately, Finn insisted they stop at inns for meals. No one would be searching for them this far west, and he wanted everyone nourished with warm meals if not a warm bed.

Maire enjoyed the ride and never complained, her mood uplifted by the adventure. She'd once confessed to AJ, while they'd both been Reginald's captives, that she'd be willing to sleep anywhere as long as it was under the stars. No one questioned her right to make up for lost time, but regardless of her smiles, she was still touchy whenever someone mentioned the stones or how well the incantation worked. She continued to blame herself for the lost two days, and nothing would change her stubborn mind until Stella was rescued.

They arrived at Hensley's estate late in the afternoon of the following day. The four horses pounded down the drive, only slowing when they reached the fountain in the circular drive. Stableboys ran toward them, probably having heard the fast-moving group approach. A minute later, Rodgers, Hensley's butler, stepped down to greet them, a group of footmen on his heels. He stopped to speak to Finn, but they were too far away for her to hear what was said. Seconds later, Finn raced for the stairs, taking them two at a time.

"Will you be staying overnight?" Rodgers didn't seem fazed by the abrupt entrance.

Before anyone could answer, Mary's voice cut through the bustle of activity. "What excitement! I can't believe my eyes. I didn't think I'd ever see you all again." She raced toward the group. "Rodgers, why haven't the footmen taken their bags?"

"It's not his fault, Mary." AJ answered quickly before she considered Rodgers would have been able to speak for himself. But as Mary hugged her to the point of cutting off her air, she caught Rodgers's nod in her direction. A thank-you without a smile. Butlers.

"Sorry for the road dust," AJ continued. "We rode straight here from Hereford."

"Hereford. Without stopping?" She'd left AJ and was giving Maire a once-over. "You look so much healthier than the last time I saw you. Such a beautiful child."

Maire laughed. "I'm more than a child, but I'll take the compliment. We did have a short sleep."

"Well, now we must see to rooms and something warm to eat." She glanced at Ethan and was heading his direction when Hensley stepped next to him.

AJ smirked at Maire, who'd also noticed Ethan's relieved expression.

"Rodgers, I need Tommy. Quickly now."

The butler turned toward one of the stableboys, who was still holding reins while the footmen removed bags. He snapped his fingers, and the boy handed the reins to the boy next to him and raced toward the stables.

Shouts and commands floated from the stable as another lad, this one in his teens, raced toward them. Hensley gave the boy a note then waved for the rest of them to follow him inside. Before AJ disappeared through the front door, the first stableboy ran out with a frisky coal-black beast behind him. He'd barely handed the reins to Tommy before the lad jumped into the saddle and nudged the horse. They were flying down the drive as the front door shut behind her.

Hensley waited in the foyer with Finn. He gave Mary a nod only a wife could understand.

"I'll see to your rooms and have cook prepare a lunch service." Without another word, Mary bustled off.

Something twisted in AJ's stomach. She'd never seen Mary leave so abruptly. They were supposed to be a surprise, yet Hensley hadn't seemed that shocked to see them. She glanced to Finn, but he wore his poker face, and it irritated her that most times she still couldn't read past it.

Hensley cleared his throat. "Let's go to my study."

He waited for the four of them to find a seat in the spacious room before taking his own in a leather wing chair. Gentle flames flickered in the hearth, leaving the room pleasantly warm. The faint scent of cigar lingered, hinting where Hensley had spent most of the day. When AJ spotted the short stack of envelopes at the corner of his desk, the inkpot still open, she absently nodded at her correct guess.

"Should we be concerned about the young lad who just raced off?" Ethan asked what AJ had wondered.

"We'll get to that, but first I'd like to hear your story. I predict, if you don't mind me saying, that once again trouble follows you." Hensley rested his hands across his stomach, no larger but not any smaller than the last time she'd seen him, which would have been seven months ago in this timeline.

"And as always, your prediction is correct." Finn leaned forward, an elbow resting on the armrest. "Several days ago, based on our timeline, someone came for the Heart Stone. They appeared through the fog while the four of us were away. Unfortunately, a good friend of ours was at the inn at the time, and we believe she was mistaken for AJ. They took her and disappeared back into the mist."

Hensley didn't move, but his brows lifted a fraction when Finn mentioned Stella being taken. Finn pulled the kidnapper's note out of his jacket pocket and leaned over to hand it to his mentor.

Hensley nodded as he read. "Did you use this incantation?"

It wasn't the first question AJ expected, but it would have come up at some point.

"No." Finn glanced at Maire but decided to take on the role of spokesperson for the group. "I wanted to arrive earlier than the date on the note. Maire studied her notes and was able to create a different incantation. We weren't sure it would work, but we landed pretty much where we wanted."

"Two days too late," Maire muttered as a reminder to the group she was still buried in self-recrimination.

"What was your destination?" Hensley stood and fussed with his waistcoat before placing five glasses and a bottle of Jameson on the table in front of the sofa. There were plenty of reasons for having Jameson on hand, yet AJ's gut said Hensley had been expecting them.

"Hereford," Ethan chimed in. "We'll need men, and I'd hoped the earl could be persuaded to help."

"And was he?" Hensley finished pouring and handed out the glasses.

"He agreed without any convincing." Ethan smiled, obviously pleased the earl had his back.

Hensley settled back in his seat, the glass of whiskey perched on his stomach. "He knows the dangers of the stones. The question now is how did someone else discover their secret, or did we leave someone alive we shouldn't have?"

"We rode like hell to get here," Finn said. "The meeting is only three days away, but it was imperative to inform you of the situation and see if you knew where the *Daphne Marie* might be. We aren't planning to cross the Channel with the war still on, but..." He shrugged. "It seems we always end up at the monastery." He sat back, took a long sip of his whiskey, and waited for Hensley.

The man stared into the flames while he turned his glass in a circle, first one way and then the other. He always seemed to carry the weight of the world on his shoulders. "The lad you saw leave is one of my best riders, so I only send him out on emergencies. He's the only one that can handle that damn stallion, and the only one I'd trust with him." He turned his attention back to his visitors. "Early this morning, I sent a message to

Jamie in Bristol. The *Daphne* is in port, and I had a new assignment for him. Just before you arrived, I received another courier with urgent information that overrode my earlier need for the ship, which I have no doubt is being prepared for departure as soon as the tide is favorable. So, Tommy would have been sent, one way or another, to deliver my request to hold sail until my arrival."

"We don't have the time." Finn rubbed his face.

AJ didn't see him get frustrated often. He would want to see Jamie, but a message would have to do if they were to reach Basingstoke in time.

Hensley set the whiskey down, and his expression turned grave. "I'm not sure the meeting will be happening."

"It has to." AJ couldn't help her high-pitched outburst. She'd pushed thoughts of Stella and what nightmare she must be living to the farthest corner of her mind, then forced herself to ignore it. That was the only way she could put one foot in front of the other. The only way to keep her perspective. And now it was cracking, bits of shard already crumbling away.

Finn squeezed her hand. "Breathe."

She sucked in air, but never took her pleading gaze from Hensley. "We have to get Stella back."

Hensley held up a hand while Finn put an arm around AJ and pulled her close. "The last time I've had these many dispatches in a single day was during our last bout with Reginald. If this were London during the season, it would seem strange without them arriving every hour. But out here, close to Bristol, it's quite the rarity. As I mentioned, the last messenger arrived an hour before your horses trampled down my drive and was my original reason for sending Tommy."

AJ bristled at his sidetracking until he gave her his full attention.

Her stomach rolled like the *Daphne* in a storm. "Just say it."

"The message was from Beckworth. Gemini or her men could be headed this way. He's on his way to Southampton with plans to sail to the monastery. And he has Stella."

158

14

———

Beckworth steered his horse down a narrow trail as they approached the small village, satisfied as the path skirted the quaint community. When he reached an old storage facility, he circled it before coming to a stop in a nearby copse.

He nudged Stella, who woke with a start.

"I'm okay." She sat up, looking a bit disoriented and glanced around. "Where are we?"

"A small hamlet. I think we'll be safe if we stay out of sight. Gemini's men wouldn't expect us to hide this close to a village."

"Are you sure? It wouldn't take them long to find us if they tried."

"True. But they can only guess how much of a head start we got. They'll ride fast, covering as much ground as possible, making assumptions on how far we might have traveled. Then they'll turn around and search more thoroughly."

"Squeezing us until they have us surrounded. Can I get down?" Her snappish tone surprised him, but she'd been in the saddle for longer than she was used to.

"Yes, of course." He dismounted then helped her down, holding her elbow when her legs gave way, but she quickly recovered. She didn't say anything when he led her farther into the trees with the horse trailing after them. He stopped next to a hedgerow. "Sit here."

She didn't argue and dropped like someone cut her strings. "I'm going to check things out in town, maybe see if men have already been through. I need you to stay here."

"Why can't I go with?"

She wouldn't make it ten feet. "It's too dangerous to light a fire, and you could use a hot meal."

She licked her lips, and he couldn't seem to pull his gaze away. "I wouldn't mind that. What do I do until you return?"

He grinned. "There's a reason I put you next to the bushes. You can lay down, roll under them, and get some sleep."

"Is that supposed to be funny?"

"From what I've seen, you seem to enjoy hiding in them."

"I'd rather have a weapon."

His humor drained away. "That's not something to be taken lightly."

"I agree. I take firearms quite seriously. You must have gotten a weapon while visiting your friend."

"That's not the point." Gemini had taken his sword, but he still had his blunderbuss and a dagger. Eleanor had a firearm, but he wouldn't think of leaving her defenseless. "You don't even know how to fire a flintlock."

She folded her arms across her chest, and even though she stared up at him from where she'd sprawled, she looked irresistibly formidable. "I watched Ethan load one when he was training with AJ. I just need a quick refresher."

He wasn't going to argue the finer points. The last thing he needed was gunpowder blowing up in her face. Assuming she didn't shoot him first. "We'll discuss it later. Will you promise to stay put?"

"Where would I go? Besides, I could use some sleep in a

horizontal position." She laid down, then scooted backwards under the bush.

"I'm leaving the horse here. If you leave him alone, he'll leave you alone."

"AJ never told me what a funny man you were. You can be assured the two of us will keep to our own company."

After a second glance back, he disappeared into the trees and raced behind the storage facility to enter the far end of the village. He worked his way toward the inn, maintaining a steady pace as he moved from building to building until he stopped behind a stack of crates near the smithy. The inn was across the lane and one door down. He hadn't seen anyone who might be one of Gemini's men, but there hadn't been many people out and no one seemed interested in him. After another long scan, he pulled up his collar and crossed the street.

The inn was smaller than most but otherwise similar in setup. A handful of customers filled tables near the hearth, but after a quick glance to see who'd come in, they all returned to their meals and conversations. Once he'd purchased breakfast and chatted up the innkeeper, giving him a long story about highwaymen and how he was on his way to London, he stepped out of the inn and hugged the wall as he studied each building. Dugan's men had been clever, and while those who survived had joined Gemini, it only took one long night of drinking with them to learn most of her gang were simple mercenaries. While they might be thick, it didn't make them any less dangerous.

He made a beeline for the tiny mercantile two buildings down from the storage facility while he juggled two mugs and a burlap bag. He strode past the store then ducked behind it. He stopped long enough to glance back. No one appeared to notice or follow him.

His pace slowed when he reached the copse. Birds chirped

and flitted from limb to limb, but other than his horse munching on the long grass, there were no other sounds.

Stella was well hidden under the shrubbery, and for as much teasing as he'd done, he had to give her credit for smart thinking. They made excellent cover. He found a spot near her but let her sleep while he arranged their breakfast.

Rich aromas floated from the opened burlap bag—warm bread, thick slices of bacon, and fried eggs. Within a couple of minutes, she stirred and rolled to one side to face him. Those vivid green eyes took a moment to focus, and she scanned her surroundings before she pinned her gaze on him, then the food.

She became a whirlwind of activity, crawling out from the bushes, leaves stuck in her hair, her overcoat caked with damp earth and twigs. She didn't bother standing as she inched her way over on hands and knees to settle next to him, her tongue running over roughened lips.

"Is that coffee?" Her voice was rough from sleep. Though she spent most of her time on horseback napping, she would need a solid evening of rest. They both did.

He handed her one of the mugs. "How long have you been in this time?"

She sat cross-legged and closed her eyes as she took her first sip. Her face scrunched with displeasure. He agreed it wasn't the best coffee, and having been in her time, and knowing AJ's addiction to the brew, he'd wondered if Stella would have the same negative reaction. But she didn't say a word as she drank half of it down before cradling the mug in her lap, her attention moving to the food. She placed an egg between two slices of bacon and finished it off before he'd taken his second bite. She licked her fingers before tearing into the bread.

"Didn't they feed you?"

She glanced up, and her cheeks blushed. Even through the

dirt-stained face, he couldn't remember seeing anything quite so lovely.

"Three times a day, but it was always hard bread, partially moldy cheese, and jerky. I didn't bother to ask what the jerky was from." She set the food down and grabbed her mug with both hands. "I barely got any water." She touched her cracked lips, no doubt a bit dehydrated, which might explain her fatigue. "But coffee? Other than the dregs they left me the first morning, this is the first since I've arrived. Maybe this—" she lifted the mug and took a sip, "—will stop the headaches."

"Headaches?"

She nodded as she pulled another piece of bread apart. "When you drink as much caffeine as I do, and then it's abruptly taken away, you can get headaches. For me, they last three or four days."

"Another coffee addict?"

She stared at him for a moment, then smiled. A generous, carefree grin that he'd bet she did regularly back home. It was the first one he'd seen on her, and if she'd taken his breath away before, this time, he might need someone to thump his chest to get his lungs working again.

"I forgot how much time you spent with AJ. Coffee is only one of the things we have in common."

"Don't tell me. Wine being the second."

"You must be Beckworth if you know her that well," she teased. Her gaze moved to the last piece of bacon.

"Go ahead. I've eaten more recently."

She nibbled at the bacon while cleaning up their debris, stuffing everything back in the bag. "What's next? We're only two or three days from the meeting."

"If I only knew where that might be. Gemini was tight-lipped about the location, and while I plied her men with alcohol before stealing you away, I thought someone might slip up. But I don't think anyone other than her and Gaines knows where they're to meet Murphy."

Her earlier exuberance faded as her serious look returned—all narrowed eyes and thinning lips. He plucked a twig out of her hair before she had a chance to slap his hand away.

She scowled, but ran a hand through her unkept hair, picking out more errant leaves. "Isn't that where AJ and Finn should arrive?"

"Maybe."

"Gaines left an incantation. The one he used wasn't completely accurate but seemed close enough."

He nodded. "I've been thinking about that. Didn't you say Maire and Hughes were still in the future?"

"Yes."

"You haven't time traveled before or spent time chasing the books or the stones like the rest of us, but you're a smart woman. What's your take on Maire's knowledge of the stones?"

She finished her coffee, and checking to find he'd finished his, she plucked a handful of grass and used it to dry out the mugs before placing them in the sack. "I think she knows those books almost as well as the druids. You think she'll modify the incantation."

"Possibly. If she has the proper notes to guide her."

"She has Sebastian's journals as well as her notes, and..." She hesitated, then shrugged. "Well, she's modified them before."

He studied her as she set the bag to the side then made herself busy cleaning the mud from her coat. It seemed there was more she didn't feel comfortable sharing, still not trusting his intent. He understood. If AJ didn't trust him as he thought she had, his words would have no effect on Stella. Only his actions, and thinking of AJ again, maybe not even then. It was possible his time with the duke had left an irrevocable stain.

He ignored the tightening in his chest and repositioned

himself to a spot farther away from her. "Since we don't know what Maire will do with the incantation, we don't know when or where they will arrive. If I know Murphy, he'll want to be here well before the meeting."

"To get help."

He nodded. "Without a hostage, Gemini will still go to the meeting spot, expecting Murphy. But if he gets my message, he might not bother."

"What message?"

"When I went for supplies, I gave Eleanor a message to send to Hensley."

"Because that's where he'd go if he had the time." She tugged at her hair. "Then why don't we go there?"

"Gemini knows Murphy worked for Hensley as I do now, and she'll have sent men, assuming she didn't have them stationed there in the first place. She's too unpredictable, and by taking you, I've disturbed the hornet's nest. I don't know if she's given orders to capture or kill, and I can't take the risk."

"But that would put AJ and Finn in danger."

"Possibly, but they'll be well armed and expecting trouble. With any luck, they'll be gone before Gemini's men arrive."

"Gone where? I thought you said they wouldn't go to the meeting."

He nodded. "With any luck, they'll be on their way to Southampton."

"Now I'm lost."

"Not to worry. I'll explain on our way." He stood and grabbed the burlap bag. After rearranging items in the saddlebag, he dropped a package in front of her. "This should help you blend in more. You can change behind the trees, but give me your coat first. I need to make it look—not so foreign."

She grumbled as she removed the coat but didn't say anything else as she opened the package to find a pair of pants and a shirt. He'd originally requested a dress, but with her inexperience with horses, riding sidesaddle seemed dangerous. She wasn't gone long before she reappeared holding her pants up with one hand and her soiled clothes with the other. They were too large and, based on the rolled-up bottoms, too long as well. The shirt, while also ill-fitting, would be close enough, especially with her coat over it.

"Here, I brought you boots. Let me get you something to tighten the pants. I'm afraid that was all Eleanor had. I didn't think a dress appropriate for riding." He handed her the boots in exchange for her soiled clothes, then added them to the saddlebag before removing rope, from which he cut a section.

Stella took off her old boots. Under the dust and mud, they appeared to have been a dark red. She stared mournfully at her broken shoes, sighing as she glanced down at the stodgy ones Beckworth had brought for her.

"If it helps, they were very nice boots."

His words seemed to startle her, and, for an instant, moisture filled her eyes before she blinked. He tossed her the rope then turned away. "I think it would be best to hide them under the bushes. Your feet will do better in the ones I brought you."

She had stuffed the boots under a bush and was tying the rope to hold up her pants when the sound of hooves broke the peaceful morning. Beckworth grabbed her and pulled her to the ground. He didn't cover her mouth, the fear in her gaze was enough to know she wouldn't say anything.

"Stay put," he whispered. "I'm only going to the edge of the trees to get a better look." He waited until she nodded.

He crouched as he crept to the trees, quietly pushing through the surrounding bushes. Four horses had stopped in front of the inn. Three burley men were still in their saddles and scanned the area. Beckworth barely breathed, not wanting them to catch the movement of leaves or branches. A few minutes later, the fourth man stepped out from the inn and mounted. They chatted for a moment, and Beckworth assumed they were discussing the tale he'd given the innkeeper. Would they believe it?

After another minute, the four men kicked their mounts and raced out of the village, heading north toward London.

He scurried back and untied his horse, glancing around for signs they'd been there, but Stella was already kicking dirt over where she'd crawled out from under the bushes then ran her boot over where they'd sat, encouraging the grass to straighten. He'd have to make a point to ask if she'd been on the run before. She seemed rather adept at it.

Without asking questions, she waited for Beckworth to check the saddle before he helped her up. He kept the horse to a walk as they left the copse and worked their way south of the village, keeping an eye on the road behind them.

Assured he didn't hear returning horses, or anyone paying them any attention, he nudged the horse to a trot for a mile before breaking into a full gallop. The men might not go far before considering they'd been given false information, or they could ride all the way to London. Not wanting to take a chance, he leaned over, forcing Stella low over the horse's neck, and urged the beast faster.

15

Beckworth kept a fast pace after leaving the village, but whichever road he selected, and whenever he found a spot to rest, they were soon forced to move on or change direction. At their first stop, he'd barely retrieved the food Eleanor had provided before four horses, riding hard, raced by on the road. He couldn't be sure if they were the same men who'd stopped at the inn that morning, but he kept their break to a minimum.

He backtracked to a more westerly route before turning south again. At their next stop, they moved farther into the dense foliage, but when he heard horses, he crept through the trees in time to catch sight of two men moving slower and scanning the landscape—searching. Maybe not for them, but he had to consider it a probability. Gemini seemed to have men everywhere. Did she have that many men to cover all his possible routes, or had she risked sending most of them south, anticipating his move? It was too late to turn back. Her men could be anywhere by now, and there were still several ways to reach the coast and find a ship, though the less known points meant smugglers. But that was preferable to Stella falling into Gemini's hands.

When they were forced to double back for a third time, they passed through a small hamlet he'd been to several years before and an idea struck. Stella would probably complain all night, but they'd be safe and warm.

"We can't keep doing this. It's two steps back for every step forward." Her tone reflected his own dour mood, and he couldn't argue her perspective.

He glanced down as he skirted the horse around the village and noted for the first time the four small braids in its mane. Stella worked her fingers through the hair before separating strands to start another one. Once she completed it, she gave the horse a gentle scratch before gathering another section.

"I'm familiar with this area, and I know a place where we can get a good night's sleep. Then I'll determine our next steps."

"Should I feel comforted by that? It seems like we're just going in circles. This rescue wasn't planned out very well."

He couldn't remember the last time a woman left him speechless. She'd seemed compliant enough after breakfast, but her irritability grew after each stop. Perhaps it was the headache she'd mentioned earlier. She obviously required more coffee, but he made an attempt to appease her.

"I admit, I'm a bit perplexed by the number of men we've run into. While I can't be certain they're Gemini's men, it would be foolish to consider otherwise. And while the route might change, we still have a variety of options to reach our final destination."

"I don't think you mentioned where that is."

"Didn't I?"

"No." The word couldn't sound any more final.

"Hmm. Well, I think it best we wait until we get to our evening stop. Then we can have a good chat over a fire."

"We'll be able to have a fire?"

He smiled at the immediate improvement in her tone. That was better. "Yes. Without any worry about being seen."

She snorted. "I don't suppose you have marshmallows in that saddlebag of yours?"

"No." Blasted women.

An hour later, he led them up a small trail. Stella nestled against him, and with her soft trembling, he assumed the closer contact was to escape the bite in the air. But the higher they climbed, he couldn't miss her growing tension.

Twilight had descended when he stopped next to the base of a craggy hill. The darkening sky revealed nothing but several groupings of trees surrounded by brush with early spring growth.

"Where are we?" She leaned back into him, though her body was rigid.

"Our evening abode. I know it doesn't look like much, but this is just the outside." He dismounted and haphazardly tied the reins to the low branch of a tree. "Stay on the horse while I make sure we're alone."

"I wouldn't think Gemini's men would be waiting for us up here."

"They're not my concern."

"Oh."

After checking the perimeter, he glanced up to view what he could of the rocky hill, scanning for the telltale signs of fissures. A three-foot-wide opening, partially hidden by scrub brush at the base, ran up the rock face, narrowing the higher it went. He considered walking inside, but with the darkening skies, he had to ensure this wasn't some animal's home.

Stella stood next to the horse and stroked its neck as she watched him. He couldn't decide between being pleased by how quickly she'd grown comfortable with the animal or irritated she hadn't paid attention to his instructions. He gathered wood from the surrounding area and piled it close to the entrance. He used his flint to light the tips of a branch to use as a torch.

He returned to the crevice and stuck the flaming torch inside. Nothing scurried about or growled, so he took that as a good sign. There weren't any tracks other than his, nor was there any scat. He stepped inside and lifted the flaming branch. The cave was twenty feet in diameter. Plenty of room. He walked the perimeter, keeping an eye on where the smoke went. The last time he'd been in one of these caves, which would have been several years ago, the smoke traveled upward to an open gap. In this particular den, the smoke disappeared about ten feet up. He'd lucked out on his first try. Maybe good fortune was turning their way.

He dropped the torch in the middle of the space and hustled outside to retrieve more wood. Once he had a good-sized pile, he added dry leaves and smaller branches to the fire until he'd built a strong flame. He turned to find Stella standing in the entrance.

She held several items in her arms and when she noticed him staring at her, she shrugged. "I thought I could help." She glanced around the cave. "There's not much room in here."

"More than enough for two."

She gave the space another scan, then took a hesitant step.

"Is there a problem?"

She shook her head. "It's just a bit small." Her voice was barely audible, and she focused on the fire.

Could she be scared of confined spaces? First horses and now tight places. A distraction was in order.

"Is the horse still here?" His tone was light, and he held back a grin.

She gave him an eye roll before her lips twitched. "He's fine. I think he likes me."

"He does fancy the ladies."

She studied him long enough to make him wonder what she

was thinking, but then she turned back to the fire. "I wasn't sure what to bring without knowing how long we'd be here."

"We'll overnight here. I know the accommodations aren't ideal."

"They'll do." She set down blankets and the bundle of food before placing a branch on the fire. Then she added another one crosswise before tossing in more leaves. The fire sparked to life again, lighting her face in a golden glow.

"Have you camped out before?"

She shook her head. "A couple times when I was a kid, but I've built many a fire on the beach."

"If you can keep that going, I'll bring in the rest of the supplies." He strode to the entrance, then turned to make sure she'd heard him. She stared into the flames, already miles away.

When he returned with both saddlebags, she'd made a makeshift sleeping area halfway between the entrance and the back of the cave. He'd prefer if she slept farther toward the back, but with her discomfort in small spaces, having the entrance close would lessen her anxiety.

She was sitting up, her head down as she played with something in her lap.

He dropped the bags near the fire. "What are you doing?" When he stepped closer, he wasn't sure what to make of it. She was folding a piece of paper, her fingers moving quickly, until she held up a small figure.

"What is it?"

"What does it look like?"

He held out his hand. "May I?"

She gave it to him, and he held it up to the firelight and turned it this way and that.

"It looks like a swan."

She grinned. "Well, thank the stars. I've folded that paper a dozen times already—probably more—and it's impacting my results. The wings won't hold their form. I need more paper."

"How did you know how to fold it like this? Can you do other forms?"

She smiled as if she had a secret. "It's a Japanese art form called origami. I seem to have a knack for it. And yes, there are dozens of shapes, but I prefer birds and fish.

He handed the swan back to her. "So, how did you get that bruise?"

She rubbed her jaw, winced, then shrugged. "Jessup and I didn't agree on a particular matter."

Based on his brief chats with Gemini's men, he had some idea of what the disagreement was about, but it wasn't his place to pry. "I'm sorry you had to go through that."

She lifted her head, satisfaction glowed from her eyes, and she gave him a bitter grin. "He only tried once."

He nodded his respect and decided to leave it at that. It had been obvious early on that while she might be out of her element in this time period, she hadn't lost her wits and retained a healthy sense of survival. He added two logs to the fire, waited for the flames to rise, then made up his own bed for the evening. Once he settled, he noticed Stella unfolding the swan, then once the paper was flat, she turned it and began folding from a different angle.

"So, AJ didn't have many good things to say about me." Beckworth didn't pose it as a question and meant it more as a conversation starter. He caught her cringe, and he chastised himself for bringing it up. Just because it bothered him, there was no reason to make Stella uncomfortable with his own insecurities. When they met up with AJ, he would ask her directly.

"I wouldn't go that far." She tossed her hair back, gave him a quick glance, then went back to the swan. "She mentioned you knew quite a few street urchins in London."

He tilted his head, not sure he'd heard that right. It was an odd statement, and he couldn't fathom how that conversation would have come about. Perhaps AJ had recounted their run through the streets of London in an attempt to catch up with Reginald, his now dead half-brother. At least she was talking. "It's no secret I grew up on the streets of London and still have many good friends there." He couldn't help giving her a grin when she glanced over. "I could find my way around the city with my eyes closed simply by the different smells."

She wrinkled her nose. "That couldn't possibly have been pleasant."

He barked out a surprised laugh. "In many cases, you are quite correct." He tugged at his sleeves then leaned back against the cave wall, pulling a knee up and resting an arm over it. The memories spurred a melancholia for the old days. "But they weren't all bad. There were Mrs. Brubaker's meat and potato pies you could smell two blocks away. And, of course, the flower vendors in Whitechapel. I would walk until I was in the middle of them then take a deep breath." He tilted his head back, closed his eyes, and inhaled. "You could tell what month it was by which fragrance was the strongest. My favorite month was May."

"Lilacs?"

His eyes opened, and he regarded her. "Yes. Lilacs."

She puffed up the blanket that would be her pillow and laid on her side, head propped on her hand. "My garden has two lilac trees. They're both purple and put out the most heavenly scent. I fill vases with them in both my home and office."

His interest piqued, he urged her on. "You have a garden?"

Her smile was filled with a mixture of emotions—pleasure, longing, and maybe satisfaction. "It's a wonderful garden. I try to keep a variety, but I have my favorites. It took me two seasons before I managed the right selection to produce blooms from the first of spring through the end of fall. Though I've been lucky to find two species that provide winter flowers."

"Marvelous. I wish there was time for you to see the gardens of Waverly before you leave." He straightened his shoulders and lifted his chin. "I think they would pass muster with a fellow garden aficionado."

She laughed. "I'll admit, Maire and AJ both mentioned how lovely your gardens are."

"Really?" He beamed with pride, and she gave him a lovely smile before something he couldn't name flashed in her eyes and she dropped her gaze to the fire.

Silence grew, but neither seemed bothered by it. After several minutes, and for a reason he couldn't explain other than it was a moment they had both shared, or maybe he was overly tired, he confessed, "I remember seeing you in Baywood."

She sat up. "What?"

"Baywood. While I was there."

She stared at him for moment, her gaze unfocused. No doubt trying to recall the incident. "You mean when AJ and I went to that restaurant? You were there, right? AJ thought she saw you crossing the street."

At first, he couldn't remember the moment, then it came to him. "By the antique store."

"How did you know to use me to find her?"

"What do you mean?"

"You put a tracker on my car."

"Ah."

She'd caught him off guard, but as much as it pained him, he understood why it might be her first thought. He'd still been the enemy back then.

"I admit I was a bit crazed at the time, living with two nutty sisters, and wondering if I'd ever get home. When I saw you with AJ, I immediately recognized you."

She appeared perplexed. "Recognized me?"

He gave her his best don't kid a kidder look. "Come now. I'd been in Baywood for three months by then. You don't think I saw the advertisements with your saucy smile and fabulous auburn hair plastered all over town and not recognize you?"

It was difficult to tell in the firelight, but she might have blushed. "Good grief. It makes me sound a bit egotistical."

"The only thing I saw was a woman taking a chance by putting herself out there as one of the best. In this time, that simply isn't done, and it's a shame it's taken so many years before becoming fashionable." He frowned. "That isn't quite the right word."

She snorted. "No, but I get what you're saying. And you took the chance that following me would lead you back to AJ?" When he nodded, she chewed her lip. "Where did you think to find a tracker? Hell, how did you even know to do that?"

"The sisters thought of it. A GPS system I believe they called it. Louise talked one of the neighbors into loaning it to her, or maybe he gave it to her. To be honest, I hadn't paid much attention to her rambling until she mentioned I could track someone with it." His melancholy returned. "It was a difficult time for me, but Louise and Edith weren't that bad. They took me in, after all."

Stella laid on her back and stared at the ceiling, and he considered letting the topic drop, but something made him persist. "The day I was remembering was when I found the note on the moped."

She rolled back to her side but didn't respond.

"I didn't realize until recently that you meant to cause a distraction. I'd been frustrated at not finding AJ's vehicle and had been turning away."

"The letter hadn't been delivered yet, and by then, we knew

about the trackers. I was worried you'd walk away too soon, and I couldn't think of anything else that might slow you down."

"Who was that man you were with?"

She squinted as if replaying the scene. "You mean Adam? That's AJ's brother."

He held her gaze, unable to look away. "I can remember what you wore."

She blurted out a chuckle. "Yeah, right. I can't even remember that."

"It was an orange and pink wrap over a sunny yellow dress. And you wore matching shoes the color of sunflowers. I think Louise said they were called high heels, which I suppose makes sense."

She stared at him with an awed expression. "That was exactly what I was wearing."

He'd said too much. It had been a foolish thing to do. He stood. "I should make sure we're still alone. Get some sleep. I want to start early." He never turned back before slipping out, but he felt her gaze follow him until he stepped out into the cold night. Something had fundamentally shifted. The responsibility for keeping her safe outweighed his own welfare, but he convinced himself it was nothing more than an inherent debt he owed AJ.

16

"What do you mean he has Stella?" AJ's words were cold and deliberate. What the hell was going on? How had Beckworth become involved in this? He would know the incantation, and he still had one of the smaller stones. Yet she couldn't think of any reason he'd willingly get involved with the trouble the stones created.

"I've come to recognize that look." Hensley's gaze was shrewd, but she held his stare. "It's not what you think. He hasn't betrayed you. While on another assignment, he was contacted by someone claiming to be Gemini."

AJ relaxed, and she took a deep breath as the band clamped over her lungs released. Of course, he hadn't betrayed them. She trusted him. It just didn't make sense how he could have ended up with Stella or why he decided to go to the monastery.

"We've heard the name Gemini before." Ethan brought a chair over and sat next to Maire. "Some type of information seller, if I remember correctly. Did you say Gemini was a woman?"

Hensley nodded. "Yes, on both counts." Maire huffed from the corner, and Hensley chuckled. "I do remember someone mentioning Gemini might be a woman. Beckworth and I laughed about it during his Christmas party. Anyway, we believed Gemini might have been the source that inspired Reginald to take up where the duke left off."

"Why would this person contact Beckworth?" Finn shook his head when a knowing spark lit his gaze. "Of course. He knows about the stones."

"I don't have all the details," Hensley continued. "But his assignment might have encouraged Gemini to seek him out. I can't tell you the goal of his original mission, but his role was to convince certain parties that he was a double agent, pretending to work for me while gathering information for others."

"Similar to what Gemini is so good at," Maire volunteered.

"Exactly." Hensley's expression changed, and his shoulders slumped. "We knew very little about Gemini, believing him to live in the shadows, using others to move his information around. Though whether his goal was mere financial gain or something sinister..." He shrugged. "The main point is that while he was on our radar, we weren't actively pursuing him. As it turns out, Gemini is a woman, who seems to have built a network almost as impressive as mine.

"Beckworth was told not to investigate Gemini, but that changed after I received a letter from him almost a fortnight ago. He'd been abducted by someone claiming to be Gemini, who wanted him to consult on something the Duke of Dunsmore had been working on. They heard he was in the information business, which only demonstrated how well Beckworth was performing his assignment. They promised to contact him when they were ready to proceed with their plans. And to prove how insidious they are, they claimed to have a mole at Waverly. Fortunately, Beckworth, being more devious than most, was able to send a letter explaining this latest development without anyone being the wiser. His decision, which I would have agreed with had I been able to voice it, was to play along."

"And you believe this Gemini traveled to the future and took Stella?" Finn's jaw ticked, and AJ sensed his earlier frustration was turning to anger.

"More likely someone in her employ." Hensley's upper lip curled. "She doesn't seem the sort to get her hands dirty. You also need to know that Beckworth and I met Gemini without realizing it. In fact, so did Jamie and Fitz." Then he mumbled under his breath, "Especially Fitz."

AJ stifled a snort. Not the most likely candidate, but she'd always suspected Fitz carried a special bad boy appeal for some women.

"Anyway," Hensley continued, "we met her at the holiday gathering I mentioned earlier. Several noblemen and their wives were present, including a Lady Penelope Prescott, who we believed had traveled with the Singletons, although we later determined that was a fabrication. I thought you should know, should you run across her in disguise."

"So, how did Beckworth end up with Stella?" Ethan redirected the conversation back to what they all wanted to know.

Hensley scratched his stomach and looked a bit chagrined. "According to Beckworth, he rescued her."

***

Hensley's words echoed in Finn's head. Beckworth had rescued Stella. On the surface, this was good news. His actions removed Stella from an unpredictable and dangerous trade with Gemini, especially when the exchange was on the captor's turf. But from the intelligence information Hensley had shared, this wouldn't resolve the issue with someone searching for the Heart Stone and might have made the situation worse.

Gemini was a planner and a woman. A dangerous combination he'd faced before when involved with one or two of Hensley's missions. From his experience, when someone screwed with their plans, everything become downright treacherous. And the one item Gemini required to ensure the retrieval of the Heart Stone—her hostage—had just been taken from her.

"Where's the Heart Stone from this time period?" He should have asked earlier, but it had to be in a secure location to force Gemini to use time travel.

"In Buckingham Palace." Hensley responded without hesitation. "Beckworth handed it over to Langford a month after his return to Waverly. I received confirmation from Langdon a fortnight later stating it was in a safe location within the palace. Only one other person knows its location."

"Don't tell me. Beckworth." Ethan received disbelieving stares from the women, but Finn knew better.

Hensley shrugged. "He required Beckworth's assistance with the hiding spot. I have no idea what that means, and Beckworth pretends he has no idea what Langdon is talking about and mutters about the war making him mad as a hatter. Either way, I don't think we need to worry about it for another few years when he's promised to return it to Elizabeth."

One issue they wouldn't have to worry about, but as Finn glanced around Hensley's study, another concern developed. They were only a handful against how many? Hensley retained a small team of well-trained men, but Finn wasn't convinced it would be enough if Gemini's men were on their way. "How many men does Gemini have?"

"You think she'd actually come here?" Ethan asked, then stood to pace a short path between his chair and the door before answering his own question. "Of course not. She would send men instead, hoping to catch up to Beckworth and Stella on the way."

"Mary is already packing for the London season." Hensley response was no different than someone suggesting they leave in advance of stormy skies.

Finn jumped from his seat. "She should pack light. Have the rest of her trunks brought later." He raced into the hall in search of Rodgers.

Ethan followed behind him. "What else has you worried?"

"Gemini appears to be a planner. If she was the one spurring Reginald, she's spent months, maybe years, plotting."

"You think she already has men here."

"Aye, maybe before she sent someone to the future."

"Expecting us?"

"No." He stopped in the foyer, glancing around, not having the first idea where Rodgers would be. He stared at Ethan, suddenly remembering their conversation. "I think Gemini might want to keep an eye on her enemies, just in case. I know Hensley wants to go to the ship to discuss options with Jamie, but he and Mary need to get to London, and they'll require guards. They can be our decoy."

"If she has men here, they wouldn't know who we are."

Finn headed toward the stairs that led to the basement where Rodgers and the housekeeper kept offices. "They might think we're part of Hensley's spy network with helpful information. Hensley said multiple messengers have come and gone all day. It's impossible to predict what anyone would make out of that."

Ethan chuckled. "I'm living part of it and still can't grasp it myself."

Finn couldn't argue the sentiment. He'd just reached the stairs when a voice called from behind.

"Can I help you, sir?" Rodgers stood at the end of the hall, his hands clasped behind his back as if he'd been standing there for hours.

"I believe Hensley still has the spare coach he uses when his newer one isn't available. We'll need a team of four ready to depart for Bristol in an hour. Hensley's coach will leave at the same time. He'll require his entire guard to escort him to London. They are to remain with the coach at all times, and not let Hensley or Mary out of their sights. Do you understand?"

Rodgers's demeanor transformed from stuffy butler to Sergeant of Arms within a single breath. "Will you be in the carriage, or do you need two horses?"

Finn considered his options. Then a fond memory triggered a new possibility, and he gave Ethan one of his more dangerous grins. "Remember that trip from Bart's when AJ had been injured?"

"The highwaymen?"

"Aye." Finn turned back to Rodgers.

"Say no more, sir. I'm aware of the story. I'll have your weapons loaded in the coach as well as two loaded muskets with the coachman. He's a steady shot. Although I believe an additional man with the coachman would be best."

Finn smiled and squeezed Rodger's arm. "Good man." Before turning away, another thought occurred to him, but he wanted to ask Hensley first. "Thank you, Rodgers."

The butler bowed his head. "Lunch is being served in the dining room. It will only be a small respite, but the nourishment should see you safely to Bristol." Then he disappeared into one of the side rooms.

"Is there anything else we can do?" Ethan asked, his brows knit in concentration. The man was as tired as he was. It was easy to see in the dark shadows under his eyes and his slumped shoulders.

He grabbed Ethan around the shoulders and turned them

toward the stairs leading to the second floor. "Let's take time to get cleaned up, then get the women to the dining room. I'd like to get their opinion of Gemini."

Ethan trudged up the stairs, his face more dour with each step he took. "We thought we had it bad with two women. Now there are four involved."

Finn stopped long enough to give him a long stare. "Four?"

"Stella."

"What does she have to do with it, other than requiring a rescue?"

"You must be utterly exhausted to say that. Remember who our girl is, and who she's with."

Finn sighed. "Chaos. That's what we can expect. Utter chaos."

The team gathered around the carriages as they waited for Mary to finalize items with the housekeeper. AJ kept on eye on Finn, whose blank expression conflicted with his clenched jaw as footmen scurried to load more trunks. He'd wanted to leave an hour earlier when the carriages were ready, but Hensley refused to be rushed, forcing everyone back to their rooms for a short rest before completing a leisurely hot meal.

The extra time allowed the group to review their plans, but she'd hoped for a longer rest. At least the ride to Bristol would be short and there would be time to sleep on the *Daphne* once they set sail.

When Mary came down the steps, followed by two lady's maids, Finn's sigh was audible. Hensley, who'd also been watching Finn, patted him on the shoulder.

"What was the one thing I always counseled in your younger days?"

"Patience," he muttered.

"Those men, if they're out there, aren't going anywhere if they've seen the number of messengers today. An hour won't change the outcome."

Finn released a long sigh, and his features relaxed. "Aye. Someday I'll be as wise as you."

Hensley barked out a laugh. "Perhaps wise, but your Irish blood will always demand immediacy."

Finn shook his head, but his ready grin was genuine. "There's no arguing that." And with a graciousness that was most likely urged by guilt for his impatience, he reached Hensley's carriage before the footman. "Allow me." He opened the door as Mary approached.

Before she stepped in, she embraced him with a fierce hug. "Everything will turn out, and you'll get your friend back. We might even see you in London. Our homes are always open to you and your friends." She tugged out a hankie and dabbed at her eyes. "I do so hate saying goodbye to you, never knowing if this is truly the last time."

"We appreciate your hospitality and friendship. And where the stones are concerned, one never knows what the future holds." He winked, kissed her cheek, which created a lovely blush, then assisted her into the coach.

He shook hands with Hensley, who pulled him close. A few whispered words were shared, but AJ couldn't read her husband's face to know whether it was a heartfelt goodbye or new information he needed to know.

Before she could ask him, Ethan steered her to their coach, and she climbed in, plopping next to Maire, who was already priming her rifle and musket. She reached for her bow and set the quiver in the corner for easier access. Her nerves, already on edge, weren't comforted as they usually were when she reached into her pants pocket to squeeze the Heart Stone. Convinced they would settle once they were on the move, she reached for Maire's hand and was relieved when she received a strong squeeze in return.

When the wheels began to turn, the women hung out the windows to catch sight of two supply wagons that pulled ahead of the coaches. Both wagons had two men on the bench, one driving and the other with a musket. The same as the carriages. In the back of the open wagons, a large canvas had been spread to shield the cargo underneath.

When the convoy reached the end of the drive, the wagons and carriages picked up speed. The first wagon turned right with Hensley's carriage close behind along with ten armed guards on horseback. AJ and Maire ducked back in, each grabbing onto a window ledge as their coach made a left turn at what AJ guessed was a speed just under the tipping over point. For a split second, she noted Finn spurring his mount within a few feet of the wheels before she was flung away from the window.

Once the conveyance straightened, they each reached for their weapon of choice. AJ knelt on the floor, an arrow nocked. Maire positioned her rifle on the window frame, the musket miraculously still on the bench across from them.

Their first hurdle was behind them with no sight of Gemini's men. At lunch, the group had discussed possible places where either coach could be attacked. The entrance to Hensley's estate was the obvious choice. After that, there were several places within a two-mile radius from the manor where dense foliage could hide men on horseback.

To be safe, the supply wagon would lead them to the docks in Bristol. Hensley's coach would follow the other wagon to the first busy village fifteen miles away. If there were no signs of trouble, Hensley would continue with his guards.

The coach maintained a solid pace for ten minutes with Finn and Ethan sticking close. The women relaxed but kept their weapons close, each focused on the landscape for any sign of trouble, neither speaking. They passed a narrow crossroad marked with nothing but a single elm tree and not a single rider in sight.

A couple miles farther on, the coachman yelled, "Riders!"

"And behind." The voice sounded like Finn's, but it was hard to tell as the carriage picked up speed.

Maire laid down her rifle and stuck her upper body out the window, checking in front and behind the coach. When she slid back in, she picked up the rifle and double-checked the pan. "It looks like two behind us. I couldn't see much with the wagon in front of us, but there might be four, maybe six men blocking the road. Possibly more in the trees."

AJ plucked three more arrows from the quiver and laid them within easy reach. "I hope our surprise works."

"And that everyone follows the plan so we don't fire on our own."

AJ's mouth went dry at the thought of hitting a friendly. She picked up her bow and nocked an arrow. Her gut twisted in anticipation of the next few moments.

Voices streamed through the window, but with the sound of the wheels and thundering hooves, she wasn't able to make anything out. Unable to resist, she stuck her head farther out the window, taking a quick glance behind and spotting the two riders Maire had mentioned, who were making every attempt to catch up.

When she turned to scan the front, her heart thumped against her ribs. Six men lined the road, their horses stomping back and forth as the men fought to hold them in place as the wagon and coach barreled toward them. She glanced back inside, but Maire had also stuck her head out.

The men blocking the road divided and split their forces to both sides of the road. When the wagon drew closer, the men on horses began firing just as the man on the coach bench did. Then the canvas in the back of the wagon flew back and four men, each holding a musket, rose and fired. A second musket waited for them while two men, braced against the front of the cart, quickly reloaded the weapons.

She ducked back in and drew her bow, loosing two arrows in rapid succession without a second thought as the sound of Maire's rifle rang through the coach. Within seconds, they were past the men, and she stuck her head out the window, searching for Finn. He was pressed low over his horse and appeared unharmed. The men blocking the road had scattered, a couple lay on the ground.

After a quarter mile, the landscape cleared of trees and the wagon slowed, forcing the carriage to do the same. Before stopping, the wagon turned to the left while the carriage made a right, creating their own blockade.

Finn and Ethan rode between the conveyances. They jumped from their horses, tying the reins loosely before climbing the carriage. The scrape of their weapons moved across the roof as they crawled to their positions.

The women positioned themselves in front of Maire's window and watched the road. They didn't have to wait long. Four men raced toward them, but when they drew near, they slowed before coming to a stop out of range of weapons fire.

"They wouldn't be foolish enough to come closer, would they?" AJ couldn't imagine anything Gemini could offer being worth riding into what would assuredly be their death. The men were outnumbered more than two-to-one with no cover.

"Men do strange things for money. But no, I think they're trying to make some point before heading back."

Just as Maire said, several minutes ticked by before they turned in unison to head back for their dead or injured. Maire released a sigh as AJ placed her unspent arrows back in their quiver. The coach rocked and boots scraped the side as the men jumped from the roof. The door swung open, and Finn stuck his head in.

"We don't think they'll be back, but the wagon will follow us to the docks. We'll keep a steady pace, but not as fast as before."

"What about Hensley?" AJ would be devastated if he or Mary were injured.

"We won't know until we reach Southampton. Hensley will most certainly send a messenger, but I doubt he had as many men to contend with, if any at all. My guess is when they saw the ten heavily armed guards, they decided to pluck the less protected carriage. And with the number of messengers in and out of Hensley's estate, the majority heading to Bristol, we seemed the safer bet. Now sit tight, and we'll be at the docks before you know it."

AJ couldn't help herself, and before he had a chance to step back, she grabbed his jacket and pulled him in for a quick kiss. "Stay safe, husband."

He grinned. "Will you ever get tired of saying that?"

"Never."

Then she pushed him back out the door and took her seat. She ignored Maire's smirk, preferring to maintain her vigil out the window as the group journeyed on. With the battle behind them, her focus returned to Stella and Beckworth, new fears for her friends increased. How many men were they running from? She closed her eyes, unable to imagine how Stella was faring, but after dredging up the worst possible scenarios, she turned from the window and rubbed her face. The activity from the last two days, this last chase into Bristol, and her worry over Stella had zapped the rest of her strength. To top it off, she pictured Stella and Beckworth in their own war with each other. Would the two of them kill each other before they made it to Southampton?

17

Stella woke before Beckworth. She had vague memories of him keeping the fire going through the night, but now nothing remained other than the glowing orange of a single log. At some point, he'd also replenished the stack of firewood. She pulled her blanket tight to fend off the chill and knelt to feed the fire, using a stick to stir up the embers. Satisfied with the growing flames, she surveyed the cave and their supplies.

She found a suitably flat rock and pushed it close enough for the fire to lick its edges. After digging through the saddlebag, she found a coffee pot, added coffee and water from one of the skins, then placed the pot on the rock to cook.

Through all that, Beckworth slept, and with nothing else to do until the scent of brewed coffee filled the air, she watched him. AJ had been right. He was a handsome man. More than that. He was beautiful. A face that would look good whether he was laughing, screaming mad, or sick as a dog.

After the last few days, as mad and terrified as she'd been, she'd kept her wits, and she had AJ to thank for that. Without the advantage of hearing her journey, she might still be curled up in that old farmhouse—or possibly dead if Gemini was truly bent on revenge for Dugan's death.

She depended on Beckworth for her safety until AJ and Finn caught up with them. For now, they were on the run, and she had to trust that his goals were the same as hers. Trust. There was that word again. He knew the players, he knew this time period, and was in a better position to predict what everyone would do. Except for Gemini. And from their first conversation, she knew the woman would be unpredictable. But wouldn't going to Hensley's be the better option? Yet, if AJ and Finn did go there, whenever they showed up in this timeline, they might already be gone before she and Beckworth arrived. They could end up chasing each other for months, always a step behind.

She glanced at Beckworth and tried not cringe at her single lie, making him think AJ didn't trust him. The hurt in his eyes when she'd made him doubt the opinion of someone he considered a friend plagued her. She was such an asshole.

From the first moment he'd seen her, he'd never divulged her identity. She might not agree with his plan, but as far as she could tell, he was trying to help. He might be playing some game, and if she spent her time second-guessing his motives, she might miss her opportunity to meet up with AJ and Finn. He said there was one place she would be safe, somewhere AJ would know to look. Her stomach wrenched. The stones. She had to remember this was all about the stones. Oh god. No. They were heading south to the coast. Was he taking her to the monastery?

Her stomach did a flip just thinking about a sea journey, and before she could work herself into a tizzy, the call of nature lured her out of the cave and into the frosty morning air. A light fog hung low in the trees, and she scanned the area before stepping out from the bushes that covered the cave opening. Only the chatter of birds greeted her, and she stayed close to the rocks that lined the cave system until she was far enough away to take care of business.

On the way back, she noted the horse appeared to be asleep, his head bowed toward the ground, one hoof flexed. Its ears perked as she stepped back toward the entrance, and she released a muffled cry when she was seized from behind. A hand covered her mouth as she was lifted and carried into the cave.

Once she was set back on her feet, she pushed Beckworth away. "What did you do that for?"

"At first, I wasn't sure it was you." He stepped back and ran a hand through his hair. "Then I might have been a bit overprotective. You shouldn't have left the cave."

She straightened her shirt and retied the rope holding her pants up. "I had to relieve myself, and I wasn't going to do it in here."

"Then you should have woken me. Anything could be out there." He flung a hand toward the entrance then stared at the pot sitting next to the fire. "You made coffee?"

"It's not ready yet. I just put it on. Besides, I checked the area for signs of strangers, and your horse didn't seem to be aware of any predator."

"You checked the horse?"

She busied herself with finding mugs. "To be honest, I didn't do that until I was on my way back to the cave."

He sat next to the fire and added another branch. "That was smart thinking, even belated. You seem to have a good sense for self-preservation. I'm sorry if I overreacted." He handed her a roll with cheese and jerky. "It's not much. We can go back to the village and get you something warmer."

She took the proffered food and nibbled at the cheese. They ate in silence until Stella checked the coffee pot, pouring a small amount in a cup before blowing on it to test it. Somewhat satisfied, she poured a small amount in both mugs, then set the pot back on the rock.

"It needs a few more minutes but this will warm us." She passed a mug to Beckworth. "What are your plans?"

He chewed a piece of jerky then swallowed it down with a sip of coffee. "I didn't realize how many men Gemini seems to have working for her. It could be the same men covering a similar search pattern, but I don't think so. I'm concerned she might have paid additional mercenaries to search for us, either to capture or report back. But..." He shrugged and took a bite of the bread.

"Just finish it. I'd rather know what trouble we're in rather than think everything is roses and unicorns."

"What? No rainbows?"

She barked out a laugh. "I think it will be a while before I see anything so comforting again." She sobered at the thought, then shook her head, already sorry for the duplicity of her next words. But she had to know for sure he wasn't playing her. "Just stay honest with me. It's the only thing I ask."

"And a simple enough request. I assumed she would expect us to flee to Hensley or the earl."

"Maybe she sent a few men in those directions but kept most of her gang south. She must have had a hunch on where you would go."

"I should have known it would take another woman to understand Gemini's motives."

"I'm not sure I know her motives, but doesn't everything happen at the monastery?"

He finished the mug and handed it to her, and she watched his expression as she filled both mugs. It never wavered, and her stomach churned.

"I can't go there."

His eyes narrowed. "Why not? Sebastian will protect you. I'm sure AJ told you there were dozens of secret tunnels."

"How do you know that's where AJ and Finn will go?"

"Because that was what I wrote in my note to Hensley." He leaned toward her. "Are you all right?"

She wiped the sweat from her brow. "I'm fine."

"You don't look it."

Was now the best time to tell him there was no way she was getting on any ship? "I think I need a change of food."

He took her leftovers and wrapped them up before stuffing them in a saddlebag. "Let's have more coffee, find some breakfast, and try again for Southampton."

"What about Gemini's meeting with Finn? She'll still want to make that, right?" She refilled the mugs then folded her blankets.

He considered her question. "She lost her bargaining chip, but it would be foolish not to have someone at the meeting place. But she'll likely send Gaines rather than go herself. That seems to be something she does regularly."

"And you're positive she didn't give you a clue as to where this meeting place is?"

He shook his head. "I tried to pry it out of her men, but they were clueless. And I would have picked up on anything she might have let slip. She's very careful."

"If Maire changed the incantation, and they arrived someplace else, do you think Finn would go to the meeting place?"

"It depends if he reaches Hensley after my message arrives. If they don't get my message, they'll have no choice other than to go, expecting to find you there. But if they got my message, they should head directly to Southampton.

When Stella quieted and turned to stare at the fire, Beckworth offered her a piece of encouragement.

"One thing I've learned about Murphy: Sooner or later, he

always shows up. Trust that his first thought is finding you."

She nodded. He was right. Eventually, they would find her, assuming she stayed alive that long. "I'll reiterate an earlier point. I need to learn how to handle a flintlock."

Beckworth tossed out the dregs of his mug and handed it to Stella. He picked up a canvas bag he'd used as a pillow and stuffed it in the saddlebag.

Stella stood to clean out the coffee pot, but her pants began to slide down again.

"I'll also try to find a smaller pair of pants at the first mercantile we come across. Although I don't think a young man's size will fit like they did on AJ."

Stella retied the rope, snug enough to cut off air. "Are you saying my hips are too large?"

He grinned and stood. "I would never disparage a woman's shapely curves. I'll wait outside if you can bring the other saddlebag once you finish packing."

Stella watched him go as she picked at the oversized pants. AJ had a slimmer, more athletic frame and would have no problem wearing a smaller size. Maybe it would be better to find some shears along with needle and thread. She was handy at sewing. Then she smiled. He'd noticed her curves. Hmm.

When she finished cleaning the mugs and pot and met Beckworth outside, she noted the saddlebag sitting next to a tree.

He gave her a quick once over. "I think we need a hat to cover that red hair of yours. It's a wonder Gemini didn't know you weren't AJ. I would have thought someone would question the ginger-colored hair." He motioned her over. "Come on, up you go."

She handed him the saddlebag, which he placed next to the other one. "You typically put the bags on before we mount."

"Yes, but I want you to get a feel for the horse without me on it."

She was fairly certain all the blood had drained from her face. "Why?"

"In case you find yourself on your own. You need to know the basics of riding."

"You plan on ditching me somewhere?"

"Not intentionally."

The thought he could be injured or killed during their race to safety hadn't occurred to her. A deep hole opened in her gut, just before it tightened into a soul-crunching knot. She reached for the pocket that held the tiny beaded purse, and while it should bring a sense of comfort, it didn't. Right now, her survival depended on him. He was right. If anything happened to him, she would need transportation, and having her own horse only made sense.

"I'll keep hold of the reins the entire time." He waved her closer.

She swallowed her fear. The horse was well-trained, and they'd gotten to know each other. She let him help her up, and he led the horse in a wide circle as he explained the basics of riding—steering the horse, stopping and starting, and other typical commands. He explained the saddle and the bridle, and after thirty minutes, she felt more comfortable, but not enough to take the reins when he handed them to her.

"I think we should save that for next time."

He chuckled. "Fair enough, but you did well."

She couldn't help but smile, rather pleased with herself as he resettled the saddlebags on the horse before mounting behind her.

She remained silent as he turned them down the trail. The horse picked its way around rocks and through trees. Her stomach clenched as the thought of sailing returned. She wasn't sure which worried her more—Gemini's men or getting on a ship. This would be a good time for AJ and Finn to show up.

18

AJ stared out the carriage to the ship anchored at the end of the pier. The *Daphne* rocked gently, her yards fixed long ago from the damage she took on their last voyage. Men scrambled around the deck, preparing her for sail, but all she saw was the ship that first appeared out of the mist in Baywood and the arrogant captain who stole her heart.

She stepped down from the coach and reached for Finn's hand. He pulled her to him, and they watched the men, no words spoken between them. But they weren't necessary. She laid her head against his shoulder while he soaked in the memories. While he had years of stories with the ship, she had her own strong connection to the *Daphne*, and a collection of memories that were humorous, terrifying, and intimate.

He kissed her forehead as footsteps approached.

Jamie stepped next to Finn, but he didn't speak. He must have some inkling as to Finn's thoughts as he gazed upon his past.

After some time, Finn clasped Jamie on the shoulder. "She looks fine. I've heard you've done well with her."

Jamie, who'd become a well-seasoned captain and ladies' man, preened at the compliment, though a touch of pink was visible on his sun-kissed cheeks. "I've learned from the best."

"Your flattery won't buy much."

Jamie grinned. "Aye, I was talking about Lando."

Finn laughed. The first true one AJ had heard since they'd discovered Stella had been kidnapped. At times, he seemed more worried than she did, but she suspected he suffered from unwarranted guilt. No one could have predicted someone would travel to the future looking for the Heart Stone, let alone kidnap someone in the process. And with any luck, this short trip to Southampton would restore his spirit.

Jamie turned when Ethan and Maire joined them. "You're welcome to board. We're meeting in the galley."

Ethan gave the *Daphne* an appreciative glance. "She looks good."

"That kind of talk will just go to his head." Finn patted Jamie on the back. "I hope you have the Jameson ready. It was a hell of a ride getting here."

"Fitz!" Jamie called.

The short, muscle-bound second mate hurried up the dock, a huge grin on his face. "Well, look at that. It's my lucky day. I believe I won the bet." He reached for Finn's hand that was already extended before being pulled into an embrace.

"It's good to see you, Fitz. And what was the bet?" Finn's smile was infectious as Fitz pulled away, seeming a bit embarrassed by the exchange, though he grinned in return.

"Two actually. One on whether we'd seen the last of you. The second on what year you'd return."

"And did you win both bets?"

He shrugged, but he puffed his chest out and made a show of tugging his pants up. "I have a reputation to uphold."

Everyone chuckled while Fitz nodded at the women and shook Ethan's hand. "I need to run a quick errand, so hold your tales until I return." He sauntered off, but his grumbles flowed back to the group. "Can't believe we're dealing with those blasted stones again."

"At least his sentiments match our own." Ethan gave Maire his arm before leading her to the ship.

Jamie fell in step next to Maire, and their laughter trailed away, leaving the two of them alone again.

She slipped an arm around her husband's waist and leaned her head against his shoulder. They returned to their quiet reverie, broken only by the strong thrumming of his heartbeat.

After several long minutes, he took her hand. "Let's meet the old girl and see what stories she has to share."

She let him pull her along, grinning at his sudden eagerness to board. But she understood his need, and wherever they were headed, she trusted the *Daphne* would shepherd them safely.

Finn's muscles sensed the ship the minute he boarded, and his legs melded with its movement, aware of every nuance. When AJ pulled away, he kissed her hand before she left him alone to greet his old friend.

It was like coming home, and years of memories flooded him as he walked the deck. He scanned for recognizable faces and was surprised by how many sailors remained from when he'd last captained the ship. Several worked the rigging and either waved or reached out to shake his hand. He couldn't help grinning like the young ship rat he'd been when he'd hidden away on an old merchant vessel, instantly aware that this was the life for him. At least for a while.

He monitored the men's work as they prepared for sail while he tested the rigging and ran his hands over the well-oiled masts. Once he reached the bow, he steadied his legs and clasped his hands behind his back, his focus on the water. A handful of ships began their journey up the river, while others headed back toward the Irish Sea. A moment of wanderlust filled him, but it dissipated almost as quickly as it rose.

If they'd returned for any other reason than a rescue, he'd enjoy another run on the *Daphne*, but these few moments of pleasure wouldn't last. They had a missing family member on the run, probably more scared and wary than AJ after her first jump. At least she had the benefit of three months of his tutelage before their falling out, leaving her to fend for herself. Thank the heavens she'd found Maire.

Of course, Stella was with Beckworth, so she wasn't alone. Hensley had given him every assurance that Beckworth could be trusted to keep her safe. Even AJ had been relieved at hearing the news, though she still worried about Gemini's men, and with good reason. Perhaps if he didn't have such a sordid past with Beckworth, his own uneasiness would settle. But Beckworth wasn't the issue.

Finn had trouble finding a motive behind the events. Was Gemini simply an earlier player in the business with the stones they hadn't accounted for, or was something more insidious at play?

He released his breath as his old mentor's voice sounded in his head, "You need to work on your patience." And that was the crux, he was never good at the wait-and-see game. He sucked in the scent of the docks—crisp, tangy air coming off the water, pitch and tar from the ship, and pipe smoke. When they returned home, he would take AJ on another long sail, this time just the two of them.

For now, their focus had to be on Stella and getting her home. The lump in his gut said it wouldn't be easy. Nothing about the stones ever was. Someone let the genie out of the bottle and, once again, their small group were the only ones capable of putting the stopper back on.

With one last look at the sails and rigging and noting how well the crew worked together, he headed for the galley. A sense of pride filled his chest; Jamie had become an excellent captain. Fitz met him at the door, and they were laughing at one of his tall tales as they approached the group. They sat around a table filled with cheese, meats, and breads. Pitchers of ale and wine circled an unopened bottle of Jameson.

"How does it feel to be a guest on the Daphne?" Jamie picked up the bottle of whiskey.

"I'll admit it will be difficult not to bark an order or two once we set sail, but I'll do my best to stay out of the way." Finn took an open seat next to AJ and gave her a reassuring grin.

"There will be none of that." Jamie opened the bottle, pouring a fair share in each mug while Ethan poured wine for the women. "You'll be put to work just like Ethan. And if I'm right, I noticed AJ give the crow's nest a fond look."

AJ grinned. "Just tell me where you need me, and I'll be there."

"Then let's toast to good friends and another adventure. May this one bring us all home safely." Jamie lifted his mug, and everyone followed suit. "Sláinte."

Ethan caught everyone up on the kidnapping and the harrowing drive from Hensley's while the group dined on the cook's leftovers. Jamie moved trays out of the way to clear a spot for a map that displayed the southern part of England, the Channel, and the northern coast of France.

"These lines here—" Jamie pointed to three dark penciled lines that ran from three different ports, "— have proven to be the safest courses to cross the Channel. They can shift east or west by twenty miles, depending on what the Royal Navy is up to. The French tend to ignore smugglers unless we sail right up their backsides."

"And which port will Beckworth head for?" Finn had a good idea, but the war could quickly shift how safe a port might be.

"The logical place would be Southampton. It's a larger port with more ships. If he has your friend, he'll want to find a friendly ship."

"He won't find many." Fitz sat back, a long, white clay pipe sticking out of his mouth. A faint spiral of tobacco wafted through the room. "He'll have to pay good coin for a captain to take a woman on board."

"And when did you take up smoking?" Finn asked.

Fitz pulled out the pipe and gave it a grand look. "Since I found this beauty at a shop in Dublin. The shopkeeper set me up with this fine tobacco. It reminds me of Ireland."

"At least he's using it as intended." AJ's comment earned a chuckle out of Ethan. He and Finn were the only ones who knew Jackson and his propensity to use his pipe for smokeless contemplation.

"What about the meeting with Gemini at Basingstoke?" Ethan asked. "If we're headed south, we should try to meet up with Thomas. If we can take out some of her men, it might change the game enough to reduce the pressure on Beckworth and Stella."

"Then Southampton would be best. From what I heard this morning, it's still a friendly port." Jamie pointed to the city on the map. "From there, it should be less than a day's journey. Horses should be easy enough to procure. I'll send Fitz and Lando with you while men search the town for word of Beckworth. If I have to move the ship, they'll know where to find us."

"Where is Lando?" Finn had noticed the big man missing but assumed he'd have come back with Fitz.

"I sent him for more powder and food stores when I received Hensley's last message."

"I understand you've already met Gemini?" Finn had asked the question of Jamie, but he glanced at Fitz. "If she's as smart as she sounds, she'll have men at the ports, most likely keeping an eye out for the *Daphne*."

Jamie rubbed his chin while he stared at the map. "We met her at Beckworth's hunting party last Christmas. She had an eye for Beckworth the whole weekend, though Fitz knows her better."

Fitz shook his head. "I knew that Lady Prescott was trouble," he growled and clenched his pipe.

Finn wasn't surprised by Fitz's dalliances, even with high-born ladies. He wasn't sure what he said to them, but they never had a complaint. And he suppressed a smile when he considered their satisfaction probably had nothing to do with small talk.

Maire cleared her throat. "Fitz's romantic escapades aside, did you learn anything useful from her?"

"What about that Gaines fellow?" Fitz pointed his pipe at Jamie. "He followed her around like a lost pup."

"Hensley didn't mention him." Finn should have asked to read Beckworth's letters. It had nothing to do with trust. He didn't question what Hensley told him. But sometimes, the way a sentence was worded, or the choice of word used, could change the meaning or provide a secondary clue. Hensley knew the man better than him, but still, he should have thought to ask. He grew restless, the charm of his old ship already wearing off. "I think we've gone over all we know. Let's find our way to Southampton and see what fate has in store for us in Basingstoke."

"Fitz, help AJ and Maire to their cabins so they can get settled." Jamie rolled up the map and stored it. "I could use Ethan and Finn topside."

Finn watched his wife and sister follow Fitz. "When did you get more cabins?"

"I had one of the cargo holds divided in two. Since the war started, I've occasion to provide passage for an unlucky soul requiring a quick exit out of England or France. They can still be used for cargo when necessary."

"You'll be sailing a cruise liner before long." Finn slapped him on his shoulder as they mounted the stairs, Ethan following behind.

"I'm not sure what that is, but I doubt I'd be interested."

Finn laughed. "That would be a wise decision."

When they reached the deck, he pulled Jamie to the side while Ethan hovered close, keeping an eye on the men.

"Listen, Jamie. There were at least eight of Gemini's men chasing us. I'm not sure if there were more who followed Hensley. If we assume she sent men to Hereford, it would be only a handful. We don't know the number of men she has working for her, but Hensley thought there were quite a few."

"Which means the bulk of them will either be at the meeting place or chasing Beckworth."

"If they know about the stones, they know about the monastery."

Jamie considered Finn's words, then nodded. "She placed men where Beckworth might go, but she'll be hedging that he went south. The only remaining question is whether they have their own ship."

Ethan's expression reflected his own concern. "Is it worth going to the meeting place?"

Finn's jaw tightened. "We don't have a choice. We need to let Thomas know what's going on and take a chance Gemini, or maybe this Gaines will be there. But it's a helluva risk. There's no doubt in my mind she has a ship."

Jamie shrugged. "Then I have one more task while waiting for you in Southampton. Find her ship."

19

Stella's head bumped against Beckworth's shoulder, jarring her awake. They'd been traveling for hours, and after studying the shadows on the road, she judged the time to be mid-afternoon. Even with a decent night's sleep, she'd fallen asleep again. The smooth repetition of the horse's movement would lull an insomniac to sweet dreams.

"Sorry if I woke you. I had to get off the main roads, which has forced us to narrow trails with small creek crossings." Beckworth's warm breath tickled her neck.

She shot up, then fidgeted, his arm tightening around her as it did any time he thought she might tumble off. "Where are we?"

He chuckled. "That's a good question. We're still heading south, for the most part, but I'm not familiar with these particular back roads. There are three villages in this area, all fairly close together. Until we run across one, our exact location will remain a mystery."

She should be concerned about them being lost, but the only thing she could focus on was their destination. Maybe she didn't have to divulge her issue with boats. There were other solutions, like dropping her off at a nice inn in Southampton where she could wait for AJ and Finn to show up. AJ knew how sick Stella got on a boat. But what if they sailed directly to France after hearing she'd escaped Gemini? Did she want to risk missing them and then find herself on her own?

"If Gemini has most of her men heading south, maybe we should turn back for Waverly or Hensley's. I doubt she'd expect that."

After a few minutes of silence, she assumed he wouldn't answer. She wasn't a whiner, and putting her attempts at irritating Gemini aside, she didn't want to become one. The last thing she needed was for him to dump her somewhere because he couldn't stand listening to it anymore. But she was bored, cranky, and not getting nearly enough decent coffee. She slumped back against him. The soft rhythm of his heartbeat thrummed against her back, and it settled her.

"It's not a bad idea." He startled her with both his sudden response and the fact he'd given her suggestion some thought. "But AJ and Finn will be expecting us in Southampton, and I don't know of anyone who could pass along the message that we'd turned around."

"But you're assuming they'll come by ship. What if they're on horseback, or in a carriage? We might meet them on the way."

The shake of his head tussled her hair, and she knew she'd taken the request as far as she could.

"I'm sorry, luv, but as you've seen, there are dozens of roads they could take to get there. And while they might be traveling with their own small army, the chances of running into them are not odds I'd want to risk." He gave her a gentle squeeze. "Cheer up now. I know it's been a long day. It won't be much longer, and we'll find a place to rest, let you stretch your legs, and with any luck, get a nice warm meal. You're probably in need of coffee."

"At least you remembered the coffee."

"I wish you could have met Eleanor. She has a story or two of when she wasn't very pleased by how well my memory worked."

"Eleanor is the woman you went to for supplies when you left me in that rotted-out cabin."

"She and I have been friends since our early days in London. We both had rough beginnings until she found a place as a dressmaker for the theater. She has a knack for makeup and clothing. I was nothing more than a natty lad the first time she took me in and hid me from the guards."

"Natty lad?"

"Pickpocket."

"A tough beginning indeed." She pictured a scrawny, knock-kneed kid, racing through the more affluent neighborhoods of London, searching for an easy mark, doing whatever he could for a meal. "Eleanor lives alone?"

"She's quite self-sufficient. And though it's rare, God knows she doesn't ask nearly enough, Waverly is always at her disposal for whatever she needs. Barrington, my butler, knows her from those early days and keeps watch over her when I'm gone."

"Are you like that with all your friends, or just Eleanor?" She cringed at how that sounded. It wasn't that she was particularly interested in his relationship with Eleanor, but he seemed to have an overly protective nature.

He shrugged. "Most of them. At least those close to Waverly. I check in with old friends whenever I'm in London, depending on how much time I have." He chuckled. "Although I do have quite a few old acquaintances there, so it's difficult to keep up with everyone, but I do what I can."

"Do you think there might be some kind of store in the next town that might have herbs?" What a horrible segue to her growing dilemma, but it seemed as good a time as any to ask. He was probably making a list of all her faults, and she hated to give him another. But if she couldn't talk him out of going to the monastery, she had to come up with alternatives.

"An apothecary?"

That was the word she'd been groping for. "Yes."

"It will depend on the size of the village, but most have something of the sort. Do you have an urgent need for something? Are you sick?"

She snorted. "Not yet."

He slowed the horse and bent to get a better look at her. "You seemed fine this morning. Was it the food?"

She kept her head turned away, not sure why she couldn't look him in the eye. A lot of people got seasick.

He nudged her. "Now is no time for secrets. I can't properly take care of your needs if I don't know everything."

Good grief, now he was making her look foolish. Or maybe that train had already left.

"Come now, out with it."

"I get seasick, okay. I get woozy just standing on a dock."

The horse came to a complete stop. After another long silence from him—and why did it take him so long to think things through—she swore she heard a clock ticking somewhere in the trees. But it was just his steady heartbeat, and damn if it didn't comfort her.

"Well, that will make crossing the Channel problematic. You couldn't think to tell me this sooner?"

"You only told me our destination last night."

He clucked, and the horse began moving again. "Well, you're not the first traveler to have that issue. There are a couple of items that might help. An apothecary would be our best option, but I have an idea or two if we don't find one."

"The best option would be to stay in England. So, if we could meet up with AJ & Finn before we have to board a ship, that would be my top choice."

He didn't laugh, but she was positive he was holding it back. No doubt her imagination.

"So, let me see if I have this right. Scared of horses, small spaces, and you get seasick."

She hung her head in shame. He *had* been making a list.

"Don't fret. You have many good qualities to overcome your shortcomings." And though she heard the smile in his comment, he kicked the horse to a faster pace on the very narrow and debris-filled path, leaving any further comments pointless.

An hour later, they met up with the main road. Beckworth waited for several minutes before turning down it, which led them to a decent-sized town. He skirted around it, once again concerned Gemini's men would be waiting. Only one cart had gone by, and with the lighter traffic, perhaps Gemini's men had already come and gone.

He followed his same routine, leaving her and the horse behind a church near bushes she could hide in. After thirty minutes, he came back without any supplies.

Stella stood from where she'd hid behind a pile of felled trees. Rather than hide under a bush and nap after all the sleeping she'd been doing, she spent her time pacing while talking to the horse. If anyone came upon her, they'd assume she was just some crazy lady dressed up like a man, who might have gone a little mad.

"What about the hot meal?" Her stomach had grudgingly gotten used to the hard tack they were forced to eat, but she wanted something different. Her cranky bells were clanging.

"I wanted to do some shopping first."

"I should be mad I didn't get to go with, but I can't seem to find the energy to care."

He removed three differently colored muslin pouches from his pocket. "Each of these herbs have properties to settle the stomach and help thwart seasickness. This brown one has ginger, which should prove to be the most useful. It can be made into a tea. Actually, all of these can, but the woman at the apothecary warned that this one—-" he held up a red bag, "—-has a horrible taste so a pinch or two in a savory meal would be best. She also believes it was the best of the three for settling a bad stomach."

"If only we had a savory meal."

"Ah, and that would be my surprise."

When she perked up, he grinned. "I thought that might interest you. The woman also mentioned that a group of six men rode through two hours ago, searching for a red-headed woman and a handsome man."

A single brow twitched up. "Were those her exact words?"

His grin grew to a breathtaking smile, and he shrugged. "Close enough."

She laughed. "So what's the surprise?"

He tucked the bags back in his pocket and untied the horse. "It means we're going to the inn to get that warm meal I promised. Maybe with a cup or two of hot coffee."

She didn't have to be asked twice. Coffee was what she needed. Her fatigue most likely came from her state of mind, but the lack of coffee wasn't helping. The headaches had lessened, but she just wasn't her old self. AJ hadn't mentioned any of these ailments from her first jump, but she hadn't been on the run since the first day arriving in this century. Not that she wanted to compare her dilemma with AJ's, but so far, the only time she'd felt truly safe had been the evening in the cave.

Beckworth reminded her to keep her head down when he led her through an alley and across the main street to an inn. There were only a handful of customers, who barely glanced up as the two strode to a small table in the corner of the room, farthest from the door and close to a warm hearth.

The innkeeper didn't appear interested in who they might be, and after serving the food and drink, left them alone. Stella wolfed down the stew, and whatever powder Beckworth had tapped into her portion didn't seem to affect the taste, though she doubted she would have cared. The bread was warm and the coffee, while not great, was better than she'd tasted since arriving. There had to be a better way to brew the coffee Eleanor had provided. There was promise in those beans if she could brew it right. Maybe a press would be better than boiling it.

"You should have some ginger tea, or maybe the peppermint." He shuffled the herbs, laying them out for her to choose.

"I've used ginger before, but it would be best to save it until just before boarding." She shivered. What was she thinking even getting close to a boat? "And I'd rather try the herbs individually first to see how I react."

He nodded. "That makes sense. Finish up. I'm going to see about some fresh food for the road."

She used the last of the bread to mop up the remaining stew, already feeling her energy returning. After finishing the last drops of coffee, she wished she'd been holding her favorite travel mug when Big and Tall dragged her through the fog. She was fairly certain they didn't have to-go cups in this century.

When Beckworth returned with a brown bundle, she asked, "Is there a general store?"

"Yes. On the other end of the street. Is there something specific you're looking for?"

"Another coffee pot. I don't know. I want to look around." She was thinking some type of plunger to act as a press, but he'd think her crazier than he already did.

He stared at her. "What's wrong with the one we have?"

"I think there's a better way of brewing Eleanor's coffee."

"You know we're on the run for our lives."

She stood and gave a last longing look at her empty mug. "And I run much better when my mind is functional. We need better coffee."

She didn't wait for him as she headed for the door, remembering to keep her head down, the sound of his boots scraping the floor behind her. When she exited the inn, she took a quick glance about then turned toward the direction of the general store.

They were a few feet from entering when a man stepped from around the corner of the building. She stared at him, too surprised to lower her head. Seconds later, Beckworth pulled her behind him then moved them back a step. She glanced behind but didn't see any other men who could be a problem. Then she peeked over Beckworth's shoulder. She didn't recognize the man, but from what Beckworth said, that crazy gangster woman could have well-paid mercenaries scattered everywhere. Not that it mattered at this point. Whoever this particular man was looked dangerous enough.

"You wouldn't happen to be Beckworth, would you?" The man's smile was definitely a leer, and he was missing a couple of teeth. He didn't have any visible scars, nothing that said much about him other than his dirt-encrusted clothes that suggested he'd been on the road a long time.

"I'm afraid you have the wrong person. Perhaps you'll have better luck at the inn." He continued backing up as he spoke, and she peered behind, ensuring a clear exit.

The man advanced until a burly man stepped out of the store, almost knocking into the mercenary. Beckworth took advantage of the situation and turned.

"Run."

She didn't need prodding and raced for where they'd left the horse, which unfortunately was closer to the inn. The boots she wore weren't the best for running, but she ignored the discomfort and the yelling behind them. Beckworth was faster, and he grabbed her arm to drag her along.

They ducked down an alley toward the back side of town. She spotted their horse, but rather than run to it, Beckworth pushed her to the left through a stand of saplings. After several more yards, he positioned her behind a larger tree.

"Stay there."

She opened her mouth to ask what he was doing, but he was already gone, running to another large tree fifty feet away.

Gemini's man—who else would chase them through town— slowed before picking his way through the younger trees, then turned toward an older one where Beckworth hid, a pistol in his hand.

"If you just give me the woman, I'll let you go. Gemini has a score to settle with you, but she's willing to wait. She only needs the woman for now."

Beckworth stepped from behind the tree, the hand with his pistol behind his back. "I'm not sure if I should be offended or relieved."

The man stared at Beckworth with a bewildered look. She guessed he wasn't much for witty comebacks. Pressed against her own tree, she was caught between not wanting the man to see her, especially if he didn't know where she was, and desperately needing to see what was happening.

"You don't have to make this difficult." The man took a step to the side and craned his neck, spotting her. "Just ask her to come out here."

"I suppose if I told you this wasn't the woman you're seeking, you wouldn't believe me."

The man's brows narrowed. "You're Beckworth, right? So that makes her—" he pointed the gun haphazardly in her direction, "—the woman Gemini wants."

"I had a feeling you'd say that."

The man didn't have a chance. Beckworth had been ready, and before the henchman brought his pistol up, he swung his arm out and fired. A flash erupted from the mercenary's gun as he fell to the ground. A branch above her head cracked, and Stella yelped as she jumped away.

"Are you all right?" Beckworth yelled as he raced toward the downed man.

"I'm fine." She brushed leaves from her hair and stared, probably wild-eyed, at the still man.

Beckworth checked the man's pockets, removing a stuffed muslin bag that jingled with coins, a knife, and a folded piece of paper. He stripped a small leather pouch from the man's belt.

"Stealing from the dead." She'd never seen a dead man before, at least not seconds after being shot. The whole incident had shaken her. The thought of being dragged back to a hostile Gemini gave her cold chills, but the gun pointed at Beckworth had terrified her as much as when it had been pointed at her. What would she do without him? The cramping around her chest must be fear of being left alone. What else could it be, unless she was having a heart attack? More likely, a panic attack.

Now that the moment had passed, slight tremors took over. She glanced at Beckworth, who was reviewing the folded note.

"He won't need the coins or the ammunition, but we will."

She crept closer, wanting to see what was on the paper, but she couldn't stop staring at the man. His eyes gazed at the sky. Not in the way one might watch the clouds go by, and not as if he was checking the weather, but in a cold, unfocused way with a touch of surprise, as if he just found his keys in the fridge next to the milk.

How could he look so shocked when he'd been the one to start the fight? Maybe he didn't think he would be the one to die. But dead men didn't talk, so she would never know.

He'd said they would need the coins. She squeezed the ones in her pocket that she'd stolen from Gemini. They would need transportation on a ship. Up till now, he didn't seem short on money, so she hadn't seen a reason to confide her own stash. Was that a sign she didn't trust him yet? She would give this entire event a more thorough review once they were on the road with more numbing miles ahead of them. For now, she needed to stay in the moment. Someone would have heard the gunfire.

Beckworth stood, the paper already tucked away, and grabbed the man's arms to drag him away.

"Stop," she ordered, and was surprised when he did.

"We can't leave him here."

"I know." She bent and retrieved the man's pistol before patting the dead man's chest, somehow needing to give him a final send off to whatever God he believed in. "Okay. You can hide him somewhere."

"Ah, how silly of me to forget the pistol."

Once he had the man tucked under a bush, he left her long enough to find the man's horse. He searched the saddlebag and turned with a coffee pot in hand. "I guess we don't need to stop at the general store."

"Well, there's a positive outcome to all this." Her response had been dry, but she couldn't stop her lips from twitching at his large grin.

"Exactly." He pulled out a blanket, and after reviewing everything else, closed the pack. With the coffee pot and blanket held in one arm, he held out his empty hand.

"What?"

"The pistol."

"Finders keepers."

"I think for now, it would be best—" He didn't have a chance to finish.

"Here's what I know." Stella fisted her hands and placed them on her hips, exaggerating the motion for extra emphasis. Then, with hair falling in her eyes that she brushed away with the hand holding the gun before reclaiming her indignant pose, she explained the situation to him. "I was minding my own business, in my own century, when some asshole attacks me in AJ's kitchen and drags me back to this century. I've been bruised, battered, starved, dragged over miles, almost raped, shot at..." She huffed out a breath, mentally going through her list to see if she'd stated everything, then raised a finger when Beckworth appeared ready to speak. "I'm not finished."

She spent another second reviewing her list, then continued, "And I'm not getting nearly enough coffee or wine to make any of this acceptable. If you think I'm going to continue following you around in the hopes of finding AJ and Finn in these conditions without self-protection, then we're not going any farther." Something seemed missing from the list, but based on Beckworth's slack-mouthed expression, she probably got her point across.

After a few moments, he recovered, and a slow smile appeared. "Well, luv, I was simply going to suggest I hold on to it until you get proper training, but since it doesn't have any powder, I suppose you can carry it." He gave her a wink, then patted the horse on its rump, directing him toward town.

Once the horse had wandered off, he gave her a stern look. "I've made a list of my own."

She held back a smirk, as difficult as it was, but she might have given him a slight eye roll. If this was the list of her failings, she didn't need a refresher, but it was unrealistic to think he'd let her get by without reviewing it. "I'm willing to listen."

His lips twitched. "I'll give you a lesson with the pistol so you don't blow your fool head off. But not until you complete a full riding lesson." When she didn't comment, he added, "On your own."

She might be questioning whether to completely trust him, but right now, she was pretty sure she hated him.

20

AJ wiped the sweat from her eyes. They'd ridden hard the day before after docking at Southampton just before sunrise. After meeting up with Thomas and his fighting men in Overton, they left for the farmhouse outside Basingstoke. They stopped two miles from the farmhouse to meet up with Thomas's surveillance team.

Five of Gemini's men had circled the farmhouse within a quarter-mile perimeter, but with that small number of men, they couldn't cover all the possible deer trails. The surveillance team had determined the gaps and selected several vantage points their team could use.

With the meeting date the following day, the team bunked with the horses, reviewing their strategy after a cold dinner. They left two hours before sunrise and rode to a spot just short of the monitored perimeter. They left the horses with one of the men, and everyone moved into their predetermined locations.

AJ scratched her shoulder and fought the urge to stretch her legs. An hour earlier, a group of ten men rode into the clearing and took up their positions, not once looking up. She returned her focus to the farmhouse. It had seen better days. The front door hung from one hinge. The windows were covered over with old boards that had been haphazardly nailed as if someone had been in a hurry to leave.

Two men sat on apple crates, one on each side of the door, muskets laying across their laps. The man on the left chewed something, and when he spit over the uneven porch railing, she guessed tobacco.

She glanced at the tree to her right. Finn had climbed to the first branch, high enough to get a clear picture of the clearing. She sat one branch higher, a spot Thomas assured her would better if she was using a bow. Her quiver, with double the normal amount of arrows, was tucked into a notch within easy reach.

Ethan and Maire shared a tree on the other side of the clearing, a few yards beyond the farmhouse. Ethan wanted Maire to stay with the horses, but she grabbed her musket and ducked through the undergrowth before he had a chance to object. The two would catch anyone running to or from the back of the house.

Finn would have to walk into the clearing. His job was to confirm Gemini or her second-in-command was there with an ultimate goal to capture if possible. Her job was to make sure he walked back out. Lando and Fitz were their ace in the hold. They didn't have a specific assignment. Fitz and Lando hid in bushes on opposite sides of the clearing. They would go where needed and when needed once the action started.

In addition to the earl's men, Thomas had stopped at Waverly on their way south, where he picked up an additional five well-trained men, leaving their count at twenty-three. The Waverly men would take out the five sentries once Gemini entered the perimeter. The rest of the men were positioned a hundred yards out and would move in once Gemini reached the clearing. Until then, it was anyone's guess whether they would be outnumbered. At least they had surprise on their side.

AJ scanned the area, keeping her movements slow and steady, tracking every movement, any leaf, for signs of men hiding in bushes or behind trees. She counted ten men plus the five at the perimeter.

The sound of hooves, riding fast, came from the north. Finn shifted so his back was against the trunk, the spring leaves dense enough to give him cover. She followed his lead and moved back a few inches, unhappy when a branch blocked him from view.

Ten horses raced into the clearing, coming to abrupt stops in front of the farmhouse. The riders were all men, and one stood out as he strutted to the porch. The others dispersed in a semi-circle around the clearing. These men appeared organized and were probably well-trained. They would pose a challenge, and she shook off her fear for Finn.

She focused her attention on the leader. He seemed familiar. Was this the traveler who had kidnapped Stella? She lifted her bow with infinite care and nocked an arrow. The team had discussed taking out whoever led this exchange, but if it wasn't Gemini, capturing him could yield longer term results. She hadn't agreed with their assessment. If this was the man who took Stella, all bets were off.

She refocused on the leader, but images from the inn's security system played through her mind like a kaleidoscope until she closed her eyes to stop the repeating reel. To her, Stella had been missing for almost two weeks, but for Stella it had only been a few days. She knew that, but when Finn held her during the night as she held back the tears, he repeated the same mantra that all would be well, she wasn't alone. If anything happened to Stella, she'd never forgive herself. She'd always been worried about Maire wanting to return to this century. It never occurred to her that her best friend could be catapulted to the past. Stella was tough, but she'd never wanted to time travel. Was she getting enough coffee? It wouldn't be up to her standards. She had to be giving Beckworth a hard time. AJ had seen Stella when she was off coffee. She stifled a snort. It wasn't pretty.

She aimed her arrow at the leader's head—so tempted—but she released the tension and lowered the bow when she caught sight of Finn striding into the clearing. Two of Thomas's men followed a few steps behind, one to each side.

"Is Gemini here?" Finn's slow Irish drawl was relaxed, almost lazy, and though she couldn't see his face from her position, he'd be flashing his everyone-loves-me grin.

The leader, a broad-shouldered man with a surly face, stepped to the edge of the stairs, hands resting on his hips. "That would be me." He squinted in the bright morning sun.

"Is that so? I heard a rumor Gemini was a woman."

A few of the men gave each other sidelong glances, but the man posing as Gemini never flinched.

"Some days Gemini is a woman, sometimes he's a man." He puffed his chest with his last words. "I assume that makes you Finn Murphy."

"It does. Now, where is my wife?"

Gemini, if that's what he wanted to be called, seemed to deflate, confirming they didn't have Stella. The only thing left was whatever Gemini had planned for this meeting. After lengthy discussions over dinner and several mugs of ale, the team determined Gemini's only play was to take Finn by force and hope he had the Heart Stone.

"I might ask the same thing of the Heart Stone."

"Let's see AJ first, then I'll show you the Heart Stone."

The man gave Finn a long, hard stare before turning to the seated man on his right, whose musket now laid across his arms rather than his lap.

When the man stood, Finn yelled, "For king and country." The call sign to fight.

Gemini's men moved first but hesitated with Finn's unexpected battle cry. That was the point, a few seconds of an advantage.

She didn't hesitate as she loosed an arrow toward the porch, hitting the second man on the apple crate in the right shoulder. With any luck, he was injured enough to stay out of the fight.

When she glanced at the clearing, Finn and the two men with him had scattered while Gemini's men were assessing what happened. She took aim at the first apple crate guy, who now knelt on the porch, his musket resting on the top of the railing. He would pick off her team one by one. She loosed her second arrow without thought then closed her eyes for the briefest of seconds when the arrow pierced him in the neck. She sucked in a breath. There hadn't been any other option. They were the ones who came to her home, took her friend. She hated what she did, and would have nightmares about it, but they weren't done yet.

Her next arrow was already nocked, and she searched for the Gemini wannabe, but he was no longer on the porch. He would have gone after Finn, who should have gotten one shot off before running back toward Thomas's men.

AJ calculated their numbers to be equally matched. This fight would come down to experience and training, which should give them the advantage. In addition, most of their team had worked together before. Everyone knew their job and would perform it without question, which led to AJ's dilemma.

She wanted to jump out of the tree and find Finn, worried that she'd lost sight of him. Her first job had been to protect him while he was in the clearing. Once he gave the command to fight, her role changed to keeping an eye on the clearing, lending aid where needed. She forced Finn out of her head and searched the clearing for members of her team.

Fitz chased two men toward the back of the farmhouse. His broadsword was lifted above his head, and though it was two against one, it appeared the two running men were outmatched. Some of Thomas's men were in the clearing and were holding their own, so she trained her arrow on the edges of the clearing.

Within seconds, she spotted a man sneaking up on Maire's position. She had her musket trained on someone in the clearing and wouldn't notice the man, who clearly had his gaze locked on Maire.

AJ monitored his movements and readied herself for him to walk into her target zone. Before he took the next step, she loosed the arrow. It caught him in the side, and he dropped. He flopped around but no longer seemed a threat. When she glanced back at Maire, she was still focused on the clearing, never knowing how close she'd been to danger. Or, as AJ would prefer to think, Maire felt confident enough in her team to watch out for her.

The responsibility gave AJ renewed commitment as she expanded her focus to the bushes and trees. Gunfire lessened and grew fainter. Either Gemini's men were fleeing, or her team was retreating. After another scan of the trees, she turned her attention to the clearing. Only a couple of men continued to fight; others were either down or had moved off to the trees. Lando ran through, knocking out the remaining opponents from behind, leaving team members to clear out.

AJ had stored her arrow in the quiver, planning on climbing down, when white-hot pain pierced her side. She glanced down. A dark red stain spread across her shirt. The pain doubled her over, and she gripped the tree, moisture pricking her eyes.

Please don't be a gunshot. Please don't be a gunshot.

She slid the quiver over her shoulder, or thought she had.

Instead of falling against her back, it dropped to the ground. No one seemed to have noticed. In fact, there wasn't anyone around. The fighting had either moved elsewhere or, as she suspected, most of Gemini's men had ridden off.

Her movements were stiff as she climbed down to a lower branch, doing what she could to protect her right side. She'd steadied herself, ready to shimmy down the trunk, when a shot rang out and a branch snapped above her. She dodged to the side. Her movements weren't fast enough, and the branch clipped her on its way down. She held on to the trunk but didn't have the strength to slow her descent. Her injured side scraped the bark on her way down. The pain was so unbearable she had to let go. Somehow, she retained enough sense to bring her arms over her head, yet she was unable to quiet her screams as she fell.

She hit hard, and the pain in her side intensified until blackness crept in from the edges. Just like when she fell off the damn horse.

21

———————

Beckworth led the horse down a side trail that branched into several smaller ones, forcing the horse through the trees while Stella, her head ducked against his chest, kept her hands over her head in an attempt to fend off the branches that seemed to constantly reach for her hair.

She'd been quiet since the previous afternoon when he'd had to kill Gemini's man. The pistol she'd removed from the body had been tucked in her coat pocket, and she touched it several times an hour as if it might have magically disappeared since the last time she stroked it.

They'd ridden for several miles in a southwesterly direction, and only got a few hours' sleep before he forced them back on the road. She'd been in shock at first, and seemed to recover quickly, but her continued silence this morning concerned him, as did the piece of paper he'd found in the dead man's pocket.

The map had been sketched quickly, or the person drawing it was just bad at maps. But even with the poor road markers, and assuming he understood the badly scrawled names and the inconsistent spacing between the towns, it was easy enough to see the various roads led to Southampton. Gemini had guessed his move, or had hedged her bets, and sent men in two different directions—Hensley and the coast.

Southampton was a big town that would be teeming with soldiers, but even in a city as large as London that had hundreds of guards, bad things happened all the time. Any approach to the seaport would be tricky, and after yesterday's altercation, he'd determined Stella required her own self-protection. And if she said she could handle a weapon, he should at least test the option. He smiled. She'd actually demanded a weapon, and he appreciated her tenacity.

They soon broke out of the dense foliage into a quiet glade with a narrow creek that ran along the tree line. They could replenish their water, build a fire, and take time for lessons. He'd originally been in a hurry to put distance between them and Gemini's men, but if they were surrounded by them, the best course would be slow and cautious. The meeting with Gemini was to take place at some point that day, if it hadn't already occurred.

If Murphy had shown up for it, and he suspected he had, they would soon be headed south themselves. Perhaps they'd run into them before he procured a berth on a ship to France, but he doubted it. Murphy wouldn't take any chances. He would garner a company of men for the ride to Southampton, and they wouldn't have to take the tiny side roads he'd been forced to take. If they ran into them, all the better, but he couldn't afford to bet on them for help.

He stopped next to a tree and dismounted, tying the horse while Stella scrambled off. She was adept at getting on and off the horse without his assistance and had taken a liking to it. If his plan worked, and she was cooperative, they would leave the glade with her more confident and independent. She required the appropriate skills to survive if anything happened to him. It was imperative she reached the monastery.

Stella removed items from the saddlebags, correctly assuming they'd take time to eat. While she reviewed their food staples, he selected branches and twigs to start a fire. When she saw his actions, her mood lightened.

Without asking, she removed both coffee pots—he still had no idea why she required two unless she didn't want to wait to brew a second pot—the coffee, and blankets in addition to the food.

Once she noted where the fire was being built, she tore a piece of muslin from the provincial backpack she'd fashioned out of various sacks she'd pilfered along the way, dumped coffee into it then placed the muslin in, before taking both pots to the stream to fill. He found several flat stones that he set in a ring and started the fire. Once she was back, she set one pot on a rock to cook.

"Are you making tea? Perhaps some of that ginger herb you have." Beckworth was curious, never quite knowing what to expect from her.

"No. I'm not fond of tea. I'll drink it when I have to, but I don't think we're there yet." She'd plumped up the blankets into two seating areas before walking around searching the ground.

He was tempted to ask what she was looking for but found it more interesting to watch and learn. She found another rock and hefted it to set between the two blankets. Once settled, she poured a small amount of coffee on another strip of muslin, and using a small rock, crushed it. She studied it, moved a portion around with her fingers, then appearing satisfied, dumped the coffee into the second pot which she set next to the first one.

"Why did you do that?" He'd never paid attention to how coffee was made. Grounds, hot water, coffee. It seemed simple.

"I don't think the problem is the quality of the beans. It might be the roasting, but I think it's more how we're brewing it. The coffee is ground, but not very fine. You don't want it too fine, but I think it needed more grinding. I'm running an experiment. Depending on how this turns out, I might try brewing a pot using the French press method."

"AJ never complained about Eleanor's coffee. She seemed to like it."

She shrugged as she set the food on the rock and began splitting up portions. "Your friend probably bought the coffee that way. I bet if you watched her make the coffee, she probably ground it more before making it." She set out two mugs and poured water from the skin, then she waved for him to sit. The rock had been made into a dining table. She was continuing to adapt to her situation.

He sat on the second blanket and stared at the mug of water. "I should have thought to purchase a jug of ale."

Her eyes sparkled with what he'd determined was a combination of humor and longing. "Next time see if they have a jug or two of wine." She paused and tilted her head. "Did you drink wine when you were in my time period?"

He nodded. "Not at the sisters' house. They had horrible taste in wine. But when I scraped together enough money from what little the sisters gave me to run errands, I found a restaurant or two that had very good wine."

"How does it compare to this time period?"

"It depends on the wine maker. The larger the town the better chance of finding decent wine, but you get what you pay for at the inns, and most don't have a choice of what they can purchase, especially with the war. But I think you'd find it...good enough."

She snorted. "Anything alcoholic would be sufficient at this point."

They ate while the coffee brewed. Once she was satisfied the coffee was done, she poured a small amount from both pots and nodded for him to try them. He drank the coffee from the first pot. The muslin filter didn't work as she'd anticipated, but the coffee didn't taste any different than before. When he sampled from the second pot, his eyes widened.

She laughed and took the mug from him, testing what was left in the mug. "I knew it. A little more grinding was all it needed. Maybe more time to steep but so much better than before."

He couldn't argue, and by the time they finished the second pot, the first one had more time to steep, and was an improvement. Now that Stella found the coffee more to her liking, perhaps her headaches would go away and she wouldn't be so fatigued.

After she'd filled herself with coffee, she stood and pulled out her pistol. She tested the weight with one hand, held it up and aimed it at nothing in particular, before waving it at him. "Okay, let's get started."

His brow rose. "It's not that I don't trust your word, but we'll do this in stages."

When lines appeared on her forehead, he smiled. "I'll show you how to load the pistol, but no firing until you ride the horse for a solid ten minutes."

She huffed out a deep sigh accompanied by an exaggerated eye roll. "Fine. But we're not leaving here until I've had time to practice with targets."

"Sorry. I dropped my arm when the pan flashed. I wasn't sure what to expect." Stella stuck her arm toward him, her fingers closing in and out. "I need another cartridge for a second shot, don't I?"

He considered her request. She'd followed his instructions

for loading and priming the weapon, and even with her flinch, she'd gotten closer to the target than he'd expected.

She struck one of her indignant poses. "I'm going to need to practice to improve my aim. Otherwise, why bother with a pistol? You might as well give me a rifle so I can at least swing it like a bat. I'll admit, I'm pretty good at that as well."

He could have responded, almost had, but she was so fascinating to watch. She moved from one emotion to another so fluidly, probably without even knowing it. He didn't want to break the spell.

"They don't require that much powder, and you have the extra pouch with the paper cartridges."

She paused, and he almost smiled, knowing something new was crossing her mind. He was sure to hear what it was and kept his expression blank while she considered her new idea. Then she held out a hand and wiggled her fingers at him again. When he simply stared, not understanding the gesture, she stomped her foot, and her fingers wiggled faster. Yes. That certainly helped explain everything.

"The cartridge pouch. The one you lifted from the dead guy. That's mine."

He wasn't sure what boggled him more, the fact she claimed ownership of stolen property, or that she maintained a straight face, because she had to be joking. But her determined expression never changed, and when he considered the last couple of days and what he'd come to know of her, he should have expected she'd crave more control. He couldn't blame her.

He picked up the pouch. She'd been trained on loading powder from a flask and how to prime the pan, but the paper cartridges were easier to handle. When she made a grab for the pouch, he pulled it back. "Three more shots, and then you have to get back on the horse. We'll trot this time."

She snagged the leather bag and gave him a look of exasperation before holding the pistol under her arm and ripping open a cartridge.

"Do want me to show you the steps again?"

"You don't need to." Her tone was level. All business as they said in her time.

He itched to prime the pan for her, then chuckled to himself. An image flashed of him following her as she raced to a tree and engaged the enemy then waited for him to reload her musket before she sprinted for the next tree.

She glanced at him before she poured a small amount of powder in the pan, closed the frizzen, then dumped the rest of the powder in the barrel of the pistol, followed by the ball and the paper from the cartridge. She rammed everything down, then faced the targets.

She hit the targets with all three shots. He was impressed and would have said something, but her smug expression made him scowl. Instead of the ten minutes of riding lessons she'd committed to, he made her ride for twenty and somehow felt better when she returned his earlier scowl after dismounting.

They drank another pot of coffee and ate leftover pork and cheese sandwiches before returning to the road.

After a few miles, he tried conversation. "Who taught you to shoot? You mentioned you'd had some practice before."

"My father. He made sure all of us were well-versed in firearms. Going to the range was like a family picnic."

Her tone said it was anything but a pleasant experience. "You have brothers and sisters?"

"Two older brothers."

He wanted to ask more, but her body had tensed when she mentioned her family. That didn't mean he couldn't skirt around the topic. "Did you grow up in Baywood?"

She fidgeted in the saddle. "Will we be stopping for a break soon?"

They had just started, so he didn't take her question seriously. "Soon."

When she didn't answer his question, he wasn't sure whether it poked too close to family, or she wasn't in a talkative mood. So he turned his thoughts to Southampton and what they would find there.

"I was born in the Midwest. As soon as I was old enough and had enough money stashed away, I traveled as far west as I could until I ran out of land. I lived in Astoria when I first arrived. That's on the northern tip of Oregon. When I got my real estate license, I tried to find a broker that fit my style. You might have noticed I'm a bit of a free spirit."

"Really?"

She elbowed him. "Anyway, I found a woman broker who was of like mind, and she took me in. She taught me everything she knew before she died."

"I'm sorry."

She pushed her hair back and fiddled with the horse's mane. "She had cancer and fought a brave battle. Do you know about cancer?"

"I've read snippets about it. Old Bart would know more."

"Another friend?"

He chuckled. "Yes. He doesn't live far from Waverly, but in the opposite direction of Eleanor. He was a well-known surgeon in London until he moved to the country."

"Well, it can be a horribly painful death, but she went peacefully at the end. She left me her business and all her contacts." Her sigh was wistful, and he imagined she was smiling. "I was still quite young for a broker and needed a change. I took long excursions down the coast and found Baywood. I sold the business in Astoria and started over in the same building where my office resides today. Although at the time, I lived there, too."

"An entrepreneur."

She laughed. "Yeah. Who would have thought a big mouth like me would have found something I'm so good at?"

"Being an estate agent requires an ability to work with people and have a good head. You seem to have the right qualifications."

"I suppose."

He found her humility refreshing—no guise, no manipulation, and no filter. Nothing like the women he was used to—except for the sharp tongue. That seemed to transcend time.

"How did you meet AJ? I guess I'd assumed you were old friends from childhood."

"It seems like that." She was braiding the mane again, swaying with the movement of the horse, no longer grabbing on to him or the saddle. She startled him when she tilted her head back and laughed. "I had to think back to when we first met. It was at Joe's. Did you go there while you were in town?"

"It doesn't sound familiar."

"Wow. Best po' boys on the West Coast. Back then, Joe still owned the place, before he retired and moved to Florida of all places. But he was a big sports fisherman, so I guess it makes sense."

He wasn't sure he understood most of what she said, but this was the most she'd spoken since they'd met. And it was good for her to talk about something other than her troubles.

"Joe's is a restaurant, but it has a great bar. His bartenders made the best drinks, even back then. It was a Friday night, and I'd had a horrible week. I was still establishing myself and getting to know the area. I stopped in to have a drink, maybe meet one or two locals. I was getting to know the bartenders pretty well."

He snorted and received another quick jab from her elbow.

"Joe's was the place to be on a Friday night, especially for singles. Most tourists had no clue about the place, and Joe liked it like that. Anyway, I noticed this woman sitting alone at a corner table, sipping on a beer with all these papers spread around her. A couple men had wandered by and, well, I watched for a while, curious how she'd handle them. A smart woman might use all that paperwork as a ruse to get guys to stop by, and though she smiled when she spoke with the brave ones that did, they all moved off pretty quickly. She was pretty and looked like a college student, so unless she had the world's worst breath, I didn't understand why the men walked away so quickly."

"Perhaps they instinctively knew they might get stabbed in the shoulder one day."

She snorted. "Or perhaps twice?"

"Good lord, she does tell you everything."

She patted him on his leg, and a jolt went through him at her touch. "Anyway, I walked over and introduced myself. We hit it off, exchanged numbers, and the rest is history."

He stared at the spot where she'd touched him. "You're not getting off that easy. Tell me why the men didn't stay."

"Are you truly interested, or just hoping for something to hold over AJ?"

"I thought you'd be more willing to share the juicy bits."

She finished a braid and smoothed it along the gelding's back. "And?"

"All right. I'll admit I wouldn't mind having something to tease her about the next time I see her."

She laughed. "That's more like it. Even after all this time, she still blushes easily." She paused a moment, and he suspected it was to find the best way to tell the rest of the story.

"She was a fledgling reporter back then. Her editor tossed her all the easy stuff."

"The boring stuff."

"Yeah. But it was Baywood. Nothing exciting ever happens there, so pretty much everything is boring."

"I read her stories about the historical buildings. Those were well done."

"Yeah, she really enjoyed investigating them. She has Ethan to thank for those."

"Hughes? Really. That seems like an interesting tale, but you haven't finished this one."

"Just remember you asked for this. So, she had clippings of old newspaper articles spread around the table along with some notes and her journal for a series idea she was researching. A couple nights a week, she'd stop by Joe's because it gave her a different perspective. She hadn't meant to stop on a Friday, but her week sounded worse than mine. The men must not have glanced at the headlines or they would have taken her words for the joke they were."

When she hesitated, he nudged her. "You started this."

"And now I'm sorry I did."

"It can't be that bad."

"Each time someone approached and asked her what she was working on, she told them she'd discovered several mysterious deaths in the county. No one could figure out what was going on. They were all men who seemed to have died from natural causes, except they all had one thing in common. Their penises had been stabbed numerous times."

He felt his own shrink back as if dowsed in freezing water, but he couldn't help but laugh. It was audacious, but he would expect nothing less of AJ. "I see why the men fled so quickly."

Stella laughed with him. "I couldn't stop snorting. And, of course, I'd had a couple martinis by then, so I added a line or two to help accentuate the story. As you can imagine, the two of us cooked up a pretty good tale."

He wiped his eyes, not sure it was all that funny from a man's perspective, but it was easy to picture the two women, heads bent close, conceiving stories to keep the men from bothering them. "I have to admit, I'm not sure that's something I could tease her about."

Her mirth was evident. "I didn't think you'd get the outcome you wanted, but with enough imagination, I'm sure you could come up with something that didn't specifically name the male anatomy."

"To be honest, in this day and age, the only place you'd hear anything like that would be a very late night at a gentlemen's club or a brothel."

"Or a women's garden party?"

He laughed again. "I'm not sure I know of any woman who would use that word in conversation." He considered the women he knew. "Although, I believe Dame Elizabeth Ellington might use the word. She's more progressive than most."

"AJ mentioned her and seemed intimidated by her. But, I think she'd be a hoot."

The sisters had often used that word. He wasn't sure it applied to Elizabeth, but he'd give anything to see her and Stella match wits at Waverly. Though he doubted that would ever happen. Stella would be going home once she made it to the monastery.

He kicked the horse to a faster pace. "Let's make a quick stop at the next village, then see what awaits us in Southampton."

He wasn't sure if she knew she was doing it, but her hand clutched his as they picked up speed, and he hoped the touch reassured her as much as it did him. They would need all the luck they could muster to find safe passage across the Channel.

22

AJ woke when someone nudged her. She kept her eyes shut while she assessed the blazing pain in her side and what had created it. The scent of gunpowder filled the air. They had been fighting Gemini's men, she'd been shot, and then she'd fallen from the tree. Now, all was quiet except for faraway gunshots and the sounds of heavy breathing. Had she been bumped by a boot? Was it one of Gemini's men?

"AJ. Wake up."

Her eyes popped open to find Finn staring down at her, deep lines wrinkling his forehead. The best thing a woman could wake up to. Then she screamed when he prodded her side.

"Sorry, lass. It can't be helped. We need to see how bad it is."

"Let me pass so I can get a better look." Maire elbowed her way past Fitz and Lando.

"Why don't we all give Maire and Finn some space?" Ethan pulled men away. "She doesn't need an audience. Did anyone see what happened?"

AJ didn't want the men to go, she wanted to hear the story, too. Finn shifted to sit behind her, resting her head in his lap which allowed her to watch the activity around her, but a moment of darkness edged her vision, and she bit her lip to fight the pain.

"What of Gemini's men?" Finn asked.

"They're all gone except for two we've kept for questioning." Lando hovered a few steps away, his gaze focused on Maire's activities.

The sound of cloth being torn gave her an inkling of what was coming next, and she grimaced as Maire pulled the fabric away from her wound.

"I was chasing some dolt across the clearing when I happened to glance up and saw a man pointing a rifle up a tree." Fitz stood next to Lando, also watching Maire, but he fidgeted, his feet moving back and forth as if not sure whether to stay or run. "I knew AJ was up there. I changed direction, but I wasn't going to be fast enough, so I shouted at him to drop the weapon. I probably should have kept my mouth shut, but I think it startled him."

Finn nodded encouragement, but she sensed his worry when he reached for her hand. "You probably saved her life with your quick thinking." Like everyone else, he was focused on what Maire was doing, which hurt like hell each time she poked.

It seemed everyone had a front row seat except her. Though she'd been partially raised, with her shirt pushed up to expose the wound, she didn't have a good angle to see what Maire was doing.

"I agree with Finn. This could have been much worse if the man hadn't been startled." Maire ripped more fabric. "It's a flesh wound, but the bullet took a bit of muscle with it and might have nicked a rib."

"That would explain the pain." Finn tore his gaze away and looked up at the men. "We'll need something to wrap it."

"And see if that water is warm enough yet. I want to clean the wound before we bandage." Maire wiped her hands on a rag before reaching into a pocket for small packets of herbs.

Lando, Fitz, and Ethan ran off in different directions while the other men remained in a large circle, a couple with their backs to them, watching for anyone who might sneak back.

"What happened to the man who shot me?" She wasn't sure she wanted to know, but Finn's words comforted her.

"Fitz took care of it."

She'd have to find a way to thank him, no matter how uncomfortable it would make him. And the thought made her smile until Maire began poking again.

Ethan returned first with two shirts. She was either losing track of time, or they'd moved the horses closer for him to have returned so quickly. Fitz followed close behind with a blanket. She wasn't sure how that would help until Finn placed it around her shoulders, and she noticed she'd been shivering.

"I need water. I might be going into shock."

"You are." Maire's tone was matter of fact, her professional nurse attitude in full swing. "Where's that water?"

Fitz had already taken off, presumably to get drinking water. Lando's large body came into focus when he placed a pot of water next to Maire.

"Thank you, Lando. Does someone have a coffee tin? I'm sorry to keep shouting orders."

Two coffee tins were passed to her immediately. Someone must have brought a saddlebag over.

Maire filled both mugs with water before turning away. AJ heard something being ground. When Maire turned back, she set the two tin cups next to her before dropping powder into one of them. When she began wiping and dabbing the wound, AJ tightened her grip on Finn's arm. Whatever had been in the water stung like hell. After drying the area, Maire applied a paste that was warm, soothing, and carried a minty scent.

"Let's wrap it, but we can't sit her up any farther until we have the paste secure." Maire ripped part of the shirt Ethan handed her and made a gauze-sized pad to settle over the wound. Then, with Ethan's help, she managed to maneuver a piece of shirt beneath AJ before bringing it around her middle to tie the ends together.

Maire dumped water from one of the mugs then made up another concoction, which she gave AJ to drink.

Already expecting the worst, and not disappointed, she choked down the nasty drink.

"That should help with the pain, but it might make you a bit drowsy."

"It's best we move in case Gemini's men regroup." Ethan helped Maire collect her medicine, cook pot, and cups.

"Let's see if you can stand." Finn helped her up.

The pain lessened to a dull ache, probably reduced by the tight wrapping that squeezed her middle. She managed two steps before Lando held her steady while Finn mounted his horse, which one of the men had brought over. Then she was lifted and passed up to Finn.

"I can ride on my own." AJ struggled to get down until Finn trapped her arms and kissed her temple.

He whispered, "Let a worried husband hold his wife in his arms. Everyone knows how strong you are."

She relaxed into him, her mother's words of advice, given during her birthday party at the inn, floated back to her. Let Finn be the man he was meant to be. "I'm sorry I worried you."

"Not your fault. It might be a bit jolting, but we need to move fast, at least until we put a few miles behind us."

"I'll be all right as long as I'm with you."

He kissed her forehead, and it was only minutes before their large group moved south. Two of the nearest men wore bloody bandages, and she worried over how many they might have lost, but when she tried to count them, her vision blurred. She cursed Maire under her breath. The woman had given her a sleeping potion, and even with the stabs of pain as the horse raced down the road, she couldn't keep her eyes open.

When she woke, she found herself in a room she didn't recognize.

"There you are." Maire gave her a sweet smile.

"You drugged me." AJ's mouth was dry, and the room tilted.

"You should have expected that."

"I'd hoped you'd changed."

Maire's laugh made AJ grin. As if that would ever happen.

"Sit up and drink this." Maire held out a mug to her.

She eyed Maire suspiciously, and while she did sit up, she didn't take the mug.

"It's only water." Maire made a cross motion over her heart, her smile never changing.

AJ took the mug and sniffed it, which earned her an eye roll. She took a chance and sipped. The water was cold, refreshing, and tasted absent of any drugs. She glanced around the room. "Southampton?"

Maire shook her head. "Finn was worried Gemini's men went that direction, so we've only traveled as far as Winchester. There are wounded men to care for. You're not the only special one, you know."

"What about the *Daphne*?"

"Fitz went to find her. We'll stay here while we wait for word. Finn and Ethan went out with a few of the men to gather supplies. They should be back soon. Until then, feel like something to eat?"

AJ nodded, and while Maire left to go downstairs, she checked her bandages, which appeared to have already been changed. She wanted to take them off and see the wound for herself, but if she did, Maire was sure to give her another sleeping potion, this time hidden in her food.

She took the opportunity to get out of bed with nothing on but her tank top, undies, and Maire's careful wrapping. A saddlebag lay against the wall, and she inched her way to it. For the most part, the pain had subsided to a fraction of what it had been, but she soon discovered certain movements stabbed like blades of ice, and she blinked back the tears. She pulled out a clean pair of pants and shirt. Her previous ones were nowhere in sight, and she hoped they hadn't been tossed.

When Maire returned, she balanced a heavy tray along with clothes tucked under an arm, and she kicked the door shut with her boot. "It's good you're up and able to move about. How's the pain?"

"Manageable. It only hurts when I move my right arm too much."

Maire nodded and placed the clothes near the fire. "You should try to use the arm as much as you can even if it hurts. It shouldn't impact the wound, and there's no sign of infection. I found someone to wash your clothes, but they'll dry faster by the fire."

"Do you have the Heart Stone?" She hadn't seen it anywhere, but Finn wouldn't leave it lying around.

"Finn has it."

She ate the stew with gusto, only stopping for a bite of bread or chunk of cheese. "I can't believe how hungry I am."

"You slept through the entire night from what Finn said."

Her eyes grew wide. "It's morning?"

"A few hours past."

The door opened, and Finn stuck his head in. "Just making sure you're presentable." He opened it wider and was followed in by Ethan, Lando, and Thomas.

"We heard back from one of Thomas's men who went with

Fitz." Finn sat in the chair opposite AJ and stole a piece of cheese. "They found the *Daphne*, but she's no longer in Southampton. The port is thick with Gemini's men. Fitz spotted the man claiming to be Gemini but didn't see the woman herself."

"Before Fitz sent Thomas's man back to us, he was able to locate Jamie." Lando gave AJ an assessing gaze that made her fidget. "He moved the ship to Poole, and so far, no one has taken interest in her."

"What about Stella and Beckworth?" AJ shifted in her seat, and it seemed everyone noticed as she bit back the pain, but she forced a smile.

"No sign of them." Ethan leaned against the wall, his arms crossed, a mirror image of Lando.

"Beckworth's smart." Thomas's grudging praise surprised her. After all Beckworth had done, Thomas still didn't trust him. But that was probably true for several of the men, who didn't know all he'd done for them. "He would have scouted the town before going in."

"He must have anticipated Gemini moving men into town or seen them lurking at the inns." Finn filled a mug of ale for AJ and then one for himself.

"Or no one saw them because the real Gemini is holed up with Stella, and who knows what she did to Beckworth." AJ sat back and rubbed her side. She wanted to scream.

"Let's not get ahead of ourselves." Finn took her hand and held on. "There's no evidence of any of that."

"My man said the men are watchful." Thomas poured mugs of ale for the rest of the group. "It might be they're looking for us, but I think Beckworth is still out there somewhere."

"I agree." Lando took the cup Thomas offered. "The little man has shown himself to be quite slippery. Which means he went to a different port. I can think of a couple possibilities, but

Jamie knows him better than me. They spent many hours playing chess on the Channel crossings. My bet would be Poole or Bournemouth, which is where Jamie typically docks."

"Aye. And if he can't find the *Daphne*, he'll find another ship." Finn glanced to the window before turning to AJ. "We need to move now. It's a long ride to Poole, but we should be able to make it before midnight. It won't be an easy ride."

AJ sat straighter, not looking forward to what came next. "I'll manage. If it takes until dawn, I'll make it." Nothing would stop her from finding Stella. And as she stared down the men in the room, no one questioned her resolve.

23

____

Beckworth stopped the horse a half mile from Southampton. He'd ridden closer than he should but didn't want to be too far away since he'd go the rest of the way on foot. The road had gotten busier as they approached town, which made sense with the war. Even before that, the road from London to Southampton could become overburdened with carts and carriages since it was one of the main ports to cross the Channel.

Stella had been upset since he'd shared his plan that morning. At first, she went through a dozen reasons why it was a bad idea. It might have only been two, but she repeated the various options so often it seemed like more. Then she stopped talking all together. Her disposition hadn't improved after a full pot of coffee at breakfast and again at lunch, which meant the magical brew would only appease her to a point.

When he turned the horse down the third narrow trail of the day, she heaved a sigh. After the dilapidated structure came into view, she moaned her discontent.

"Are there any farmhouses in England that don't come with broken floorboards and gaps in the wall? Or am I just the lucky tourist who gets to see the real England."

Her ability to bounce back to sarcasm made him chuckle. "I keep forgetting you're an estate agent. You must be used to selling much finer homes. However, in England, you'll find that the finer homes are typically occupied by owners or renters."

"I see your point." She jumped off the horse before Beckworth had brought the horse to a full stop.

Beckworth hid his grin. It wouldn't do for Stella to be told how well she was doing with the horse. From what he'd seen, she could adapt to any situation, but she seemed to prefer playing down her accomplishments. He understood her reasoning with the horse. It was one thing to master trotting a horse, but racing at top speed to avoid Gemini's men was a different matter. Maybe he should remind her he wasn't going to leave her to fend for herself. Although he thought it would be obvious by now.

She strode off to check the structure and was back in five minutes. "There's only one door, but there's a spot in the back I can squeeze through if I need to." She glanced up at him when she noticed he hadn't dismounted. "What?"

He jumped down and led the horse toward the back of the house. "You're becoming a fine runaway. You learn quick."

"It's called survival skills. I might have been a bit out of sorts when I first arrived, but it's all coming back. I suppose I have your thieving ways to thank."

If she'd meant to be hurtful, he disregarded it and chalked it up to her cranky temperament. She followed him as he led the horse behind the house and tied it behind a tree. He returned to the front and stepped over rotted boards to enter the house.

The floor was filthy, with months—possibly years—of debris and dirt that had blown through the gaps in the wall. A rickety chair and table, the only furniture remaining, sat in front a cold stone hearth. He checked the opening in the back where a board had been pried off, rotted away, or was purposely removed by squatters for a quick escape.

"Only take what you absolutely need out of the saddlebags. You won't have time to pack up if someone comes searching." He turned and returned to the front door.

"I remember."

"And stay in the house if you can, the weather looks sketchy. It will be easier to monitor the area without anyone seeing you."

"I know."

"I shouldn't be long, but it could be a few hours, depending on what I find."

"We went through all of this at breakfast and again at the lunch stop."

"If anyone comes snooping, sneak out the back and wait with the horse. Chances are they'll only take a quick look before moving on. But if needed—"

She didn't let him finish. "If needed, I'll shoot them and drag them under a bush."

"I was going to say, ride north until you lose them, then try to find your way back to the last town we visited and hide until I can catch up with you."

"Oh. Well, I suppose that would work as well, but you'll have a lot farther to walk." She all but ran down the steps, dodging the weak boards, and disappeared around the corner of the house.

He waited where he stood. She wouldn't want or need an escort. When she returned with an armful of items that she laid out in front of the hearth—a package of leftover food, a skin of water, and a book she'd found at a mercantile. She opened the book and took out one of her folded art pieces. She pulled at a corner here, a tug there, and a swan emerged. She handed it to him.

"You never mentioned what possessed you to learn...what did you call it? Origami?"

She gave him her first smile of the day. "I'm surprised you remembered." She tucked a strand of hair behind her ear, her toe pushing a stack of leaves to the side. "I was going through a self-improvement phase and took several classes—cooking, some painting, stained glass, several others. Nothing stuck except gardening and this." She sniffled but didn't turn away.

She missed home. He understood. She had become part of a unique group of people who knew what it was like to be displaced by time without knowing if they'd ever see home again. He understood quite well.

"And what is the significance of giving me this swan?"

Her smile, if a bit melancholy, returned, and it was all he required to remind him of his mission—getting her to safety so she could return to her own time.

"Proof of life."

He grimaced. "I've heard that phrase."

"If the sisters kept you in front of that TV, I imagine you have." She hesitated then pushed the swan into his hand. "I don't know if there's any place where you could leave it that AJ or Finn, even Ethan and Maire, would spot it. But if any one of them saw it, they'd know I've been there."

"For all your idiosyncrasies, you are a smart woman."

"Flattery isn't going to get you off the hook for leaving me here with the horse again."

"You like the horse, and I distinctly remember you mentioning the horse liked you." The swan flattened easily, and he tucked it in his pocket. He stared down at her. "It will only be a couple of hours. If you get sleepy—"

"I'll crawl under a bush and deal with the rain if it comes."

"Do you always finish people's sentences?"

"I find it faster. Now go, the sooner you leave—"

"The sooner I'll return." He winked at her. "You're not the only one that can do that."

She didn't say anything but managed a weak smile before nodding. He wasn't sure what made him do it, but he brushed her hair back and lifted her chin so she would meet his eyes. "I won't be long, and I will return."

He felt her gaze on him as he jogged down the trail, his chest tightening at leaving her. Had he been foolish to leave her so close to town? He considered doubling back twice. It was a solid plan. Gemini wouldn't bother scouring the woods this close to Southampton. It was a risky move, and he was betting that she thought of him as the simple viscount who'd reported to Dugan and the duke. And that thought was the only thing that comforted him as he followed the road to the port city.

***

Beckworth slipped behind a stack of crates across from the docks, and as he expected, there were several ships, but he'd have to walk the piers to check each one. He'd taken the extra time to skirt around the town and come in from the east side. If Gemini's men were paying attention, they would know he'd been following a more westerly route and would assume he'd arrive from that direction.

That decision had delayed him when he came upon a massive encampment on the north side of town, most likely filled with soldiers from the British Army waiting for a ship. When he managed to sneak past them, he'd arrived at the docks in time to hear at least a dozen or more horses racing off amid angry shouts. He'd considered it might have something to do with Murphy, but with so many military men at the port, it could have been anything, and since they were heading west out of town, he'd never catch them to confirm one way or another while on foot.

He scanned the docks, but the two Royal Navy vessels blocked his view of the other ships. A light drizzle had greeted his arrival and would drive many inside, leaving only sailors preparing ships to weigh anchor with the next tide. He pulled up the collar of his jacket and hunched his shoulders, grateful his clothes had the look of a weary traveler or the local drunkard. With his head down, he added a limp as he walked the docks, only glancing up long enough to identify a ship. He occasionally paused near a dark ship to watch for anyone who might be following him. If Gemini's men were here, they were mostly likely inside drinking.

If he'd hoped to spot the *Daphne Marie*, it was at best wishful thinking. He had no doubt she'd be close, but there were dozens of ports where Jamie could have docked. And there were plenty of reasons why the young captain wouldn't or couldn't dock in Southampton. So he wasn't surprised when he didn't find the ship among the dozens he'd walked past. Stella would be disappointed.

When he doubled back, he found a quiet spot next to a naval ship. The inns and pubs that lined the street were busy, and while it might be advantageous to roam through a couple, it wasn't worth the risk. His focus had to remain on their journey to France, and while he hadn't spotted anyone that might be one of Gemini's men, it would be safer finding transport at one of smaller smuggler ports.

Before leaving the docks, he checked his coins. He'd carried a fair amount when he'd ridden to meet Gemini, not expecting to find himself on the run. With Stella to care for, he'd been careful with his spending, but finding a ship to transport them during war time would be tricky. If it wasn't for the coins he took from Gemini's unfortunate mercenary, their trip across the channel would have been precarious at best. As it was, he might still be short.

He limped away from the docks and prying eyes. He couldn't say if any of the men moving from pub to pub were Gemini's men, but he knew they were out there. He could sense them if not pinpoint them. The business district had long closed for the day, but he continued to amble through the streets until he found the shop he wanted.

It was easy enough to break in, and pushing his guilt aside, found parchment, quill, and inkpot. He quickly wrote two letters, sanded them, then sealed them in envelopes. After a search of the shop, he found several coins in a tin stuffed with old newspaper print, which prevented the coins from rattling around. Smart man. It was a small stash, four crowns in all. He stared at them for some time before he took two and put the others back. He hated to do it, but this was their lives, and it might be months before the shopkeeper noticed the missing coins. Eventually, the money would be replaced, and to ensure it happened quickly, he reopened the letter to Barrington and added a subscript of where to send four crowns as repayment for the shopkeeper's assistance. It was the best he could do to assuage his conscience.

Before leaving, he noticed a small stack of newspapers. He took six and left two schillings on top of the stack. The streets were quiet when he exited the shop, and he took a more direct route back to the farmhouse.

The earlier drizzle increased to a steady rain on his way back, leaving him soaked by the time the farmhouse came into view. With the poor weather, he expected Stella to be in the house, but he made a quick perimeter check. His horse was where he'd left it, but no sign of Stella. He approached the cabin with some wariness, and stayed close to the house before mounting the steps to the front door.

He raised his voice to be heard over the rain. "Stella?" When he didn't receive a response, he tried again.

The telltale sound of a flintlock being cocked, barely heard through the rain, made him pause. He hadn't seen anyone following him. "Are you trying to decide if you can trust me?"

Without answering his question, she stepped around the corner of the house, barely a shadow in the dim light. "I'm disappointed you're alone."

When she stood only a couple feet from him, he shook his head. She was wet from head to toe and shivering. "Let's go inside." He waited for her to move first, which she did without hesitation, probably as eager as him to get out of the rain.

It wasn't any warmer inside, but she'd put wood in the hearth, which was in better shape than the rest of the place. Beckworth lit the fire and turned, finally able to see her in the firelight.

She took off her boots and set them and her raincoat by the fire.

"Why are you wet?" Beckworth found a spot near the fire and watched her wring out her hair.

"A couple riders came by about a half hour after you left. I sneaked out the back, but they stayed on their horses and talked for a while. I didn't feel comfortable waiting in the house like a sitting duck."

"You should dry off as best you can. And you might as well make some coffee."

"We're not staying the night, are we?"

He shook his head. "We need to find a ship, and it would be safer to travel at night. More so now that it's raining."

She nodded. "I'd like to change into some dry clothes."

It wouldn't take long for their clothes to get wet as soon as they started riding, but dry clothes would be warmer than riding off in damp ones. "I'll check on the horse and make sure no one followed me."

After another perimeter sweep, he pulled out his previous change of clothes, considered the contents of the bag, then closed it. He was fortunate Stella had insisted on rinsing clothes the last time they had a fire. He swiftly changed on the porch before going in and placing his pants, jacket, and shirt next to Stella's raincoat.

"If you want to change in the corner, I'll keep my back turned." He opened the package of food. Not much left but cheese and a hard roll he managed to split into two. "The coffee smells good after the long walk in the rain."

She returned and set her clothes next to his. "It should taste better, too. I think I have the grinding figured out. Now it's just fine-tuning the measurements."

Several minutes of silence passed while both watched the flames. Stella set a swan on the floor between them.

"Should I be worried that the *Daphne Marie* wasn't in port?"

"No. It would have been a miracle to meet up with them. There were two Royal Navy vessels in addition to a couple British patrols and several other ships. And though I couldn't pinpoint any specific man as being one of Gemini's, they were out there. There's a slight possibility that Jamie hasn't shown up yet, but he probably decided on a safer port. I believe I mentioned there are several ports along the coast, many of them used by smugglers and local fishermen."

"And why can't we wait until morning?" She poured the coffee and passed a mug to him.

"It might take some time to find the right ship. We'd have better luck if we were at a port where I could monitor them."

"It's raining."

"I agree it won't be a pleasant evening."

"We have to ride all night?" Her voice rose an octave, but

then she shook her head. "Sorry. I'm just tired of being wet and cold."

He was close enough to reach out and brush the hair from her face, but he didn't think she'd appreciate the gesture. Her hair was drying quickly, and light copper strands shone through the deeper auburn color. He didn't know how to make it any easier on her.

"I was originally thinking Poole, which is one of the ports Jamie used on one of our Channel crossings. But Bournemouth is closer and would probably better suit our purposes."

"I'm not sure I want to know what that means."

When he didn't respond, she waited a full fifteen seconds before her loud sigh filled the room.

"Tell me what that means."

"It means smugglers. I think they'll be our best option for crossing the Channel safely."

"Would it really be so bad to just wait until morning?"

"There's no guarantee the rain will let up by then, and all we would have done is waste time."

"In a dry place with a warm fire."

"Are you a romantic, Miss Caldway?"

She smirked at his question. "Not currently. A romantic would expect a fur rug in front of the fire and scented candles." She tilted her head in a manner he'd come to recognize as her mentally running through a list, and she didn't disappoint. "Of course, there would have to be wine. In crystal goblets."

He snorted. "And I imagine music would be playing in the background?"

"Maybe some soft jazz."

"Hmm. I remember Louise playing jazz when she was in a particular mood to annoy Edith. What about what your era refers to as classical?"

"Like Bach?"

"Or Mozart."

"I was always partial to 'Clair de Lune' by Debussy."

"I'm not sure I'm familiar with that one."

A horse whinnied, and they both froze, but only for a moment as Stella began gathering supplies. He grabbed her raincoat and boots, then her hand as the items she'd collected fell to the floor. He led her to the back of the cabin and pushed her through the gap seconds before the front door crashed open.

<hr>

S tella struggled to get her boots on, then her coat, thankful to feel the heaviness of her pistol in the pocket. Her hands shook as she checked the pan; the black powder she'd loaded earlier looked dry. She set the pistol to full cock.

"I'm sorry to say this cabin is already occupied. I believe there's another one a mile to the east." Beckworth's flippant words were greeted by silence.

She peeked through the gap and focused on the two men outlined by the firelight. One had reached for his pistol, the other his sword. She closed her eyes for a second, replaying the loading of her pistol after Beckworth had left for Southampton and nodded to herself when she was positive she'd done it correctly.

The men were closer than the targets she'd practiced with earlier that day. Was it still the same day? They were all blending together. She pointed the pistol through the gap, keeping her eye on both men and Beckworth.

The two men peered around the cabin. "Would you be Beckworth?"

"I'm not sure I'm familiar with that name." Beckworth

stepped closer to the fire, his hands stretched toward it as if seeking warmth.

Stella didn't know if he'd purposely given her a clear shot or if he had another plan in mind. Since the man with the gun wasn't aiming it anywhere specific, she waited.

Beckworth picked up a branch and tossed it in the hearth. "If you don't mind. It's getting chilly in here again. Maybe because you left the door open."

The man with the sword turned to shut it. Stella snorted. His momma must have taught him some manners before he became a stupid thug.

Beckworth took that moment to drop and roll as the other man took aim.

Stella didn't hesitate. She blinked from the flash but didn't drop her arms. The man stepped back, firing wildly into the ceiling. She searched her pocket for another cartridge, but she wouldn't be fast enough. It didn't matter because she couldn't take her eyes off the room and the macabre scene where moments ago they'd been discussing romantic evenings by firelight. Good grief.

Her shot had gone wide, but then she noticed the man with the sword had fallen, and the first man, not seeing his partner down, tripped over him and fell, arms swinging.

Beckworth took that moment to grab his jacket and pistol from the hearth before racing toward her. He squeezed through the gap while the men in the cabin swore and yelled at each other, probably flustered as they untangled themselves. She didn't have a chance to peer through the gap to confirm her assumption because Beckworth grabbed her arm and pushed her toward the bushes where they'd left the horse.

"Our supplies." It was funny what one thought about when running for their lives, but she would miss Eleanor's coffee beans. She was so close to brewing a perfect cup.

"We'll get more."

She stuck the pistol back in her coat and would have tripped several times if Beckworth hadn't kept hold of her, nearly dragging her over fallen twigs, rocks, and puddles. The rain increased, and the horse had turned its back to the wind.

"Go left, I'll go right." The words were muffled by the rain. The men could be yards away or right on their tail.

Either way, they spurred her on, and when they reached the horse, she climbed on while Beckworth untied the horse. In a flash, he mounted and forced the horse through the trees. It was a slow pace, and, in the darkness, it was difficult to see, but the men wouldn't run around on foot for long.

After several long, anxious minutes, they broke out of the trees onto a narrow trail, and he kicked the horse to a faster speed while she waited for the sound of a pistol. But other than shouts fading away, the only sounds were the beating rain, the pounding of their horse's hooves, and the fierce thrumming of her heart.

Neither spoke until they turned onto a wider road, and he slowed the horse to a more sustainable pace.

"Are you all right?" Beckworth's grip on her lessened now that neither of them was a hair's breadth of being snagged off the horse by an errant branch.

She trembled, unsure if it was from the cold, shock, or both. Everything happened so fast, she took a moment to replay the event, then she reviewed it a second time.

"I shot one of them. He wasn't the one I was aiming at." Even to her, the words seemed too hushed for him to hear through the rain and the horse's thudding trot through the mud.

"It was an arm wound. He'll survive. Your quick action was a perfect diversion."

She straightened a bit, thankful for his words. Whether he meant them or not, they gave her peace of mind. "My nerves are shot to hell. We left Eleanor's coffee and the rest of our food behind, as well as our second set of clothes. Thank you for at least rescuing my boots."

"I'm sorry for that. I should have been more diligent."

"Are we that important that men would be riding around in this weather to find us?"

His arm tightened around her waist. "I think they were just trying to find a place to get out of the storm."

"The men who came by while you were gone?"

"Most likely, but we're close to town, so it might have been others. Gemini probably sent men out to widen their perimeter since we haven't shown up yet."

"Will they follow us?"

"Doubtful. They would expect us to try for town, but we're heading farther west. I don't think they'll expect that, but I've been unable to guess Gemini's game until recently. Based on a hand drawn map I found on the dead man, it seems she's been trying to steer us toward Southampton, most likely from the minute we escaped."

He leaned into her, and whether he did it on purpose or not, she appreciated the additional warmth his body provided. "I'm sorry you didn't have enough time to dry or get a decent rest."

She didn't respond, unwilling or simply too tired to yell in order to keep the conversation going. But she relaxed against him, her way of telling him it was all right. The only indication that he understood was the tightening of his arm around her waist as they settled in for their long ride to Bournemouth.

24

The scent of decaying fish, salty air, and human waste were the first signs they'd reached their destination. If only Stella could have been transported to a time when sewers had been inverted. Scattered lights broke through the trees, confirming her guess, but it was impossible to see anything else in the dark, the dim moonlight hidden behind clouds.

The rain had let up a short time ago, but it didn't make a difference. Her hair was dripping wet, and her clothes hadn't faired any better, even with her raincoat. The poor garment was hardly recognizable anymore. When Beckworth had wanted to purchase a different coat, she didn't just say no—she'd been adamant to the point of stomping her foot. It was the last remnant of her own clothing besides her bra and panties, she had left. She grinned, remembering his only response had been a lifting of a brow. From some of the stories AJ told her about the aristocrats in this century, Beckworth had probably dealt with all forms of female temperaments.

At the time, she had no desire to see Waverly, but after spending time with him, she had to admit she was curious about his home. She could only imagine his gardens from movies of this era or in magazine spreads. What was he like when he was the consummate viscount?

She glanced around when he turned down another road and the scent of the Channel became stronger. It had to be close to morning, but lights still blazed from a few buildings. Several ships floated at the pier, and her heart raced. Was one of them the *Daphne Marie*?

Beckworth steered the horse for the buildings that bordered the docks. Men stumbled about, moving from what had to be one pub to another. She'd expected him to leave her in some rundown building outside of town like usual, but she didn't ask questions when he rode past several buildings before turning into a narrow back alley. The town was larger than she'd expected for a smuggler's port.

He pulled the horse to a stop between two buildings, both with back doors and oil lamps that cast a yellow glow.

"If I promise to be right back, will you stay put?" He gave her a stern look, but it didn't matter.

She might have nodded, but the only thing she was aware of was being tired, wet, and cold. All she wanted was someplace dry. Another ramshackle cabin with a hard floor and passable hearth would be a blessing. When had AJ given in to the loss of twenty-first-century comforts?

AJ had somewhat of a soft landing into this time period, having Finn by her side for most of it. Stella had been dropped into the middle of a nightmare. Granted, she had Beckworth, who saved her from Gemini's wrath and continued to protect her. If she ever saw AJ again—no, *when* she saw AJ again, she would definitely point out the extra hardships she'd endured. She grinned. They would laugh about it as they listed out the reasons why one had a more difficult experience than the other.

But they would be doing it over a bottle of wine on her back porch or with martinis at Joe's. Damn if she couldn't almost smell the po' boys. When did she last have a decent meal that wasn't greasy stew?

Her head popped up when she realized she'd been daydreaming. She glanced around, not remembering Beckworth leaving her, too busy being lost in her own pity party. The street was quiet, even the pubs were slowing down, and the alley looked deserted. She dismounted, remembering her promise not to wander off, and leaned against the building, feeling less exposed.

She tipped her head back against the rough boards that somehow grounded her to the moment. The silence was a blessing after the long ride. He never stopped for a break, only slowing the horse to a walk for a couple miles before returning to their faster pace. She couldn't remember a more miserable time. Yet there she was, standing in a dark alley in some smuggler's port during the Napoleonic Wars while on the run from some madwoman. She didn't care who might be listening—she laughed. Out loud and hearty enough to make heads turn, her laughter continued. She was a mess—physically and emotionally—but she felt alive. She'd slept on nothing but hard ground, was chilled to the bone most of the time, and terrified when they raced through forests and glades with dangerous men chasing them. Hell, she'd shot a man. A bad man, but still. And she couldn't stop laughing.

Beckworth stepped up slowly. He didn't say anything, and when she gave him a sidelong glance, he appeared confused, or maybe that was concern. Yes. She'd finally gone mad. Then he quirked his lips which immediately turned into a wide smile. Oh, yeah, he was gorgeous, even when wet. And that made her laugh more.

"All right, I believe it's time to get you inside and dried off. Then I'll take the horse to the stables."

She reined in her laughter, but it was difficult, and a few snorts escaped as he led her through a back door and up a narrow staircase. Once they reached the second floor, he opened the first door on the left. Stella immediately walked to the window, which gave her a partial view of the docks.

She turned in a circle, taking in the gaudy decor, before her gaze locked on the small hearth with a low-burning fire. That explained the warmth, but most of the lighting came from two oil lamps. Before she could ask where they were, she noticed he was still in the hallway.

"Warm up. I won't be gone long. Keep the door locked until I return."

She lifted a brow, still grinning. "I'll behave myself." She lifted her arms. "We have a fire. I couldn't ask for more, except dry clothes."

He grinned, and there was something mischievous in his gaze. "I'll see if I can do something about that."

When the door closed, she stripped off her coat and hung it from a hook by the fireplace. She removed her shoes and quietly begged not to be surprised by more of Gemini's men. Then she eyed the bed. She doubted it would be anywhere near as comfortable as her own bed, but it had to be better than the hard ground or wooden floorboards she'd been sleeping on the last couple of nights. Yet, it was off-limits until she had dry clothes and hair.

A table with two chairs sat between the fireplace and the bed, a single sideboard with one of the oil lamps was placed against the far wall, and an upholstered chair hovered in the corner. She plopped into a chair by the table and leaned back to give the room a more thorough look. If this was an inn, they had gone to some expense to add decor, though the sheer fabrics and strong perfume smell seemed odd. But she had nothing to compare it with since she hadn't seen any of the rooms at the inn Beckworth had allowed her to visit.

She closed her eyes but worried she'd fall asleep and tumble out of the chair, so she laid her head on the table and waited.

The knock on the door startled her, and she sat up, wiping a bit of drool from the side of her mouth.

"Stella. It's me."

She gathered her energy and dragged herself to the door. Her stomach growled. What were the chances there was a kitchen downstairs?

He strode in, his hair and jacket still wet, but his pants and shirt appeared new. "Fortunately, the stables aren't that far." He held two bundles under his arm that he dropped on the bed, and a clay jar in his other hand that was probably filled with ale. From his pocket, he produced something wrapped in paper. She didn't catch an aroma, so assumed it was leftover bread and cheese she hadn't seen in his saddlebag.

After serious consideration of the clay jar, she trudged to the bed and noted one bundle was damp. When she opened up the thin towel, she found his wet clothes. She placed them by the fire and on her way back to the bed noticed him fussing with the wrapped package. Was he ignoring her, or was it her imagination?

When she unwrapped the next bundle, she could only stare. Then she made another slow circle to scan the room before picking up the sheer, lacy robe and pinning Beckworth with an icy glare.

"You brought me to a brothel? I thought you called this a boardinghouse." She placed her fists on her hips, the robe dangling from one.

"That's what they call them in smuggler's ports." He didn't seem fazed and had already uncorked the jug.

When the red liquid hit the cup, she licked her lips, the frilly lingerie and where he'd brought her fading. "Is that wine?"

He smiled as he handed her a mug. "I thought you could use a treat and maybe a little courage to get out those wet clothes and into something dry. I realize the clothing might be questionable, but there should be enough layers there to cover you properly."

She glanced at the bed. He had brought several pieces of clothes. She sipped the wine, grimaced, but finished it all. "I don't remember AJ mentioning how bad the wine was.

He shrugged and took the empty mug. "You'd have to go into the better part of town to find decent wine. Smugglers aren't as discriminating. The ship's captains, certainly. But the sailors? No."

She eyed his clothing. "How did you find clean clothes that fit?"

His expression turned sheepish as he poured her another drink. "How about one more and then get out of your wet things? I promise to turn my back."

"You had a spare set of clothes in your saddlebags." It wasn't a question, but he understood the tone well-enough.

"Eleanor keeps clothes for when I visit to help with the more difficult chores. I sometimes spend several days fixing this and that. It saves from having to pack anything."

She took the mug and drank half of it down. The wine, if it could be called that, might not be smooth, but it was working its magic.

"I think another jug might be in order. You can change while I'm gone."

She continued to give him the evil eye as he backed out of the room, but he winked before shutting the door. Her earlier laughter was all but forgotten as she picked through the garments. With a suffering sigh, she reviewed the pile and had to admit that, by sheer luck or design, the skimpy clothes appeared clean, could be layered to protect her modesty, and the robe would hang below her knees. That was something.

She stripped down to her undergarments that she'd fortunately washed the day before. Woolly socks were tucked in the center of the bundle, and she eagerly stripped off her damp ones. After all the layers were on, she slipped on the robe. It would never be a fashion statement, but she was warmer, and her feet thanked her, even if the socks were itchy.

When the knock came and the door opened, she mentally slapped herself for not locking it, but he didn't say anything as he set another jug on the table.

"We probably don't need more wine, as tired as we both are, but we should eat, and we'll need something to wash it down. I'll get us a pitcher of water tomorrow so we can have a more thorough wash."

He'd only given her a quick glance before opening the paper with their cold dinner. When she sat, she pushed back her still wet hair and finished the last drops from her mug. She pulled the paper closer and split up the food, but he stepped away from the table. When he returned, he dropped two of the sheer fabrics that had covered the sideboard.

"It's not the best, but it should help with drying your hair."

She must have been tired, otherwise she would have thought of it, and she pulled them to her, laid one over the other, and proceeded to wrap her hair as if they were towels. "Thank you."

He lifted a brow as he chewed a slice of pork. "I know this isn't ideal, but it would be one of the last places Gemini's men would think to look. At least, I hope so."

"Did you look for the *Daphne Marie*?" It was a stupid question. He would have said something by now if he had. Unless he hadn't checked yet.

"I did." His sympathetic glance said it all.

"Will we sail in the morning?"

He shook his head. "From what the woman who runs this place told me, there are four or five ships departing tomorrow afternoon. She didn't know their destination."

"Does that mean I can sleep in?" She took a bite of cheese and chased it with wine.

He grinned at her. "As long as you'd like." He eyed the bed then returned to his meal.

Up to now, she hadn't been bothered by their close proximity. They slept next to each other, tucked into their own blankets when huddled by a fire, and she suspected that was for safety should Gemini's men show up. While on horseback, she used him for support, warmth, and comfort. But sitting in a cathouse with a single bed brought an intimacy she hadn't expected.

She drank more wine.

They remained quiet as they ate, but the bed that was so inviting thirty minutes ago seemed to loom and mock. Was she supposed to sleep in it alone while he spent another night on the floor? The bed wasn't as large as she was used to, but there was enough space for two and, fully clothed, it wouldn't be any different than their sleeping arrangements on the ground. The fact that the bed was a foot off the ground shouldn't matter. Somehow it did.

"So, tell me about your childhood." She spit it out, not really thinking about the question, just wanting to get thoughts of the bed out of her head.

"What?"

She shrugged. "We're having dinner with a jug of wine. We've discussed gardens. You've asked about my childhood. I thought you might want to share something of yours. I guess we already know enough about your father, but what of your mother?"

His gaze dropped to his food, and he ripped off small chunks of bread that he placed in a circle around the cheese and meat. He lifted a shoulder. "I was born in the poor side of London. My mother lived with her sister and her husband at the time. I was five when my uncle decided we weren't providing enough to stay, so we moved to the shanty towns along the Thames. She found a job as a cleaning woman. With nothing to keep me occupied during the day, I began running with kids who worked for some of the crews in town."

"Crews?"

"That's what I called them, but to everyone else, they were gangs."

"Hoodlums." She finished her share of pork and sat back with her mug, still picking at the cheese.

He gave her a bit of a grin. "Young entrepreneurs in search of investments."

"You stole from the rich?"

"There wasn't any reason to take from those as poor as the rest of us."

"Your own redistribution of wealth."

"In a way." He wiped the breadcrumbs from his hands and finished his wine. He poured more and lifted the jug to her. She held out her mug. "They were small jobs, picking pockets mostly."

"You needed a crew for that?"

"It was safer in numbers. One or two would create a distraction while the other got close enough to grab a purse."

"And your mother was okay with this?"

He took a long sip from the mug, his eyes unfocused. "She understood the situation we were in. The money I brought in after a couple hours of work was more than she'd see after a week, slaving away from early morning to early evening cleaning up after others." His tone turned bitter, and he must have seen the concern in her expression. He shook his head, and when he continued, his voice returned to normal. "After a couple of years, I moved up in the gang, finding new ways to expand our jobs."

"It must have been a difficult life for you and your mother."

"When you're born to it, it's just a fact of life."

"But your mother hadn't been born into it, had she?"

He met her gaze. There was sadness, perhaps regret, hidden in his eyes. She could only guess, because she doubted he'd ever admit it, but it seemed that guilt haunted him.

"No." He drained his mug and set it down but didn't let go of it. His grip tightened, as if he was trying to make a fist. "She was born into service, like her mother, but she worked in a grand house and slept in a warm bed. Until the duke took a fancy to her."

AJ had told her this part of the story, and she didn't need to hear more. She didn't want to ask, but it seemed worse if she didn't. "And your mother now?"

He tugged at his sleeves and stared at the remnants of their meal.

She blinked and stared at his sleeves. He'd rarely touched them since they'd been on the run, yet AJ had sworn it was one of his prominent affectations. She found it interesting but tucked the topic away for later.

"My mother died in an unfortunate accident."

She'd suspected his mother was dead and, as curious as she was, didn't ask about the circumstances. "How old were you?"

"Old enough to take care of myself, and I had the crew."

"So, no regrets?"

He considered it for half a second. "No. It was a decent enough childhood, better than anyone could expect being poor in London. What about you?"

She snorted. "I think I shared enough for you to know the answer to that. I'm not close with my family, but I have a thriving business. I have a home that gives me nothing but joy. What more is there?" She hoped he didn't ask about the men in her life, or the lack thereof.

He watched her to the point she wanted to fidget. Then a slow smile appeared. Her chest tightened, and the room seemed a bit warm.

"No regrets?"

She relaxed. It was an easy answer. "My childhood taught me fortitude and perseverance. It forged, for good or bad, who I am today." She pushed her mug away.

"And that is something to be grateful for." He stood and removed his jacket, then glanced at the chair in the corner.

"Don't be silly. I think we're both adult enough to be able to share a bed. I'm guessing we won't have such a luxury on the ship." She could have turned twenty shades of red. Not an hour earlier, she'd stared daggers at the bed, knowing damn well it was plotting against her. Then the mention of the ship made her stomach gurgle. Or it might have been the bad wine. Either way, all her insecurities about sharing a bed vanished.

She expected him to give her some argument, but he didn't. When she studied him, she noted for the first time his hollowed-out eyes and paler than normal skin. While she'd spent most of her time napping in his arms, the only time he'd slept was during the night, but that was when he wasn't standing guard. He had to be exhausted.

He waited until she'd climbed into bed, which was no more comfortable than the one in Gemini's cabin. But it was better than the floor. Once she was settled, he added logs to the fire and doused the lamps. He shoved the curtains open, shedding silver light throughout the room.

She barely noticed when he slipped into bed and turned his back to her.

"Good night, Stella."

She turned and gave him her back, comforted by his way of giving her privacy. "Good night, Beckworth." She listened to his light breathing as he settled into sleep. She was pulled under soon after, feeling safe for the first time since arriving in this nightmare.

25

Lando brought their horses to the front of the inn where Finn waited for the women. Thomas's men had already ridden off to ensure the road ahead was clear. No one expected Gemini's men. Now that the meeting had been a disaster, it would be foolish for Gemini to focus anywhere but the ports.

"We should stay on the main road to Poole." Lando turned when Ethan walked up from the south end of town.

"Are you expecting someone?" Finn glanced at Ethan, who held up a sack.

"More herbs for Maire. She wanted her supplies restocked before we board." Ethan tossed them each an apple. "So, what's this about keeping to the road?"

Lando ran a hand over his closely shaved head. "It's a route we've used several times when needing to get to London but wanting to stay off the road from Southampton. If something changes in Poole, Jamie will be able to get word to us."

"Where's Thomas?" Ethan bit into the apple and wiped juice from his chin.

"He's scouting ahead. We'll meet up with him five miles out." Lando used his knife to slice a piece of apple.

The door to the inn opened, and Maire stepped out, followed by AJ. Her pace was slower, and she walked with a slight hitch, her lips thin from what Finn assumed was pain. When he glanced at Maire, who gave him a slight shake of the head, he sighed. AJ was irritated with him. She didn't look at anyone as she limped to a horse.

"Can you breathe?" He ignored her grumpy mood. Her face was pale, and it wasn't all from pain. She hadn't slept well, even with one of Maire's potions. The closer they got to the coast, the more stressed she became. They'd all wanted to catch up with Stella before crossing the Channel, but no one more than AJ. And there was nothing he could do except be there for her. He'd rather have a foe he could use a sword against, but he tamped down his own worry. It only clouded his thinking.

"You didn't have to make it so tight." She scratched at her side and gave him a particularly evil stare.

"You'll be thanking me in a couple of hours when the bandages begin to loosen. Then all I'll hear is how I made them too loose in the first place." He tried not to grin, but when her expression turned downright unpleasant, he'd known he'd failed. Maybe if she stewed over his overly protective requests she wouldn't think about her ribs or Stella.

"Take it from another one who's been in your shoes." Ethan handed the sack to Maire, who opened it and went through each of the individualized packages before nodding and stuffing them in her pack. "A tight bandage will make you feel awkward, but it will make the ride tolerable."

AJ didn't actually growl, but it was close enough for everyone else to turn away, their lips twitching as they held their humor in check. Finn suspected most of the discomfort came from her torn muscles rather than a sore rib. Either way, the ride would be uncomfortable, and they had a full day ahead of them.

When she tried to mount, she couldn't stand on her right leg long enough to get her foot in the stirrup. At that point, everyone led their horse away to give Finn and her their privacy. They all had their pride, and all had been injured and understood what AJ was going through. And none of them would want sympathy.

"Let me help you up." Finn stepped closer when she tried again and almost tipped over. "You're spooking the horse." He kept an even tone, hating how much she hurt.

"I can do it."

He laid a hand on hers, removing it from the saddle. When she tried to pull it away, he didn't let go. He bent his head low. "I know you're worried. I understand how frustrating it can be when you're not a hundred percent, but if you keep it up, Lando will take your horse, and you'll ride with me."

He recognized the stubborn set of her jaw and was prepared to do exactly as he warned, but she expelled a large breath and leaned her forehead against the saddle.

"I can't believe how stupid I was to not see him."

His released his own sigh. He'd been wrong on all counts.

When he'd seen her fall from the tree, he'd swore they'd go home right then. But this mission wasn't solely about Gemini's plans for the stones. If necessary, Hensley and his team would eventually take care of the problem. This was about Stella and getting her back. And until they did that, he'd suffer in silence while Maire doctored AJ's wound. At the time, he'd been grateful she hadn't hit her head again when she'd landed. And he could have kissed Fitz for his quick thinking in diverting the shot.

He'd assumed her bad temper had to do with Stella, but he should have known better, and he blamed it on his own worry over their friend. "It was chaos. You couldn't have had eyes everywhere. That's why we have a team."

"Fitz shouldn't have had to save me."

He turned her so she faced him, but he had to lift her chin to force her to look at him. "And how many of our men did you save with your well-placed arrows."

"That's not..." She huffed and rubbed at her side. "I see your point."

"So, let's get you in that saddle. You're lucky to be riding at all." He braced her right side and gave her a gentle push.

She grimaced as she swung her right leg over the saddle, but once she was astride, she wiggled until she found a comfortable position. When she nodded, everyone else mounted.

They kept to a walking pace, with Ethan and Maire leading the way and Lando in the back. Finn rode behind AJ so he could watch for any signs of fatigue. She leaned into her right side, and at first, he second-guessed letting her ride on her own. But she stayed in that position without swaying, and he assumed it was less painful. Riding with him wouldn't stop the pain, it would only make him feel better to hold her.

They caught up with Thomas's men five miles out of town as expected.

"Nothing but farmers and your normal travelers. The British Army would stay on the road to Southampton." Thomas's report wasn't anything more than Finn expected.

"Stay a mile ahead of us. We'll stop in Ower for a break." Finn didn't glance at AJ. Her movements on the horse would be enough to tell him when she required a break, but he wouldn't make it about her unless necessary.

Thomas's men waited for them at a quaint inn at Ower. The cook was already preparing more food for their large group. Finn took AJ and Maire for a stroll around the small hamlet while Lando and Ethan helped the stable boy feed the horses. After lunch, Maire insisted on checking AJ's side, and Finn found them a quiet place behind the inn. Once a new bandage had been placed over the wound, Finn set a tight wrap.

"Will that do?" He kept a close eye on AJ, but she seemed to be in better spirits.

"Yes. I see what you mean about a tighter bandage. I'm sorry I've been such a grouch."

He kissed her forehead. "As long as you don't remind me of what a stubborn ass I was during my recovery from Reginald's not-so-delicate care, I'll let you work through what you need to."

"Thank you."

"Enough with you two. Let's get moving." Maire winked at Finn after closing up her healing bag and walked off toward the waiting horses.

"She's been bossier lately," AJ grumbled when Finn helped her mount.

"She always gets that way when she plays healer to a group of soldiers. You're not the only one being difficult with the first aid." He nodded toward Thomas's men, several recovering from their own wounds that Maire was overseeing.

"I suppose I saw some of that when she patched up sailors on the *Daphne*."

"Aye, but the sailors put up with it because she's my sister, whether I'm still the captain or not. But Thomas leads soldiers, who tend to think of themselves above pampering."

If nothing else, their banter appeared to relax her as they started their next leg of the journey.

They were two miles from their next stop when a rider raced toward them. One of Thomas's men.

The rider pulled up on his reins, bringing his horse to a quick stop. "Fitz waits for us in Ringwood."

Before he could stop her, AJ took off at a gallop, forcing the rest to keep up. He let AJ set the pace all the way to town before he passed her, racing for the inn, and jumping from his saddle the second his horse stopped. After tossing the reins to one of

Thomas's men, who'd been lounging outside the front door, he ran and caught AJ as she fell from her mount.

A muffled cry escaped her lips, and her whole body shook.

"My impatient wife. What did you hope to accomplish with that foolish ride?" He carried her into the inn, Maire only steps behind.

"Take her to the back corner for more privacy." Maire all but pushed Finn toward that direction, but he wasn't listening.

"Innkeeper!" he bellowed. "We need a room. Just for a couple of hours. I'll pay for a full night."

The innkeeper, a tall, thin man with spectacles and a straggly beard came running, wiping his hands on his soiled apron. "Second door on your left. It has a hearth if you need it."

Maire had changed direction with Finn. "We'll need a pitcher of water and coffee if you have it."

The innkeeper waved at a lad, who jumped up and ran to the kitchen.

Through all of it, AJ couldn't speak. Her lips were pressed firmly together, her face as white as the wool on a newborn lamb, and she was probably as weak as one.

He laid her on the bed and unbuttoned her shirt while Maire set her bag on the table. The lad arrived a couple minutes later with the water and a coffee service that he placed on the table, his eyes wide as he watched Maire grind herbs.

"Should I fetch a barber?" The lad glanced from Maire to AJ, who struggled as Finn removed her bandage.

"No. She's just had a long ride and needs rest. That's all we need for now." She gave him a pointed look, and he nodded quickly before racing from the room.

"He probably thinks we're a band of highwaymen." Finn pulled the bandage off. "Stop fighting me, woman. You're not leaving this room until Maire's had a look. If you want to know what Fitz rode to tell us, you'll calm down."

"I'm fine. I just need to sit." AJ plucked at his hands, but she had little strength to do anything more.

He stared at his wife, noted the stubborn set to her jaw, and played her game. "All right. If you can walk to that door on two legs, we can all go back downstairs. Crawling doesn't count." He stood back, hands on hips, watching while she surveyed the distance. Maire had paused in her work, waiting to see what AJ would do.

He had to give her credit as she rose to a sitting position, the old bandage hanging from her open shirt. But when she tried to move her legs to the floor, she fell back, her head thumping on the pillow. "Damn it."

There was nothing else to say, and Maire went back to fixing her concoctions before taking a look at the wound.

"It looks angry, but I think that's from being rubbed against the other bandage. There's not much I can do about that until she's on board the ship and can give it some time to heal. She doesn't have a fever and hasn't lost any blood, so I think it's just the combination of pain, jostling, and worry that has her so worn out. I have a pain medication from Bart that shouldn't make her too drowsy."

"Will she be able to ride?"

"I think so. But it would be best if she eats well before we leave."

When Maire had replaced the bandage, she left everything on the table so they could wrap AJ with the larger bandage when it was time to go. Then she nodded at Finn. "I'll send some food up. She needs to eat it all."

"I'll see to it."

When the door closed, he prepared for her wrath.

"We're missing the news. Can't you have Fitz come up and tell us what's happening?"

He shook his head and handed her a mug of coffee. "You'll

know soon enough. After you've rested and had a good meal. I'll not have anything riling you up any further. Not yet."

"Stop babying me." She took the coffee and gulped two swallows.

"Then stop acting like one."

Her eyes narrowed, but she didn't seem to have a retort, which surprised him.

"Whatever's happened, there's nothing we can do to change it." He calmed his voice, sorry for his outburst.

"But what if we're needed in Poole?"

"We're a good three hours from there if we push it. If we walk the horses, it's closer to four. And if you don't get a good rest, it could be longer than that. Let's be smart about this."

She beat a fist against the bed, somehow not spilling any coffee. "I hate being injured. I feel so useless. All I'm doing is holding everyone back. Maybe we should have gotten a coach."

He sat next to her and pulled her to him. "Take it from one who's ridden in a coach while injured, it's not any easier. And if I remember correctly, I irritated you and Maire sufficiently enough that you sedated me."

She smiled. "You knew we did that?"

"Not at first. But once my head cleared, I had a pretty good idea there'd been a reason for foisting so much water on me."

A knock on the door heralded their lunch. AJ ate with gusto, and the food seemed to be what she needed. She was able to stand on her own and took the time to wash the road dust from her face before turning to him with her arms raised.

"Get the bandage on, and let's go see Fitz."

AJ managed the stairs without any hesitation and set Maire's bag next to her. "It's all there. I think I put everything in its correct place."

"You're looking more chipper than an hour ago." Maire

opened the bag and checked all the packages. AJ didn't seem offended by his sister's possessiveness—perhaps obsessiveness would be a better description—for her herb bag.

"The food helped."

"I would have expected more of a ruckus about Fitz's news." Finn smiled as he watched Jamie's first mate devour a bowl of stew.

"And he might have shared that information if he'd stop eating long enough." Maire rolled her eyes when Fitz winked at her.

"And he refused to say a word until the two of you joined us." Ethan stared at Fitz with suspicion. "I have a feeling he doesn't have as much to share as we hoped."

Fitz ate a chunk of cheese, followed by a thick slice of bread, then swallowed it all down with a long gulp of ale. "And I'm afraid Ethan is correct. Jamie was still collecting information when he told me to find you. Beckworth and Stella have boarded a ship." He raised his hands when everyone started talking. "I have no idea where to. That's all the captain knew. The men he sent to Bournemouth are positive they left, but they were still piecing together which ship."

"That's not surprising. Beckworth doesn't do anything the easy way." Finn kept his eye on AJ, who'd gone still. "I'm guessing there's more to share since we were already on our way to you."

"Gemini isn't looking for just Beckworth and Stella." Fitz gave Maire a glance and pointed his mug toward her. "She's also looking for the translator."

Everyone turned to Maire, and Finn's chest tightened, though he wasn't surprised. Based on Maire's expression, neither was she.

Maire slumped in her chair. "It seems it's still not safe to be in this century, but as long as we all stick together, I should be safe enough, especially if they don't know where I am."

"Which is why Jamie sent me. He wanted you to be aware should you run into any of Gemini's men."

Finn stood. "Then if you're done with your repast, it's time we get on the road."

26

Beckworth whistled as he jogged across the lane to the boardinghouse. He didn't have anything to be jovial about, but the sun was out, the gulls were active, and though he'd had no luck finding passage on the first two ships he'd visited, the captains had given him names of two other possibilities.

The sun was getting high, and though Stella had been sleeping soundly when he'd left, she'd tossed and turned a good portion of the night. He hadn't noticed her do that before. So why now? Was it having to get on a ship, or that AJ hadn't been here waiting for her?

When he'd first woken, he'd turned to find her asleep, her hair spread around her head like an auburn halo, her face so peaceful. But the image that forced itself front and center had been from the night before. She'd been leaning against the building in the rain as wet as a London sewer rat, yet she had a mystifying glow about her. Even with her hair clinging to her head in wet clumps, her face lifted to the sky in laughter—she'd been breathtakingly beautiful. The other memory that came to mind when he thought of her had been that day in Baywood with her brightly colored wrap flowing about her. As stunning as she'd been that day, it didn't compare to the woman he'd glimpsed last night. It was probably nothing more than the way the lamps lit the alley, but something had seemed different about her.

When he reached the boardinghouse, he entered through the front door and strode straight to the kitchen.

"Hello, luv." Beckworth spotted the cook pulling bread out of the oven.

"The man with the fancy words expecting something special." She scowled at him as she laid the pan of loaves on the counter.

"I thought the extra coins would be enough to soothe your harsh tone." He gave her his best smile and checked the coffee pot hanging near the hearth. "The coffee smells wonderful this morning." He noticed the buckets on the counter. "I still have to check on my horse this morning. Can I take care of those scraps for you?"

She gave him another scowl over her shoulder, most likely ready to hurl more tart words, but then she squinted, and though she didn't smile, her face softened. "The chickens next to the stables would appreciate them if you had a mind. But don't think that will win you any favors."

"Of course not." He held a hand to his chest. "I am a gentleman."

She snorted and went back to tossing a large chunk of bacon in a pan.

Beckworth picked up both pails and was almost out the door when the cook yelled, "While you're feeding the chickens, tell Mrs. Morrison that you're picking up the eggs for me."

He smiled. "Shall do."

Thirty minutes later, with a heavy tray in hand, he kicked lightly at the door to their room. When he didn't hear anything, he kicked a bit harder. There was rustling, then the door was pulled open, and a ginger-haired devil in layers of alluring clothing stared at him, pointing a pistol. He almost dropped the tray.

"Oh, thank god. I'm starving." She lowered the pistol, laying it on the table before running both hands through her hair. "I miss my hairbrush. I miss a fresh change of underwear. And most importantly, I miss my toothbrush." She rubbed a finger over her teeth. "But if that's coffee I smell, it will be a good start."

He grinned at her complaining. In the few days they'd been together, he'd come to realize her grumbling was a sign she was in a good mood. Perhaps the tossing in her sleep was normal for her. Something stirred below his belt, and he dropped the tray with a resounding thud.

He cleared his throat. "I'm not sure if the coffee will compare with what you've been able to make with Eleanor's beans."

"It smells the same, so we're halfway there." She poured the coffee then fell into a chair. When he offered her a plate, she shook her head and pointed to the mug. "Priority."

She brought the cup to her nose and whiffed, took a small sip, then shrugged. "Not bad for a whorehouse, but I guess they need to keep the girls on their toes."

He almost choked, but then she leaned back, her face pointing toward the ceiling, her eyes closed. She had a long, delicate neck, and would look marvelous moving about the balls in London, her dark auburn hair piled on her head to show off that lovely décolletage. He'd be the envy of every man there, even with her saucy tongue. Elizabeth Ellingsworth would adore her.

"I take it the coffee meets with your approval."

She opened an eye with a ready smile, then sat up. "It's either pretty good, or I'm getting used to your barbaric standards."

Beckworth grinned. "I'm hoping the food can gain your approval as well."

She rubbed her hands together and looked at the eggs, bacon, sausage, biscuits, fruits, and pastries. "How much did this all cost? We still have a ship to find." She faltered a bit on the last sentence. Perhaps that was the reason for her restless sleep after all.

"Hardly a worry after the chores I helped with."

"So when do we see about a ship?"

He narrowed his eyes. "Why are you so eager to sail?"

She snorted. "I'm not. But I've been giving it some thought. If we can't find AJ and Finn, and they know you plan on going to the monastery, then they could already be on their way there. One way or another, that's where they'll end up, so I'd just as soon get this over with."

She held up one of her little pouches of herbs and tapped a tiny portion into her eggs, then mixed it all together with a slice of bacon. "I thought I'd start taking the herbs now and throughout the day. I should have enough to get me across, but I don't know how long it takes to cross the Channel."

"It depends on the blockades. They change, which is one reason smugglers tend to flock to the same ports. They can pass along information regarding the best crossings. My best guess is two days. And about a ship, I'll need you to stay in the room while I talk with the captains." He gave her a quick glance, and when she set her coffee down to give him a pointed look he hurried on. "I've met with two captains so far, but they aren't the best choices. One wouldn't even consider bringing a woman on board. Even with your pants and shirt, maybe a hat, it won't take long for the men to figure out you're female."

"AJ never seemed to have a problem."

"Because she's only sailed on one ship that, at the time, was owned and captained by the man who is now her husband. Then she found ways to ingratiate herself with the crew."

"Ingratiate. You mean be nice and pitch in to help?"

He grinned. "Of course. I wouldn't suggest anything else." He rubbed his shoulder. "I wouldn't want to garner her wrath."

She snorted. "You mean you don't want her to stab you again."

"Exactly."

"Would a red-haired woman be considered worst luck?"

He hadn't considered that, but it was risky to discuss while negotiating a berth. "Interesting question. I imagine that would come down to what country the ship hails from or the preference of the captain."

She waved her fork at him. "I am not sleeping with the captain. I don't care who he is."

He grinned. "I merely suggest that he might have a red-headed sister that you remind him of. I suppose cajoling would work. You seem to have a knack for talking."

Her eyes narrowed as she pushed her plate away and retrieved her cup of coffee. "And what do I do while I'm waiting for your return? How long will this take? I mean, how many ships are out there?"

"Enough to not give up hope. And that reminds me." He reached into his jacket pocket and brought out the newspapers he bought in Southampton. "I thought you might be able to make use of these."

Her eyes lit up, and she examined a single sheet. "To make my swans?" When he nodded, she began folding. "This will work better than what I had before." She flipped through the stack. "I might try working on a fish. Charlotte, AJ's niece, has her favorite, but I think she'd like to try a different fish."

"Then it's settled. I'll make sure a fresh pot of coffee is sent up."

He placed everything but the coffee pot and mugs on the tray.

"Do you think it's possible the *Daphne* is close?"

He fiddled with the edge of the tray then tugged on his sleeves. "Likely. The meeting was yesterday, and I'm sure Murphy had every intention of going in the hopes of dealing with Gemini."

She just nodded and dipped her head, focusing on her first swan.

"I'll keep an eye out. You know that. But it would be dangerous to ride from port to port in the hopes of finding them. We would just as likely run into more of Gemini's men."

She nodded again, and he thought he saw a tear, but she swiped her hair from her face and was either able to brush the tear away at the same time, or he'd imagined it. He wished there was something he could do to ease her anxiety. She probably worried more about AJ than her own plight. But no words would bring her comfort.

Getting her to the monastery was what she needed. He opened the door then picked up the tray. "Make sure you lock it."

She set the swan aside and stood, refusing to meet his gaze. He walked away, leaving her to her privacy.

<hr>

Stella stared up at the tall sails as if she were Don Quixote and the imposing ship her windmill. If she only had her trusty sword. She stood alone on the dock, tucked next to a stack of crates waiting to be loaded onto a nearby ship. Her focus was on the one next to it, where men bustled about the sails with myriad ropes that ran from the deck railing to the masts and yards. How did the sailors get around without strangling themselves?

She reached for her pouches of herbs that didn't bring much comfort now that she was moments from having to board. Her stomach lurched at the thought, and as strange as it was, the motion sickness from the cruise she'd taken while on vacation in France with AJ and Finn resurfaced. It had to be her imagination, but the realization it had taken half a day before she'd felt like herself, and that had only been an hour boat ride along the coast, almost made her turn and run for the stables in search of Beckworth's horse. This boat ride would be two days, assuming there wasn't trouble along the way—or a storm.

She was still staring at the ship when Beckworth returned.

"The captain says it's time to board. I have to warn you, the accommodations aren't what we originally discussed. It seems he agreed to take on extra passengers once he decided to make a stop in France."

"What does that mean exactly?"

"You'll see. For now, keep your head down while we board. He says his crew isn't as superstitious as most when it comes to women on board, but it's best we stick together until we dock in France."

"Great," she muttered but didn't offer a protest as he touched her elbow and steered her toward the gangway. She almost balked at the last second, but he must have been expecting it because he took her arm until she stood on the deck.

He moved her to the side as other passengers boarded, but she couldn't take her eyes off the masts. She remembered the *Daphne*, sort of. She hadn't paid it much attention. Was it smaller than this ship? She lifted her gaze to the top of the mast where she spotted the crow's nest. Her stomach made a soft protest when she recalled AJ chattering nonstop about how much she enjoyed sitting up there, watching for the Royal Navy.

"We better get to our spot before someone else claims it." Beckworth guided her across the deck and around men racing from one place to another.

"Have you sailed a lot?" Maybe if she talked and got her mind off the ship, she wouldn't have dark thoughts of being trapped in the hold, being tossed around like a pinball. Her stomach made a queasy sound. She glanced at Beckworth, but he hadn't seemed to notice, his focus on a point across the deck just below the bow.

"We're staying on deck?" Stella's instinct to turn and run screeched like a banshee. If Gemini was so interested in getting to France, maybe she could find her way to Hensley's. He could write letters, and she could sit out this part of the adventure. But would he be in Bristol or London? The idea suddenly seemed daunting, and she turned to Beckworth, who was staring at her. At least he had the decency to appear sheepish.

"We were supposed to have our own tiny storage room one deck below, but someone had better coin than me." He seemed to have difficulty looking at her and stared at their little corner of the deck instead. "The captain assured me we could use spare canvas to make a cover. I thought with being behind the quarter-deck and next to a railing, we should be able to create an acceptable shelter."

He set the saddlebag down, tugged at his sleeves, then ran a hand through his hair as he glanced around, perhaps searching for the canvas.

She sighed, wishing she'd told him about the coins she'd stolen, but it was too late now. "Well, I shouldn't get as seasick on deck. Something about being able to watch the horizon."

"Has that worked before?"

"No."

He pulled out a blanket and laid it on the deck, then wandered off to the other side of the ship, returning several minutes later dragging a piece of canvas. It looked like a spare sail. She grabbed an end as he positioned it, but she was useless. The canvas sheet was heavier than it looked.

A deckhand ran over and helped Beckworth position the canvas using rope and a couple of stacked crates to provide a three-sided lean-to. There was extra canvas that could be dropped down to enclose the shelter on all four sides. She'd been in worse, though she couldn't think of an example at the moment.

No. Not true. Playing hostage with Gemini in that first decrepit cabin with Jessup sniffing after her had definitely been the worst place—ever. She glanced at Beckworth, who'd settled another blanket on top of the first, then laid a wrapped bundle on top.

She knelt next to him. "I don't think eating is a good idea." She placed a hand over her stomach, but she couldn't tell if the gurgling was hunger or early stages of motion sickness.

"I think it best to eat tiny portions throughout the day. And it will give you an opportunity to take your herbs. Tea will be a luxury."

"Are you going to mother me all the way to France?" Stella pushed the blankets around to find a comfortable spot.

"If need be. But these next couple of days will be a good time to relax and get some rest. You've been through a lot. It's not easy being on the run. We'll be able to take short strolls around the deck, but most of our time will have to be spent here."

"It's a shame you didn't bring any wine."

"I'm afraid all we have is water."

"And no coffee."

He grimaced. "No."

She fell back and groaned. "I think I'll start that resting now. Maybe I won't open my eyes until you kick me to say we're in France."

"Oh no. Sit up. Just a few small bites then you can sleep."

After they ate a small portion of the stash they'd brought, Stella noticed the motion of the ship. They'd left port, and she stepped out of the shelter to watch the land disappear, amazed at how far they'd traveled in such a short time. Maybe the trip would be faster than expected. She glanced up and threw an arm across her forehead to shield the glare.

She turned her head and grinned. "At least we have sunny skies."

27

"Cairo!" AJ paced the galley, not believing what she was hearing. Could this possibly get any worse? She almost wished Beckworth hadn't rescued Stella. But that meeting with Gemini's men had immediately gone bad. Gemini, or the man posing as her, could have escaped with Stella, or she could have been injured. Maybe they wouldn't have even brought her to the meeting.

"That seems to be more of a detour than we planned on." Fitz had collapsed on a bench, resting his boots on a nearby table. She might be the injured one, but Fitz had spent more time on horseback the last two days than she'd cared to think about.

"Sorry, can we go back to the beginning?" Ethan asked. He'd missed the first part of the conversation, having returned from taking the horses to the stables.

Jamie handed him a cup with two fingers of Jameson. Everyone had one, including AJ and Maire. It would seem the rest of the news would warrant something stronger than wine.

"I didn't have a lot of men to spare while we loaded cargo and fixed sails. I feel a storm coming." He ran a hand over his head; he seemed to carry the world on his shoulders. She'd seen the same look on Finn when he made difficult decisions that didn't always work in his favor. "I sent men when I could to search for Beckworth."

"Not an easy task." Lando stood near the stairs, head half turned to keep track of the shouts from the men on deck preparing for their departure. "He could be standing twenty feet from you, and you wouldn't know if he didn't want you to. He learned to change his speech, even his physical appearance, to blend in."

"And if they were running for their lives, he could easily hide them, almost in plain sight." Maire nodded, almost approvingly. AJ had seen Maire run hot and cold in regard to Beckworth, which was understandable after being kept a prisoner at Waverly for almost two years. Yet, even as a hostage, the two of them had discussed art, books, and fashion.

There were so many layers to the man.

"He's one to most assuredly do the unexpected." Jamie grinned, and his burdens, whatever they were, slipped from him, leaving the young man she remembered first meeting in Ireland. "Seems they stayed overnight at Miss Lucy's board-inghouse."

When the men grinned, Maire rolled her eyes.

"What does that mean?" AJ asked.

"It means they overnighted at a house of prostitution," Maire supplied.

AJ shook her head and looked to Finn as if he could clear up what had to be a misunderstanding. "That doesn't make sense."

Finn considered the information then laughed. "Of course, it does. It would be the last place anyone would expect them to be, assuming any of Gemini's men were there and searching. The real question is where did they go from there?"

Her head spun, not believing Stella would stay one minute in a brothel, and almost missed the rest of the story.

"That's what took the men so long to figure out what happened. Beckworth arrived with Stella well after midnight. We confirmed that with the boardinghouse. He helped with morning chores, but Stella never left the room."

"Wait. When you brought me and Beckworth from France to search for Maire, we arrived here in Poole." AJ inched to the edge of her seat. It was all she could do not to pace. "Wouldn't he think to check here before booking passage on another ship?"

Finn rubbed her back. "It would have been a tough call. They'd been eluding Gemini's men for three days, probably spending their nights out in the cold. Stella would be worn from the miles on horseback. He would have taken the easiest option available to get them to France."

"He might have considered coming here if he couldn't find the right ship in Bournemouth," Jamie added. "My men were finally able to piece together the rest. Seems he'd been talking with various sailors and captains, at both the docks and the inns. He never focused on one ship, so it was damn hard to pin down which one he actually left on. But once again he was sly, and if I didn't understand why Hensley finds him to be of such high value as a spy, I do now. He talked his way onto a ship heading for Cairo."

"And this was where I came in." Ethan nodded. "No one would have given it a second thought."

"Why Cairo? I'm missing something," AJ sputtered, still not believing Stella would be on board a ship, during a time of war, heading for Cairo like it was some pleasure trip. Not Stella.

"This captain makes various stops along the way, and one of those stops is Saint-Malo," Jamie said.

"Only a day's ride to the monastery from there, but it's a busy port." Ethan nodded with apparent approval of Beckworth's actions.

"Aye, it will be difficult to dock there, but we have options.

Fortunately, we have a couple of Irish passengers looking to flee England." Jamie passed Finn a long glance before they both turned to Fitz and Lando. They smiled in return, so AJ assumed it was some scheme they'd run before.

"How fast is the ship?" Finn would be running calculations in his head, already planning various scenarios. How easily she could read him now.

Jamie frowned. "She's a French ship and rides heavy, but she has a lot of canvas. We'll make up time, but they'll be in port a few hours ahead of us. And I won't want to stay long."

"Just long enough for us to disappear into town while you unload enough cargo to pay the French bounty fees. Then you can sail to the monastery."

Jamie nodded. "You'll need to be careful. It might only be a day's ride, but we don't know if Gemini has men in France. She discovered the stones and incantations from someone. And if she has a ship, we never found it."

"And you'll need to avoid French soldiers." Ethan gave Finn a knowing glance from their own encounters with them. "Maire and I will stay on the *Daphne*. We can't take the chance someone will spot her. But if you need me, I'll go with you."

"I think it would be easier for AJ and me to go alone." Finn slid her a glance, and she nodded her agreement.

"I'd feel better if I could send Fitz or Lando with you." Jamie glanced at the men.

"I'll go." Lando didn't hesitate and only beat Fitz by a breath.

"Get some rest. We leave within the hour. There's bread, cheese, and some pork that cook left for you." Jamie stood and headed for the stairs. When Fitz and Lando turned to follow, he waved them off. "That goes for the two of you as well. I'll see you at morning watch."

The three-hour race from Ringwood to Poole had zapped most of AJ's energy. Now that they'd eaten and she knew where Stella was, she was wired. She'd asked Maire for a sleeping aid, knowing she'd stare at the wooden ceiling all night otherwise.

The cabin was cozy with only an oil lamp to light it. The bed was large enough for both of them to fit snuggly, and a table with two chairs was squeezed into a corner. A small bookshelf, washstand, and an extra chair rounded out the cabin.

On the sail from Bristol, they'd spent most of their free time in this cabin, and her skin warmed as she watched her husband. Her one constant through all of this.

Finn climbed into bed next to her and put an arm around her as she snuggled next to him. "Stella's a smart woman, quite capable of taking care of herself. And, as much as I hate to admit it, Beckworth is also intelligent and excellent at preserving his backside. If anyone can escape Gemini's men and find their way to France, it would be those two."

He was right. At least Stella was on a ship bound for France. She turned pale and sat up. "Oh my God, how will Stella survive the crossing?"

"What do you mean?" Finn had half risen with her.

"Stella gets horribly seasick. It took her an entire day to recover from just one hour at sea when we visited France. How will she manage a Channel crossing?"

He leaned back and stared at the ceiling. Then he smiled. "I wonder how well Beckworth can clean up vomit."

She didn't answer—couldn't answer. He was watching her, and it was wrong to laugh at someone else's suffering, but she couldn't stop the giggle that grew to a chuckle, and then the full-on shrieks of laughter when Finn joined her. It was the release of stress. The days of worry culminating in something so simple, so tangible.

When the tears of laughter turned to tears of sorrow, Finn pulled her into his arms. He stroked her hair until her sobs turned to hiccups and then silence. She held him tight through all of it, then she rubbed her nose and sniffled.

"Stella saved me, you know." She turned into him and leaned her head against his shoulder, his skin prickled under her warm breath.

"I don't think you ever told me that."

"It was when my father died. I was a wreck. My whole world fell apart. After the service, I took a leave from work and shut myself in my apartment. Stella waited a week, then she'd stop by and knock. I wouldn't answer, and she'd go away. She never called; she only came by. Every day at the same time. For the first few days, I barely noticed. My mother called, then Adam tried. They stopped by a couple of times, then they stopped trying. But not Stella.

"By the end of the second week, there was nothing left in the fridge, and I'd pretty much polished off what little I had in the pantry. I wasn't eating much as it was, so it took a while to run out of food. Worse, I was running out of coffee and had drained all the alcohol. I called the local grocery store, and they delivered two bags of groceries.

"When I answered the door, I found the hall filled with bags of food, coffee, and wine." She snorted. "The delivery guy must have thought I was a hoarder. Then I found myself waiting for her knock, and I'd wait for her to leave before opening the door to see what she'd left me. She obviously noticed the bags were gone and had rightly assumed I'd finally seen them. One day, there was a bouquet of flowers. The next day was a pie from Donna's. The day after that, I left the door ajar."

"She's the best. But I have to ask. Was it the pie that made you leave the door open?"

She sat up and punched him in the arm.

He dramatically rubbed his arm as if she had the power of a comic book heroine. "My mistake. It had to have been the wine."

She laughed. "If I had to choose only one thing, it would have to be coffee."

"Of course. I should have known." He pulled her back down and kissed her forehead. "We'll find her and take her back home, no matter what."

She took his hand and slipped her fingers through his. "Make me forget about all of this. Just for a small while."

He rolled her over and rested on his elbows to gaze down at her. "That's what husbands are for."

"Making someone forget?"

"Doing as their wife commands."

His kiss was tender and inviting. She let everything go and gave into his increasingly demanding lips. His touch burned through her, igniting her senses. Something was different. Everything was more—consuming. It wasn't anything she'd ever felt before, but it broke open something deep inside her. More powerful than the most amazing orgasm. And her love for this man ran so deep she could hardly draw a breath when intense ripples flowed through her. Before the night was over, Finn took away all the pain and filled her with the most peaceful bliss. All she had to do was hang on.

28

The ship lurched before slamming down and rocking to the side. Water flowed underneath their soaked blankets and seeped into her pants. Stella held onto a rope with one hand and Beckworth's hand with the other. She licked her lips and tasted the salty brine of the sea.

The ship settled, but it was an illusion. A tease. But they would have a few minutes to listen to the wind whip at the canvas in an attempt to tear it from the ropes tying it down. She took the opportunity to crawl past Beckworth, her stomach wrenching. This would be the third—no, the fourth time—she'd puked since the storm started, but now it was nothing more than dry heaves that made her stomach muscles ache.

She'd only crawled a few feet, but it was enough to soak what small portion of her clothes had been dry. Beckworth gripped her waist and tugged her back, but he hadn't pulled her far enough when another wave hit them, and she tumbled across the deck, saltwater splashing her face. She swallowed a mouthful, the brine burning its way down before she choked it up. The night was eerily dark, but she could make out the white canvas and had risen to her knees when someone tripped over her.

"Damn, woman." Arms pulled her up and pushed her toward Beckworth, who grabbed her and dragged her back to the shelter. They both fell again when the ship abruptly shifted direction.

Her mind drifted to the lower decks. Was being dry but sick as death better than drowning in the fresh air? She'd been surprised how well she'd done the day before. Beckworth escorted her around the deck in between her long naps. He kept her arm tucked through his and glared at anyone who stared at her too long. Whether it was the herbs or the sunny day, she'd kept down the small meals he'd portioned out to her.

When they were both awake and confined to their shelter, they discussed an array of topics, most of it centered around social structures of their two centuries and fashion. She'd never spoken about clothes with a man before, and discovered he had an amazing eye for color and lines, which came out when he spoke of art, his plans for refurnishing Waverly's decor, and his desire to add more color and variety to his gardens.

"AJ told me about the first time she met you." She tilted her head as she gave him a quick once over. "She said you wore periwinkle breeches and tailcoat." Her gaze dropped to her hands, but she gave him a quick glance and caught the twitch of his lips.

"I don't think I own anything in periwinkle." His gaze wandered, and several minutes passed before he gave a slight nod. "Yes, I do remember that day. I was surprised Murphy came in a coach and not with a small army to demand his sister back."

"Why didn't he?"

He picked at the edge of his sleeve though he didn't tug on it. "I can't say, but I assume he wanted to get close to the duke. He knew the man was pulling all the strings, he just couldn't prove it." He hesitated. "And I'm sure he worried for his sister's safety. Then I told him his sister was in London even though she was in her rooms in the east wing."

"You wanted him out of the way." She folded one of the newspapers he'd given her. The shape of a swan slowly taking shape. When he didn't answer, she glanced up. "What?"

His gaze assessed her, and he gave her a touch of a smile. "You're correct. I wanted him gone so I could prepare for France. He'd given me the stones, and I forced his hand to leave AJ behind. I knew there was something different about her, but I couldn't put my finger on it."

"I guess you were in for a surprise."

He startled her when he burst out with a laugh. "You have no idea. AJ and Maire had Dugan's men running in circles. Well, the first time was Hughes doing, sabotaging their coach and forcing Dugan to overnight in the open. But who would have thought two women could cause such trouble?"

"Well, now you know better."

He snorted then laid his head against the canvas. When the silence stretched, she finished the last folds of the swan and tucked it between the newspapers in the saddlebag.

"They were turquoise." His eyes were closed, but his lips— had she noticed before how full they were, how soft—were turned up in a smile.

"What?" It was all she could think to say. Anything more would be nothing but a stammer.

"The breeches and tailcoat. They were a lovely shade of turquoise, and I think the waistcoat was a matching paisley."

She laughed. "AJ said you looked like a peacock."

"Really? Peacocks are regal."

When she snickered, he lifted his chin and would probably have preened if the shelter had been high enough for him to stand.

"Well, the peahens seem impressed when the male fluffs those long tail feathers."

Her snicker turned to giggles, and Beckworth laughed with her. If he'd been trying to keep her mind off the sway of the ship, he'd been doing a good job of it.

"Stella!" Beckworth yelled, jarring her out of her musings.

Right. This wasn't the time for daydreaming. They were sprawled on the deck inches from the shelter. No. *She* was sprawled on the deck. Beckworth knelt over her trying to get her attention.

"Are you all right?"

Did she look all right? "I'm wet, cold, and my stomach's attempting a prison break by way of my esophagus. I'm peachy."

"So in other words, you're fine." He grabbed her under her arms and half dragged her into their shelter. Before he could follow, someone screamed.

A woman.

Other small shelters dotted the deck. The captain was either a humanitarian or was lining his pockets with more passengers, a couple of which were family groups with small children. Either way, it wasn't her place to judge, but now, someone was in trouble.

Beckworth glanced at her, and she waved toward the darkness. "Go. But be careful."

He grinned. "Worried about me?"

"I'm worried who will get me to the monastery if you fall overboard."

"So I was close." He winked before she could respond and disappeared into the storm.

Someone managed to keep a lamp going in a tiny shelter no bigger than a pup tent, but it provided enough ambient light to make out a group of men, but it was impossible to tell if any of them were Beckworth.

Someone yelled, but the voice was muffled.

She waited fifteen minutes before her anxiety overrode all common sense and encouraged her to do something stupid. Two men, their heads down as they struggled in the wind and rolling deck, pushed forward in the direction Beckworth had gone.

She crawled out of the shelter and made it ten feet before the ship rolled and dropped out from under her. There was a momentary feeling of weightlessness before she slammed into the deck. She cried out when her hip grazed against something sharp. Probably a nail.

Somehow she'd landed closer to the group of men. An elaborate shelter had been built using crates and barrels to make a tent-like structure with enough height to stand up in. One of the waves had taken out half the shelter, the barrels collapsing on the tent. Someone, or more than one, might have gotten hurt.

She rose to her hands and knees, then cursed her timing when the ship bobbed again. With nothing to hold onto, she rolled toward the railing. Images of being washed overboard and the terror of drowning crippled her critical thinking. Of all the times. Then the ship righted itself, and she gripped the deck with her fingernails.

She glanced around, searching for something she could use to stand and brace herself. Something nowhere near the railing. She spotted the mast ten feet away. It might as well have been a mile, considering she couldn't take more than a couple of steps without being pitched to the deck. Though the distance appeared daunting, it was in the direction of Beckworth.

Determined to do something other than roll into a ball, she began her trek on hands and knees. She was halfway to her target when she spotted a person-sized lump laying near the door that led to the galley and cabins. The form shifted with the rough motions of the ship.

Curious, she changed direction and continued toward it. As she drew closer, it was easy to see it was a person, but she couldn't see a face. Not sure what to do, she nudged what she assumed was a shoulder.

A moan was the only response.

She moved closer and leaned over the person. Long hair was plastered to the person's face, and she could now see the outline of a diminutive figure.

A woman.

Was this the one who had screamed rather than someone from the collapsed tent?

She didn't want to roll her over in the rain, so she crawled around the body and wiped the strands of hair away, now able to confirm it was a young woman—more like a teenage girl. At first, she appeared to be unconscious, but a grimace of pain marred her pretty face, and she held one arm over the other one.

"Can you hear me?" Stella yelled over the storm.

The girl didn't move, but her eyes twitched. Then she released another long moan and clutched at her arm.

"Did you hurt yourself? We should get inside." She gently touched the girl's shoulder, which elicited a broken cry, but her eyes opened to slits.

"Can you sit up?" Stella lifted the girl's shoulders. "It looks like you injured your arm. Can you stand?"

The only response was a moan that turned into soft pitiful cries.

Stella scanned the area. The men were still repairing the shelter while others seemed to have their hands full keeping the ship upright.

The girl's lips moved. Stella bent down but couldn't understand what she said. What she did notice were the girl's blue lips and tremors. She had to get her someplace dry. At least the door to the galley was close.

She stood, and when her legs seemed capable of holding her upright, she grabbed the girl under her arms as Beckworth had done to her. Careful not to jostle the girl's bad arm, she dragged her toward the door, grimacing at the soft moans that grew louder with each step.

When she reached the door, she leaned the girl against the wall. She tugged on the stout wooden door, but it wouldn't open. Tired of nothing going her way, she planted a foot next to the door and yanked. The door gave way sooner than she expected, and she fell, landing firmly on her backside. She didn't want to think about how many bruises she'd have in the morning.

Thankful the wind kept the door open, she forced herself up once again. She managed to get the girl down the first step when a man stormed up the stairs.

"Sabine!"

The voice was French, and she wasn't sure if he was yelling an obscenity or the girl's name. When he reached them, he glared at Stella.

"I found her on the deck. I think she hurt her arm." She was still yelling though it wasn't needed in the stairway.

He continued to speak in French, and Stella wasn't sure what to do. He lifted the young girl into his arms, wincing at her moans, his steps light. Halfway down, he turned and stared at Stella, then nodded before continuing down the stairs.

Gratified she was able to do something to help, she glanced down the stairs. It would be dry and safe below. But she couldn't leave Beckworth without knowing he was safe, so she turned to crawl out the way she'd come.

The wind shifted direction, and the opened door came roaring back, slamming into her head. She went down like one of Mohamed Ali's opponents.

She blinked. Her head hurt and darkness blurred her vision.

Strong arms wrapped around her, and she thought someone kissed her forehead.

She was too tired to open her eyes, but she was fairly certain she heard someone say, "Why can't you stay put?"

Beckworth carried Stella back to the shelter, hating to place her on the wet blankets, but everything would be soaked until after the storm passed. The rain had lessened, and the seas were calming. They were through the worst of it.

"Sir?"

He'd just set Stella down when he heard the soft voice and turned to find a young lad standing behind him, a bundle tucked under his jacket. Beckworth had seen him the day before and assumed he was the captain's cabin boy.

"Yes." Beckworth eyed the lad, who seemed focused on Stella before dragging his gaze back to him.

The boy carefully pulled out the bundle and handed it to him. "The captain sends his regards and wanted to thank your lady for caring for his niece."

The captain's niece? Was that why Stella had been coming up the stairs?

"Thank you, and give my regards to the captain." He accepted the bundle, and with one last glance at Stella, the boy was off.

Beckworth unrolled the blankets to find fresh bread, cheese, and meat wrapped in paper along with a skin. He opened it and gave it a whiff. Wine. He smiled. Someone was going to appreciate that when they woke.

He studied the shelter and the new blankets. The deck was too wet to waste the dry blankets, so he stuffed two in the saddlebag. He pulled the soaked blankets away, pushing them out of the shelter. The wet deck would have to suffice for now. After dumping the water that had collected on the canvas, he found the driest place available and pulled Stella to him, covering them both with a single dry blanket.

He nodded off to sleep but woke when he felt her stir.

"Is everyone okay?" She mumbled the words, her eyes never opening.

He gave her a quick once-over, sighing with relief when he didn't find any major injury. When he pushed her hair back, she winced.

"A couple people were bruised when one of the barrels toppled, but they should be all right. I think they were more scared than anything."

He caressed the top of her head and found a small lump. The door had smacked her in the head, and he should have checked it straight away, but he'd required rest as much as Stella. "Just sleep. It will be better in the morning."

She snuggled closer, and he leaned back, returning to his scattered dreams. He woke again when she began a continuous string of mumbling. He bent close to hear what she said, but the words didn't make sense. Even through her soaked clothing, he caught her light scent. It smelled clean, with a touch of floral he couldn't place until he realized it must be her natural scent. His lips twitched. It made sense an avid gardener would smell of flowers.

The rain had stopped, and he felt the smooth movements of the ship as it sailed through calm waters. A bit of the moon shined between the clouds, wind filled the sails, and based on the glimmer of light on the horizon, it would be morning soon.

Stella had calmed, her sleep-filled murmurs silenced. The deck had mostly dried, so he put the dry blankets down then repositioned Stella next to him, pulling the first blanket over them.

His thoughts turned to their arrival in France and how to deal with the French authorities, who would be waiting at the dock. This would be the tricky portion of his plan. They had two choices. Find a way to sneak off while the inventory was being inspected, or walk off with the rest of the refugees. Both options came with risk, but their best choice would be for him to do all the talking since he was the only one who could speak French. He should be able to come up with some story to weave, possibly connecting it with their need to get to the monastery.

He hadn't realized he'd fallen asleep again until he felt Stella struggle to get up. Night faded as light rose on the horizon, and the thinning clouds gave way to sky that promised a beautiful morning.

"Are you going to be sick?" Beckworth watched as a light blush rose on her cheeks.

"I'll be all right. My head hurts."

He should get her some water, but he didn't want to move. Her body had warmed through the early morning hours, and he was simply too comfortable. But he convinced himself he was doing it for her. That he shouldn't jostle her and aggravate her head injury.

"This might help." He reached for the skin, taking a sip before passing it to her, surprised the captain had provided what had to be one of his finest bottles.

She took a sip. Her eyes widened, and she drank more. "Have you been holding out on me?"

He chuckled. "It seems someone did a good deed for the captain's niece."

Her forehead wrinkled as she took a longer swallow. She nodded, then winced. "That's who she was."

"Let's sleep a little more. We should arrive in a few hours unless the storm blew us off course."

"God, I hope not." Then the skin slid from her fingers as she nodded off.

A ray of sunlight poked him in the eye through the gaps in the canvas and rope and woke him from a fitful sleep. Stella was already awake, her head resting in the crook of his arm, her gaze a little fuzzy.

"How do you feel?" He was tempted to move that strand of hair that kept falling in her face.

"Like someone hit me with a baseball bat."

"Hmm. That would have been the door to the galley."

She touched her head, and when she made to sit up, he pulled her back down. "Just rest a bit more and let the sun take the bite out of the air." He couldn't fathom why he was so reluctant to move and settled on the fact he had a responsibility to deliver her to AJ healthy and in one piece.

After several hours of rough seas, they deserved rest. She was as pale as the canvas that covered their tiny enclosure. Her herbs were gone, and while the ship was currently enjoying a smooth sail, the wind could change the conditions in a heartbeat.

"You've had a harrowing evening." Unable to resist any longer, he brushed back her errant strands.

"I don't know how AJ did it. I never truly understood what she lived through. And when I finally think I've got my shit together, something else is thrown at me, and my brain freezes."

"You know, when AJ first arrived in this time, she wasn't alone. She had Murphy and Hughes watching over her. You have no one here you can trust."

"I wouldn't have escaped from Gemini or gotten this far without you."

He wasn't sure what to say, so he gave her shoulder a gentle squeeze then let an awkward silence creep between them.

After several minutes passed, she lowered her head and mumbled, "I lied."

The words were spoken so lightly, he wasn't sure he'd heard correctly. "What was that? I didn't hear."

She lifted her chin a fraction of an inch. "I lied. Back on that first day, when I was being obstinate, and you suggested us going separate ways." She hesitated, and her cheeks grew flushed. "I never lie. Not really. I might stretch the truth, but only to help. Like when a home buyer gets cold feet at the last minute, but you know they love the house, would be really happy there, so you mention there are other buyers ready to snap it up. I imagine that's true enough most of the time, but I don't really know that." She released a small snort, then rubbed her stomach. "I suppose I sometimes fib when I'm trying to get out of a sticky situation."

"It's best to just say it. We still have a few hours left at sea, and I won't care how miserable you feel, I promise to badger you the entire time."

She laughed. It wasn't her hearty laugh, but it made her lift her head, and their eyes locked. "I didn't mean for it to be hurtful. I was scared and unsure who to trust."

When she lowered her head, he lifted her chin. "I have a rather tough hide. It comes from all those years on the streets and several more under my father's tutelage."

Unable to lower her head, she closed her eyes. "I think I'd rather have your anger."

What could she have lied about to create such anguish? He waited, giving her the time to tell him or change her mind. He wouldn't really push her.

She sucked in a ragged breath. "I lied when I said AJ didn't trust you." His breath hitched, and she squeezed her eyes shut. "She trusts you with her life."

He turned away, fussing with the canvas to force the pockets of water in the roof to drain away. Only a few drops leaked out since he'd performed the same ritual several times throughout the evening, and the rain was a couple of hours behind them. But he didn't know what to do with his hands.

He tugged at his sleeves, and she caught his arm. She slid a hand down to his and gripped it tight. "I'm very sorry. I didn't mean to hurt you when I said it." She shook her head and peered out across the deck. "I was mad, alone, and scared. I thought I could trust you but—"

"But my actions and words with Gemini made you second guess yourself. I understand."

Her body tensed, and she withdrew her hand. "That doesn't make it right."

He didn't have a response and couldn't think of a safer topic. Then, like a miracle, the young cabin boy returned. He sat up, thankful for the interruption.

"The captain wanted you to know his niece is much better. He thought you could use a warm meal before we dock. It will only be a couple of hours, the storm helped us along." He handed Beckworth a tray, then scurried off.

"What's this?" Stella eased up. Her hair was wild like the woman herself. "Is that coffee?"

"We have a bowl of porridge for each of us and two mugs of coffee." He set the tray between them. "Will your stomach be able to handle the porridge?"

She laid a hand on her stomach and nodded. "It's growling. But you might want to take half of mine, just to be safe." She grabbed the coffee before the porridge and, after a few sips, her shoulders relaxed.

"Here." He passed her his mug. "I think this will serve you better than me."

She hesitated, though he could see the anticipation in her gaze. "Are you sure?"

He nodded.

"Thank you."

When they were finished with breakfast, he stood and picked up the tray. "I'll take this back to the galley. I wanted to speak with the captain about docking, but don't worry, I'll be back soon with some water."

He didn't think he'd said anything wrong, but her brows furrowed when she glanced up.

"Thank you for watching over me."

For some reason, he couldn't come up with one witty retort. He responded with a simple, "Of course."

He mentally kicked himself as he walked away. No one could blame her for what she'd said. But he'd never admit how painful it had been hearing AJ didn't trust him.

He wasn't angry with her. Disappointed maybe, but what did he expect? Would he have done any better in her shoes? He certainly hadn't been himself while in her time period. In fact, he was embarrassed by how he'd behaved, even if he'd been in survival mode. There'd been no trust then.

It had to mean something now for her to admit to her lie. She'd easily relaxed against him after the storm and had snuggled closer until he could feel every inch of her pressed against him. It was an unconscious act on her part, but didn't that say more than mere words? She instinctively felt safe with him. A lightness displaced the hurt that had risen to the surface, and a little bit of the darkness that filled his heart chipped away.

29

Stella stood at the rail and watched the port grow closer. Several ships were docked, but she was too far away to make out any details, the people nothing more than ants scurrying around their anthill. The town was the largest she'd seen since arriving in this time period. She squeezed the coins in her pocket. Maybe she could get new clothes to wear, or just find someplace to take a bath and wash her hair.

Boot steps from behind made her turn. Beckworth's hair was as tousled as hers in the coastal breeze, but he looked rather chipper in his rumpled clothing. He was smiling, but he did that a lot, so she couldn't get a true sense of his mood, or his intent, until she could see his eyes. She couldn't read him completely, like when he might be weaving a tale, or withholding information that might disturb her. And while it drove her crazy, the sentiment was difficult to be mad at.

"What did the good captain want?" She turned back toward Saint-Malo as he stepped beside her. She surprised herself when she reached out to grab his hand.

Based on the slight widening of his gaze, it might have shocked him, too, but he squeezed her hand in return. "Don't worry. The captain wants us to join his sister and niece as they depart the ship. We'll be part of their service."

"Oh." She held back a sigh, grateful he'd read the seizing of his hand as a sign of fear. And when she considered her actions, maybe he wasn't far off the mark. It wasn't that she was afraid. The worst part of the journey was over. But he was safe. She trusted him to protect her, and though the pistol she carried in her left pocket gave her a sense of control, it was knowing he had her back that brought her comfort.

She gave him a sidelong glance, noticing, not for the first time, how he kept his hair tied back except for the tendrils that refused to be tamed. Just like him. Although she preferred the short cut he'd worn in Baywood—short on the side, longer on top. What the hell was she thinking? And what had they been talking about?

Something about the captain and leaving the ship. "If the captain just offered to include us in his entourage, what was your original plan for getting us off the boat?"

"I was still formulating one, but I had two very strong options."

"Then thank the stars I saved the captain's niece."

He chuckled. "I don't think she was in a life-or-death situation."

"You tell it your way. But you weren't the one rolling around on the deck aiming for the very short railing."

"I stand corrected. Thank you for the foresight to save the child and find us safe passage."

She beamed. "Any time."

They both grinned and stood shoulder to shoulder as they watched the ship sail into the harbor. Earlier that morning, they had worked together to tear down their shelter, restoring everything to its rightful place. They'd washed their faces with cold water, leaving their hair to fate. When she glanced at him again, she was somewhat perturbed that his disheveled appearance made him appear roguish, while her hair looked like something a tornado might leave behind.

Before she knew it, the ship was moored and men began unloading. The captain waved them over, positioning them between his sister and niece, who smiled sheepishly at Stella, and two other women who must be their lady's maids. Stella kept her shoulders back and her head down as they disembarked and were met by French soldiers. The captain stopped and conversed with them while Beckworth gripped her upper arm as if she might take flight. Because why not run off in a country where she couldn't understand the language and had no idea where she was going? If her eye roll explained any of that, it was lost on him because his stern expression never changed.

After several minutes and periods of jaunty laughter, the soldiers let them pass. She remained passive, not daring to look at anything other than the cobblestone road and Beckworth's boots, feeling solace in their unfaltering steps. They were well past the soldiers, but something about this place didn't feel right to her. Maybe it was the number of people strolling about. For the last several days, it had been just the two of them and the occasional village. She usually loved crowds, but right now, there seemed to be eyes everywhere.

When they turned left down a street, Beckworth murmured something in French then took her hand and strolled into the first alley he came to. He ducked behind a stack of barrels and pulled her next to him.

"The trip over was more costly than I planned for. I'll need time to determine what options we have."

"How far are we from the monastery?" At this point, she'd be fine with walking, but thoughts of a hot bath could easily distract her.

"It's a good day's ride by horse. Around two long days on foot."

She grimaced and chewed her lip while her fingers brushed her coat where she'd hidden the coins. Now would be the time to tell him, but would he see it as proof she didn't trust him?

"You know you're rather transparent when you have something you don't want to share."

Her brow lifted. "How do you know I'm not developing a master plan to solve our problem?"

He considered her, and his gaze warmed. Something stirred in her, and she glanced around the barrels to check the alley and wait for her cheeks to cool.

"If this were the first day we'd run, I wouldn't have a clue what was rolling around in that head."

That caught her attention. "And after only a handful of days, you think you can read me now?"

His steady gaze never changed, and he tilted his head, as if a different angle might validate his thoughts. When he smiled, a small ripple of pleasure flowed through her. Good grief. How was it possible she felt more intimacy with him in a smelly alley than all the times she'd been pressed against him in the saddle or laying in his arms, sick as a dog.

"With all we've been through, it seems like we've known each other for weeks."

She laughed. It was true, and the spell she seemed to have fallen under broke. "All right. But I don't want you to think I didn't tell you about this because I didn't trust you. I honestly haven't thought about them because you seemed to be doing fine keeping us alive."

"I'm intrigued." He leaned against the building, arms crossed over his chest. With his unkempt beard, he looked what she'd imagined a highwayman would look like. At least what she'd expect from a romance novel.

She glanced up and down the alley, then up to the windows of the two-story buildings. When she didn't see anyone, she opened her coat, fished around in a pocket, then pulled out the small, beaded pouch.

His brows lifted, and then his eyes glimmered when she opened the pouch and dropped the coins in her palm.

"Will any of these get us a horse?"

<hr />

Beckworth stared at the coins in Stella's palm. Five crowns and several schillings. He understood why she'd held this from him. These coins could save her life should they be parted before AJ and Finn found them. He could get them to the monastery one way or another, but he appreciated her willingness to help.

A good night's sleep, a horse, and a warm meal would make for a more pleasant ride as they spent the next day evading French patrols.

He closed her palm. "Let's find a room, then we can discuss our next steps. Although it's only noon, it's too late to start for the monastery. I don't think it would be good to overnight on the road."

She rubbed her back. "I could use a night on a bed softer than a ship's deck. And a fire, and wine, and then coffee in the morning. Do I have enough coins for that?"

He chuckled. "More than enough." He grabbed her hand. "Come. It's been some time since I've been here, but if the place is still open, I think we'll be safe for one night."

He led her down back alleys and side streets, keeping a brisk pace, their heads lowered. Ten minutes later, they neared the Channel east of the docks. Four years since he'd visited. Back when he'd worked for the duke. He'd had some row with his father, Dugan snickering from his place by the door, and he'd needed space. Space from his father, from Dugan, from the monastery. He'd ridden to Saint-Malo to put a full day's ride between him and the duke's madness, searching for whatever comfort he could find.

His lips twitched. At least Stella wouldn't be surprised by the choice.

L'éventail Bleu was quiet this time of day. Most brothels were located near the docks, closer to their customers. But for the more select clientele with the coins to spend, no one minded walking a bit farther. Would Colette still be there after all this time? He slid a glance to Stella. Good God, he hoped not.

Stella returned a perceptive stare. "Is this another board-inghouse?"

He tugged at his sleeves before striding up the stairs. "Yes." It didn't require anymore explanation.

"Do any of the rooms have fireplaces?"

"I believe so, but I've haven't been here for some time."

"I see."

He sensed humor in her response, and he straightened his shoulders. When they were inside, he pushed her toward one of the sofas in the greeting room.

"Wait here while I see about a room."

When she opened her mouth, he gave her a stern look. She rolled her eyes, but closed her mouth, crossed her arms over her chest, and turned to take in her surroundings. He was already making a list on what might appease her, and besides a hearth and a hot bath, a bottle of good French wine came to mind.

Thirty minutes later, they were in a corner room on the second floor with a window and a fireplace. He explained her coins and how much he'd paid for the room and what he would pay for the barber, trying to give her some sense of how much money she had.

He turned one of the coins in a circle.

Stella leaned back in her chair. "What is it?"

"It's nothing."

She snorted. "I can read you just as easily, you know."

He lifted a brow but wouldn't bet against her. "I understand why you didn't tell me about the coins." He waved her off before she could interrupt. "But I can be trusted."

"I know, but sometimes survival skills just take over. With my family, you got good at hiding things. I guess the old ways just kicked in." She spread out the coins, first putting them in a line, and then she shoved them into a pile. Her smile was impish. "Everyone knows you need three basic items when on the run."

Part of the answer was simple enough. "Coffee, wine, and, I forget, what was the third?"

"An ally who doesn't talk too much."

He gave her a wounded look that turned into a grin as he poked through the small collection of coins. "I'll take one of the crowns, a sixpence, and a few schillings. Keep the rest safe, just as you've been doing. Should the opportunity arise to borrow coin from someone less deserving, keep in mind this a game of survival. But don't put yourself at unnecessary risk."

She nodded as someone knocked.

Beckworth let in two maids, one with hot water and towels and the other with coffee service. When they were gone, he tossed her the stack of newspapers.

"Clean up, make your birds, or take a nap. I won't be long, then we can have that warm meal I promised." He could have sworn he heard her growl before the door shut.

An hour later, he whistled as he made his way back to the boardinghouse—clean, groomed, and his clothes given a good brushing. His casual stride was deceiving as he discreetly scanned his surroundings. Stella might think him paranoid, but he circled the building twice before entering through the back and taking the stairs to their room.

He only managed two steps when he entered, barely registering closing the door.

Flames danced on candles sitting in the middle of the table. Two sets of plates, bowls, silverware, and glasses had been carefully arranged. A fire blazed in the hearth, and mouthwatering smells from the pot hanging near the fire filled the room. Plates of bread, cheese, and pastries filled in the rest of the table.

She'd been busy. Six swans perched at various spots among the platters of food, and she sat on the bed making another.

"What's all this?" Beckworth placed a clay pitcher on the table and removed his jacket. He took a moment to watch Stella as she finished her swan. Hair fell into her face, and she pushed it back several times, seemingly unaware of her actions. Her hair wasn't long enough to tie back, though it had been thick and soft in his fingers as it dried while she'd laid in his arms. She needed a hair clip.

"Since you were busy arranging our transportation, I thought I'd take care of the meal." She stood and stretched her back, then placed the current swan with the rest of the flock. She tapped the pitcher. "Can I only hope what that might be?"

"If you think it's the best wine a schilling can buy, then you'd be correct."

She lifted a brow. "A schilling? I need to pay more attention to the monetary system here. I could get robbed blind not knowing how much things cost."

"You didn't have to barter with the cook?"

She wrinkled her nose while she lifted the pot from the hearth and placed it on the table. The heady aroma of the thick lamb stew made his stomach grumble. "I don't think she likes me."

"She's not fond of the English."

"She seemed fine with you."

He chuckled. "I think she was more enamored with my coin purse. If she had an inkling of how poor I am at this moment, she'd probably have called the guards."

"That's comforting."

She ladled stew into their bowls, then poured the wine. He wanted to help, but she seemed to enjoy having something to do.

"So, what's the plan for tomorrow? I take it you found a horse?"

He nodded. "It will be ready in the morning. A quick breakfast then on the road at first light. We'll have to be careful with French soldiers on the roads, but we should arrive at the monastery an hour or so after dusk."

"Do you think AJ and Finn are already there?"

He finished a bite of the tasty stew, then chewed a piece of cheese while he considered her question. "It's possible. The *Daphne* is a fast ship, but she probably got caught in some part of that storm. Based on when Gemini planned on meeting Murphy, I'd say we missed them by mere hours. A day at most."

"And they would dock in the small bay at the monastery because the stairs are still viable. Why didn't we dock at the town near the monastery?"

"How do you know so much about the monastery?" He sipped wine. "Never mind. AJ again."

She used a chunk of bread to mop up stew. "Actually, AJ and Finn arranged for several of us to spend last Christmas at a villa near the monastery. I've been through the main building several times, as well as some of the tunnels."

He sat back. "I didn't know that."

She picked up her wine for the first time, sniffed it, then rolled it around in her glass before testing it. Her eyes brightened. "This will do." She took a long sip, and he watched her delicate neck as she swallowed. "So why not the port closer to the monastery?"

He shook his head. "It's small. Most dock here if not farther east in Calais. I was lucky to find anyone willing to sail this close to the monastery."

"After the last few days, I almost feel like walking, but I'll take a horse over another boat ride."

"You did well on the ship."

She sat back, holding her glass of wine close. "I did get sick."

"Only the one day, and I think the storm was a decent excuse."

"Well, AJ and Finn better show up. I'd rather not have to endure another crossing."

Her words sliced through him, and his chest tightened. How many days before she'd disappear into the fog? A day—two at the most?

"We've gotten this far. I'd say your luck is holding." His tongue felt thick as he forced the words out. What was wrong with him?

"Well, knock on wood." She rapped the table with her knuckles.

"Why don't we clean this up then finish our wine in front of the fire? We need to be up early."

They talked for another hour before they collapsed on the bed, both turning on their sides, their backs to each other. Beckworth listened to her steady breathing before nodding off.

Muffled cries woke him. He sat up, barely able to make anything out, the fire nothing but embers. Stella struggled next to him before she fell off the bed. No. She'd been dragged off it.

He jumped up but only made it a foot before someone kicked his legs out from under him.

"What the hell?" He was kicked in the stomach but managed to crawl away. When the boot came a second time, he caught it and twisted as the man lost his balance. Was it Gemini's men? How had they found them? "What's going on?"

He stood and stumbled toward two dark shapes struggling with Stella. She wasn't going quietly.

Beckworth tracked one of the men, coming up from behind while Stella kept them busy. She was a hellion. He kept his eye on the second man, who brandished a knife, its shiny blade reflecting the available light.

He crouched as he considered how to get around the first man before the second man had time to do anything with the knife. But their movements were unpredictable as they grappled with Stella.

Something slammed into his head.

He turned and caught the shadowy form of a woman before he collapsed on the floor. The rough wood scraped his face. He pushed up until he was on his hands and knees, but they'd already dragged Stella to the door, then someone punched her, and she went limp.

He bellowed with red hot rage, but before he could do anything, the second blow dropped him into oblivion.

"Hello, Teddy."

Beckworth's eyes popped open, and he winced. He wasn't sure which was worse—the hammers slamming away in his head or the spotlight that pierced his eyes. He dragged his hand through his hair and grimaced when he found a walnut-sized lump.

He used the bed for support as he stood and wobbled. His headache intensified for a moment before returning to the original pounding. Who'd hit him? He glanced at the bed, the hearth, and then the window. Stella was gone.

Then it registered that someone was calling him, and he spun around too fast. He grabbed the bed then sat before his legs buckled. "AJ?"

Her expression went through several emotions—anger, confusion, concern. After all this time, he could still read her. He ignored Murphy, who hovered behind her.

"I need your help." He glanced down, thankful he'd slept in his clothes.

"Where is she?" Each word was uttered slowly and firmly, not a hint of a smile on her face.

He stumbled to the window and clutched the frame before shoving the curtains aside. Morning lit the horizon, the street empty, yet he pictured Stella being lifted into a carriage as if it was occurring now rather than the hours that must have passed since she'd been taken.

"Where's Stella, Beckworth?" Murphy's tone was deceptively soft, and he caught the edge in it.

A heaviness filled him, almost crushing in its weight. His expression was bleak when he turned to AJ.

"They took her."

THANK YOU FOR READING!

I hope you enjoyed the adventure and the new budding romance between Stella and Beckworth

Coming in 2023
The final two chapters of *The Mórdha Stone Chronicles*
The Servant of Stone (Book 8)
The Book of Stones (Book 9)

A friend has been taken. The enemy searches for the Translator —Maire Murphy. A race begins to put *The Book of Stones* back together. But before they can discover the final secrets of the Book, they must find their missing friend, and nothing will stop Beckworth from doing whatever it takes to find Stella.

(This is a placeholder cover)

Keep reading for a preview from *The Servant of Stone* - Book 8

Enjoy!

THE SERVANT OF STONE

Saint-Malo - France - 1805

AJ Moore-Murphy stood inside the doorway. The room had more appeal than the typical inns she was familiar with, but of course, this wasn't any ordinary inn. This was L'éventail Bleu, an upscale brothel on the coast of France. It was a tactic Beckworth had used when he'd rented a room for Stella in Bournemouth while evading Gemini's men in England.

After watching Beckworth stumble around the room for the last five minutes, Stella nowhere in sight, she touched the tips of her ears, positive there would be smoke if not downright flames coming from them. All the miles and all the worry, she'd been so close. Now, within mere hours, they'd missed her.

"Where's Stella?" She kept her tone light but firm. What she wanted to do was stand in front of his face and scream at him. Stella had been on the ship when they'd arrived in Saint-Malo. Finn had confirmed it before tracing Beckworth to this brothel.

Beckworth stared out the window, his gaze on the street

below. Maybe Stella was running an errand. But if that was true, why did Beckworth look like someone had just gutted him? When he turned toward her, she could barely hold his stare. The hollowness, bleakness, failure—a mirror into his tumultuous soul.

She had to maintain focus, or she'd be swallowed up by such despair.

"They took her."

She sucked in a deep breath and almost choked on the scent of stale perfume. She counted to ten, but her mantra for inner peace wasn't going to work. Not for this.

"Who took her?" Her words were measured. She tried for the same tone as before but caught Finn's side glance and knew she'd failed. Instead of steady reassurance, she'd only managed the edge of calm, her emotions clearly leaking into outright fear with a side of anger.

Beckworth's gaze fell away, and his expression became dazed. He kept reaching for his head. Had someone attacked him? She glanced at Finn, who shrugged.

This was a Beckworth she'd never seen before, even at his darkest hour when he'd been stuck in Baywood, Oregon. There had been fear then—and a definite bleakness at the thought of never going home. But he still had a spark. That instinct for survival. Now, it seemed as if his inner flame hadn't been reduced but utterly extinguished.

Before she could ask for Finn's advice, he was already on the move. He strode to the table, picked up a clay pitcher, sniffed it, and then grabbed one of the goblets. Red liquid streamed into the cup, and she almost smiled, knowing how much Stella must have appreciated the wine. It was doubtful she'd seen much of it while on the run.

He approached Beckworth, wine in one hand, his other outstretched toward the bed. "Come sit down."

When Beckworth didn't move, she thought Finn might force the issue, but after a few minutes, he moved on his own, ignoring the bed and stumbling to the table where he collapsed on a chair. When Finn placed the wineglass in front of him, Beckworth picked it up and drained it.

Finn pointed to the other chair and waited for her to take a seat. That was when she noticed the swans, several of them, arranged around the candlesticks like a centerpiece. Tears stung her eyes when she picked one up—proof her friend had been there.

Finn sat and rested a hand on her arm before glancing at Beckworth, whose focus had turned to the swan in her hand. He tapped the table until Beckworth turned a startled gaze to him as if he'd just now realized Finn was in the room.

"Tell us what happened."

Minutes passed before Beckworth poured the last of the wine and ran a hand through his hair several times, wincing when he touched what appeared to be a sensitive spot. After a long sigh, he turned to AJ.

"I thought we were safe. At least for a night. We'd been running nonstop, and after the ship and storm, she needed to rest." His voice was rough, probably the first words he'd spoken since waking. He held her gaze. "She's been so strong. You'd be proud of her. But we had a hard time staying ahead of them. I originally thought of going to Hensley, but Gemini was certain to send men there if she hadn't already. The earl seemed too far to run, though maybe that would have been the best." His voice trailed off, and he pushed the empty goblet away. "The only place that seemed safe and out of reach was the monastery." A slight smile touched his lips. "Everyone always ends up there."

She flicked a glance to Finn. Those were the exact words he and Ethan constantly drummed into her. If this were any other day, Finn would have teased her about it, but his expression remained stoic. This wasn't any other day.

"Gemini? Is that who you've been running from?" Finn asked.

Beckworth shot a look at him and grabbed his head again. "Yes, although I haven't seen her since we escaped from an abandoned farmhouse south of Basingstoke."

"Basingstoke. You were there?"

He nodded. "Her men were everywhere. I thought heading for a ship would be the last place she'd think to look, but with the stones involved, I should have known better. We were halfway to Southampton when I discovered she'd sent most of her men south." He glanced around the table, looked in his empty cup, and pushed it away.

"Was it her men who took her from this room?" Finn managed to keep his tone supportive.

Beckworth snorted. "I don't know. Gemini might have discovered what port we sailed from. There could have been one or two of her men hiding in Bournemouth, but I never sensed them. It would have taken time to get word to her, wherever she was hiding. It just doesn't make sense." He gave Finn a quick glance before settling his gaze back on AJ. "If it had been her, or even Gaines, that took her, they wouldn't have sneaked in. Gemini is too prideful. She would have made her presence known, and I seriously doubt you would have found me alive."

Finn pointed to his head. "Maybe she thought she'd killed you."

"She wouldn't have taken a chance with something as unreliable as a hit on the head." He touched his head and winced. "No matter how effective at knocking me out."

"How did you meet Gemini in the first place?" Finn's question surprised her. Hensley had already told them, but as much as she didn't want it to be true, perhaps Beckworth had an ulterior motive. The question had to be asked.

"She'd been watching me since she wormed her way into my holiday hunting party, playing the role of Lady Penelope Prescott. No doubt one of many parts she's played. Her trusty bloodhound, Gaines, followed me to London and noticed the shady characters I'd been meeting with. They assumed I was running my own information ring outside Hensley's purview, not realizing it was an assignment orchestrated by the spymaster."

He leaned back in the chair and gazed about the room. His eyes were unfocused, either from the realization Stella was truly gone or from the hit on his head. "Gemini knew about the duke and Reginald and more than she should have about the stones and the books. She thought I could fill in the gaps from what she'd already learned." His wicked laugh sent chills down her spine. "One of Gemini's weaknesses is making assumptions before validating her facts."

"Whatever possessed you to run instead of playing out the role? You could have gained valuable information from her." Finn, having worked for Hensley for many years, understood the advantages and the risks of playing out a lead. He'd spent eighteen months time traveling to find the Heart Stone.

"And you were in the same town where Gemini had set up the meeting with Finn." AJ couldn't keep her mouth shut any longer.

Beckworth's brows shot up at that, and he gave a derisive snort. "Why doesn't that surprise me? No wonder she wouldn't reveal the location of the meeting."

She glanced down at the paper swan she'd been holding to find the poor thing had been mangled in her clenched fist. Regardless of her attempts to straighten it, the swan's wings drooped. She stuck the wilted figure in her pocket, her original fear stoking the flames of anger. "So, why did you run? Another couple of days, and we could have gotten you out of there."

Beckworth pushed out of his chair and paced the room, his arms waving. Whether anger or fear drove him, she couldn't tell and wasn't sure it mattered. He was no longer the confused viscount. "Well, excuse me. I thought you would be more interested in removing Stella from the middle of danger, not have me guess at whatever plan you might have cooked up. Gemini never revealed the location of the meeting. I had no idea we were in the vicinity, and none of her men had been aware, other than perhaps Gaines. And god knows I tried. I spent an entire evening getting them good and drunk."

He turned and gave her a scathing look. "Oh, and Gemini discovered who killed Dugan."

She paled. "So?"

"Gemini and Dugan were lovers. And while she's now intimately involved with Gaines, she still pines for Dugan. I worried she wouldn't wait for Murphy's arrival before killing the person who took her lover from her. She is a bit mad."

She glanced at Finn, and though his gaze was tender, the heavy hands of guilt settled on her. "I'm sorry." The words were bitten out. She ran her hands through her hair before picking up a goblet and throwing it at the wall, where it bounced before rolling toward the window.

Beckworth ignored her outburst and tugged at his sleeves. "We still have an advantage. Whoever took Stella didn't just select a random person in a boardinghouse. We have to assume the people that took her are either working with Gemini or a rival faction."

Finn pounded a fist on the table. "That's all we need, two different groups searching for the Heart Stone." He stood, and it spurred AJ to follow. The room seemed to press in from all sides.

"Either way—" Beckworth moved to the bed and pulled on a

boot. "—There's only one reason they took Stella. Someone still believes she's you. They'll want to barter to have any hope of getting the Heart Stone. And we know where they're going."

AJ shook her head. "The monastery."

* * *

When they exited the boardinghouse, Lando waited with four horses, three of them complete with saddlebags and weapons. AJ's bow and quiver hung from one saddle.

"Hello, little man. It's been a trial catching up with you." Lando nodded to one of the horses. "Hope you don't mind me picking up your ride."

Beckworth scowled. "How many times have I asked you not to call me that?"

"Not enough to sink in, I'd imagine." He tossed Beckworth a small wrapped package before handing one to AJ and Murphy. "Your breakfast. You're welcome."

Beckworth stuffed his meal in his jacket pocket, not particularly concerned about squashing it. Then he threw his saddlebag over the horse before taking its reins. The lump he'd received was still sensitive, and he pushed on it until tears formed. He deserved the pain—needed it. After everything they'd been through, he'd allowed Stella to slip through his grasp. He shouldn't have been so brash strutting around town, thinking they were safe simply by stepping foot in a different country—war or not.

Once everyone was mounted, he followed them as they maneuvered through the edges of town, keeping their heads down and avoiding anyplace soldiers might congregate. They walked their horses until they were a couple of miles out of town, giving them time to eat while moving, although he noted AJ only picked at her food.

He wanted to say something. To apologize for losing Stella. For not taking better care of her, although he wasn't sure what else he could have done other than perhaps take her elsewhere. Maybe they should have gone to London after all. They could have waited for Hensley if he wasn't already there for the season. He had contacts Gemini wouldn't have known about. If only she could have seen the flower vendors in Whitechapel. It was too early in the season for lilacs, but the daphne would be in bloom. He could have dressed her in the finest gowns and introduced her to Elizabeth Ellingsworth. There were so many other things he could have done had he been thinking straight.

AJ gave him side glances, but Murphy kept her close to him. He couldn't blame the man and didn't think it had anything to do with him. Murphy and Lando were both watchful, keeping eyes out for French soldiers if he had to guess.

She had to be curious and would want to know everything there was to know about Stella. How was she holding up? Was she scared? Was she getting enough coffee? He snorted. And then his thoughts shifted to Stella. Was she frightened by whatever new circumstances she found herself in? She had adapted to every situation he'd put her through. Would she brave without him? His worst fear was that she'd blame him for failing her. No. He wouldn't think that way. She'd confided not more than a day ago that AJ trusted him. That she trusted him. She'd be spitting mad and defiant but had to know they'd come for her. That he would come for her.

Then another thought raised the hairs on the back of his neck. Had they found her pistol or had Stella been able to keep it hidden? It hadn't been in the room, and he'd scoured the place, making sure he had what little of her belongings had been left behind. He'd even stuffed the swans in his pocket.

They rode for several hours, keeping a steady pace, then turned down a small trail that followed a creek until they were a quarter-mile off the road. They rested the horses while Lando pulled out another wrapped package for everyone.

"What do you think is waiting for us at the monastery?" AJ moved her food around, nibbled at a bit of cheese, then sat back with her skin of water.

Murphy shrugged. "The monastery doesn't have any protection, and it would depend on the size of Gemini's force, assuming it's Gemini that took Stella. The *Daphne* should be in the bay by now."

"And would Gemini know of the iron door?" Lando asked. He kept his gaze on the trail, the forever watchful sentry.

AJ and Murphy turned to him as if he were one of Gemini's inner circle. "How would I know?" He stared off to the trees, sensing their gazes on him. He let out a sigh. "I don't remember her mentioning the monastery, only the stones. She knew the book had been split into pieces but didn't indicate if the information was recent or what she'd learned from the duke. The largest surprise for me, besides Stella being mistaken for you, was this new incantation that allows a traveler to select a specific day and location, though it seemed it wasn't completely accurate. Gaines showed up two days late from his jump to the future, and I got the sense the jump they tried before had been more accurate."

"She didn't give any other names? Who might have given her the incantation?" Murphy's questions were reasonable, so he played the game.

"No. She gave me what she knew, or suspected, was common knowledge. I can confirm she doesn't have the stones, though she seemed to know where they were. She also suspects two are missing."

"How the hell does she know that?" Murphy seemed skeptical, and he couldn't blame him. He'd been mystified himself.

He shrugged. "For some reason, she suspects you have one. She'd probably piss herself if she knew I had it." He'd picked up a stick and had been drawing odd shapes in the dirt. He scratched through them, realizing they had been designs for a new garden bed. Something he'd wanted to share with Stella. He stabbed at the dirt until he'd created a small hole. Could he make it large enough to bury his head in it?

"There was one thing I found odd," he continued. The others had gone back to their meals and inner musings, thinking he'd finished with what little he knew. He held their rapt attention again, and AJ's expressive gaze, full of hope, almost broke his heart. "Gemini was obsessed with locating Maire."

Murphy straightened. "We'd heard she was looking for the translator. We assumed it was Maire."

He nodded. "It was one of the questions Gemini wanted me to ask Stella. Of course, she thought I was speaking to AJ, so it was a logical assumption I might garner an answer. She assumed if anyone knew where Maire was hiding, it would be AJ."

"Was that her exact word—hiding?" Murphy asked.

He thought back to their conversation. "She assumed Maire was in hiding, continuing her translation of *The Book of Stones*, or at least a section of it. And she also assumed Hughes was with her. She never gave any consideration that they might have jumped to the future with you."

"Well, that's helpful." Lando sliced a piece of apple with his knife. "Not good that they're looking for Maire, but they have no idea the two of them are with us."

"So she's on the *Daphne*?" He asked.

"What if her men went to the monastery? What if they have her?" AJ's voice rose an octave with the last question.

Murphy laid a hand on her shoulder. "You're getting ahead of yourself again. Neither Jamie nor Ethan would let her off the ship without knowing the conditions at the monastery. Jamie would have sent Fitz and a small team in first."

She jumped up to pace back and forth. "You're right. I hate going back to the monastery when we don't know who's running the place." She stopped and gave Murphy one of her pleading looks. "Maybe we should try the iron door first, and if that doesn't work, we head down to the beach and signal the ship."

"An excellent idea." Beckworth stood and gathered the remains of his lunch. "The three of you should head for the ship while I enter through the front door."

The three of them were repacking saddlebags when they turned and stared.

"What is this, little man? What game are you about?" Lando's words should have cut him, but he understood their confusion.

"I have no desire to get myself shot, but we need someone inside, and I have a better chance of talking my way in than any of you."

"You should at least wait until we've checked with Jamie." AJ's concern for him was touching, if unwarranted.

"Beckworth's right." Murphy took AJ's packaged leftovers and skin. "We can monitor from the road. If guards are outside, we'll know the monastery has been compromised. But it's also possible they won't have enough men to post sentries. After five minutes, if Beckworth doesn't wave us in, we go for the stairs and the ship."

With somewhat of a plan, they rode back to the road in time to meet a small group of travelers headed in the same direction. After a few short words, Beckworth ascertained they were getting as far from Paris as possible, heading for family along the coast.

When they grew closer to town, Murphy suggested they stop at Guerin's Inn in case they had news of the monastery. But two miles shy of town, Lando called a warning.

"Four riders. They've grown closer the last few miles, but now they seem to be pacing us." He turned toward the road they'd traveled and pulled out a spyglass. "They appear to be French soldiers."

"Let me have your field glasses." Murphy held out his hand to AJ.

When she gave him the binoculars, Beckworth scowled. "Are those mine?"

AJ gave him a wicked grin. "If you mean are those the ones you stole from the sisters, then yes, they are."

He snorted. "Edith had several lying about the house. I doubt she even knows they're gone."

"They're wearing uniforms, but something is off about them." Murphy continued his surveillance. "Ah, that's the problem." He handed the field glasses to Lando. "Their uniforms don't seem to fit well."

"They're staying back with the size of our group. They'll wait until after town, then try to overtake us before we reach the monastery." Lando handed the glasses back.

Murphy smiled. It was that friendly smile that didn't reach his eyes. The one he'd come to know well. Murphy had a plan, most likely a devious one.

"Aye. But let's see if we can change the setting a bit. Our visit to Guerin's will have to wait for another day."

After another mile, a narrow road branched off to the southwest. Rather than follow their fellow travelers, they bid farewell and took the road that skirted the town. When Beckworth lifted a brow, Murphy flashed his grin.

"This road leads to a cave Sebastian uses to store his smuggler's inventory. Ethan and I helped unload a cart or two while we waited for a ship to England."

He said nothing more, knowing the story of how he and Hughes had followed AJ after they'd left for England on the *Daphne.*

The terrain was rocky and would be difficult for carts to travel, which was why the smugglers' cave had remained safe from French troops. And he noted there were also several opportunities for the perfect ambush. They traveled a half-mile past a trail Murphy said led to the cave before he stopped to set their trap.

Murphy and AJ would stay with the horses and cover Lando and Beckworth, who would hide behind a grouping of large boulders until the riders passed. Their decision to leave no one alive, assuming they weren't indeed soldiers, made AJ irritable. Still, she seemed to understand Murphy's reasoning —take them out here or face them again later when the numbers might be against them. For now, they were evenly matched.

Everything went without a hitch. The four men were focused on the narrow road and not their surroundings. When he and Lando quietly closed ranks behind the men, an arrow took one to the ground, who Lando dispatched immediately while Murphy's shot rang true. Beckworth shot the third man while Lando wrestled the last man to the ground.

The four of them gathered around him. Blood seeped through the shirt near his abdomen, and he grimaced in pain. Beckworth was surprised the man had fought as hard against Lando with what appeared to be a severe injury. The struggle for survival wasn't anything to take lightly.

AJ stared at the carnage. "Maybe we should have confirmed they weren't really French soldiers."

"While we didn't plan to, they would have been a problem," he said.

"Sebastian would have talked to them." She walked away when the man continued to stare with unrepentant defiance.

"We don't know who has control of the monastery, and we don't need to fight two fronts." Lando took weapons and coin bags from the dead.

Beckworth glanced at the others. "Why don't you ride ahead? I'll see what our friend can tell us." He sighed when he caught Lando looking to Murphy. "Fine, Lando can help. We need to hide the bodies anyway. Give us thirty minutes."

When he and Lando caught up with AJ, he put her mind at ease. "They killed the soldiers just outside Saint-Malo. Lando took the horses back to where the road split and sent them back the way they'd come."

"And the last man?" Murphy asked.

"He was stubborn and native French. Of that, I have no doubt. But other than what happened to the soldiers, the only thing I was able to get was a single name—Belato."

AJ's head swung up at that, her brows knit together.

"Do you know who that is?" Murphy asked.

She squinted, drawing her brows closer together, but then she shook her head. "I've heard the name before but can't remember where or when."

"Let's keep moving." Murphy took the lead, and they followed single file.

Beckworth let everyone go on, insisting on watching their back. He stopped every quarter mile or when they crossed a ridge, waiting to see if anyone else followed. It gave him time to resolve what he'd done to the mercenary. God knows he'd done worse in his time but thought he'd grown beyond that. But with every question he asked of the man, he never really saw him or the blood as he worked for answers. All he saw was Stella. The way she'd looked with fear when he'd first spoken with her. Or her greater fear when he returned to her room later that evening, when all she saw was someone sneaking into her room after everyone else had passed out. The look in her eyes when she stared at the dead mercenary he'd shot. But then he remembered how quickly she'd adapted. She didn't want to kill anyone but hadn't seemed to mind when he had to do it. She understood survival.

When his vision finally cleared and he stared down at the man, the defiance now erased by fear, his senses returned. The man had been bleeding out from a shot to the stomach, and there wasn't any way to save him, even if he had a mind to. He'd been surprised when the man grabbed his wrist, his strength waning but firm enough to hold on.

When the man pulled him down and whispered the name into his ear, he questioned if the man had given him a false lead. Until the man uttered his last words, a thin trail of blood leaking from his lips and staining his teeth.

"They're all mad."

After ten minutes and no one else appeared on the trail, he turned and spurred the mount to catch up with the others. The last few miles were uneventful, and they didn't stop until they reached the final curve in the road that took them to the monastery. They left the horses and moved cautiously over the rocky terrain to see what Beckworth would be riding into.

"Oh god, they've already posted guards." AJ had a hand to her throat, no doubt worried about Maire.

"They're guards, all right, but not mercenaries." Lando moved the spyglass in a slow line before dropping it. A huge smile added sparkle to his gaze. "They're sailors."

Murphy laughed. "Jamie has added a defense perimeter."

They scrambled back to their horses and raced to the inner courtyard. The sailors guarding the front of the building raised their arms in greeting and opened the doors for them. They'd barely dismounted before Maire raced out the foyer doors to greet them, Hughes a single step behind.

Tears streamed down her face, and his chest clenched. Not Stella. Please don't let this be about Stella. AJ had gone pale as she caught Maire in her arms.

"Sebastian is gone. They took Sebastian."

THANK YOU FOR READING!

I sincerely hope you enjoyed reading, *A Stone Denied*.

The last two books of the series will be coming in 2023.

Until then, you might be interested in my new series, *Of Blood & Dreams*, a paranormal romantic suspense series. Suspense and mystery...with just a pinch of spice.

Seduction in Blood - *Book 1*
A thief. A vamp. A walk on the wild side.

Cressa Langtry is the best cat burglar on the west coast. But she owes a large debt to the wrong kind of people. Her only way clear is to steal something for the city's notorious and ancient vampire – Devon Trelane.

Devon Trelane can't forgive the one man who cost him a seat on the Council. Luckily, a thief has fallen into his lap. A woman with the skills he requires to take down his greatest enemy.

There's only one hitch—a simple business arrangement becomes complicated when their dreams collide.

Available at all retailers - ebook, print & audio
Pick up your copy today!

Want to know when my next book will be available?
Sign up for my newsletter!
Or follow me on Amazon, Goodreads, Bookbub, Facebook, or
Instagram)

As an additional thank you for signing up for my newsletter, a free copy of *A Legacy of Stone* is available for download. This prequel to the *Mórdha Stone Chronicles* introduces Lily Mayfield, the last Keeper of Stones...until AJ that is!

LEGACY
OF
STONE
EXPANDED VERSION
KIM ALLRED
A MÓRDHA STONE CHRONICLE STORY

ABOUT THE AUTHOR

Kim Allred lives in an old timber town in the Pacific Northwest where she raises alpacas, llamas and an undetermined number of free-range chickens. Just like AJ and Stella, she loves sharing stories while sipping a glass of fine wine or slurping a strong cup of brew.

Her spirit of adventure has taken her on many journeys including a ten-day dogsledding trip in northern Alaska and sleeping under the stars on the savannas of eastern Africa.

Kim is currently working on the final books for the Mórdha Stone Chronicles series and the next books in her sizzling romance series—Masquerade Club.

For more books and updates:
www.kimallred.com

facebook.com/kim.allred.52831

instagram.com/kimallredauthor

bookbub.com/authors/kim-allred

amazon.com/-/e/B07CQY2J8Y